I0640788

LYNELLE CLARK
MULTI GENRE AUTHOR

LOVE AT WAR

Their enemies tried to outsmart them.

Obedience their only defence.

LYNELLE CLARK

An Inspirational Love story.

COPYRIGHT

Book cover design: Canva

Proof Reader: Magda de Korte

Betareaders: Tony Nordin, Magdel Roets, Isak de Lange and Alta van Zyl.

Translations: Google

Scriptures taken from the King James Version, Amplified Bible and English Standard Version.

Paperback ISBN 978-1-928535-14-0

Printers: Minuteman Press, Trichardt str, Boksburg

Not suitable for sensitive readers.

Contents

Measured in seconds, time's algorithm captures infinity within each movement. Worlds change and fragments become relics. Fashioning a new set of rules to profit from your only choice.

Tick...

PROLOGUE

20 September 1995, Pretoria, South Africa.

BEATEN AND WORN-OUT a young Sonia reached the front door of the motel. The usual buzz in the place were eerily quiet. No one to notice the bloody hand palm as she tried to support herself. All the way to the entrance the emptiness extended. Through the grimy glass, the emptiness enclosed the parking lot. The security guard not in his usual place.

Blood trailed her every step. Anxiously, she followed the cement path. At the boomed entrance she curled into excruciating pain and collapsed. Her head hid the ground. Immediately grime attached itself to her sweaty forehead but it was the last of her problems.

Three things happened in one moment.

A cork-like release followed by a blood clot landed between her feet.

A woman screamed. Then Sonia fainted.

A curse revived her, her view blocked by pedestrians.

The sick sensation of the rejected foetus left her paralysed and she adjusted her head to the place he laid. Helpless. Small. Defenceless.

He was all she had in this world. Another curse caused her to move once more. A black woman clicked her tongue in a sneer.

Her sins under public scrutiny.

At her feet blood covered his body—a fist under the cheek. A dark red stain on the cemented driveway.

One Jacaranda flower dropped on top of him, just like a heavenly garment. The act so minute, but understanding whispered. He was in a safe place—a better place. Far better than her motherly offering.

From there things happened swiftly. People gathered around her. One man's soft, endearing words reached her befuddled mind. The pain only a dull throb, and she was cold.

"She must be drunk."

"What kind of mother is she!"

Her client appeared in front of her. His condescending insolence endorsed the crowd's whispers, and he left with no inclination that he knew her.

The next moment they placed him on her breasts. His tiny form blueish, and she shielded him with trembling hands.

Sirens filled the air. The faint smell of petrol fumes released an oppressing heat. The merciless sun left her powerless. A shadow shielded her as an uniformed man covered them with a soft blanket.

Focused on her son, she burnt every perfect part of him into her mind. He was her courage, the reason she still breathed. Tears formed as she closed her eyes— blackness, her only solitude.

***

AN ETERNITY PASSED before she opened them in an altered world. Everything was different, brighter and clean.

The sting of disinfectants confronted her and a woman hovered above her. She whistled a well-known song, one she had learnt at her mother's knee. Her compassion stirred her spirit and tears stung a bruised cheek. Enclosed behind a curtained area the bed was soft.

"What is your name?" The woman's voice crisp and clear.

Startled she looked at her. She could not remember the last time she used her actual name. Brandy, no, that was not correct. She was never a Brandy.

"Where is my baby?"

The woman lowered herself. "He's in the Father's hand, child. Do not fear. He will look after him." The soft hand brushed her face.

"Cry, my child. We will take good care of you. When I come back, we can discuss it."

She isolated her with a white sheet—warm, pressed, and clean.

More tears filtered into the pillow; stained with regrets and why's. When she returned the day had passed. Night changed into day before pale blue eyes appeared again.

"How are you?" A covered plate drew her attention.

"Better, thank you."

"Eat something. I know it's not the best, but it will strengthen you." The nurse lifted the lid and she inhaled the aroma of the food. Her intensive stare never left as she ate with gusto.

The woman dragged a chair closer, her features more prominent in the daylight. She did not imagine the kind-heartedness.

"Can you remember what's your name?" The matron spoke when she felt satisfied and placed the spoon on the table. Satisfied, a feeling long forgotten.

"Sonia." She cleared her throat and repeated: "Sonia Main."

"I am Matron Sally van der Walt. So happy to meet you, Sonia." In the motherly irises she found no judgment.

"How old are you? Can you remember?"

"Nineteen," she replied uncomfortable under the scrutiny. The last time she had experienced this kind of acceptance, was when her mom was alive. How long ago was that?

"What are your plans for your future?"

"I don't know," and she pulled the sheet towards her. Her shame hidden.

"Today I want you to rest, get stronger and then, when willing, we can talk about your future. God has not forgotten you, my child. You have come to the right place. God's plans are greater than what you can see. Never forget that."

Tock …

Sephanje 3: 17.

The Lord your God is amidst you, a Mighty One, a Saviour [Who saves]! He will rejoice over you with joy; He will rest [in silent satisfaction] and in His love He will be silent and make no mention [of past sins, or even recall them]; He will exult over you with singing.

Amplified Bible, Classic Edition.

PART ONE

LOVE IN CONFLICT

1

Iraqi desert, March 2019.

SHOCKED HE STARED AT THE EXPLICIT PHOTOS.

Excessive perspiration dripped from him, unnoticed. The boiling heat; airless.

His attention arrested with the terrible images engraved in his mind. The betrayal left him in utter devastation.

Before long, uncontrollable hatred replaced the shock as he tossed them in the corner. It connected with a filing cabinet with a thud.

His marriage was a farce!

Vile tasting disbelief infiltrated his mouth. Balling fists pressed against the desk, his vision blurred. Automatically his fingers massaged his temples and pinched himself.

His lovely wife of twenty-five years. How could she? He had been home in February when they celebrated it, and now this.

He picked up the crumbled pictures and straightened them. The digital date and time on each caught his scrutiny—captured adequately over four years—the last one the day he left. Her track of deceit adequately defined in each emotion and position.

It joined the rest of the discarded pack. His personal world had tilted in seconds: from virtuous to depraved in a heartbeat.

The uncomfortable silence stifled the office and chairs moved. Colonel Curt McGee avoided the staff, disgraced.

He swiped the images from the table and collapsed back into his seat. Anger tightened his jaw which framed the day-old stubble.

"Sir, is everything okay?" Curt looked at his aid, speechless.

How could she? We made love that last day. We assured each other of our devotion. I was the luckiest husband on earth. The next night she was back in her lover's arms and by the roguish looks, enjoying herself.

"I'm going for a walk!"

"YES, SIR!!" THE COLONEL'S normal straight shoulders slumped, the long strides weaker.

Doug regarded the coloured prints with unease. The woman was in an appealing encounter. Buck naked, the guy pounded into her. Her hips held in a fierce grip. She was a looker.

Footsteps on gravel propelled him into action and jumbled them together, shoved it back into the large envelope marked in bold letters: Colonel Curt McGee. He then placed it in the desk's drawer.

He straightened as Sergeant First Class Ralph entered the office. A deep frown creased his rugged face. He glanced through the workplace.

"Is the colonel here?" the stern voice thundered. His DNA formed with military precision. The broad shoulders and perfect stance brooked no-nonsense.

Doug saluted him and the moment he acknowledged him, he relaxed.

"Just stepped out, Sir."

CURT WALKED TO THE FURTHEST end of the camp. How could she? Sand drifted into the warm air. And with that person? More sand floated upwards. Out of breath he glanced around, his throat parched.

A jeep pulled up and he waved the soldier closer. The private saluted, but he demanded the keys with a careless gesture. He jumped in and stepped on the accelerator. The engine roared into action as it left the camp in a dust trail.

"That bitch!" he groaned, banging the steering wheel, with tears evaporating in the drive.

Fifteen minutes later Curt stopped at the local tearoom, the owner a well-known patron of the town. Usually Curt refused his subtle offerings, but today he wanted to forget.

Once inside he removed his shades. It took a few seconds to adjust to the dimness.

Elaborated carpets, curtains and cushions divided the room into sections. The cosy place was a favourite amongst the military staff. Satisfied that he had the place to himself, he relaxed. The owner manned the battered counter to the right of him.

SAMER SLEIMAN, THE PROUD owner of the establishment, met Curt with a slight bob. He beamed with pleasure. "Ah, my favourite officer," he said, twisting his hands with the unexpected fortune.

"What do you have?" Curt asked with added interest.

"I have anything you want, my leech." Sleiman fawned with submissiveness.

"Bourbon?"

"Ah, an excellent choice, my leech."

He scrutinised the colonel. Allah has blessed him with an unusual feast; one he will savour, he thought with a smirk.

He had waited for this officer to cave.

He hated the western capitalists. They walked into his place as if it belonged to them. It irked him every time he came face to face with one of them. He made money from their drunken debauchery with no guilt.

"Any other pleasures?" Samer's hands gestured two boobs in front of him. Curt did not understand the illustration until the penny dropped.

"Yes."

"Room?"

"Yes."

"Now I can entertain the officer in my modest abode," and the ugly face transformed into an uglier mug.

"Follow me, my leech," he ordered with arrogant confidence. Samer led the way deeper into the dimmed place. The steady gait of the client energised his own pace.

The depilated stairs led to a darkened hallway. At the door of a shabby room Samer stepped aside as the officer entered and closed it with a wicked grin. It took him minutes to collect the beverages and called for his wife's niece. She would do.

Back in the room the officer showed no interest when he approached him. With undeterred greed, he spoke: "You will love this, my leech."

Samer presented the bottle with a well-known bourbon sticker. For the first time the officer's attention perked while he opened the cap. He filled a glass with the rich amber and served it. The officer sniffed the content and rolled his eyes.

Samer knew it was the best batch of bourbon he had bought. The apt name of Heaven's door with its distinctive flavour, a favourite amongst the rich Americans. Today was undeniably an outstanding day to open the case.

PLEASED WITH THE label Curt swallowed the golden liquid, the burning sensation a welcome sensation and he smacked his lips. As he caught the greed filled face, he snatched the bottle from him and ignored the gleeful chuckle.

"Bring another!" he ordered, tossing money on the bed.

Samer bowed. "I have a present, with your permission."

He waved towards the door. A woman, enclosed in black, approached them.

"I'm sure she will pleasure you, yes?" The owner pressed the girl closer. Quietly he watched her approach. When she stopped Curt removed her hijab.

Hell, she is younger than my daughter! With scorn he looked at the man directly behind her, his beady eyes sinister and smug before it returned to the girl. Outraged he wanted to dismiss her, then paused. A moral fight inside weighed him down.

"Does she please you?"

"Isn't she too young?" Long black hair protected the face, her gaze diverted to the floor.

"No, my leech, I assure you she's twenty," Samer replied, smacking her on the butt. She shrieked and blushed. Her nervous giggle echoed through him. This was not him.

Curt groaned; she was someone's daughter.

He knocked back another swig, then got to his feet. Dust motes swirled upwards with the motion and she coughed. A small hand protected her mouth.

He touched her hair and let the silk glide through his fingers. Huge, scared eyes stared at him, her innocence a sharp contrast to the environment they were in.

With a sneer he pushed them aside and left; bottle in his hand.

2

The area of Bentiu, South Sudan, Africa. April 2019.

SONIA MAIN WATCHED the human line intensely.

It often included women and children. Even early in the day sweat coated them with a glossy sheen. No one bothered to swat the persistent flies away—silence their only resolution. The ragged tent was not adequate, and a lengthy line trailed listlessly outside the tent.

It was the last day at this camp. Tomorrow they would continue to another line much bigger than this one, the war-torn country in desperate need of help.

In partnership with David Sulliman, her interpreter, they examined the patients. He was of average build, his constant smile exhibited pearly whites against the darker skin. Based in South Sudan for two years, they had developed a good working relationship. He genuinely cared about his fellow countrymen.

"David, she needs to see the doctor." Sonia pulled an older woman from the line-up. Her concealed face was feverish at the touch.

"*As-Salam Alaykum, awewe,*" he greeted the woman and showed her where to go. With slow steps she met Alice inside the tent.

"It will be another long day," Sonia said.

"Yes, it will," came the answer.

Armed with the vaccine she followed him, the clipboard present while he spoke to each person. Scanning the crowd, she shifted her attention to the landscape. The deserted area gave no hope of rain. Each breath laboured, the patients a mirrored image of the countryside, as barren as the parched earth.

"They reported another case of diarrhoea." David broke the silence during a break.

"Head Office promised to look at the quality of water." Sonia redirected her attention back to her work. "They sure can send more tents. Food and medicine are much-needed."

"The critical needs are dire," David said.

"And personnel. We need more help," Sonia said.

"You know they struggle with trained personnel." Medical personnel were difficult to find. The hours, heat and minimal luxuries held no appeal for many.

"The war doesn't help," she stated.

A sudden outcry interrupted them and both scanned the people. A woman wailed as she gripped her abdomen. The next moment she fell. Wisps of dust swirled upwards before they spread over her. Impassive bodies stood aside.

"I got this." David motioned and went closer. Sonia administered the child's drops while monitoring David. By the time she reached them, the woman was comatose. Her black skin strained over a thin frame; dull eyes stared upwards.

"She is unresponsive," David said with trepidation as Sonia knelt next to them.

"Stretcher!" Sonia called when she detected a faint pulse. The heartbeat was cumbersome.

"What do you think?" On closer examination, she replied: "She is losing the baby," and stood aside as the two soldiers approached.

"Be careful with her." In her delirious state the woman slumped around on the stretcher and Sonia calmed her with a warm touch on the arm and reached the tent with no incident.

"Here." Sonia directed them towards a bed in the corner. People pushed against them before they stepped aside. With only cardboard on the worn springs, she pulled a sheet from an empty gurney.

"Lay her down." The acrid stink of rotting flesh and sickness made breathing difficult.

"Doctor ... "

"What's wrong?"

Soft weepy sounds immersed from the patient's lips.

"The baby will not make it," the doctor whispered. A lonely tear trickled down the woman's frightened face.

"Doctor Wek will help you," Sonia said with a calmed tone. Her own heart rate already galloping.

"I struggle to find her pulse, Doctor," Sonia informed him.

The woman cried. A sudden spasm pushed blood-water from her legs. Sonia glanced at Doctor Wek knowingly, her own heart in pain.

The doctor's face was a blank canvas as he explained to the woman what had happened. More water stained the white sheet and with it came the foetus. In sync with her baby, the woman's last breath slipped from her parted lips.

Oh, Lord, no! Not again. Please!

Blocking her line of thought, Sonia turned back with a sheet. Dr Wek stood aside as she swathed her. Afterwards she notarised the death.

Another death in a senseless war no one cared about.

3

"LET'S GO PEOPLE. We must be at home before dark," David called. Sonia closed the van's backdoor. David hitched the trailer as she took her seat, the sliding door the last act of the day.

Children ran alongside them, their energy appreciated as they waved at them. Amidst the poverty they still beamed with joy.

Behind them the sombre landscape displayed tints of orange and deep yellows from the last sun rays. It softened the harshness and tedious state.

As they sped away, a boy waved at them in his run. Up ahead his donkey's gait a two-step as the cans jiggled from side to side.

Each trip to the refugee camps met her with humbleness, the children's toothy grins a personal highlight. What she valued most was their carefree attitude. They cherished life in every moment. With only the bare minimum, they seemed unworried about the future.

For the medical staff it was crucial to venture out to lift the tremendous burden. The influx of exiles gave them no rest while they suffered. She could leave, but the South Sudanese people had no choice. To help them, remained the closest she could come to excellence.

At the hospital they filed out—a tired but satisfied group. Sonia unpacked the van like a robot.

"We will help you."

"Thanks, Alice."

"They shot a doctor today," David informed them when he returned.

"Where?" The weight of their predicament oppressive.

"Khartoum—trapped with protesters inside a house in Buri. They shot him without reason," David said.

"I don't understand this wave of murders. We are here to help them," Sonia said.

"These people have no consciousness," Alice replied.

"We have to be watchful," David agreed.

Reluctant and uneasy Sonia removed the bags with filthy linen. "Take this and I will take those bags inside."

"Thanks, Alice." Sonia placed the clean linen inside the marked crate and closed the lid.

"Good night, Sonia."

"Goodnight, Alice. See you tomorrow."

In the compact kitchen Sonia drank a supplement she always had at hand, showered and went straight to bed. Lathered with enough Tabard, she added a flimsy sheet as a shield against unwanted night crawlers.

It was well after eleven when she flicked off the light. A thick blanket of darkness wrapped around her. A miserable sense which devoured you if you were not careful. Restless she stared out the small window, her thoughts far away. The moment she fell asleep, the woman's face intertwined with her own. It haunted her till she woke. Drenched in sweat she reached for the water. Once her thirst was quenched, she laid back.

The soft mattress's peaceful embrace drew her back, but sleep evaded her.

When the orange globe tinted the sky, she prayed. A solitary commodity that kept her sane. The constant battle for self-control became worse in the last couple of days.

Sticky after the night's heat, she made her way to the showers for a refreshing spray of cool water. By 6h00 she left.

"*AS-SALAM ALAYKUM, SONIA*. What a fine day to do what we love."

"*As-Salam Alaykum*, Alice."

Alice Abiodun was a local nurse and a dear friend. Her animated nature boosted her energy.

"Here comes David." She waved as he parked. David was the driver, interpreter, their only bodyguard and liaison.

"*As-Salam Alaykum,* Dr Wek." He greeted the group. He joined them two months ago and proved to be an asset to the area. His volunteer work gave him the opportunity to serve his country and he did his work with no complaints.

The stoic face of the porter appeared; a set of yellow teeth exposed. "Nurse Main, the matron wants to see you right away."

"Thanks, Max."

"What's up?" Alice said.

"Not sure."

"Hurry, we have a distance to drive today," David said.

At a quick pace she entered the hospital entrance, shivers ran along her spine. With a brief prayer she followed the white corridor. Time and age stained the painted walls. The morning shift rushed around. Lively sounds stemmed from the hospital's walls. The smells and sights were familiar.

At the connected building, a replica of the other, Sonia knocked on Matron Nyanath Haleema's office door at the end of a long corridor.

"Come in." The distinct voice of the woman coached her inside and met her with a broad smile, pristine in her uniform.

The cramped space held the bare minimum of furniture: a wooden desk with an office chair and two visitor chairs. One personal item displayed her family in a silver frame. It included her beloved husband, a local doctor and three children - two boys and a lovely girl. The children's presence damped her desires. Her choices did not allow room for a family.

"Sonia, I am sorry for the delay. I must introduce you to Major Scott. He's with the United Nations." At that precise moment two pairs of astounded eyes locked. Years spooled back to the day the door closed. Her perfect world turned into chaos.

Her unease changed to anger. A desire to harm swept through her, but she steeled herself.

"Is everything good, dear?" the older woman asked.

"All is fine." She loathed to lie; sure that the crimson would give it away. In the dim office light she hoped the older woman would not detect it.

"Sonia, this is Major Brady Scott."

A muscular hand extended towards her, but she ignored it. It remained in the air for a second or two before he let it fall to his side.

"He is here as an observer for the UN," she explained.

He could work for the devil for all she cared. His presence disrupted her world, which she so delicately closed off. Her fingers bit into her palms. *How did he find her?*

"I need to run," Sonia said.

4

HALEEMA'S FACE WAS A question mark. Sonia ignored it. She had no explanation to give. The quicker she got away, the better.

"Can I offer you water?" The director of nursing asked. Sonia paused.

"Water will be fine." Her voice's irritated tone betrayed her inner turmoil and accepted the bottle with trembled fingers. With heavy knees she took a seat.

He took the seat next to her. Brady Scott, the only man she gave herself to as an eighteen-year-old. Naively, she believed him. Alert she adjusted but the proximity left no room for distance.

His arm brushed against her every time he moved. She shifted her chair. Hate an actual emotion that threatened to erupt. Bile threatened to overpower her.

"Sonia, Major Scott's orders are to observe. He promised he will help wherever he can." Her heart thumped. Could this get any worse?

"Good," she acknowledged.

"He has to look at the water supplies since diarrhoea is the primary concern. He will note the general state of the camps and so forth. You know the drill."

"Yes," Sonia replied. Of all the people employed by the UN, why him? How could she cope for an entire week with him?

The tensed silence stretched for seconds longer before Haleema continued: "If you have no other questions, you can go."

"Thank you for your hospitality. I appreciate it, Matron." Brady's jovial voice brought a gag on, and she rose.

Sonia left first, in long strides. Her sneakers squeaked on the nylon floors and echoed through the busy corridor. She did not want to be near him, ever.

A food trolley with empty breakfast dishes rumbled past her.

Why God?

"Sonia." He kept with her pace; she moved faster.

"Sonia, please!"

"I have nothing to say to you, Major Scott," and stretched her steps. She would play her part for this week, but that was it.

"Sonia," his voice dipped in frustration. He caught her arm and spun her towards him. "Please."

"What?" Hatred erupted as she glanced at his hand. Brady removed it.

"I didn't know …," he started.

"You didn't know what, Major?"

"I didn't expect to see you here." He moved closer. Her heart rate picked up and she folded her arms, her knuckles white.

"Get away from me."

With a dismissive look she picked up her pace to the entrance. Her team waited outside the double glass doors. Alice's gaze turned to the entrance before she looked at her watch. Time was important, by six they must be on the road.

In search of the water bottle, she sighed. She had left it behind in her rush to get away.

"Do you have an extra bottle of water?"

"Yes." Alice handed her a spare. Her gaze focused on Brady. Half-heartedly she made the introductions.

"Major Brady Scott will join us for the next few days. We should cooperate with him."

David moved first and greeted Brady with a cheerful handshake. The rest followed while she got in the packed van. Once seated, she took a long swig.

"Are you okay?" Alice asked, then peered at Brady.

She brushed through the curly hair. "Yes, thanks Alice," and arranged her hair in a scrunchy she had nearby. From her worn bag, the only possession she had left from her parents, she removed sun block.

"You sure? You don't look well?"

"Don't worry, I am fine," she clipped. Her aggravation was palpable.

"Do you know the man?"

"Alice, please drop it." It came sharper than intended. It grated her enough without the persistent questions. Instead, she focused on the throng outside.

A military truck roared past them and drowned Brady's responses to the men.

She closed her eyes; a headache pounded a staccato behind her eyelids, the window a resting place as she prayed for patience, wisdom, but mostly for peace.

David started the van once the sliding door closed.

THE TOWN BUZZED with people. Their wares balanced on their heads, ready to barter in Bentiu.

Scattered trees lined the gravel road. The rest of the countryside was dry, black and barren. A slight breeze caused toll bushes to cross the veld in a flurry. The rising sun held no promise of rain.

Once they left the busyness behind, the road snaked to the north; dust trailed behind them. The potholes caused uncomfortable moments inside the cabin.

Yet the conversations were amicable. Brady's voice broke the monotone trip. He peppered Dr Wek with questions which the doctor answered in a cool tone.

A heavily pregnant woman hustled towards town, four children behind her. Each balanced a can on their heads, waving at them.

She had to admit Brady looked good. The white shirt which spread over a broad chest, the muscular hands in a flurry as it talked with him. It brought back many memories. The shades concealed the bluest eyes she could drown in.

But time left its mark. His laugh lines were deeper, his skin battered from exposure. The crew cut which framed his face gave him a sharp square appearance that was coated with grey. He was still good looking. Back then, his hair had a natural blond wave.

They talked about a future. That was twenty-five years ago. Brady promised her the world and she believed him. She had nowhere to go, no family to turn to. It was only him.

Then he left. No word, no note or phone call to explain his sudden absence, the streets her only choice. The things she did for survival still left her disgusted.

5

SUDDENLY THE VEHICLE stopped and it yanked her back to the present.

"Be quiet," David demanded as he opened the window. "No sudden movements and no heroics," he said.

Alarmed, Sonia noticed the barricade in the road: burning tyres, barb wire and rocks littered it. Ten boy-soldiers' weapons trained on them.

The eldest approached David. At twenty years of age he looked ominous.

He looked inside the van, meeting her with a scrutinising glare. She covered herself with the scarf.

"Papers!" Reaching for the bag she passed hers along with the other documents to David, who handed it to him. For the longest minutes he studied the papers, then the van. Every muscle tensed as they waited for David.

"Get out!" the leader ordered in threadbare English. David tried to appease the youth, but the soldier was adamant to search them.

Another soldier tapped against the slide door window with his rifle. Alice, the closest, opened it. They pulled her from the van. One touched her face and she shrieked.

"What do you want?" Brady demanded as he followed. "Brady, quiet," she warned the moment she stepped from the cabin. Alice stood closer to Sonia. Their hands locked.

The leader marched around the van. "What's inside?" he demanded. Brady moved forward, but David shook his head: DO NOTHING STUPID, he messaged. Sonia held his arm.

"We are on our way to Yida Refugee camp. We are with the United Nations and Red Cross, see."

David showed him the banner. "We help the people."

Another soldier examined every window tentatively. At the back he stopped.

Sonia held her breath, her face concealed behind a scarf. All their supplies were there. Without it, they could not continue.

One boy looked at her and she pushed deeper into the van's protection, Alice's closeness a silent strength.

Still the questions continued. David kept his calm throughout the negotiations. During a pause Sonia lifted her gaze just in time to witness as he handed the leader his wristwatch and laptop. The older boy showed Dr Wek to get back in the front, then Alice followed. Sonia moved along, then he stopped her. One youngster, no older than fifteen, grabbed her. She yelped, fighting against the hold.

David intervened: "Please, she is part of the team. She must go with us," he explained.

"No! No!" the leader yelled. A heated debate ensued between them, his grip painful on her arm. Her heart raced.

"Let go of her!" Brady manoeuvred his larger frame between them. The boy's grip lessened, but his eyes blazed. It caused an uproar with the soldiers. Another attacked Brady.

SONIA HEARD THE PUNCHES, but his body shield remained. His bulky frame her only lifeline.

"Please, Lord. I don't want to stay here. Please help us," she prayed. Her body pressed into the metal.

"Please, here are my shoes," David offered. The punches stopped and Sonia peered from the scarf. He let go of Brady. The release gave her time to jump into the van and fell in Alice's arms.

When she looked back, David handed them a packet of cigarettes and a bottle of brandy. Cheers erupted as he hurried inside the van and closed the door.

6

THE TENSION IN THE VEHICLE remained while David shifted the gears and sped away. Shaking hands clutched the steering wheel. His face masked with sweat.

"Thank you, David," Dr Wek said.

"It was close; you have done well. And our supplies are still intact," Sonia said.

A nervous giggle slipped from Alice. "Thank You, Lord." And the group said: "Amen."

"Are you okay?" Brady leaned on the back of the bench.

"Yes, thanks." Her parched throat combined with the headache did not help. With shaky movements she opened her bag and searched the content. Once she found the tablets, she swallowed them with mouthfuls of water.

"I owe you an apology," Brady said to David.

"Don't worry. These youngsters are out to prove themselves. They only want luxuries, nothing more."

"I will make sure you get at least your watch, laptop and shoes back."

"Don't be concerned about it." His accent was heavy this time around.

Once back on the road, silence filled the cabin. David received water from Alice.

Just after 12h00 they stopped at the refugee camp; welcomed by a group of people. The camp was larger than the ones they visited. Another medical team was already hard at work.

"*As-Salam Alaykum*, Ibrahim." David greeted the head of the team. "Let me introduce you to Major Brady from the United Nations."

Introductions continued while Sonia and Alice carried the supplies to the erected tent. When Dr Wek joined, the team greeted him cheerfully. Doctors were a rarity in these parts and highly revered.

The multitude gathered nearby. During a break she noticed Brady as he interviewed the camp's chiefs, the notebook well used folded in his hand with ease as he scribbled every grievance they had.

This camp was better organised. With educational programs in place, the jovial mood buzzed around them. The U.N.H.C.R. or the United Nations Refugee Agency did its best to ensure a future for the people.

I hope he jotted security as of the utmost importance. Today we were lucky. It could have been worse, Sonia thought.

She relished the updated version, then stopped with the comparisons. *He was part of her former life. No reason to go there.*

Terrified and tired people arrived at the camp later in the day. "What happened, David?"

"New arrivals. It seemed they had fled from a village kilometres from here. They are in a bewildered state."

"Should I come?"

"No, Ibrahim will call if they need help."

Alice bumped against her. "Look!" On the outskirts of the camp more UN military vehicles arrived.

"Sonia, Alice, they need help with the supplies," Brady called and rolled his sleeves on his way. A lengthy line extended between the trucks and tables. Lines of refugees formed behind the table.

The flurry of movement added more people to the existing masses. Experience caused them to evaluate and give what was needed. They promptly sent those with medical needs to the medic tent. The teams worked in harmony till late.

There were no deaths that day.

EARLY MORNING SONIA enjoyed the silence of the first light.

"Can we talk?" Brady's closeness shocked her.

"No," her antagonism clear. Frustrated fingers ran through the crew cut. She remembered those hands, the long limbs, the clean-cut nails which could make her purr in want.

"I want to talk to you."

"You said enough twenty-five years ago," she clipped.

"I know I was acting …"

"You were not acting, you walked out on a pregnant me."

"I …" He tried again, at a loss for words.

"We had a boy, his birthday would have been September 20th." Removing a curl, she sighed. "Leave! You are good at that."

He tried again. "LEAVE!" Her face contorted into pain and hurt, and he left.

She slumped in the dirt and touched her barren tummy; one tear found its way to the dusty earth. Her son's body flashed before her. Grief overwhelmed her, even after all these years it stayed with her.

As the first rays touched her dark curls, she calmed.

7

Iraqi desert.

EMOTIONALLY DRAINED CURT STARED out the window. It took two days to become sane again, days from which the owner of the tearoom profited.

How Clark got him into his room unnoticed, he did not know. Alcohol obscured these days in a haze of oblivion.

His aid needed a raise for what he had put him through. Between him and Phillip's visits, he cleared his head. In the end the lifestyle was not him. His stern religious upbringing told him as much. The anger remained, and now he drowned himself in work.

"Contact Vivian," Phillip said.

"I fear what I will say to her."

"No matter. Get this over."

The chaplain was correct. With a deep sigh, he dialled the number. When she did not answer, he left a message. In the afternoon he tried again and left another message. On day three she finally answered.

"Hello, Love."

"Vivian, why don't you answer your phone?"

"I am busy."

"I can only guess. Did you receive the divorce papers?"

"Yes, I don't understand. Why?"

Stay calm, he cautioned himself. "Because you don't honour your vows," he breathed out. He wants out, now!

"That is your word against mine. The answer is no."

He looked at the phone, not sure he heard her. "Vivian?" The line was dead.

DAMMIT, Vivian! He dialled her number, but a busy tone greeted him.

"DAD, I HAVE SENT you the letters I have found."

"What letters?"

"Love letters. It spanned over a long time between her and several men." After a deep breath he composed himself. Just the ammunition he needed to solve the problem, he thought with a smirk.

Something was off with Jillian, her cheery self, subdued.

"How are you?"

"Good. Just busy."

"How are your studies?"

"Good, thanks, Dad," she clipped. Doug appeared. "I have to go, sweetheart. Speak soon."

"Speak soon." So soft he had to strain his ear, then she was gone.

Leaning back Curt took a large gulp of water. The discussion with Jillian muddled.

"SIR, YOU NEED A BREAK." Doug studied his superior officer. The strain of life was visible.

"Permission to talk, Sir?" Though the colonel did not give him his attention, he went ahead.

"I won a holiday to Malta." That had the result as the commander stirred.

"Did you say something, Sergeant Clark?"

"Yes, Sir." He smiled at the motionless face staring at him.

"I won a break away. It is not much. I want to give it to you, Sir." The bemused look on the colonel's face gave away his surprise as he leaned back in the chair. The late afternoon sun coloured his hair in taints of gold.

"You want to send me away?"

"You need it, Sir. The men complained you drive them too hard."

"When is this break away supposed to be?"

"This weekend, Sir, in Malta," a sacrifice he made gladly. The colonel needed it more.

"Malta …" He stopped for a while. "Small island south of Italy," he murmured.

"Yes, Sir, that's the place."

"How do I get there?"

"The ticket covers a round trip to Rome where you will board the plane, heading out at 11h00 am on Friday."

"That means?"

"You leave at 21h00, Thursday, to catch the flight at midnight."

"The red-eye?"

"Yes, Sir. You need this, Sir."

"I will think about it." He turned to his paperwork. A haggard face filled with doubts and worries.

That was Doug's cue to leave. He did not understand the urgency about the trip, but obedience was better than sacrifice. He had learned this at the foster home back in the States.

Behind the workshops he found a quiet spot and prayed. The colonel needed a Saviour ... now more than ever.

Once done, a sense of peace settled in his spirit. He broke out in a joyful whistle on his way to the mess.

God will make a way.

8

25 April, Bentiu, South Sudan.

"I DON'T POKE MY NOSE where it doesn't belong, but do you know the major?"

Last night Sonia handed the report to Nyanath and dashed to her room without a word. She needed time alone. The last three days were brutal. Brady's presence tired her more than her work.

She could not avoid the conversation, even if she tried, and placed a bag in its compartment.

"Yes, it's a long story."

"This will not influence your work?" came the question as she touched her shoulder.

"No, never, I assure you." Sonia met her gaze before she busied herself and stacked the blankets in the compartment. Her eyes burned from tiredness.

"Do you want to talk?"

"No," she said and closed the door, meeting the soft mocha eyes. A tear materialised.

"When last did you enjoy a weekend?" The sudden change in topic took her unawares and she fingered her hair, her mind blank and blushed.

"That long!" She laughed. "Well, I think it's time for you to take a break. Let me see what I can do for this weekend and inform you of the details when you return." Dumbfounded Sonia stared at her.

"It's time to go!" Dr Wek broke her trance.

Sonia placed her shoulder bag in the van.

"Get this behind you. Whatever troubles you, you must get through it."

It was true. She had to deal with Brady and rethink her life. The baby's death would not be in vain.

"Thank you, Matron. I can make my own arrangements."

"No dear, let me. You have worked hard these last couple of months. Every person on the team enjoyed a restful time away. And yes, I have checked. Since you came to us, you never took a holiday or a weekend." Sonia smiled. She could not argue with that.

Voices reached them and Haleema cut the conversation short: "When last did you eat?" Sonia could not remember.

"Get food in you. You are no good to me sick." She touched her arm in encouragement.

"Sure," she replied.

"I have to run."

"Make it quick!" David said.

While washing hands she realised what a mess she looked. Her normal tan was pale, even with the makeup. From her pocket she removed a lipstick, applied it and left.

Once she turned the corner, she walked into an unmovable wall. She yelped in surprise as firm hands grabbed her and pinned her against the wall in one quick movement. She gasped at the sudden intrusion. Brady Scott's warm breath tickled her cheek.

Their gazes locked and her senses went into overdrive. He smelled great. Clean and … no. She stopped herself and anger replaced the infatuation.

Her feelings for him died a long time ago. Firing eyes returned his stare, and he let go of her arms.

"You are ignoring me for three days now. You don't give me time to explain."

"I hate you," she hissed out.

She fought against him, but he was too strong for her to move him even a fraction. Steal arms had caged her.

"Let me go, Major," she spat out.

"No, they can wait a few minutes."

Then she punched him. Immediately he backed away.

"Please listen," he insisted, but she hissed out: "Let me go, Major," and then he did something unexpected.

He kissed her—hard. With all the strength she possessed, she pushed him back, then slapped him.

"You will never touch me again, is that understood, Brady," she whispered through clenched teeth. "Never!"

"I am so sorry. Please let me explain."

"You said you loved me, and then you left me." This time a sob developed. "You felt nothing for me. Not for me or our son. You left." She stepped away.

Brady stepped closer and repeated his apology. "I am sorry, sweetheart."

She scowled. "You have no business calling me sweetheart. Leave me alone!"

This time he stepped back. In her rush she wiped away the traces of her turmoil, straightened her clothes and add more lipstick to her bruised ego.

HE DID HER A GREAT INJUSTICE. The news floored him. He and his wife struggled to have children. He had hoped to meet the child one day.

He remembered the day he heard the news. He was ecstatic. For hours he proclaimed his love to her as they made love. He declared his devotion to her.

Seeing her he realised he still did. He loved Christa, but theirs was a comfortable relationship, their love a quiet stream with no currents. Sonia's love was passionate, and she gave unconditionally. Just a slight brush against her skin would kindle her desire. It saddened him to learn she had not found love. The man she commits to would be one lucky person.

Quietly he trailed her through the camp. Her sweetness towards the refugees moved him.

He remembered the day he saw his father. The shock on their faces brought him back to reality. His father used his influence and shipped him off to an army camp at Upington, Northern Cape. He had no means to contact her, and after three months of basic training she had disappeared. He had just turned twenty-one.

The landlord removed her. Sick to the stomach he could only guess her whereabouts. He had searched everywhere with no success. He could not blame her for acting as she did.

"Please Lord, soften her heart."

God forgive me, but I still love her. How can I go back to Christa? His thoughts dipped in sorrow. He knew he had to continue with his own farce. He could not turn his back on another woman. Not now, no matter his feelings.

Dark shades masked his distress. With a notebook in his hand, he approached the crowd. He volunteered to come, his ever-growing resume: his motivation to excel. He never expected to find her here.

Brady kicked at a loose stone and dust veneered his boot. He grimaced. His life stretched before him as a dust cloud with no change.

Concentrate man, he chastised himself. *To dwell on this will not help. Rather pour your energy into the work.*

The enormity of this country's plight was horrendous. The shortage of food and water great, the pitiable living condition of the people worse.

Security, another importance, particularly for the staff. They did miracles every day, but with the added danger it was a risk that exposed them even more.

He looked towards the small posture of the nurse, bended over a patient. A wretched cry from the woman filled the air, the weight thereof immediate as Sonia walked away. He noticed how she wiped her face.

"What happened?" he asked Alice.

"The woman lost her baby." The simple comment punched him in the gut.

He found her inclined against a leafless tree; her back turned to the camp. Standing behind her he waited till the shoulders relaxed.

"I am sorry for your loss; I never meant to hurt you."

She kept quiet, then moved. An arm brushed against him.

"I am sorry for that woman who lost her baby," he continued. This time she looked at him.

"Really? You are sorry. What part will you understand?" Her tone low and dangerous.

"My wife had lost a baby. Ever since we struggle to conceive again."

She gasped: "You are married?"

"Yes, seven years - without success of a child." Turning towards her, he continued: "You must believe me, my father tricked me. I was helpless back then."

SHE LOOKED AT HIM QUIZZICALLY. "Why?" His news floored her. Miserableness made way for curiosity.

"Because I had to. My parents forced me." His gaze on the landscape.

"Your parents?" She remembered them. They were never fond of her. Coming from a mining community, she was beneath their class. The Scott's never accepted her.

"Yes, I told them you carried my child, but they didn't care. My father enlisted me. Before I could get away, they dragged me away. All communication severed." He removed his glasses and cleaned them before he concealed his eyes once more. Never meeting her watchful gaze.

"I tried to contact you after the basic training, but you were not at the flat. I was going insane with worry and searched for you, but had to return or face jail time."

Silently she examined Brady, her own hurt so real she struggled to believe his version. She hated him. It kept her going; motivated her.

"The landlord evicted me. I didn't eat for days," she peered at the surroundings. A slight breeze played with her curls. "I slept with men for a meal while my body ached with the pregnancy. The things they did with me I don't want to remember." Her disgrace was enormous and Brady wrapped her in his arms. With her face buried in his shoulder, she cried.

Once calmer she pushed him away—the sadness replaced with disdain. "Because I was underweight, starving in fact, he came too early. A police officer took us to the hospital where the nurses helped me. A benefactor enrolled me in the nursing program. Here I am, re-experiencing the events through the many women in this god-forsaken country." Her voice laced with frustration.

"I am sorry for what I have done to you. I should have fought harder," he sighed. "I still love you, Sonia. You always had my heart," he assured her.

She stopped him cold.

"Please go, Brady. It isn't true. There's nothing more to say."

"If only …"

"There's no if's, Brady. You're too late." She pushed him away.

Brady watched her disappear into the medic tent and his shoulders drooped.

Yes, he was too late, and he lost.

9

SHIELDED EYES FOLLOWED SONIA'S retreating
back before it sculpted into a frown. He observed the
white man as he slumped with defeat and clicked his
tongue: "*Nu lalaki bodas teu terang kumaha ngatur
awéwé,*" (The white man does not know how to manage
his woman.) He grinned.

"*Éta awéwé anu kuring nyarioskeun ka anjeunIt.*" (It is
the woman I told you about) the soldier said. Well-
hidden from prying eyes they followed the woman as she
did her duties.

"She knows the white man's medicine. She can help," he
explained.

"Why do I need another woman?"

"You don't have one like her. She is a healer." He
glanced at the leader. "If you don't want her as a woman,
I will take her."

Since he saw her on Monday, he was obsessed with her. His prestige would grow even more with her at his side.

The leader snickered: "You don't know how to please a woman, and that one is trouble."

"I have learned," he hissed. The older man waved him to silence.

"No, you're right. I can use another woman."

"You right, she is trouble," the youngster replied. He wanted her from the moment he saw her.

"We must plan this carefully; too many eyes," the leader said.

"No, we can do it when they leave."

"No, I don't trust the white man." The leader nodded in Brady's direction.

"We do it when she's alone."

Iraqi desert.

"SERGEANT CLARK, WHERE is the vehicle report? Ralph put it on my table. I'm sure of it."

After a quick search, Doug handed it to the colonel. "Here it is, Sir."

Curt snapped it away. "Get me, Saunders!" he ordered.

Curt peered out the window. The phone conversation he had with his daughter disturbed him.

Jillian never cried. The truth disclosed through tears shocked him to the core. It was not fabricated from a young, deranged woman looking for attention. No, rather from a much abused one. *Why didn't they tell him any of this earlier?*

How could Vivian do this?

Her lover seduced Jillian, and she did not stop it. Even his son, Mark, two years younger than Jillian, suffered abuse under the man.

He was still motionless when Clark and Saunders returned.

"Sir?" the sergeant said.

Startled Curt looked at both and barked: "At ease!"

"Take a seat."

With the temperature at 47°C, their clothes were saturated with sweat. A slight breeze filtered through the flaps, but it made no difference. The fan did not disturbed the air either.

Curt offered them water and returned to the report, the shortages of parts for the vehicles, serious.

When a soldier approached Doug with a message from radio control, they stopped. He relayed the message to the colonel in a hushed tone.

Curt excused himself. General Cartwright wanted to meet.

"Good day, Curt." The impressive figure of the general appeared on the screen. Friendly greetings exchanged before the general came to the point.

"Private T. J. Cummings has allegedly murdered a woman. They said you refused to send the file."

"Yes Sir, I did."

"Why?"

"Something is off with this case. Before I hand them the file, I want to speak to Cummings first, sir."

"He is no longer under your command after he deserted his post."

"No matter, General, he needs help. I don't think he did it."

"I don't care what you believe. Send the file and get it done."

Curt did not like it. That the general phoned him, meant someone higher up demanded it.

He had been optimistic about Private T. J. Cummings' future. His knowledge made him an asset. He lived in the country his entire life; he knew the area and spoke the language fluently.

Back then Curt hoped the soldier would explain the events which triggered the AWOL. No one had seen him ever since, until now.

Why would he murder someone? It was not his nature; he was military potential. Now he faced jail.

Back at the office Ralph awaited him with another emergency and sent the file to the mailroom. With it he sent hope that all would work out for him and that his future would not be marred by this case.

The envelope marked:

TOP SECRET General Cartwright.

10

Thursday afternoon, Iraqi desert, 25 April 2019.

"SIR, IT'S TIME TO GO."

"Why?" Curt asked without looking at his aid. Doug smiled. The man had forgotten about the getaway.

"The chopper will take you to Bagdad at 22h00," he informed him undisturbed.

"You delivered the file?"

"Yes, Sir."

"Good. I will get my stuff ready."

"Here is the itinerary and your tickets."

"Thanks, Doug. It has been a while since I have been this excited about a getaway."

"Enjoy, Sir."

CURT HAD CHECKED THE WEBSITE. If it resembled the pictures, he should enjoy the stay.

At 20h00 he rushed to his quarters and changed into civvies. From the shelf he grabbed an overnight bag, throwing in the necessities. At the last moment, he packed a dress shirt and pants. Maybe …

The mirror showed a person of confidence—a faint grin enhanced the attractive face. He still had it and stretched. The broad shoulders looked great under the shirt and the denim gloved his narrow hips sporting well-toned legs underneath.

The moment he sat in the chopper he relaxed.

All the worries would be Monday's problem.

The younger man was kind enough to offer it to him, and he will not disappoint him.

He laid back and listened as the pilot went through the checklist, and then lifted. The swooping blades overpowered every other sound. God, he loved it; shutting his eyes with appreciation.

Once in the air his thoughts drifted to the children. Guilt: a strong emotion he had to deal with. Vivian's lover left emotional scars on his boy. Mark did not know where he belonged. He always believed his children should find their own path, but he will let go of that resolution if he had too. The military a good straightener.

Jillian also struggled, and with the added pressures of her studies she barely held on. There was more to the story. Nevertheless, she did not confide in him. His children needed him.

Rattled, he prayed—something he neglected for years. The weight of parenting lay heavy on his heart. He could only speak to One Person.

21h00 Bentiu, Thursday evening.

BACK IN HER ROOM, a knock disturbed the quietness. In no mood to receive visitors, Sonia opened the door. Haleema greeted her with a soft smile. She opened the door wider. "Come in, Matron."

"Thank you, Sonia." The door closed with a soft click.

"Please sit." She watched as the matron examined her living space and followed her gaze. Except for a table which sported an empty vase, a handmade frame, a gift from the matron's daughter and a wired beaded rose, there were no other memorabilia. A decorated lamp in the room's corner removed the sombreness.

When a yawn escaped, she covered her mouth.

"I do apologies for my late intrusion. I know how tired you must be. It was a long week."

Haleema lifted her hand before Sonia could respond. "I have wonderful news I had to share with you. I know this is unexpected, but I took the liberty to book a holiday," she said, her soft voice filled with care.

"You can't go on like this. You need a break."

"But …"

"No buts. You will leave early tomorrow morning to Khartoum. There my uncle will meet you and fly you to Cairo. An Alitalia flight will take you to Valetta, on the island of Malta. I have a nephew who works at the Excelsior Grand Hotel. He arranged everything. Your visit includes a stay of two nights and three days."

When Sonia finally understood the meaning, she embraced the woman. Shock made way for surprise but raised her spirit tremendously.

"This is a wonderful surprise, thank you."

"You deserve this holiday, dear."

"I didn't expect this, though."

"The best part is that the spas are inside the hotel." She handed her a white envelope. Tugged inside gift vouchers waited.

"The island is small enough to stroll or to rent a scooter to the places they recommend and maybe have a romance." Warmth spread over her as her friend chuckled.

"Move on, Sonia; find someone to love and cherish. You have so much love to give." She stared at her friend.

Was her loneliness that obvious? She could not even remember the last time she had a relationship. Romance, the last thing on her mind.

"This is such a surprise. I never thought you would actually do this. Thank you."

"You are welcome." About to leave, Haleema stopped and turned. "The weather is sunny, pack your bikini."

"Yes, Ma'am." She giggled, the sound so unfamiliar to her. Her insides flipped with the unexpected adventure and she fell on her bed. The idea revitalising and she did an air-dance. This is something she had not done in a long time, but the act so free that a smile erupted on her lovely face.

Fascinated with the island, she searched the web. The rich history and baroque landmarks inspired her.

Tucked away at the southernmost part of Europe, it promised to be the perfect place to test the waters for romance.

The opportunity to change a good possibility and opened the door to the cupboard with renewed energy.

"Thank you, Lord."

11

04h00 Bentiu 26 April 2019.

"YOU SURE YOU HEARD CORRECTLY?" Jabu asked.

Abasi looked around, terrified of the danger. Die-hards roamed the empty streets, women of the night advertised their goods. The youth stood close to burning konkas, sipping liquor they confiscated from drunkards.

Jabu had asked him to meet at the hospital. A fierce expression marked his face that demanded obedience even if you knew it was wrong.

"She leaves tonight and will be back Sunday night."

"I can grab her at the airport. It will be the best place while it is quiet," he mumbled.

Abasi regarded him with trepidation. If not for the money he owed, he would have never done it. He admired nurse Sonia. His mother would kill him when she learned about his deceit. He knew he mixed with the wrong crowd when he lost SSP20 (South Sudanese pound) during gambling. He did not know how to repay him, but Jabu said he should not worry. It sounded good at first … information for a clean slate. He never thought Sonia's name would be the one when he agreed to it.

Jabu leaned on an old run-down jeep parked in the shadows of the dilapidated building. Talking with a person inside the jeep shielded in the shadows.

The moment nurse Main left the living quarters, Abasi stepped deeper into the shadows as she got in the taxi.

"I want you to let me know if her plans changed … and Abasi, not a word to anyone."

"Yes, Jabu." Abasi received a slap.

"Fool! You never say my name in public," he hissed while he skimmed the area.

"*Punten.*" (Sorry) Tears pricked his eyes, his lip quivering.

"Run, baby!" Jabu chuckled. "Not a word to Mommy."

Abasi ran as fast as his twelve-year-old legs could carry him the five blocks before he reached his home.

JABU SCRUTINISED THE boy as he hurried away. Jabu had a name amongst the children. Enforcing fear, a game he played with anyone who dared to challenge him.

"Well?" The leader's voice trembled with impatience, a trail of smoke the only sign of his existence.

"Is everything in order?"

"Yes, Haji." He swallowed the fear that wanted to stop him. He only had one chance to do this.

"I set it for Monday morning. The kid will collaborate with us?"

"Yes, all set, Haji. The kid's scared; he will not talk," he replied, his face a blank mask. One wrong word would alarm the leader of his deception.

"Good! I have great plans for you, Jabu."

"Thank you, Haji." He feigned humbleness and shielded the grin.

PART TWO
LOVE'S
DECISIONS

12

Valletta Capital of Malta, 26 April 2019.

"MR MCGEE?" A GREY, HALOED MAN GREETED HIM. Curt lowered his sunglasses and nodded.

"Follow me, please."

"Sure," he responded with light-heartedness. Ever since the trip began, he forced himself to think happy thoughts. The dark that hardened him left at the compound.

With excitement he had studied the brochures on the flight. Streets stretched in straight lanes along Valletta. From the air it looked like an architectural artwork. The palace with its golden roof blazed in the rising sun whilst sail ships cruised the coastline. Others moored in various marinas along the coastline—the main marina, the Grand Harbour, vexed in time were cluttered with colour. The brochures described it accurately.

The White SUV waited outside the terminal with the Grand Excelsior Hotel emblem in big bold gold prints. Curt placed his bag at the back. Inside the cab the guide introduced himself: "My name is Armanno," and proffered a chubby hand.

"Please to meet you, Armanno. Call me Curt." As he pulled into the traffic Armanno pointed out distinctive landmarks, his enthusiasm tangible.

"Where did it all start?" Curt's curiosity peaked.

"It goes back to the 16th Century. During the crusade period."

"That long back?"

"Malta has a proud history. We are the smallest capital city in the European Union. In 1813 we became a British colony and served as a way station for ships. We were an important Allied base for the North Africa and Mediterranean operations. We received our independence in 1964 and became a Republic in 1974. Our history includes the Ottoman invasion. You will find noteworthy museums here. They showcase the relics of each period."

"I never knew it's importance and the vital role it played in history. The museums are on my itinerary for the weekend," Curt promised.

"You will not be disappointed. There is always something new to discover."

They followed Route 6. The landscape changed from city to country. At a circle Armanno turned left. They continued with Triq Vincenzo Dimech road. Minutes later they entered another dense region. The imposing wall of the fortified city in view declared a World Heritage centre. It attracted visitors across the globe.

At the hotel the entrance caught Curt's attention. The circular garden boasted with two fountains. Small decorative trees lined the pathway and three limestone arches completed it. At the zebra crossing they entered the coolness of the shade. Impressive glass doors invited them inside. A serene atmosphere filtered through the marble entrance.

Tourists took pictures, fascinated with the surroundings. His attention drifted upwards. The crystal chandelier stressed the enormity of the place and gave it an elegant superiority. They stopped at the mahogany desk. Next to it a marble horse and boy stood hip high, the craftsmanship precise.

A young, soft-spoken Italian supplied him his card. "Gracias," he thanked her.

Armanno wished him well and left him in the care of a younger man. The bellboy stepped forward. "Can I carry your bag, Sir?"

"No thanks." The bellboy bowed slightly and led the way.

"This way, Sir."

Classical music played inside the lift. Mirror covered walls reflected a tired image, an image he planned to rectify.

The doors opened on the second floor. A whiff of spices accosted him at the door. He missed the brunette by millimetres as she stepped in. The smallest of smiles transformed the youthful face. A glimpse of emerald eyes met his. Then she disappeared.

"What a sight," he sighed and smiled.

"Did you say something, Sir?"

"No."

At his door the bell boy produced the card and opened it. The large canvas of translucent aqua left him breathless. From the balcony the amoeba-shaped pool gleamed like polished crystal. The cool wetness offered relaxation.

"I hope you find this satisfactory?"

"Yes," he answered, handing the bellboy a euro bill. He returned to the panoramic view and filled his lungs with the ocean breeze. Next to the fountain colourful umbrellas dotted the pool. Guests relaxed on deck chairs.

About to turn, the brunette re-appeared, her green sarong swayed with her. One tanned leg revealed itself cheekily with each step. From his advantage point he appreciated the perfect curves, the delicate shoulders of the slender body. At a deck chair she removed her sunglasses and let the material slip.

With graceful fluency she disappeared into the water. He followed her blurry outline until she re-appeared. All rational thoughts of unfaithful women aside.

His body reacted in a delicious way, a memory so vague that nostalgia tucked his body. With a final appreciative look he changed into his swimming trunks. A bright red towel draped around his neck.

Inside the elevator he tapped the rail as it glided to the main lobby. The doors swished open, and he trotted to the pool with a feeling of excitement. An empty chair next to hers waited for him and he dropped his towel. He spotted her at the far end of the pool already returning back towards him. She glided through the water with easy strokes. Sinking into the coolness he waited in her path. *Corny,* he thought with a grin. He had to see the emeralds and glorious smile. It was not possible that he imagined her smile. He needed the reassurance. The moment she touched him, he helped her to her feet. His eagerness captured in a moment of quietness.

His world, as he knew it, stopped when she smiled. Twin dimples appeared in an open face. The emeralds glitter with enjoyment and he could not help himself. He laughed, a deep belly laugh that released the ache in his heart.

A momentous second ... a turning point of his entire world.

SONIA'S HEART JUMPED. *IT IS HIM!*

She stepped back and shielded her face. Water dripped from day-old stubble, blue eyes sparkled with merriment. His bulk dusted with a wisp of light hair, the crew cut neat. *What a hunk,* she gushed.

"I'm so sorry, I didn't notice you." Her breaths betrayed her energy kick. The encounter with Mr Hunk added to the exhilaration, a pleasant stop which removed the cobwebs she drowned in the coolness.

He was not part of the itinerary, but plans could change. Right?

"The pleasure is all mine, Ms," he said in an American drawl. His eyes displayed genuine interest.

She wiped the water from her face and to hide her admiration. Someone pushed against her and she fell into him. His arms locked behind her. His face lowered. She stopped breathing—shocked, but in a good way. She could not believe what he was doing.

"What …?"

Stunned their lips connected. A cascade of colour enhanced it. Worlds shifted and ears blocked the noise. A soft tone manoeuvred its sound waves between them, caressing the connection. They forgot all except for the here and now.

"From the moment I saw you, I wanted to kiss you." He breathed. "I call that an excellent introductory to a surprising experience." He drawled softly.

A pregnant silence followed, brought on by the unexpected link. Sonia rested against him. The rapid pulse beneath his skin mimicked her own heartbeat. She cupped it with her hand. He groaned and drew her closer.

Infinite time locked in seconds passed.

Retreating backwards, dumbstruck.

What just happened?

The distance caused cool water to fill the space she created. Bereft of a vital part, she shivered.

"Don't …" He reached out, but she shook her head. Fantasy made way as her mind registered the reality of it.

This never happens. This partnership is not possible.

"I have to go."

"I want to see you."

"I'm not sure it is a good thing."

"Why?"

"Because …" She suppressed a giggle. There was no reason not to meet. Besides, the matron ordered her to have a romance. "I will love it," she whispered and got out.

Out of character she knelt at the edge. "By the way, my name is Sonia," and trotted away. The tone's sound waves stayed with her and she smiled.

"MS MAIN?"

"Yes."

"Please follow me."

Comfortable on the massage bed her thoughts focused on the pool, the immediate connection of the meeting. They formed an undeniable bond in those tender moments.

"Ms, are you all right?"

"Yes ..."

"You are shaking, are you sure?"

No, I am not, I am terrified. How is it possible that every barrier I had erected, broke?

He is a stranger. Do not do something stupid, Sonia. You hardly know him. You read too much in the stolen kiss.

But I can have a brief romance, can't I?

The conversation in her mind quieted as she surrendered to the ministrations of the beauticians. After an hour she left the spa in high spirits. A boutique caught her attention.

"Welcome. Are you looking for a specific dress?"

"Something elegant. It's been a while since I spoiled myself."

"Let's correct that." The saleswoman smiled and led her to a colourful display of lace and silk. Brushing through the latest fashions Sonia stopped at a soft, yellow tea gown.

"The dress is a classic, and with your skin tone it will look lovely. Would you care to try it on?"

"Yes, please." In the fitting booth she agreed with the woman as she twirled in front of the mirrors. The price tag caused a deep intake of breath. It was steep, but she could spoil herself. Years of working in Africa allowed her no reason to spend. Her savings had grown in a tidy sum.

Content with her shopping spree she entered the lift.

The setting sun gave her a marvellous view of the Manoel Island Yacht Marina which she enjoyed. Taking her time to adorn herself with the things she bought, she twirled again. Her reflection showed a different person she had not seen in a long time.

Her stomach growled and she smiled. The last time she ate was breakfast on the plane. She could do with nourishment among other things.

13

AT THE LIFT, SHE FELT HIM before he stopped next to her. A tantalizing shiver danced up her spine as she watched him with keen interest.

Dressed in black pants and light grey stripe shirt with no tie, he had an impressive posture. A military man, she was sure.

Although different looking from the morning, her heart acknowledged him. Her face heated as their eyes met, and her body reacted in recollection of their closeness only hours ago.

They waited for the doors to open. Finding a bridge to cross kept them quiet, their eyes searching as their bodies remained stationary.

"Curt," he said.

"What was that?"

"My name is Curt." She laughed softly.

"You look stunning, Sonia," his voice caressed her.

"Thank you." The doors opened and he followed her. Shoulder to shoulder their reflection revealed more than what she was comfortable with, his features under a spotlight. She liked what she saw, drooling at the sight.

"Are you going to the restaurant?"

She nodded a yes. "Can we sit together?" The intense stare said more than the question implied.

"Yes, why not, since we are on kissing terms," Sonia added. This time he chuckled. The deep sound caused her to smile.

"Sorry about that, but it's your fault."

"How so?" She grinned.

"You are too beautiful, and I couldn't resist."

"So, you're easily tempted?"

"Only by a beautiful woman."

"And does this happen often: tempted by a beautiful woman, I mean?" Jealousy winked at her. Averting his stare, she berated herself for the runaway emotions. *Do not jump to conclusions.*

"No, not often." He squinted as if thinking hard and then met her gaze … serious.

"Only once," he clarified. Raising a brow he continued, "with you."

Her heart stopped for a second. He closed the gap, squashing her against him.

"You are hard to resist, nymph of the pool."

"And you are a fine-looking man," she whispered.

His head lowered. This time she met him halfway. When their lips touched, the doors opened.

Awkwardly they stepped aside when an elderly couple joined them. The couple's perceptive smiles underlined their emotions. He continued to hold her, his closeness profound and exhilarating.

Once seated in the restaurant, Sonia had an unobstructed view of the ocean. The panoramic sight, a bonus of a perfect evening, still young.

"We are lucky to have this table," Curt remarked.

"We sure are?" The place swarmed with couples, but when Curt leaned over, all dashing, Sonia forgot about them. Their fingers abruptly cut out the rest of the world.

"This day feels enchanted."

"Once we wake, it will only be a dream."

"Indeed," Sonia agreed. *Is this really happening?*

"Then we must make the best of the dream."

103

"I don't believe in soulmates, but if it was true, then this experience just changed my opinion," she admitted.

Their eyes met: "Soulmates. This is new to me. Even my actions are unnatural."

"What?"

"Brazen with a woman."

She laughed softly. "I must admit I have never kissed a stranger. Not like that."

"If I did not act, this conversation would not have happened. I would have admired you from a far. It felt right."

Her life had changed forever, she was sure. Listening to his recollection made things clear.

"I will love to spend the weekend with you. Get to know you. Will you mind?"

"No, I will not mind. I will like that very much."

His presence sealed a void Sonia suppressed for twenty-five years. His soul's window showed they agreed. It was not meaningless words. The more they talked, the more the connection grew. A love story in the making.

The hero and heroine met, fell madly in love and together they conquered the dragons. The steep castle walls were no match, and all the trouble disappeared.

Could it be true?

HE WANTED TO BE HONEST WITH HER. She would leave the moment he confessed. His desires cloud his senses. The brief kiss in the pool hooked him.

But can you trust her?

Why not?

You have no idea who she is. He scolded himself and leaned back. It severed the intimate closeness.

She whimpered, a quiet sound which echoed his own loss.

He struggled with Vivian's betrayal. Still did. To be this possessive was unlike him. Since his undivided attention he discarded his bitter emotions. What mattered was the present.

Once again he connected with her and took the smaller hand in his own, the tan covered righthand sported a faint beauty spot on the side. She was not a child anymore—a working woman that enjoys the outdoors. Long delicate fingers enfolded his own, nails short and neat. All of this he took in as he watched her.

"Is this your first visit to the island?" he inquired when their wine arrived.

"Yes, but not my last. It's a magnificent place."

"Yours?" She inquired …,

"Also my first. How do you know this place?"

"A friend planned the trip," she explained. "The pressure of work kept me busy. I am grateful she did."

He planted a kiss on the knuckle. "I'm so glad I met you, Sonia. The meeting is unusual for me, but I feel at peace with you."

"Me too. As if it was always this way."

Both sipped their wine quietly. Their thoughts an open book for each other. When he squeezed her hand, she blushed.

"I never thought it can happen like this," she admitted.

"Make two of us. Life can throw some nasty curveballs but this one I like."

"Really?" Her doubts surfaced.

Her question floored him. How could she be doubtful of a man's attention?

"Yes, I do. I'm thrilled meeting you, can't you tell?"

The momentary expression on her face spoke of mistrust: pain lurking in the depths. She tried to cover it by scanning the interior.

He should set things right, but how? This could only lead to more pain, for both of them. And he would be the snake. He squirmed when the emeralds returned and settled on him. He should walk away. He should do the right thing. He cleared his throat, but she spoke first.

"I am long past the schoolgirl crush. Once you have been burned, one tends to hide away. Love becomes a yearning buried so deep that you don't recognize it."

This time he looked at the woman. The bitter lines round the mouth, the tense shoulders, the white knuckles which held the glass. All signs she was not at ease.

"Please look at me, Sonia." He began, unsure of his own thoughts.

She turned back to him, the eyes shadowed.

"You're the best thing that has happened to me. I want to be the one that shelters you from the storm and gives you peace." He did not know where the words originated from, but was okay with it. This woman mattered.

"You are doing things to me I have not defined accurately. Please believe me, my intentions are honourable towards you."

Her evaluation of him unsettled him, but he could not walk away. Not now.

"Please talk to me?"

"Love does not come easy to me. My life is one long wail of missed opportunities and unfulfilled dreams."

"Do you think this is love?" His heart raced, expectant of her answer. He could give her nothing, and his heart was squashed. *Could he trust her?*

"I don't know. My track record is one big blot of black." She took a sip of her wine, pressed the serviette against her lips and something broke in him. He wanted those lips on him.

"We are two strangers in paradise. We don't know each other, and I will be honest. Until moments ago I was ready to leave, but listening to you my heart opens. It is ready to be filled again."

In all his life he could never understand love until that moment. All thoughts of flight filtered away and he leaned forward. "If I give you my heart, will you take care of it?"

Big emeralds considered him. She leaned closer, their lips a breath away. "Can we give each other this weekend? I need to be sure, please."

He closed the gap, lips meeting. His body reacting, his heart rejoicing. He felt elevated as he whispered, "I will love that." And sealed it. A delicate promise of a budding love no one asked for.

When she pulled back he squeezed her hand. The change in atmosphere a touchable entity. The couple had no idea what to do or how to react. Their solitude a practiced shield of protection they erected once again. However, the yearnings of their heart could not be denied.

TO BREAK THE SILENCE SONIA opened the first pamphlet. Heads together they pinpointed the historic sites they wish to visit.

When their food arrived, they enjoyed the interesting flavours mixed with Mediterranean extravagance. The food was prepared with perfection.

Arm in arm they followed the well-lit gardens around the pool till late. Deck chairs had an unobstructed view of the black waters and he pulled her into one. Together they enjoyed the harmony of nature as their souls connected at the very core, and fell asleep.

It was well after midnight that they returned. At her room he kissed her. It was a chaste kiss—delicate, with no demands.

"I will see you in a few hours," he said before letting her go.

14

27 April 2019.Valletta, Malta.

IT HAD BEEN A WHILE SINCE she had been conscious of her heart. The manner it swayed and jumped foreign but welcomed. The day turned out to be magical. Haleema would enjoy her story.

Within the darkened room lights played a hypnotic game. A slight wind danced with the curtains and fragranced the air with a fresh sea breeze.

As she dozed off a knock interrupted her, a persistent sound that forced her into action. A bare-chested Curt stood in the hallway. His hard toned body a glorious sight, but why was he there?

"Hi, what is wrong?"

"I couldn't sleep. I don't know why, but I need to be with you," he explained.

"Why?" she asked with her arms folded, her own appearance not appropriate for visitors. He brushed his face.

"I'm not sure, but I experienced the need to protect you," he admitted. "I want to assure you my intentions are honourable."

She scanned the empty hall, mystified, then stood aside, organising her sleepwear.

"I tried to ignore it, without success," he said as he slipped inside. "I'm sorry to wake you," he whispered. "I know this must sound ridiculous. It does to me."

"I don't understand, but come in."

Curious with this unusual development, she wondered whether it was a trick to get her in bed?

"That's the thing, I've never done this before." His admission sounded genuine enough. Sonia did not miss the tense shoulders and alarmed look.

"I don't understand, Curt. Why do you think my life is in danger?"

"I can't say, but the urgency in my gut says I shouldn't ignore it."

She led him to the couch. He took a seat while she folded her legs underneath her, next to him, staring worrisome into the darkened space.

As a religious man prayer was done only in the most urgent cases and alone. He was perplexed at the thoughts accosting his sleep.

"I never prayed with someone." He touched her leg reassuringly. "What must I say? I am not even a believer, but this has me stunned."

"Well, it has been a while, but my parents taught me a specific scripture in the Bible. I hope I can remember it."

"You can only try." He opened his hand and she placed her smaller one inside. Strong fingers curled hers and they bowed.

Silence followed as Sonia tried to remember, her sleepy mind not fully awake. As she thought back to more happier times, the words came.

"He who dwells in the secret place of the highest shall remain stable and fixed under the shadow of the Almighty. I will say of the Lord. He is my refuge and my fortress, my God; on him I lean and rely, and in him I trust! For He will save me from the trap of the fowler, and from the deadly pestilence. He will cover me and completely protect me with his pinions, and under his wings i will find refuge. His faithfulness is a shield and a wall. I will not be afraid of the terror of night, nor of the arrow that flies by."

Peace filled the room when she stopped and Curt squeezed her hand. "That was beautiful. Where is it written?"

"In **Psalm 91**. My parents quoted it often enough growing up in Orkney."

"Orkney?" It sounded different coming from him, and she smiled.

"Where is that?"

The sound of water reached them. It had been a while since she thought of her hometown or parents. She could hardly remember their faces, or the sound of their voices.

"It's a mining town in the Free State, South Africa."

"You are a South African?"

"Yes."

"I would have never guessed." She gave an awkward smile.

"Where are they?"

"They died when I was sixteen years old. Father was first, tuberculosis had done its work, and mom followed six months later with a broken heart."

"I am sorry to hear."

"No siblings?"

"None. My parents struggled to have children. By the time they gave up, I arrived. They were both in their early fifties then."

"Would you like to have a family?" he asked cautiously. The ongoing silence turned to unease. Sonia had dismissed the thoughts of family before. The thought tugged at her heart strings.

"Maybe one day."

"So, there are no man or children waiting for you?"

"None."

"That's hard to believe," he concluded.

She could not tell him about Brady or the baby. Just thinking of her parents made her sad. They left an emptiness. Without warning tears formed.

"I am sorry for upsetting you."

The way he said it flung open the pain of loneliness. It reminded her of a lost youth, a life so different. For the first time in her grown-up life Sonia cried for her parents, her lost youth; the years of yearning. A soft cry encompassing all her emotions. It felt clean.

Curt moved, drawing her into him, and she nestled against his frame.

"Tell me about your parents."

"My life was perfect while my parents lived. I loved school and planned to study. We were happy." She smiled. "Orkney is not much to look at, a small community that really cared for each other. The mining shaft which dominated the town amplified Orkney's smallness. It was the highest structure back then. For young people there was not much to do except for playing in the veld. My father was a shift boss until his death, Mom a homemaker. She kept herself busy with cooking, baking and canning. We had a variety of fruit trees which kept her busy. My parents were believers, their dedication and faith admirable. I guess I lost it on the way."

"Faith is not always easy; we leave it behind when our lives begin," Curt said.

"True."

The conversation quieted down as tiredness won and soon both were asleep.

The sun shone brightly when she moved.

"Hi there," he said gruffly.

"What's the time?" her voice hoarse.

"Time for lazy people to get up."

She covered an idle yawn and he chuckled.

"You are beautiful."

Her face crimson, she pulled away. "It is time to go, Mister. I need my few moments of transformation." She fluttered her lashes with a grin.

"You need no such thing, you are perfect." She slapped him slightly on the chest. "I will see you in five minutes."

"That is too quick."

"Ten?"

"Fifteen." She admitted and he chuckled.

"Fifteen minutes, and I am back."

"Okay, and Curt?"

"Yes, Sonia?"

"Thank you."

"I'm the one who needs to say thank you. You made an old man happy."

She laughed, "You aren't old."

"I'm older than you."

"Only a couple of years," she admitted.

"Okay, only with a few years." His lips touched her forehead. "You are special, Sonni," the endearing word a smoothing balm to a hungry soul.

"You are special yourself, Curt," she whispered and stretched leisurely on his imprint.

BACK IN HIS HOTEL ROOM, Curt took a quick shower.

He dressed in a faded denim and cream colour T-shirt with a black logo—a birthday gift from the children. Checking his military edition watch, he went to the grand lobby. At the front desk he booked two scooters for their trip and booked a 4-hour lunch boat tour he had seen on a brochure. The customisable tour was a huge advantage and a wonderful surprise for his Sonia.

If only it was true. He hated to keep her in the dark about his marital status. Last night was wonderful. He felt refreshed for the first time in a while. The jolt of protectiveness he experienced still not clear.

A quick prayer before he walked into a dangerous situation was the norm, but they were far away from any dangerous situation. Nothing was out of the ordinary. Who would want to harm her?

In his line of work he learned to trust his gut. It saved his life and those of his men. Last night he tried to ignore it, but it intensified until he went to her.

The prayer touched his heart. With a quick search on his mobile, he read it again. Each word calmed him, gave him peace.

He should learn it by heart, he might need it again.

15

28 April 2019, 23h00 Valletta, Malta.

"DO YOU ENJOY YOUR HOLIDAY?" Haleema's text message arrived once Sonia connected to the Wi-Fi; sent on Friday. Her phone and the people back home, forgotten. Her life rushed back to her.

"I hoped you found romance." The next message said. They sent it on Saturday.

What should she say? She had found her heart's portion. Her soulmate was an older man, a hunk with baggage, and she lost her heart.

Would she see him again? The jury was out on it.

She doubts they would understand.

Another beep announced a message from Alice, asking the same. There was enough time to reply. In no mood to text, she recorded a voice clip to both friends.

"Thank you, Haleema. Valletta was a perfect choice and I had a wonderful time. On Friday, I visited the spa and spoiled myself. You must see the dress and shoes I bought," *and Mr Right, a pity he could not fit in my bag.*

"Saturday morning we stopped at St. Andrews Bastion. They use the fortress as a wedding venue, built with limestone back in the day. It has this vintage look, submerged in a spell of historical beauty. While we were there, a marriage was in progress. They decorated the hall with an elegant style fitting to the place. I wish you could see it. The photos don't do justice to the place. The city's rich history complimented each structure, the museums informative and well preserved." *He enjoyed the trip.*

"At the Sliema Ferry a water polo game created a buzz. The skill they displayed was a marvel to watch. Our next stop was the Grandmaster Palace. Built between the 16th and 18th centuries, it seems you are stepping back into time." *Curt loved the construction of the building, and the weapons crammed on the walls gathered over centuries. But mostly, I liked it when he kissed me.* She blushed at the thought and cleared her throat.

"A trip to the Upper Barrakka Gardens granted us a spectacular view over the Grand Harbour. Pictures won't do justice, Haleema, come and experience it yourself."

I wish I could introduce you to Curt. We experienced something unexpected.

"I like you, Sonia," he had admitted during the tour. *His hands ignited my skin and we virtually made love in an alcove if not for the guide who stopped us.*

Self-conscious she scanned the terminal. Certain she was alone at the bar, she continued with her telling.

"At Grand Harbour we boarded a boat which took us to the Valletta waterfront. The shoreline was exactly as the photos showed. A glimmering city ensconced in history. Palm trees dotted the waterline, added splashes of green against the age-old sandstone." *He surprised me with the sail. Every moment was precious.*

Yet, amidst what they shared, she sensed he was holding back.

"Last night we danced. We discovered this excellent spot and swayed to the music all night long. The people, the atmosphere … I wished I could stay longer. We walked along the front and stopped at the City gate and talked. Our time limited. This morning we visited the market, but I will tell you all about it tomorrow. I bought you a gift to cheer up your office."

Sending it, she remembered their last conversation.

***

"My life is complicated, Sonia. Meeting you made me believe I can experience happiness. I need to sort my problems first." *He had held my hand so fiercely that it hurt. The more I listened, the less I was comfortable with the conversation. I was scared for the rejection.*

"I wish I met you during a better time, then I could offer you what you deserve."

"What do I deserve?"

"You deserve happiness, a family. Someone who will love you for who you are," and he touched my cheek. I took a step closer, hoping for a change.

"You cannot be that man?"

"No, I'm not that man." Tears appeared, chastising myself for allowing it to happen.

"I'm so sorry. I didn't want to hurt you."

"I am grateful for your honesty."

"You are an amazing woman, Sonia."

"All we have is this, then?"

"Yes, this is all we have."

"Let us make the most of it."

Without more words our lips united. It became a probing dance until all the layers broke; and passion stirred. The heat of the afternoon excelled hundredfold. Words lacked, so our bodies took over.

"I need you so much, take me to the hotel."

"Are you sure?"

"I want this." *The entire weekend I was cautious, my lips speaking what I longed to do. At least this unity will give me a tangible memory. He needed her. She needed him. Right or wrong, it did not matter any longer.*

At her room he stopped. "I can't do this. This won't be proper. It's not right towards you." *He had brushed wayward hair from my forehead. The touch electrifying, hunger lingered on the boundaries of my self-control.*

When the door opened, they stepped away as strangers.

I invited him in. "I understand. At least stay and enjoy a night cup with me." They were adults who could enjoy each other's company.

"I will love it." *Switching on the light, I ordered two cappuccinos. Although silent, the atmosphere was amicable. We viewed the beautiful vista in quietness.*

"Are you sure you understand? I mean—I'm no saint, but with you I want to do it differently: preserve this."

"I understand," *I assured him.*

"We share something special."

"Yes, we do, and having you will complicate the situation more."

"It's better this way."

I was unhappy and disappointed, but he had a point. As it was, it already affected me.

Nestled on the couch he got his camera and showed me what he had taken. The collection surprised me. When our cups were cold, he tucked my hand and I crawled into his lap. It was a perfect ending I did not want to interrupt.

Love and time had no boundaries, the infinite possibilities a mystery to the mortal. Once you start one, the other tests you. Only then could you truly become one in the infinite space.

In our case, only time could intertwine our lives.

16

"YOU ARE SURE ABOUT THIS?" Roger Gisemba, Leader of the Democratic Freedom Alliance (DFA) queried.

"Yes, I am sure. Jabu gave you the wrong information. The white woman will arrive on Sunday night and not Monday morning, as he had said."

Tau Gbadamosi watched the leader's scarred face contort into rage. Minutes ticked by while he sipped the brew. Though tired, he waited, caution ever present.

"Must I bring him in?"

"No, follow him on Sunday night. Report back, provided you have information. Take Kwame with you. I want no harm done to her. Her medical knowledge is crucial, as you well know. I will decide whose wife she will be. Treat her as a guest."

"Yes, Haji," Tau replied.

"She is not to be harmed; do I make myself clear."

"Yes."

"Call Baaka."

"Good night." He sauntered into his quarters closed off from view. They divided the rest of the place in an office, a radio room and an extra room used as a holding cell.

Tau could not understand why Jabu Boro deceived them. He lived in the streets of Jaman when he found him. Half beaten; Tau introduced him to the militia. The leader accepted him. Soon he proved to be an excellent soldier and promoted to Sergeant. He had made a name for himself. Now he lied to them.

What were his plans with her?

Jabu introduced the plan to them. They discussed the benefits of her presence. On Roger's orders he had followed her for two days. Her compassion with the people touched him.

Timing was everything. Kidnapping the nurse would put a target on them.

"We will take her to the main camp. She will be of more use there."

"At Fangak?"

"Yes. I considered moving. With the growing military activity it becomes difficult to move around town. They watch us like hawks. I will feel more secure away from prying eyes. As an added measure of protection, we should marry her to a worthy man." Tau's heart flipped. It did not sit well with him. He wanted her.

"The advantage of her expertise at camp outweighs the problems. We will increase our security."

With this Tau had to agree. The people needed help, and all Jabu Boro had in mind was his own needs. The betrayal extended to the people.

Roger Gisemba would make him an example. He pitied him; his death would be cruel. First a punishment and then a message. No one will question his leadership of the nation and healer of his people.

He knocked against the frame of the reed hut. At once the woman appeared. Haram Baaka Gisemba—mother of two of Roger's eight children with the third on its way; far advanced in pregnancy; the reason the nurse had to come.

Haram Baaka shuffled out the door and without a word from Tau, she shuffled to her husband's room. He bid her goodnight and left for his own room.

17

THEY MET IN THE HOTEL restaurant and enjoyed a healthy breakfast. The earlier conversation greeted with ignorant silence. What could they say?

Last night he prayed once again. The unease did not leave him, even after the plea. He should speak to Phillip about this, Curt thought.

To get away he ordered a taxi for them. He wanted their last day to be special. The driver recommended the Sunday market. It was a big event on the island.

Ancient buildings rose from cobblestoned earth, colourful balconies lined the streets and tourists sauntered the lanes. A cocoon of nostalgia. Curt took more pictures of Sonia. He was an old fool, but he wanted to remember her.

At the market they passed wooden cartwheels laden with clothes, food and crafts. At one cart she draped a coloured shawl around her. Sculpted in denim and a black lace top, she enticed him. The few moments he had with that body almost shattered his resolve.

"Are you married long?"

Surprised he checked the younger girl who spoke with curious youthfulness, then smiled. "We aren't married."

"Ah, young love. It is so beautiful." She went on, and he grinned. He peered back. At that precise moment Sonia turned.

"Are you going to propose to her?" He totally forgot about the woman transfixed on Sonia. Reality caused a lump in his throat, and he swallowed. He longed to ask Sonia to share his life. The suggestion seeped through his body, to his mind and landed in his centre: part of him.

"Are you not sure?" she asked as she shielded her eyes. "Whatever you do, Sir," she continued. "Consider it. You look great together."

"Thanks." The girl dissolved into the crowd and he felt alone.

Shooting up a prayer he opened his spirit.

"I would want to meet her again, Lord, one day, when it's sorted—if you allow it. Give me the peace I need and protect her on her journey."

As she paid for the shawl he sauntered closer. When he drew her into him, she wrapped her arms around his waist. More than ever he craved the connection as he cupped her face. Staring at her glowing face he kissed her. The picture engraved in his mind.

Sonia severed the connection and pushed him aside, thanked the sales lady and moved away. Searching for her hand they connected. Curt followed the cobble alley, his heart heavy. Not noticing Sonia's struggle alongside him. She remained silent. The hours ticking away as they enjoy the moments left.

The desire to cool down plunged them into the hotel's swimming pool. Sonia was a remarkable sight. Relaxed, a pulsating energy surrounded her. Vexed, he followed her in the water.

"I caught you, Sonni."

"So, you did," she agreed. "What will you do with me?" She fluttered her lashes.

God, he loved her. He picked her up and flung her in the water. She surfaced, sputtered and laughed. He was with her in seconds.

A ball game began and they played along. When she sank in the playful maelstrom, he panicked. He searched till he found her on the other side of the group. He held her with a trembling heart.

"What is wrong, Curt?"

"Don't disappear like that, Sonni. Please."

"I am here, "she whispered. He clung to her as if it was an evil omen he had just received.

She rocked him, kissing his face and chest. Hungry he captured her mouth.

"Sonni," he murmured. When their eyes met, desire burned in the depths. He did not want to ignore it anymore, but she must tell him or he would not stop.

"I need you," she whispered.

"Your room?"

She laughed. The sound touched his core. "Yes, let's go."

He did not recall how they got back, but they did. The connection stirred for a deeper connection as he took her. His craving's subtleness opened her. Sonia gave unconditionally. A tear appeared and he kissed it away with tenderness. Every part of her responded under his touch. He sated her thoroughly, and by the time they finally joined he had no doubt that it was the best way to end the weekend.

She explored the planes of his body lazily, and he squeezed her fondly. Words would be an intrusion, but ...

"We need to get up."

"I will always remember you," she promised.

"Maybe one day …"

She stopped him. "Don't," and he heard a hiccup. "Do not say things that will make this harder." She kissed him and ran for the bathroom.

He could not let her go like this. She was in pain. His own heart broke in two, the thought of leaving her too much. He had to love her as she deserved.

Shielded behind a steam curtain he moved in right behind her. Love proved in every touch as he began at her shoulders, the roundness of her body warm and pliable. He could not help himself and made love to her. He poured all his desires, needs and wants into the action and sealed it orgasmic.

"Sonni, love!" An idea formed. Her sadness captured in the depths of the emerald eyes.

"I will sort out my life. I will see to that," he vowed. "Give me six months and I will meet you here," he whispered. "Will you give that to me?"

"Yes, Curt," she pledged.

Just then a knock on the door stopped them. He cleared his throat, calling: "Yeah."

"Room service. We need to clean the room, Sir."

"We will be out right away."

"I will get my things and meet you in the lobby."

18

29 April, Bentiu, South Sudan.

IT WAS A DIFFICULT TRIP. Sonia cried herself to sleep. Her dreams filled with an impossible future. The air hostess covered her with a light blanket.

Minutes before midnight her flight landed. She trailed the group through customs, then moved to the luggage wheel where her overnighter waited. The weight's added memories left her with a hefty heart. The leather bag dangled from her shoulder and the colourful scarf surrounded her shoulders.

The holiday was over, and she smiled melancholy. She missed Curt already.

The night's cooler air nipped at her flesh and she covered herself with the scarf. There was no one in sight which she found strange. Haleema said a driver would pick her up and she stepped to the curb in search for a familiar face. All she saw was pitched blackness with some flickering stars and a flash far away. The sound of a skirmish unwelcome after the idyllic weekend.

When she heard her name she glanced sideways. A man bumped into her followed by a prick on her arm. It went dark as she wilted on the concrete.

Muscular arms lifted her in the back of a decrepit van with no effort. He placed her gear next to her sedated body. A door closed and they drove in a northern direction without her knowing any of it.

Another unmarked car followed; the men glared at him. They knew his intent and they were furious.

If Tau Gbadamosi had a choice he would end his life here, but the leader's explicit orders stopped him.

He would not allow him to hurt her. She was precious cargo and valuable to his people. He would stay on them like a tick on a dog.

Determined he called.

Iraqi desert

AT 05H00 MONDAY MORNING CURT strode into his office, tired and not in a great mood.

The drive was one lengthy argument with himself. The last day on a loop. The memories pounding waves into his core which crashed against a rock wall.

He was stupid. He had caved. All he wanted now was her. His consciousness berated him with each passing kilometer. He was an old bastard. Why did he promise her?

This weekend he discovered a jewel in Sonia Main. He learned her surname when he booked the same rooms … in six months' time.

He believed in second chances.

He salvaged the camera and scrolled the images as he studied her with a school boy crush. Then he transferred them to his laptop. The last picture showed a carefree woman wrapped in colour.

Then he stopped. The well-known sensation plunged him in worry and recited the scripture. Even during the flight, he prayed. It truly bothered him, helpless at the same time—like now.

He could not contact her as he never got her number. His only hope was in the God she trusted.

Since he left his phone in the desk drawer, he retrieved it. Ten voice messages.

The first one from his twenty-year-old son, Mark, and he listened warily.

"Dad."

"Son."

"I'm so glad to hear from you." A sigh escaped.

"It is good to hear from you," Curt replied.

"Why did you phone, Mark?"

"Something is wrong with Jillian. She cries a lot and I don't know what to do?"

"Where's Mom?"

"She's gone for the weekend. I think we'll see her this afternoon."

"I'll speak to her. How's work?"

"Wonderful, Dad, no complaints."

"Good, Son. Send me an e-mail, will ya? Let me phone her."

Next two voice messages were from his daughter, crying in both of them. With a lump in his throat he dialled her number. At twenty-three years of age Jillian was a beauty. Clever and witty—she was in her fourth year, studying corporate financial planning. She was always in control and precise. Never like this.

"Daddy," she answered on the third ring.

"Pumpkin," and his tone soften. She opened the waterworks. He waited before he asked. "What's wrong?"

"Daddy, I am pregnant." Shocked, he tightened his grip on the pencil.

"I don't know what to do," she whimpered.

He pinched his eyes, seeking for words, but the correct ones failed to appear. "Who's the father?" he finally asked.

If possible, she cried even harder, which gave him a moment of clarity. He was going to be a grandfather, at fifty-six.

"Neil Davis," she breathed.

At first his mind refused to believe the news, but then he clipped out the words in utter shock: "You mean your mother's lover?"

"Hm," she sobbed.

"Bastard!" It slipped out before he could count to ten. Not only did the pervert seduce her, now she was pregnant.

"Where's your mother, does she know?"

"She's with him at his penthouse, and yes, she knows. She was with me when the doctor confirmed it."

"What did she say?"

"Nothing," came the soft reply.

By then he totally lost it. He could strangle the woman right now. He breathed hard, almost squashing the phone in his fist.

"I'll talk to her," he finally said, "and we'll sort this out. Are you all right?"

"Yes, Daddy, but I am scared."

"Does Neil know?"

"I don't know, maybe," and she sniffled. "What must I do, Dad?"

Orderly stacks of paperwork waited for his attention, but they held no answers. He was clueless in these matters.

"Do you want to keep it?"

"Yes," a sigh followed. "I mean no." Silence, "I don't know. I am so confused, Dad. Please, help me." She resembled the twelve-year kid again.

Back then she was in a serious car accident. She had a painful headache afterwards and cried nonstop. He was at home when it happened and had a tough time not to put the kid, responsible for the crash, through the wall. The same sensation obscured his vision; he would do this man physical harm once he found him. Another inhale and exhale followed; he had to stay level-headed.

"You're old enough to decide, but I won't accept an abortion, I can tell you now. It's wrong, Pumpkin."

"Yes, Dad, I know," followed by a heavy sigh. "My life is over," she sobbed.

"No, Pumpkin, your life isn't over. A child isn't a curse."

"But Dad, what about my studies, my life?" she complained.

"You are almost done. Don't give up, Honey." He breathed deeply. "Please Jillian, whatever you do, don't give up on yourself or on this baby."

"Yes, Dad."

"Ok, Sweetheart. I love you."

"I love you, Dad."

"We'll talk about it again."

"Yes, Dad."

"Night, Pumpkin."

"Lord, I don't know how this all works, but please Lord, help my girl to make the right decision. Be with us. Give me wisdom, and Lord, keep Sonni safe."

19

Iraqi desert.

"EVERYTHING OKAY, SIR?" Sergeant Doug asked.

"My life is falling apart." He had never admitted defeat. He wanted to return to the island, to hold the nymph and make love to her until all his troubles disappeared, but it was a dream.

He was an idiot to believe he had a second chance of happiness. His emotions put through a ringer. It was not fair to her.

The obstacles were taxing, and he was not back a day.

"I understand, Sir."

Curt pulled himself together, straightened his uniform and took a deep swallow from the bottled water.

"Did you want to see me?"

"It's private Charlie Alvarez, Sir."

"What about her?"

"The doctor's wife arrived and confronted her in the open." Curt groaned; he did not need this.

"What happened?"

"The doctor's pregnant wife attacked the soldier."

"You're not serious."

"It was a good fight even though it only lasted two seconds." Doug grinned.

"No."

"The doctor pulled her away."

"Sir?" Ralph said as he stepped into the office.

"First Sergeant Gaines wants a word."

"Sure. Let him come in."

"Did you enjoy the break?"

"Yes, I did, Ralph." Curt straightened his uniform and took the proffered mug. "We will discuss this later, Sergeant."

"Yes, Sir."

The younger man entered the office. His stocky frame tensed as his eyes locked on Colonel McGee.

"Gaines." He was a close friend of Cummings.

"Colonel."

"At ease, Soldier; have a seat."

"Thanks, Sir."

"How can I help?"

"Private TJ Cummings, Sir. They accuse him of murder."

"Yes, Gaines, I know,"

"He wants our help, Sir. Says he is innocent of this crime."

"He sounded desperate, and I considered it best to talk to you first, Colonel."

"This is not our problem."

"He has no one else."

"Do you believe him?"

"Yes, Sir, I do. To leave him will be a shame, Sir."

"Get the private online. It's time to get better acquainted."

"Yes, Sir."

"Thanks, Gaines. I'll see what I can do."

Once they got him, Alvarez called him to the radio room. The soldier avoided eye contact. For now he will let it go.

***

"Sir, I didn't do this," the private repeated. Curt had to figure out the next move. From a military point of view, they could do nothing, nonetheless the man needed help. How, he did not know, yet.

"Who represents you?"

"A newbie lawyer, Colin Reeve, who the court appointed."

"Do you have his number?"

"Yes, Sir." Curt scribbled the number in a small notepad.

"I cannot make any promises, Private."

"I have no one, Sir. I made mistakes in my life, Sir, but I will never kill a woman. My mother would kill me if I did. She raised me well, Sir." His voice broke.

"We will speak soon."

"Yes, Sir. Thanks, Sir." With one click the communication ended.

Curt handed the phone back and stepped into the brilliant sun. His satellite phone buzzed. It was his lawyer, Chris Norton. He, too, had left two messages.

"McGee," he answered.

"Norton here, Sir."

"Any progress?"

"No, Sir. Mrs McGee doesn't want to sign."

"Reason?" An extra set of rage stewed within him.

"She says if she walks, she loses all. Reconsider, Sir."

"She had affairs all of our married life. She deceived me and my children. I owe her nothing. Even my daughter came into the line of fire."

"She doesn't see it as you do, Sir. My advice is to give her the money she requested, and she will be out of your life."

"No, never!" he hissed. "Her lover seduced Jillian. He raped her: she is pregnant." Vile burned him. "She will not get a dime from me."

"Can I have the doctor's report?"

"I will ask Jillian to forward it to you."

"Hopefully this will be the clincher."

"I won't give in to her demands."

"I will work on it, Sir."

"Make it quick, Chris."

"Yes, of course, Colonel."

Another call came through and he answered automatically. This time his irritation was unstoppable. She was the last person he wanted to talk too.

"Yes, Vivian." A deep frown marred his face.

"Now, now! Is that the way to greet your loving wife?"

"What do you want!" he barked.

"What Every Woman Wants: love and attention from her soldier." Her voice dripped of sweetness. He wanted to vomit.

"In your case, Vivian, you didn't appreciate it when you had me. This is over." The moment the words were out, the atmosphere changed.

"Never!" she hissed. He ignored her sudden coldness.

"You are aware of Jillian?"

"Yes, isn't that sweet? We will be grandparents."

"It doesn't bother you that Neil is the father?" The nearest sand pile swirled upwards.

"Is that her story, the little tramp, and you believe her?" she snorted unwomanly.

"You make me sick, Vivian. I believe my daughter."

"Neil said it could never be his, he used a condom."

"And that's okay with you?"

"She isn't as innocent as she had you believed."

"So, and what is the truth?"

"She has many lovers. Neil is just one of many."

He swallowed hard at the bile. "The test will prove he is the father, Vivian."

"And if it is, it doesn't matter."

"So, let me get this straight. You're okay with your lover sleeping with our daughter?" At this point he was astonished. *I am married to this ...*

"Yes. Neil is very energetic—if you get my drift," and she chuckled in a husky voice. He clenched his jaw.

"No, I don't get your drift? You will sign the papers, Vivian."

"I will never sign the papers, Curt."

"Why Vivian?" he finally asked.

"Because, as unbelievable as it might be, I still love you. The others, they keep me company when you are not here. I was never a military wife. You knew it from the start."

"But, yet, you want to continue?"

"We had our moments, Curt. I love you."

"You have no right to it." With a final click the call ended. The finality of it left him empty. It could not continue and disappeared around the building. He stared across the desert sand; the heat gleamed over the dunes. It covered his skin in a layer of sweat. By midday perspiration poured from every pore.

"God, me again," he whispered. *"I need a miracle."* When calmed enough, he continued. *"There is no love between us. Give me the freedom I so desperately need. Give me peace."*

20

North of Bentiu, South Sudan.

'WHY IS CURT HOLDING ME THIS TIGHT?'

She writhed against the bonds of dreams.

'I can't breathe, let me go,' she pleaded.

'You are scaring me.'

She woke with a start.

Why am I tied?

What is happening?

Confused, she looked around and realised she was moving. Except for her gear, the cabin of the vehicle was empty.

Panic flooded her reason. Frantic with fear she rolled around, kicked and screamed. After a while she stopped, sweat pouring from her.

You need to relax. Find out where you are. Wait for the right time.

The car moved at a comfortable speed, so the person was at ease. She struggled upright, the sun's rays just colouring the heavens. Cramps settled in her shoulders and hips and moved to a more comfortable position.

Then the car slacked until it stopped. From above a man appeared and before she could react, another prick pulled her back into oblivion.

***

Alarmed Sonia stirred. The vehicle slowed and she lifted herself to see barren trees, the sun setting. An entire day gone.

Where was she?

The car accelerated and she bumped against the frame. A splitting headache and thousands of needles advanced on her. The pain worsened with each movement. Her bladder piped in; she had to go. She tried to move again but it was no use.

Even the offending stench worked on her gag reflexes. The piece of rag stuck in her mouth, making it difficult. The corners of her mouth stretched.

At a sharp turn she slammed head first into the rear seat. Pain shot right through, causing the headache to intensify. The driver cursed.

Who was he?

The engine dulled and slowed. This brought on new, frightening thoughts. She was in the wilderness with no one nearby.

She thought of Curt; a tear evaporated in the material.

There was no we in their future.

This line of thought will not help you, Sonia.

You are breathing, which means you are alive. Look for an opportunity to escape. No matter how small.

The car came to a complete stop. The face of a youngster, no older than twenty, appeared, grinning an evil smirk. Even with her clothes on she felt violated. He looked familiar and raked her memories. Where did she see him?

He stretched as a roughened hand traced her leg. She squealed under the touch and kicked. A chilling laugh emanated from him; fixated on her breasts. He leaned forward and pinched a nipple through her clothing. She shrieked and tried to kick, but it was no use. He grinned with triumph as he pinched again.

Sonia forced herself to become still, her fear was his fuel. Though difficult, she relaxed. When he spoke in his language, Sonia detected the meaning behind his intentions. His gaze unwavering on her, and she forced herself to be quiet. The smirk disappeared as he pinched her again. Lifeless she met his gaze.

She did not care about his disappointment.

"I will enjoy you. No one will hear your screams. It is just you and me," his threadbare English's message clear enough.

His hands ever-present on her as he continued to touch her. He fiddled with the zipper, but it stuck in his haste.

The small reprieve a welcomed moment, but for how long?

Sonia tried to withdraw herself not to be an easy reach, but he snickered. He held her limbs still, his eyes glazed over as it travelled over her private parts, her insides in turmoil; helpless to protect herself. Lust palpable on his face.

She was in trouble and alone. Her mind in a jumble.

"PLEASE LORD," she whispered, never leaving his face.

His diabolical laugh as she tried to get deeper into the steel frame, chilled her to the core. A door opened.

Sonia struggled against the bonds. Fear leaving her exposed. The cotton silenced her screams. How much time did she have?

The crunch of gravel, heavy footsteps and the tapping against the steel body unnerved her. At the back door he stopped. The cheerful tune unnerved her. Her heart pounded as the door opened, and he appeared. A slow and malevolent grin appeared as he grabbed her feet and pulled her legs apart. She let out another muffled sound as he untied her legs. She kicked, but he pinned her with a knee. A knife emerged and he began at the denim seam. A deliberate, slow action as he cut through the material. First the one leg, then the other.

Her noises fell on deaf ears.

Once done, he strapped her legs to the frame on both sides, spreading her wide open. Helpless, Sonia shrank away as he touched her. The blade was a constant reminder of what was happening.

"Please Lord, not like this."

He grabbed her painfully. Heated agony shot right through her. A scream made her deaf for any other sound. When her abductor landed between her legs, lifeless, it stunned her. It was then that she realised they were not alone.

An older man appeared in the doorframe. His bald face contorted in anger as he dragged the man away from her and threw him on the ground. He towered over her. The descending sunlight at his back, Sonia's vulnerability under the fresh set of eyes visible. With her clothes in rags it exposed her. The moment he reached for her, she screamed.

He spoke in heavily accented English.

"I will help you. I will not harm you. Let me loosen the cables." She nodded.

He got in the cabin and worked on her bonds until she was free and covered her with a blanket. Grateful for the consideration she clutched the blanket close to her.

"You are safe, let me remove the gag." Once her mouth was clear she scrambled deeper into the van, not sure what to do.

"Please, I won't hurt you, okay." He tried to smile, but failed miserably. His anger simmering, he kicked the body in the dust.

"DON'T BE AFRAID," TAU REPEATED. Up close her features were remarkable. She was everything he dreamed about.

"Who are you?" she asked. The emeralds hypnotic, her voice soothing, even when anxious. That Jabu touched her was unforgivable. Her torn clothes and battered state not acceptable. Jabu will pay.

"You will go to a safe place." His voice was low not to alarm her, but disbelieve marred the green eyes.

Anxiously she looked past him.

"That is Kwame. Once we are at our destination, I will answer your questions."

Still frightened, she got out and covered herself. He retreated to give her space.

"I am here to help you," he assured.

The next moment she did the unthinkable … she ran.

"Miss!" He followed as she sprinted across the veld.

"Where is she going?" Kwame yelled.

"Miss, stop!" Tau really had to give it all and caught her, panting. "Why did you do that?" he barked.

"Please let me go," she pleaded. Her fear palpable, but to run stupid.

"Now, listen, woman, I won't hurt you." His breath was sporadic. "You have nothing to fear."

She struggled again, but his grip tightened. Suddenly she bent and vomited.

Unsure he peered backward, Kwame smiling at him. It would not be the last of this. Kwame will mock him, but he waited.

"Let us go, it's late. I will give you water and you can change, understood. No screaming or running. It won't help, there's no one around to help," and he shook her arm. "Understand?"

She nodded as she wiped her mouth and walked back. Stepping on a sharp rock, she shrieked. For the first time he noticed her bare feet and crouched to inspect the bleeding foot.

"Why did you do that?" he asked as he removed a clean handkerchief from a shirt pocket and wiped away the droplets of blood. "Running barefoot through the bush will not help." He ripped material from his shirt and bandaged it. The entire time she kept quiet, watching him closely.

After that she placed her weight on it, she shrieked of pain. Immediately he caught her and helped her.

"Thanks," she whispered on the way.

"No problem. Just leave the silliness aside, okay."

"WHY AM I HERE? What do you want from me?" Her fear shimmered through, but he did not answer.

At the jeep, Kwame handed her water. Sonia rinsed her mouth before she emptied the bottle greedily.

"I'm Tau Gbadamosi, this is Kwame Okiro. We will take you to our leader."

"Why?" she got out with a rasp.

"We need you in the village."

"Where are you taking me?" she asked.

He ignored her and walked to the old van and removed her bags. "Get dressed, we need to leave."

They gave her privacy as they stepped away. Once changed, Tau called her. "We will stop for food once we are in a secure area." He handed her an energy bar, which she gladly took.

Tau opened the back door, but she jerked from his grip.

"No, what's the purpose of this?"

"You will understand when we get to our destination."

"Tell me now," she demanded.

"*Anjeun langkung saé ngawartosanna* (You better tell her)," Kwame said.

He deliberated with himself. To tell her would mean more questions. He was in no mood for answering any of it. She would learn quickly that Tau Gbadamosi was no talker.

"Fangak County."

"But that's in the swamps; malaria-infested swamps," she shrieked, her eyes wide. She worked long enough in South Sudan to know the different areas and their dangers.

"Are you not a nurse?" he asked, surprised but matter-of-factly.

"Yes, I am."

"Well, you're needed in the malaria-infested swamps," he parroted.

"You're not serious?"

"Yes, I am. You will take care of the sick. My people need medical care, and you will give it to them. Are you too good to touch them?"

"No, I am not."

"Except for malaria-infected people."

"I am no doctor, and we need the correct vaccine which I don't have."

He tapped her on her cheek. "Don't you worry your head about medical supplies. We have it covered. You are a qualified nurse, we made sure about that."

"Why not visit the camps where medical staff are?"

"Our people cannot travel that far; Fangak is cut off. Now we bring you to them."

She licked her dried lips and he smiled. "You are beautiful." He reached for her face. She drew back and he grinned.

"Not only will you nurse the people, but I will enjoy your company, Sonia Main."

"How do you know my name?"

"I am well informed." He could not help himself as his thumb glided over her lips and brought it back to his. Never taking his eyes from her, he placed it back on hers.

Angered with his intrusion Sonia slapped his hand away. "Don't touch me."

He caught it with a firm grip and drew her closer. "You and I will get better acquainted, I can promise you that. If it is not me, someone like Jabu will. Believe me, when I tell you, you will be better off in my company." His stare intensive and direct.

Her response would give him the knowledge he needed. And the way forward.

The emeralds raked over him before they moved to Kwame and back. Her fear was palpable, but there was something else. It was that something that attracted her to him.

For a long time she stared at him, weighing the situation until she dropped her eyes. She was feisty and clever, things he appreciated in a woman. without another word she turned to the car.

Silently he helped her in the jeep and secured her to the armrest.

"Is this necessary?"

"Yes." A simple statement that closed any other conversations and quietly she sat back.

He slammed against the roof once as he took the front seat. He knew he had won this round but her feistiness revealed something else. For now she would play a long but he sure must be on the lookout for her. All the more reason he would stay with her. She would need protection from people like Jabu and herself.

Kwame pulled away and dust floated through the open window.

21

North of Bentiu, South Sudan.

AT LEAST HER NEW ABDUCTORS WERE CIVIL.
The other guy scared her. Sonia was not entirely satisfied
with her predicament, but glad they intervened.

The first guy ruined her clothes, clothes that had Curt's
smell on it. His unique blend mixed with vulgar. Clothes
she left in the car. At least she still had her other clothing
with Curt's fragrance, clothing not suitable for this
environment.

Your premonitions were correct, she reflected. One tear found his way down and disappeared in her t-shirt. Softly she recited the well-known Psalm. Her heart pounding. "H*elp me stay calm, Lord. You are my hope."* Her heart lifted. Faith settled in her mind, a conviction she thought she had lost. The weekend had left tendrils of faith within her. They would find her. Help would come. She had to believe that.

Clear-headed, she looked around. On the floor her leather bag and overnighter waited. She needed pills to still the pounding. It meant she had to ask for help. Not willing to cave she looked around.

At the back the lifeless abductor triggered her memory. He was the leader of the bandits who apprehended them a week ago.

"Who is he?"

Kwame replied: "Jabu."

"What did he want with me?"

"My guess." This time Tau turned. "Use you and once he's done, sell you."

This news shocked her to silence. Her faith tilted and she closed her eyes. To think of the unthinkable would-be madness.

"What is your plan with me, Lord?"

"YOU WANT HER?" KWAME SAID. Her gentle breathing the only sound from the back.

"She is pretty," Tau acknowledged with a blank look.

"You crave her?"

"Drop it, Kwame," he reprimanded him and stared at the passing landscape.

"Are you going to ask Haji if you can have her?" he teased.

Tau looked at him. "Leave it." A soft chuckle drifted towards him, but he ignored it.

He allowed his thoughts to wander. He never showed genuine interest in any girl. Women came to his bed when they needed help. He caved and enjoyed the platter provided. His wife lived with her family. He did not visit her often, as he had no feelings for her. So far she could not give him sons; everyone thought she was cursed and he avoided her.

This woman stirred feelings in him he would not admit to Kwame. He wanted to protect her and claim her. Her eyes pleased him; even her smell turned him on. She was perfect for him. He never considered taking a second wife, but she did things to him. Good things.

Kwame was smart. Maybe he was right. He should ask Roger for her hand; she would make him happy. But, if Roger found her appealing, he would take her into his hut. It would put a stop to his dreams.

He folded his arms and made himself comfortable. With eyes closed he indulged in the fantasy he had concocted of them together. A fantasy so wild that it could not be true.

FOR TWO DAYS THEY drove in an eastern direction. The White Nile ever-present as the landscape changed from region to region. Fangak's lifestyle differs from the rest of the country. It was harsher, slower and infested with unknown critters. People were fearful of the place and stayed away, her destination a prison she could not escape from.

They never stopped unless it was for food or to relieve themselves. They drove in silence. Tau never touched her again, but took care of her. The driver, Kwame Okiro, took deep puffs from the thin cigar he cradled between yellow teeth.

Each time Sonia woke she watched her abductors, and though they seldom looked at her she knew they were attentive. Their shoulders taught, eyes awake—always scanning the area for any trouble.

To avoid them she stared out the window and relived the weekend with Curt McGee. A time trapped in a distinct reality. To meet him changed her world. Their paths predestined to intertwine. His care and love touched her.

Now she felt empty without him. To lose him left her mystified.

Why Lord? Why did you allow me to see a glimpse of what could be, just to take it away? Why am I going to this place? The urgency to pray in Valletta, now plain, the Lord's protection upon her when he sent these men undeniable. For that she was grateful.

Sonia repeated the protection prayer as she remembered it, pondering each word's significance. Her faith stirred with certainty that this was a temporary setback. No matter how she would escape or be rescued. She had six months to return to her happiness.

In the commotion she had lost her phone, and all she had left was his imprinted image.

Will she be alive in six months? People disappeared in Africa without a trace … will she be a statistic?

She survived the streets of Pretoria. Surely, she could survive this. It was a matter of being smart, using her skills to her favour.

Once their eyes met a certainty crept in: Tau was her best bet to stay alive. The connection was a fleeting bypass but Tau Gbadamosi shared in that moment more than any conversation could do. He would protect her. Could she trust him?

Her thoughts stayed in a jumble. The deeper they went into the region, the more she became dependent on him. She had to be careful about this. Had she not seen how people can get emotionally attached to their abductors? Brain washed to believe that person was all they need. If she was not careful, she could become like that too. Again she shot up a prayer just as they stopped in the dead of the night. In the headlights she could see water and reeds. Lots of reeds.

"From here we will travel by boat," Tau explained. Sonia grabbed her earthly belongings from the floor of the car and joined them in the inkjet darkness. Stars sparkled brightly above them, but no moon lit the path and Sonia had to follow them with unease.

Just then she heard a loud noise and the splatter of water, and she jumped.

"Don't fret, princess," Tabu said close to her. "It is just Jabu."

"What will you do with him?"

"Haji will decide his fate," Kwame said. Hesitant Sonia could make out the small boat just big enough for them. Jabu's bundle was barely visible. Once she was inside the rocking boat a blanket was handed to her. It was cooler, but the blanket gave her the reprieve she needed. Despite it, her unease grew as they continued deeper into the swamps.

What is the condition like? What will they expect from me?

What can I expect?

First Jabu, who tried to rape her, then Tau who was forthcoming with his intent. What would other men try?

22

Iraqi desert.

ANNA STALIN NOT RELATED to the well-known
dictator; she assured everyone she met right away, was
on her way to the local town. Though heated dust
swirled around her, it did not interfere with her
happiness. Sitting at her left she could enjoy his profile
unashamedly.

Although the men regarded her as a flirt, they knew her
feelings for Staff Sergeant Brock Castledale. Her curves
and beauty attracted whistles, but her heart and body
belonged to him.

Brock stood six feet five inches of hard-toned body tall
in his boots. Bald, tanned, with the most beautiful green
eyes not allowed on a man, Anna thought. He was an
American soldier and in love with her, or so she claimed.

Inside the tearoom, Anna showered him with attention. He was gone for weeks and she missed him something fierce. Their last visit ended in a fight, and she promised him an enjoyable time. She had prepared herself as best she could and drank two pain tablets. While she did not agree with his sexual orientations, she would follow through—this time.

It was already late when they left the tearoom. High on the liquor buzz, Anna was ready for anything.

"Come, Darling, I am horny." She giggled and enjoyed the attention he lavished on her. Castledale's hands were all over her. It bordered on indecent and Samer Sleiman warned them about it a few times.

"You know what I want."

"No, I don't like that," she pouted. Fear caused her heart to skip a beat. With each encounter she rejected it which unleashed a fury of pouring blows.

Angry he pushed her away, ready to walk. Desperate, she grabbed his hand. "Please," she pleaded. "I want you."

Annoyed his brows lifted in a definite question. She choked. "Okay." Her body was already shivering. They tried it before; the excruciating pain stayed with her long after it.

Brock's face contorted into a grin, assaulting her lips with lust. He wrapped her legs around his waist and carried her to the parked jeep hidden in the shadows.

The window for change closed as his fingers probed the thin material. She whimpered at the intrusion. Taken as approval he pushed deeper. The penetration burned. At least he prepared her before he violated her. Her insides fluttered in revolt and her mind screamed. For the next few days she would walk with a limp.

Anna loved the man, but in bed he was an animal.

Give in or lose him. She saw it in his eyes.

At the jeep he opened the door and turned her. A slap on the right butt cheek stopped any protest she might have. Her dress bunched over her hips he spread her. She grunted with agony and whispered: "Can't we at least find a room?"

"No!" He covered her mouth and chuckled. It resonated through her. With the other he stroked her hard and deep.

"Are you ready?" She shook her head as tears materialised. Humiliation swept through her alcohol-induced mind.

He ignored it as he entered her. She released a muffled scream. It burned with each stretch and she clung to the steering wheel in desperation.

"You like this, Bitch?" and pushed in deeper. "Right?"

"Yes."

"That's my bitch," and he slapped her once more, her pain-soaked body numb. Once he pulled out she flopped on the seat. Pain shot right up her body to her core.

"Come, we're going to your place where we can continue this." Brock slammed the door shut. Another groan expressed her displeasure.

It would be a long night.

When he pulled away she grabbed the bottle left in the jeep and took a long, hard swig.

23

Fangak County, South Sudan.

"BAAKA!" SONIA HEARD THE second they arrived at the camp. Caught in the flashlight's beam the man shielded himself. A young woman answered him; her head covered.

They had moored against a steep bank where a soldier secured it. His rifle rested on his back. Another one scanned the area, his rifle in readiness.

Tau got out, followed by Kwame who helped her out.

"That is our commander, Roger Gisemba." Kwame freed her. Warily she rubbed her arms and wrists.

"*Salam* Haji," Tau greeted him.

"*As-Salam Alaykum*." (May peace be upon you)

"Dimana éta awéwé?" (Where is the nurse?) the man, Haji asked without acknowledgement.

"Anjeunna di dieu." Tau pointed to her as she joined them. Sonia's body ached after their midnight ride. How long they were on the water she could only guess. Right away they expected her to perform her duties.

"Datang!" Haji commanded. Without waiting he sprinted towards a darkened spot outside the flickering fires.

"Come," Tau repeated.

Sonia stumbled in her haste, got her footing back and followed. She had noticed the swift interaction between the two men. Though friendly, Tau's demeanour changed. It was clear who's in charge.

The surrounding space boasted with several reed huts with a building looming over it. Fires lit the area which left sinister spots against the makeshift walls. Smoke obscured the rest. At the back-pitch blackness encircled them.

"What about Jabu?" Kwame called.

"Lock him up! Haji would see to him," Tau responded.

They followed the disappearing man in a hurry. Disorientated and scared she followed.

Tau assured her no harm would befall her as they trailed him. His hand guided her.

The shadows danced a ghostly spiel as people watched them. Sonia's unease remained. Her uncertainty grew. Here she was totally in their power, the thought so persistent that she walked closer to Tau.

In the dark their destination flickered through a solitary window. Loud moans greeted them the closer they got.

Out of breath Sonia went inside the reed hut, the heat an overpowering presence and she took a deep breath. In the corner a fire heated a pot to boiling point. Another woman stood next to a makeshift bed. In anger she addressed Roger brashly. On the bed a woman sobbed, her condition noticeable. She was in labour.

The argument continued before she stomped out.

Just in time Sonia moved aside. Her glare spoke volumes as she disappeared.

"Please, my wife," Roger said. "You can help, yes?" he asked.

When Sonia replied, "Yes," she lowered and met her gaze as she took her pulse. "I will help you."

Big eyes stared back almost in relief. Her body glimmered with sweat. Another argument broke out between Roger and the woman just outside the door. Sonia directed her gaze to Tau.

"Please let them leave, and get rid of that fire," she ordered.

"The patient is uncomfortable."

"Sure," he said before Tau addressed them. The woman left in a huffed fit.

"Can you help her?" the leader asked.

"I will know once I have examined her. Tau, I need more light."

"Please Miss." His unease and concern touched her.

"My name is Sonia." A faint smile appeared. "Please, Sonia, help Baaka. Her other pregnancies were tough. I almost lost her with all of them." Realization struck her as she observed him through.

"You brought me here for her?" This kind of devotion was uncommon in Africa. He nodded and touched his wife.

"I will do my best."

With tender love he glanced towards his wife then at her, gave Sonia a slight nod and left. Once they were alone, the oppressive air lifted and Sonia gave a slight smile.

"Now we can finally get to work," she addressed her patient.

"He meant well," Baaka whispered and clutched Sonia's arm.

"It seems this baby wants to come," she explained after she did a quick check.

"I will appreciate it," sweat raced down her face.

"Lift your legs." The action caused discomfort and Sonia helped her. She shrieked in pain.

Tau arrived with more light and the supplies she had asked. From his shoulder a medical bag dangled.

"Where did that come from?" Astounded, she studied him. He just shrugged his shoulders and dozed the fire.

Sonia worked nonstop through the night. The birth was difficult. The woman's tiredness did not help. Fatigued after her own ordeal, Sonia pinched her eyes but kept her vigilance. At dawn she stepped out of the hut with a healthy baby boy. The man's grin faltered as he marched up to her, taking his slumbering son with pride.

"Is Baaka all right?" he asked.

"Yes, she is sleeping," Sonia replied and brushed sweaty hair away. Taking deep breaths she enjoyed the crispness of the new day. It helped her burning eyes and aching back. People clustered about all watching her from listless eyes.

Her view of the unknown place offered her peacefulness, and she inhaled it. The early morning sunbathed the reeds in golden hues and early birds fluttered in the tops.

The camp's layout was like most camps she had seen, except for the swamp … less dust and bareness. The water stretched all around them, so far back that she lost view. She was in a floating prison, detached from the outside world. Discouraged Sonia realized escape was impossible.

Sonia observed Roger Gisemba, her jailer, inches taller than her for the first time. His gaze fixed on the child he cradled. Pock marks covered his face which gave him a foreboding presence. Like Tau Gbadamosi, he was bald and clean-shaven. The old faded brown chino pants and white shirt, a sharp contrast against his dark skin. A pistol at the belt brought her predicament to the fore front.

"Thanks, Sonia," he finally addressed her. Another woman took the baby from him. Her head remained downcast. Once she had the baby she disappeared between the huts as the man entered his wife's hut.

Unsure she searched for Tau who was seated on a makeshift bench close by. He nodded and she followed.

Back inside Roger knelt at his wife's side. As he watched her, he spoke. "Your work is to help my people, yes." Sonia got the impression it was not a question, which she acknowledged. She was at his mercy.

Without showing her fear she folded her hands. "When do I return?"

He looked up, his serious gaze turned sinister; one she did not trust.

"Soon, maybe never."

The finality of his words underlined her situation. Panic rolled in waves towards her. Once he moved away, he studied her and left her alone with her thoughts. Fear stabbed Sonia's heart that she had difficulty breathing.

This would be my home. Nobody knew my whereabouts. A militia chief stipulated my work. What else will he want from me?

"Lord, why am I at this place? What plans do you have in store?" she prayed as she cleaned everything she had used and left with the basin of water. She was about to toss it into the nearest opening when Tau took it from her.

Grateful for his aid she leaned against the crude door and paid attention to her surroundings. Women were already busy with their daily chores as children circled them. They all peered at her through head scarfs while whispering amongst each other. Touching her neck she immediately knew what the fuss was about. Her uncovered head unwelcomed. Not for the first time the differences in culture became apparent. She longed for privacy and a bed. As she moved closer to the fire, Tau appeared with a reassuring grin.

"Tired?"

She nodded and rolled her shoulders.

"Follow me." Too tired to respond she followed him. Once his back was turned she saw the holster under his arm—a clear sign that her life had changed. Her freedom violated.

24

---

6 May 2019, Iraqi desert.

"YOU ARE SURE ABOUT THIS, PUMPKIN?"

"Yes, Daddy," Jillian McGee confirmed.

Curt was in contact with her doctors who verified Neil Davies's paternity. He reflected much about this. There were many things wrong in his family. The fact that he wasn't at home made matters worse. How to fix them was his primary concern, his daughter on the forefront of his mind. The thought that Jillian was not honest with him—plagued him. The phone call just proved she was honest. But, and this was where it became tricky, finding a noble way that would help mother and child.

Norton assured him the news would clinch the divorce case. The situation could turn ugly if not resolved. He'd rather not expose Jillian to the system. Neil Davies was an influential businessman. He would attract attention when this news goes public.

"What are you going to do, Pumpkin?"

"Dad, this is hard. My life is over. All my plans, my dreams," she sobbed.

"Jillian, what are you saying?" He swallowed, hard. Will this be his worst nightmare coming true?

"I will end it."

"No Jillian."

"Please understand, Dad."

"No, Pumpkin. I can't understand; this is murder."

"Daddy." Her cries became louder.

"Jillian, I can't give my consent."

"Daddy, I am a grown woman, I can choose." By now her voice was shaky.

"I realise that, Pumpkin. This child did not ask for this." He took a deep breath, "Neil's wife wants to adopt the baby," he blurted.

"Never, Dad!"

He sighed. "It's an option to consider."

"When did she call?"

"Yesterday." He waited and greeted a soldier who passed him. The conversation with the socialite was an eye-opener. All he knew about Harriet Davies was that she featured in the newspaper regularly and was commended for her volunteer work. The side he got to know was different from her role. She was a woman in pain and suffered just as much as he did. She wanted to give the baby the best possible option. He said he would talk to Jillian. Up until now he was uncertain of her involvement.

When he returned his attention Jillian sounded small: "Daddy, tell me what to do."

"Pumpkin, I cannot tell you what to do. I can only offer my opinion to you. Remember, whatever you choose, I'll be here."

"I wish you were at home, Dad."

"Yes, me too, Pumpkin. It isn't possible."

"Dad!" Silence assaulted them as he allowed her time to calm. "I'm sorry for all of this."

"It isn't your fault," he assured her.

"I love you, Dad."

"Think about it, we will talk again. I cannot stress it enough. You are not alone, Jillian, remember that."

"Yes, Dad."

He greeted her, the lump in his throat difficult to swallow. When he turned, Doug sought his attention.

The day was already halfway, his work far from done. With the problems at home he struggled to concentrate on the tasks, work he loved.

"What is happening to Private Cummings?"

"We are following up all leads, Sir. Could I take leave at the end of the month?" Doug explained the reason as they returned to the office.

"Fill in the forms."

"IS EVERYTHING alright with you, Nurse Stalin?"

Anna jumped when Captain Bogart touched her arm. She did not realise her blue eyes reflected fear to the one person she despised. Captain Bogart's frown confirmed it as she repeated her question.

"Oh, it's nothing, Captain," she assured, trying to leave. To talk to the captain was out of the question.

"Nurse." Her voice held a note of care, the Captain's stare penetrating as a frown marred her face. Anna could only summarise she spotted the blue marks on her neck and arms. She righted her uniform under the gaze.

"What's the matter?"

"No, Captain, it's nothing." She pulled her arm free; ready to run.

"If you want to talk," she whispered.

"Yes, Captain," making herself scarce. The sudden care from the witch unnerved her.

Once outside she disappeared to the back of the medics just to bump in her worst nightmare. She never thought she would fear the man she loved. Brock became this way after his return from the States. The word 'no' had no influence on him any longer.

The wall of hard flesh and vice hold pressed her firmly against him. When he lifted her, her heart skipped in icy fear. Brock's mood stopped her cold. The dim light granted her a menacing expression of the man.

"You are teasing me every time, Anna," and he shook her. "Me and the rest of the men."

"No, Brock." It was futile. He believed in his own version. "Put me down, Brock," she pleaded, but his grip tightened.

"Not tonight, Sweetheart." He kissed her with a hunger that hurts. She could taste the twang of blood in her mouth. She continued to struggle until he released her and slapped him hard. Her fear paramount. This was a mistake she regretted at once.

A devilish grin appeared. "You want it rough." Pain shot up her spine.

"No! Brock, not tonight, please! I'm still in pain from last night."

He chuckled; the ominous cackle clenched her heart. "Yeah, that was quite wonderful." He grinned, and she flinched.

"What are you doing?" Through the fearful haze she recognised the voice of Sam Gerber. The next moment he pushed her aside, but still imprisoned in Brock's clutches.

Sam grabbed his collar and punched Brock. The steel grip released her and she fell to the ground.

Stunned she watched the fight until Alexi Krasnorada joined her—his presence a shield against the fighting men.

"Are you all right?" Alexi asked. Shaken she viewed her abuser's beating, her fear replaced by relief and sadness. But it was only a fleeting awareness and reached out to him. Alexi held her back.

Sam and Alexi took no nonsense from anyone—both skilled special ops personnel, hardened by years of training between them. And the only men who could stand against Brock. Anna met them during their visits to patchwork. Over time they became friends.

Their faces were dangerous looking as they held Brock down.

"Do you want to press charges, Anna?"

"No, Sam. Let him go, please." She was shaking. The abuse she suffered, the lack of sleep and the constant pain made her weak. Her humiliation in the open.

"I am watching you, Staff Sergeant," Sam warned as he gave Brock an intimidating stare.

Although shorter than Brock, Sam did not stand back for him. What he did not have in height, Sam gained in strength. His bulk stretched the fabric of the khaki shirt. Everyone feared and respected him.

"Yeah?" Brock mocked him as they glowered at each other.

"You leave the lady alone."

"I don't see any ladies around." A hard hit pushed him to the ground, Alexi towered over him.

"You will respect the lady, is it clear, Soldier?" Sam's commanding presence loomed over him. Brock rubbed his jaw as he nodded in agreement.

"Get moving!" Alexi pushed him away. With a last glance to her Brock walked away. The expression left her terrified.

"Are you okay?" Alexi inquired.

"Yes."

"We will follow him closely from now on," Sam said.

"Has he ever given you trouble before?"

"No, not really," she whispered.

"What do you mean … no, not really? What did the man do?" Sam demanded.

"He …" Silently she fell back against the crates. Light exposed her.

"Did he threaten you in any way?"

"No, not exactly," she answered, her voice small.

"Dammit, Anna! What did the man do?" He raised a brow.

"He likes it rough, and I …"

Alexi pulled her closer when her sobs intensified, her shame coiled her neck and left her breathless. He touched it and she shrieked.

"When did this happen?" Alexi's voice gave away his intense anger.

"Last night," came the soft reply.

"You told no one?" Sam raised a brow.

"I could manage it, but he doesn't back off anymore."

How do you say no to a big soldier when you had let him use you? Her thoughts muddled with pain and tiredness. Trapped between the sand dunes she could not hide from Brock.

"We will have to check on him," Alexi hissed, and Sam agreed.

"Let's walk you to your room." Sam pushed her toward her room.

Anna knew they could not protect her. Brock would be back—maybe not tonight, but he would return. The camp's size and the brooding turmoil outside gave him enough opportunities. Sam and Alexi could not be there all the time. She had no place to hide.

She could leave, but where to? Back home she had no one. Her parents divorced years ago. Both remarried and had new families; she was not in the picture anymore.

25

May 2019, Fangak County.

"TO EVERYTHING, THERE IS A SEASON and a time to every purpose under heaven." Her mom used to say: 'It is purposeful. Time gifted enables hope.' For a long time, Sonia's hope clashed with her purpose. It had taken the marshlands to produce meaning to the quote.

Early mornings before the camp awoke, she walked unencumbered around and drank the tranquillity it offered. In the background the patrol remained with her.

At first it amazed her how much freedom they allowed her as she explored the island. It was bigger than most and housed many refugees and people in the area. The simple life offered to them enough to make a living. The peace they experienced here differed greatly from the rest of the country.

Ever since she had arrived, she used the period to reflect. Although imprisoned she is not jailed; treated as a respected guest. It was these small favours that instilled gratefulness.

There were luxuries she craved, a long soaking bubble bath, for one. Her hair required a wash, shaving would be wonderful and decent food and coffee.

Her overnighter held the essentials which she used sparingly. Baaka gifted her two dresses after her recovery and a headscarf; the gesture moved her. So far from civilization supplies were scarce.

The only other clothing she had was the yellow dress, inappropriate to wear. Happy memories clung to it. Smells, sounds and acceptance hidden within the folds. A weekend cloaked with mysterious freedom. Time gifted her hours of a connection she would love to experience once more. For now it remained a dream.

Does he remember me? She curt-tailed her thoughts once more.

It will not help you think about it, Sonia. Stay in the present. The past's dreams can do nothing to change your reality.

She scanned the area with a mixture of trepidation and uncertainty, her peace thinly sliced.

"Lord, I have accepted your path though it came at a cost. You gave me hope in the folds of a yellow dress. It holds my future, a future I would love to have. That is my hope. You are my hope. Thank you for the small favours and provision."

This morning the swamp's quietness touched her. Within a week she had found her way and worked in silence. Conditions were not perfect, but she managed.

Passing Roger's reed hut, foreboding clamped her. He was a charismatic evil she avoided. In the past week she had seen too much of his evilness which changed her views about him. Thankfully, their paths did not cross.

The structure she lived in, constructed from plastic, boasted with a small window. The crudeness afforded her enough privacy. It wasn't the Grand Excelsior with its glorious fittings or breath-taking views, but it was home. The single mattress a thin card box-like cover, the mud floor, though clean, worn but solid. The door fabricated of a blue plastic canvas barely covered the opening.

Her guards, ever-present, were young enough to be in school. They never talked, never smiled. One reminded her of Jabu, his sideways glances a tell-tale of his thoughts.

Tau was correct about Jabu.

Jabu became an example, his death a horrific experience they forced her to watch. On the day of her arrival they summoned her to watch. It remained a terrible memory and one that changed her opinion of her jailers.

Covered in blood, Jabu Boko's horrific screams shocked her. They had bound a leather string around his neck as another man held the other end. His menacing face implied doom for the youngster. Jabu's clothes were in tatters. A trail of blood followed his crawl on the ground. She was not sure, but it looked as if they had cut all his fingers. One foot dangled awkwardly behind him.

Sonia tried to hide behind Tau, but the demand brooked no argument. "Watch!"

"I can't," she had pleaded. He had drawn her face towards the scene as another scream ripped the air. Roger had hit him with a thin rattan, his cheek split and blood streamed from it.

Gone was the husband who cared about his spouse and held a baby that morning. Instead a savage appeared who had cut into him without hesitation. Jabu fell to the ground curling inwards, but the enforcer pulled the cord. His head jerked backward. Wide eyes stared at Roger as more screams followed; his mouth split in two.

Roger had lowered to Jabu's level, hindering her view, but the commotion coloured the void. Her imagination helped along with the screams of pain as Roger did his worst with him. When he rose, satisfaction covered the pocked face. Jabu's tongue dangled in the air. A blood-fall immersed from what used to be his mouth; his screams turned into wheezing; freight, his only emotion as he followed the leader's boasting. She wanted to run to him, but Tau held her back with a menacing stare of his own.

"Please, we must save him." Sonia tried to interfere, but Tau placed a thick finger on his lips. BE QUIET. Shocked she watched in horror. Roger addressed the crowd in Sudanese, the speech intimidating from the expressions of them. Only the whimpering sounds from Jabu broke the hypnotism he had. During the speech Roger concentrated on her. The black eyes flashed warnings. That stare shattered her as it communicated a message. She would never escape from him.

Then he withdrew. People scattered away to create a path.

With a flick of the wrist the giant threw the fleshy lump on the fire. Soon burning flesh pervaded the air. Wild screams emanated until it died in the embers.

She then fainted. Her next awareness was when Tau laid her on the bed.

"Why?" she urged.

"He has betrayed us. Death was the only punishment good enough."

"Why so cruel?"

"We tolerate no weakness. We accept no betrayal," he explained.

"We have to protect the people in our care, understand!" A tear formed on her cheek and he pinked it away. "Don't you worry, Sonia Main. If you listen to me, no harm will come to you." His closeness disturbed her.

"I will never leave this place," she said.

The attention Tau had given her confirmed her nightmare. He leaned closer until his lips touched her cheek. "Will it be that bad to stay, Princess?"

When he moved towards her lips, she stopped him. "Please. No."

He smiled and offered a peck, anyway. "You, my princess, will make this man very happy the day you give yourself to him."

"Never. I love another."

"He isn't here, Princess, but I am." With that Tau Gbadamosi had shut the door. The finality of it all crashed down on her and she wept. The cruel death and the nauseating smell of the food caused the loss of her stomach's content. Tau had nursed her until she felt better. Later in the day he showed her around as if nothing had happened.

The scenes she had seen that day washed away all doubts of escape, but her hope remained. That hope she cling to as she observed the camp once more.

They kept the base camp clean at all times. Reed huts clustered around communal cooking fires, at the back a store held all the supplies. Women performed their duties with amicable conversation—washing clothing along the bank, cooking and fetching water. Men caught fish from the side or ventured out on the river with dug outs. These small canoes were precarious looking, but children and men were comfortable with it. The younger kids kicked a plastic container around. The cheerful sounds, so different from Jabu's, echoed in the heated air as one scored a goal. Some children bathed in closeness to their mothers. The older men assembled in the courtyard where they discussed politics. Tau joined them often as they shared the homemade brew and lively conversation. The comforting scene brought some ease and life became unsurprising and peaceful.

The same scenario which greeted her every day.

WITHOUT FAIL TAU ACCOMPANIED her to the medical tent. They never talked. She followed him through the camp as people stared at her. His presence gave her some sense of peace as she locked her gaze on his back.

This morning there was a shift in the air. Tau's back was taught, his attention vigilant as they crisscrossed through the camp to the medical tent. A distinct sense of foreboding alerted her. Alarmed she noticed every detail about the camp. Machine guns, which were normally propped against trunks, were held tightly by the soldiers as they scanned the area. All the canoes and the motorised fisher boat lined the bank. The men stood around uncertain and the children were unusual quiet. At first sight everything seemed peaceful, even harmonious. Then why was she uneasy?

They crossed the makeshift bridge over a narrow canal, then stopped at the old army tent. Although weathered, it still had a purpose. Around the tent people sat about in a listless state. Sonia approached the children first. She acknowledged the mothers and reached for the first little boy's forehead. He was burning. Alarmed she met Tau's stare.

"What's wrong, Sonia?" he squatted. She continued with the examination, shielding her mounting distress. She rushed inside the tent with Tau following her. "What's happening?" With surgical gloves on, she rushed back to the kid.

Tau stopped her inside the tent. "What is wrong, Sonia?"

She met his stare and whispered: "Measles." She knelt next to the same boy and did a systematic examination.

TAU WATCHED IN ADMIRATION, convinced it was right to bring her. The week proved to be productive. The sick was cared for. It lifted the burden and gave him more freedom to connect with the elders. His attention was drawn to the problems of the camp. As always he liked to watch her work. Her confidence and care cemented the abduction. No matter if it was wrong, they benefited with her presence and the people trusted her.

A crease formed between the dark brown eyes showed the intensity he observed her reactions. With each examination she became paler. Dread treated through his heart as he scanned the camp; kids running around without fear. How many will they bury this time?

When she joined him with a hands-on-hips, her shoulders back, challenging him, his heart somersaulted. This was the last thing they needed right now.

"We need a vaccine, now!"

"We don't have a vaccine."

"Then we have a problem. All those kids," and she pointed to the children, running and screaming in cheer, "will be here. Death will take them. Do you understand?" Her eyes glistened with a fire he respected.

"Yes."

Without waiting for him she carried a child inside. He followed with another child. Their feeble attempt of a medical centre was not equipped for this onslaught. The three beds a testimony of their lack. Mothers scurried around them, crying. They could sense the emergency; many had lost children with the earlier outbreak. They knew this killer.

Once done, he rushed to Roger Gisemba's hut. The woman wants a vaccine and he will get it.

MORE YOUNGSTERS JOINED the tent during the day, her ever-mounting fear becoming real with each hour. Helpless she stared at a girl; her mother clutched her hand. Without the vaccine, she could do nothing. More people entered the tent area which added to her mounting pressure. "Lord, thank you for supplying in their needs."

Then her heart turned icy when a cry from Haram Baaka's hut filtered through the air. Sonia ran the moment she heard the cry and stopped inside the hut. Baaka cradled the baby with desperation, it sounded horrendous. When she lifted her tear-stained eyes, Sonia knew it was too late. The killer claimed its first prize; his lifeless body covered in Koplik spots.

"I'm so sorry, Baaka," she said and took the infant from her clutching arms.

Baaka's head dropped into her hands, sinking to the ground. She passed the dead infant to another woman. Sonia's own heart clenched as she consoled her.

"What's happening?" Roger barged in, followed by Tau.

"I am sorry, Roger," Sonia replied and left the hut.

MORE DEATHS FOLLOWED. A permanent wail hung heavy in the air. No one was thinking of sleep. The camp itself became a graveyard as more bodies were covered with a tarp, a reminder of what this sickness could do if not managed accordingly. When the first light broke through the heavens, Tau appeared. He held a medical ice box in his hand. A triumphed smile confirmed the contents of the container.

Like a maniac he and Kwame bordered the boat and sped away right after Baaka's baby's death. They knew where to find some and brooked no nonsense from the medical staff on approach.

If Sonia had more information she would have refused to use the content, but now it was a life source she was happy to have.

Sonia went for it. However, he held onto it and she frowned.

"Don't you think I need a reward?"

"What do you mean, reward?"

He bent and inserted himself in her space.

"What do you think of a kiss?"

"This isn't the time for games," she seethed.

"Oh, this is the perfect opportunity to have my way."

"You are a bastard!" she yelled.

Immediately he caught her and pulled her closer. The adrenaline of the day pulsed through him and deaf to her anger he went for her mouth. His tongue touched the seams of her lips and Sonia reacted. She bit into the soft flesh, pushed him away then slapped him. Tau scurried away in disbelief which turned into anger instantly. Noticing the people's watchful glare on him, his pride flared towards this woman who dared to defy him in front of his people. His hand lifted and she sprinted away as his curses followed her. In rage he wanted to follow but realized quickly that she had a job to do. One that would save his people.

His momentary anger deflated and he walked away. He knew exactly what they all must think of him. Sonia's reaction had put him in a bad spot. No one would allow him to forget.

BY 12H00 THE REMAINING children and younger people received an injection. Sonia's head pounded by the time she sat in the nearest chair. The heat, lack of sleep and food made her weak. She could sleep for days. Taking an aspirin she dropped her forehead against the cool fridge.

Finally, her tiredness won.

For a long time, Tau watched her sleeping form. His heart melted. How could he be angry with her after what she had done? Through the following hours she never complained, never took care of herself, nor ate. People looked at her with admiration. She had become more than just a healer. In their eyes she had become an angel … an angel he cared for.

Now it was time that someone took care of her.

UNAWARE OF TAU'S THOUGHTS a pair of muscular arms carried Sonia back to her hut. His pounding heart was the only giveaway of his growing feelings, feelings he shielded from her and the rest of the camp.

26

ACCORDING TO PUBLIC OPINION the swamps of Fangak County were the largest in the world, a haven for many refugees in a growing war. Feared and revered, rich in fauna and flora, nature ruled here.

For humans, however, the place lacked the most basic supplies. Soap, for instance, was unknown to them— money a commodity they had no use of. The swamps supplied the food; fresh water came by boats.

Schooling was another great need. Basic education non-excitant. The people were disadvantaged on every level. Survival the only topic.

After the measle outbreak Sonia slept for twelve hours straight. No one dared to wake her as Tau guarded the door. He allowed no one in, that included the leader.

Roger was not happy, but Tau could care less for his broken finger and he grumbled his reply.

During the first hour Tau sponged her as best he could. Her suffering showed on the damped sheet. He got rid of her soaked clothes and covered her with a linen sheet he had bribed from one woman. Taking care of her himself he had to be discreet in this little detail. He promised himself that he would only touch her when she agreed. Though it drove him to madness, he abstained from his desires. She was unlike the other women and would be cared for differently.

When she woke at last, he brought her food, water and tea. She devoured everything in haste, licking her fingers in such a way which made other parts twitch. The close proximity smuggled with his brain and he stepped away. As a last act Tau prepared a bath for her. It was the least he could do. Once he stepped out, he scanned the area. Certain they were alone; he walked to the back of the tent and removed some debris. Inside he heard the splashes of water which drew him to a tare in the plastic, his body sparked with a yearning he was not willing to confess. The thought of having her soon, his only solace. His determination would make it so. No matter if Roger did not agree.

Sonia Main was his woman.

SONIA WOKE FRIGHTENED AND clutched the sheet to her body. Being inside her hut with no recollection of how she got there, scared her. All she could remember was the pounding headache.

Stripped of her clothing, her underwear gave her some sense of relief. Tau entered her hut with food and cups and placed it on a makeshift table. Two women dragged a tin bath in and poured water inside. The entire scene was unbelievable. She could only watch as he prepared everything and left.

The bath was everything it promised, her first in over a week. She soaked inside the tub until she wrinkled before she washed her hair thoroughly. With care she spoiled herself with the last of her lotion. When she stepped out of the hut the morning sun kissed her wet hair and covered her head as prescribed by their laws.

How long was she asleep?

"Thanks Tau," she said the moment she saw him. The dress she had on was one of Baaka's gifts, the cotton cool one. On the first day of her capture, she realised she had lost the colourful scarf. The loss symbolised a loss of an earlier life now so distant she struggled to recollect.

"It's a pleasure, Princess."

"Please stop that."

"What?"

"Calling me a princess. I am long past a princess stage."

"To me you are a princess, no matter your age."

She blushed. "Thanks for the bath."

"I wish it could be more often."

Before Sonia could answer Roger interrupted them. "Once done, there is work to do." He commanded.

"Tau, bring the nurse." Roger marched towards the tent. A path opened for him. As Sonia passed through the throng, women smiled and men greeted her with a small nod. Children rushed to her and one small hand seized hers. She greeted the boy with a soft smile. This had not happened before.

"The people are happy," Tau said. "They appreciate your help." She nodded. "I only did my duty."

"To them it is more than a duty," he said.

"You stayed till the end and healed their children."

"It wasn't me. It was the vaccine."

"They think it is you. Who am I to differ from them?" he mocked, but the admiring regard showed more. With unease she stopped herself to answer. Although she grew accustomed to the protection he offered and the small favours she received, the look she received made her uncomfortable. During her sleep-binge he was the one who took care of her. He was the one who removed her clothing, she was sure of that. She would have to talk to him, but was hesitant. His behaviour in the tent made her sceptic.

"It came at a cost."

"That is unfortunate, but they are used to death." They entered the tent together. His last remark clenched her heart.

"As you know we face problems at camp." Roger began touching the tray with instruments already sterilized. She fisted a hand in agitation but remained silent.

"Yes, there is," she replied.

"Give me your views of the camp."

ASTONISHED WITH THE CHANGE, she forgot about the infected tray, happy to share her findings. "A water filtering process is required. Dehydration is an enormous problem," she began. "Schooling is another need. Both children and grownups will benefit from tutoring. Without basic education, people will remain ignorant." And ruled by fools, she wanted to add. Their piercing gazes met, her message clear. An excellent leader had to take care of the essentials. He had to give them skills to further them.

"What do you propose for this?"

"I need more help. In the tent, for starters. My afternoons are open. I can begin with classes, both schooling and teaching women about cleanliness, but I will require help with that." Minutes ticked away as Roger rolled the information around.

He was not a man who took orders from a woman, but she had a point. He and Tau had spoken about it, but had no knowledge themselves. Though it angered him, he knew she had a point. The people needed basic education, once she obviously could deliver.

"Make sure you get it done," Roger said to Tau and left.

"You pleased the leader," Tau remarked once they were alone.

"I don't like him," she blurted.

"He is a generous man once you know him."

SHE SHRUGGED IN DOUBT and removed the tray. "Who can I get to help me?"

"I will," Baaka said. "I am glad you are back with us." Her English threadbare, her voice filled with gratitude.

"Thanks, Baaka. I welcome your help." The two women's ease with each other palpable. Relying on each other helped them to cope with the burdens inflicted on them.

Their situations similar. Both were prisoners in a world full of hate, neglect and sorrow. The one used to be alone, being independent, the other used to be limited. Once they met on equal ground, all barriers lifted. Baaka shied away and washed the tables and beds with a brush.

"There is a man who could help; I will talk to him," Tau said, aware of the bond and eager to be useful.

"Thanks Tau, that will help."

Once Tau left them alone, Sonia showed Baaka the ropes. With the language barrier Sonia had to rely on Baaka's understanding through show rather than tell. The bond surpassed words. Sonia liked the younger woman, losing their children a bond that cemented the relationship.

Sonia relied on her knowledge of the people, and Baaka relied on her friendship and guidance.

27

ANOTHER PROBLEM THEY FACED were the ever-present mosquitoes. With her Tabard finished she had no defense to their onslaught. At night it was even worse. These mosquitoes were malaria carriers. The swamp doing its bit, creating the perfect hatching ground for them. The sweltering heat, the incubator for them to multiply.

Baaka instructed Sonia how to protect herself from the pest, covering herself with the repellent Baaka had brought her. A nasty concoction that suspiciously smell like urine, but it worked. She wanted to dismiss it, but after seeing Baaka who rubbed herself in it, she followed. After a while the stench was bearable.

Another day passed in stillness which they used to clean when Sonia noticed the stacked medical supplies.

Where did it come from? Her guess … stolen either from IRC, MSF, or Doctors without Borders. They did not get it legally.

According to the geographic maps she had seen once, the airstrip allowed small planes to land in the county, the only other link with the outside world. Raids and abductions were as common as starvation and disease. The people had seen it, heard it, and lived it all. Stories of the DFA well known.

Though she appreciated the medicine, she wondered about the people it was taken from. Were they still alive?

Every day offered its own questions. Questions who would never be answered. To ask Tau was futile. She tried once with no answer. Therefore she updated her inventory with the stock and packed it away. From an administration's point of view, Sonia noted each individual as they passed through the tent. Even so deep in the swamps paperwork was necessary. A familiar routine Sonia took seriously.

The camp had two hundred and eighty-two people on her last count. On her first day she started with a register and noted each visit. They entered the outpatients' information in another book. They were also in search of medical aid and anything else they might require, like food.

"Sonia, this is Isaac." Interrupted from her duties, she watched Tau with interest. "He knows the medical basics."

"*As-Salam Alaykum*, Isaac," she greeted him. "Where did you study?"

"I worked at a clinic in Juba. The nurses trained me," he replied in a heavy accent.

"Why is he here?" Sonia asked Tau with apprehension.

"He believes in our cause and joined," Tau said.

Isaac's gangling body bowed respectfully, a relaxed figure which instilled wisdom. He wore the same clothes as Tau but not as neat. His friendliness reminded her of David Sulliman.

"Please to meet you, Isaac. Let me show you around, then I can see what you know. Thanks, Tau."

"Pleasure …" She cut him off when he wanted to continue. His constant attention worried her. By keeping her distance, she hoped that Tau would change this infatuation he had with her.

Thoughts of escape escalated every time. She had just one problem. Since they arrived in the dead of night, she did not know her location. To flee in the unknown would speed up her death, a topic she thought about when time allowed. She had to get away, but how?

Used to be alone, this loneliness added a new depth to her thoughts. Her ruffled nerves longed for the company of her own people. At night Curt filled her dreams, his image fading with each passing day. She tried to hold on to what they had, but with nothing concrete she struggled. Once or twice she thought of Brady, but it was a closed chapter.

She prayed often. The one best thing about her abduction was her re-established connection with God. A connection she savoured with hope born from one dream.

FROM HIS OFFICE ROGER watched the medic tent hawk-like. Roger, everyone called him Haji, in respect for who he was; a father and protector of them all. But at that moment he did not feel like a father. His brooding eyes watched her, but he never approached her. The death of his youngest caused him to draw back and he seldom talked. All he did was to entertain thoughts of payback. Payback for what the white woman did to him. She was the cause of his son's death.

Also, he did not approve of the growing friendship between his wife and Sonia. He confronted her last night and told her to keep her place. For the first time she defied a direct order, something he was not used to.

He watched as she moved about the tent as if she owned it. Hatred sweltered deep within and he knew he should get rid of her, soon. Ever since this woman came to the camp, she created problems for him. Problems he had no answers for, but she was the reason for most. He was convinced of it.

That Tau was so stupid not to see it, was beyond him. He could not understand his second in command. Just look at the fool. With a final sneer he looked away and saw one of his concubines. She would do to get his frustration in control and called her over.

THE BOOMING VOICE STRETCHED across the camp and Sonia lifted her head just in time to see a young woman disappearing into Roger's hut. She glanced over to Baaka, her back to him as she busied herself with a child's wound.

His observations unnerved Sonia more than Tau. The evil underneath the surface left her scared. She was not afraid of Tau, though his advancements troubled her. In normal circumstances, they could have been friends. But lovers? ... That was what Tau wanted. She could never do that. It goes against every part of her being. Death was better than the alternative.

The other reason she wanted to escape was the nights. The drunkenness of the soldiers made them careless with their weapons. The flimsy walls offered little protection, her vulnerability highlighted. She locked her door by moving the pieces of furniture in front of the door. It gave her some sense of safety. There was always a guard at the entrance. He frightened her too.

Prayer had become her escape, pleading for rescue each night. Her hut, a prison cell and her fear real.

The food was not much. It included sorghum, maize and fish, but at least they fed her twice a day. Her fate could have been worse, but the question remained: When will they force themselves on her? She had seen the looks. Her work in Africa gave her insight into their way of thinking. They regarded a woman as an object. Even wrapped in her shawl, eyes followed her every step.

As she scanned the natural barrier of water, there was no escape route visible. The whitewashed wall on her right, with a militia insignia, bared her view to the swamps.

"Show me, Lord. I need a lifeline. In you I trust." A soft breeze touched her cheek—so soft she could dismiss it. It left a fragrance long forgotten. Frankincense. As a child her parents burned it in the house. A sweet reminder of His sacrifice. She stepped outside and filled her lungs with the subtleness. A crisp sense that God was with her.

"Sonia," Baaka called, and she turned.

"Yes, Baaka?"

"Here is a patient."

She nodded, lifted her gaze to the heavens and whispered: *"Thank you, Lord."*

28

June 2019, Fangak County.

THE WEEKS SETTLED INTO an active program. Sonia's days were divided between the sick and the students.

They cleared an area provided by Haji and sectioned it off with a reed wall. The older people used tree trunks for seats, the children used the ground. Their excitement to learn astonished her as they grasped the elementary things with eagerness and joy. It humbled her and encouraged her to continue.

Tau surprised her with a blackboard on her first day. A momentous occasion as the children inspected the structure up close. They made turns to clean it after each session.

The basic school program was all done from her experience and what she picked up through the years of nursing. Since there were no workbooks, the kids wrote in the ground, each beginning with their names. The day they could do it flawlessly, joy broke out in the camp.

"Another wonderful thing you did for us," Baaka said as she looked from her son's writing. The six-year-old showed interest from day one. A bright fellow with lots of potential, Sonia was sure off.

"Kids need education," Sonia replied with a slight bow.

"Without it, they have no future."

Baaka had joined the grown-up classes and was keen to learn just as much. Their studies consisted of reading, spelling and basic mathematics. Since medicine was Sonia's field of expertise, she also taught them first-aid. Something that could come in handy in their world.

Sonia had requested workbooks and handbooks for the fifteen pupils which ranged between 6 – 14 years, without success. They were parents themselves and the boys became soldiers the moment they could walk. Though it grieved her to see so few older kids it was at least a start.

Without the basic tools she had to plan it very well. That task she left for late evenings when everyone was relaxing. Because of refugees that joined the camp, a new pupil joined the two-hour class regularly.

The duo, Baaka and Isaac, had become her treasured allies in her day-to-day activities. Tau remained to be her ever-present guardian and supplied in every need where possible.

Though busy, Sonia knew she could only benefit with resources herself. A Bible for one, was something she would really like. As days became weeks her desire for friends and co-workers lessened, but her desire to read the Word and fill the gaps with spiritual knowledge grew day by day. This morning she laid it before the Lord once more.

While busy in the tent, Sonia went through her inventory and realized she needed supplies. Outside the tent she looked around but could not find Tau. Even Frank, the guard, did not know where Tau was. Sonia was not allowed near the store without Tau, she went anyway. She wanted to be prepared for any eventuality.

Frank was unhappy and stopped her. Even when she insisted it could not wait, he refused to let her pass.

This brought her restlessness to the forefront and to work it off, she circled the tent hoping the exercise would stop the flow of negativity. A place that caused more anger and confusion. Just behind the tent a building appeared. She had seen it after her arrival, a few times. Today, it called to her, and deliberated its significance. For an unknown reason the building stood for an answer, but she was not sure why.

"Lord, show me please. What is the importance of this place?"

Unsure of it all she turned back to the opening. When she could not find Frank, she decided to walk to the store. It was a good ten-minute walk that turned to thirty-minutes as people stopped to talk to her. By the time she got there, Roger stood in front of the entrance—the one person she had avoided until now. He addressed a fidgeting soldier when she wanted to pass him and stopped her.

"You are not allowed in here."

"I need supplies."

"I need many things. What are you willing to give me in return for your needs?"

Her heart thumped as she looked at him. His eyes roamed her body with a sneer, his intent clear. He stepped into her space, and she retreated. "I have nothing."

A hard surface stopped her cold. His warm breath hurried, his eye fixated. "I disagree, Sonia Main. How do they say it in your language?" He pressed a finger against his forehead. "Men swoon about you. Did you know that?"

"No." His closeness unnerved her and she pushed against him. His bulk too heavy for her, he chuckled. A raspy sound that grated her.

"You better believe it. There are many men who want you, but I have the power to give or keep you. Your life is in my hands."

He pressed against her. Scared, she pushed harder. He clutched her face in a vice and kissed her. Pain shot through her face, and her neck. "You will give me what I want, or you can forget about the sick and school. It is because of me you have it, not because you asked or Tau care for you. Never forget that." He planted another wet kiss on her lips and pushed her away. "Take her away!" he demanded to the same soldier. Eager to please his leader, Frank pushed her away from the wall and marched her back.

Trembled fingers tried to wipe away the sensation of Roger's touch, but it stayed. Her fear just multiplied.

Where is Tau? Lord, I need you. Have you forgotten me?

As they marched away Frank pushed her, cross with her disobedience. "Come." Grabbing her arm and pushed her to the tent door.

"You not here boss." He stumbled over the language. "You do as I say." Angry he lifted his rifle and held it against her.

Defeated, Sonia lifted her hands and retreated into the medic tent, her mind muddled. Until now she was relatively safe, but she was stupid to think that her stand in camp had changed because of what she did. She was still the prisoner. The abductee who could be killed. Her life was in danger. Escape a sure thing.

"ROGER?" TAU THOUGHT ABOUT this conversation. It had been weeks since her arrival and he wanted her. His longing grew with each passing day. Roger kept him busy, sending him on errands while he stayed at camp … errands that some of the soldiers could do. This made him furious because it was all stalling ways to distract him. His eagerness to please the man made no room for questioning him, but he wanted Sonia.

Roger glanced from the paperwork, a deep furrow between his eyes. "Yes Tau," he replied similarly and placed the paperwork on the table. Tau closed the office door.

"The woman: what will happen with her?"

"Sonia Main?"

"Yes."

"For now she is fulfilling her purpose."

"Will you ever send her back?"

"No, she is more valuable to me here."

This brought a smile to Tau's face, a smile he tried to hide underneath his nonchalant question.

"Are you giving her to someone as a wife?"

"Maybe, why?" and Roger's eyes narrowed.

"I want her, Roger. My body aches when I'm near her."

"What about Sarai?" and he grinned.

"She doesn't exist to me anymore. I want Sonia. She is strong and can give me children."

Roger stapled his fingers against his lips. Then he looked at Tau and smiled. "You, Tau, are a sly fox. You can have her at night, but by day she is mine."

Tau grinned with pleasure. "Haji, you have done me good. She will bless me, and I will name my first child after you."

"You, fox you," Roger laughed. "White women do things differently," he added and peered at his second-in-command with slyness. He was well-aware of Tau's feelings for the nurse. But he already decided about her fate. He would get his revenge and then throw her away. In the meantime he could play with the man. He's naivety opened him to be toyed with.

"What do you mean?" Tau looked at his commander. Other than Sonia Main, he never met white women. He had run into white soldiers who were unafraid and skilled, but not women.

"They like romance, not like our women who you can have right away," he mocked.

"You mean I cannot have her now?" Tau's puzzled expression caused another fit of laughter.

"No, they love to talk and receive flowers."

"Flowers? Where must I get those?" Dumbfounded he watched Roger. He had no idea about this.

"That you will have to figure out yourself," he said, still chuckling.

"I don't know about that." Sweat pearls accumulated on his bald head which he wiped away with a cloth.

"You better find out. Go now, I have work to do." Bored with the game, he dismissed Tau with a sweep of the hand.

TAU WATCHED AS SONIA left the store. He had not seen her in over a week. The gentle sway of her hips in the dress gave him a satisfied stirring. So poised and rigid. He wanted her in every way as he journeyed the slight frame with hungry eyes. At night he dreamed about her, whispering loving words to her. To see her each day and not touch her was painful. When she went into her hut and they locked it, he stood outside the door as a love-sick pup. People mocked him, but he could not help himself.

Then he remembered what Roger said, and he shook his head: talk and flowers.

Where will he find flowers? And what must he talk about? He was not a brilliant talker, not to women anyway. She was clever, brilliant. She knew things he did not know.

He loved his country, went to school, where he learned to read and write, and had a good understanding of arithmetic. That was the end of his knowledge. At age ten, he was already a soldier, and that was the end of his education. In the bush you did have books. There was no time for such liberties, not while they fought for their cause. Television or the Internet did not influence him. Kwame was the electronic and internet guru. He tried to teach him, but Tau became impatient with it all.

All Tau wanted to do was to make her his. He was running out of time. The men talked; he saw the looks when she passed—their interest growing but so far none came forward, and he thought it best to do so first.

Now that he had permission, he could pursue her. But talk and flowers? Was Roger making a joke, was it important to … what did he say: romance her? He had never done romance, did not give it a second thought when he took a woman to his bed. In the bush you take what you want when you want. Romantic ideas had no place here.

Why must she be different? He was a soldier.

This sounded complicated, he had to think.

"LORD, I NEED TO GETAWAY. I NEED HELP." The entire week Sonia was thinking about the incident with Roger. The desire to escape growing with every minute. Each time she left the hut or medical tent she scanned the area, made notes of the guards' schedules and habits. She added all information she could find to her mind's folder.

Unaware of her fate, Sonia noticed the building once more. Although rundown and obscured by the reeds, it called her. The magnetic hold tuned out everything else as she passed the tent. Kids circled her in elated banter. Frank called her "Mantri!" but she ignored it. The endearing word held no effect at that moment.

Fiza held her hand. With scared eyes he tried to stop her, but she loosened the hold. Her curiosity peaked with the building. She had to go. When the ground turned soggy, she stopped and looked at her sandaled feet. Sweat trickled down her spine, but it did not register as she watched the water.

"Lord, is this you?"

Without waiting for an answer, she rushed back and grabbed the boots at the back of the shelf. They were standing there ever since her arrival. No one ever collected them or used them.

"What you do?" Out of breath Frank followed her inside, but she ignored him. Driven to know she ventured back. People waded into the water often. They used it for fishing, bathing and cleaning their clothes. Kids played in it as well and thought nothing about the warning. She glanced back; Frank's perplexed gaze mystified as he shouted at her. She drowned it out and wavered deeper into the water, one foot in front of the other, sinking a bit with each step. Water sloshed into the boot but still she continued.

The building got closer.

Each step took her deeper into its dark depths. Water splashed behind her. This time Tau called her name. "Sonia, what are you doing?"

"She is escaping!" someone yelled.

She examined the water as something brushed passed her and clutched the dress in her hands. The sloshing came closer, and the next moment Tau was with her.

"Get in the boat! Do you really think you can escape?" Angry, he pulled her inside.

"I am …," but was cut off when she hit the bottom. More water splashed over her and she drew her feet deeper in the boat and scraped herself. It all happened quickly that Sonia did not even register it all.

Tau shouted: "Lay still." When Tau finally sat, the boat wobbled precariously to the side.

"What are you thinking, woman? Where are you going? This is not a place for a stroll in the woods." He sneered. "You will be dead. This is a dangerous place."

"I just wanted to go to that building," she explained.

"Why, it's an abandoned chapel taken over by nature?" Confused he looked at the place and shook his head.

Her silence and dumbfounded look annoyed him, his jaw clenched in surprised unbelief. For a few seconds he studied her trembled form before he put the paddle back in the water.

HOW DOES SHE EXPLAIN the urgency without knowing the reason? Why is this place so persistent in its call?

Watching Tau, she had stepped out of line. Tau's reaction as the paddles hit the water showed his annoyance. What will they do to her?

Sonia noticed the unnatural angle of her legs. When she moved, the boat rocked.

"Be still," Tau hissed. The boots smeared her dress with mud and another tare appeared.

"Answer me, Sonia! Why do you want to go there?" he demanded.

"Please, I just have to go, Tau. This is important to me," she begged.

"There is nothing for you. That place isn't safe," and he peddled closer to the bank. Frank was still shouting at her. With his weapon in hand, he ran up and down the bank till they reached it. The kids chanted her name in a choir.

"Please, Tau."

But he ignored her as the boat drifted against the edge. Angry hands grabbed her from the canoe so violently that she screamed. The movement split her skin in two. Mud invested itself in her open skin and blood ran freely down, but no one noticed this.

Another guard yelled at her. He slapped her once, twice, before Tau got to her and pushed the man aside.

"Stop!" In the commotion they fell to the ground, which added more bruises. Sonia tried to get away, but it was useless, her fear rising as she realized her predicament.

Tau's anger turned towards the guard as he pulled her up. She struggled to get her footing and fell against him, her leg a burning inferno. She tried to stem it, but it was useless as they pushed her from all sides.

A small hand appeared from somewhere in the maelstrom as Fiza grabbed her hand. Grateful for the small favour, she squeezed it. Then torn apart. Fiza screamed.

Tau ordered the guard to stay back. In the commotion, Roger arrived. First, he glared at her before he called the two men to order.

"Did she try to escape?" He addressed Frank pointedly and ignored Tau.

"Yes, Haji." Frank admitted.

"No!" yelled Tau.

"Take her away!" Frank clutched her arm and gave her a few shakes, then dragged her away.

"Tau!" Her frantic screams made a path, but he did not come.

"WHAT ARE YOU DOING?" Tau yelled as he tried to intervene.

"Leave her." He shouted towards Frank. Roger and Tau measured each other. The one filled with hate, the other with love.

"This woman causes me problems. You either control her, or I will get rid of her." Spittle spat against Tau's cheek, the unblinking squint adamant.

Get rid of her, meant no one would ever see her ever. Tau knew this. He had to do it a few times. Get rid of a woman. But not this woman. It was his woman.

"You have protected her long enough; she needs to know that she's the prisoner. She will stay in her hut without water or food until I release her. Understood!"

"Roger ..." The glare stopped him; no arguing would persuade the man. He nodded in understanding. "You will not go to her. If you do, you have signed your death certificate." Soldiers strained his movement, and one budded the end of a revolver to his neck. He fell to the ground in blinding pain, the faint call of Sonia's voice a reminder of his own failure.

He could only imagine what she had to go through. He could do nothing to calm her fears.

Being without water or food was harsh. The heat would break her will. Could she make it for the unforeseen future?

"Roger," he tried again. "Let me talk to her."

"You had enough time."

"Roger, what are you going to do with her?"

"It's not your concern."

"Take him away." Vice grips grabbed his arms. He smacked at it, then a hard blow against the temple took him to the ground. Another followed and darkness pulled him into an abrupt silence.

SHE STRUGGLED ALL THE way to her hut. People scattered away without help. Fiza screamed. Desperate to help him and watched as they slapped him. He fell to the ground in a flurry of dust. With a last awkward look towards him they pushed her into her hut. When the door closed, it cut her from the rest. She banged against the feeble door and screamed, but no one replied. Though the door swayed, it did not loosened from its hold, thoroughly blocked from the outside. When she calmed down, a foreboding silence overwhelmed her; she was in trouble.

The last rays of the sun left her in ominous shadows. For the first time since she arrived, she was alone. This added an extra level of loneliness which broke her heart. Stiff and exhausted she rose and examined her body. It resembled a hot iron of pain.

The muddy boots disturbed the stillness as she threw it aside, before it descended on her again. Quietly she observed the space given to her. The scanty light highlighted the makeshift furniture, desperation in every detail.

"Why Lord? Please tell me why?" Tears formed and she cried. Lying down on the dusty floor she cried till there was nothing left.

Once she calmed, her throbbing body reminded her what she had to do. Sonia struggled to her bag and searched its content. In the corner of the plastic hut a small pool of light allowed her some sight and she cleaned her wounds with the limited water still left of the previous day. Most of the scrapes were manageable, but the gaping wound needed stitches. This wound stretched from her knee to her upper leg. In her bag she found one bandage and covered the deepest section with it. The burning sensation lessened with her ministrations and she drank the last two tablets to dull the worst pain.

Once on the bed, an old hospital bed that had seen better days, she realised her world had become smaller. Her freedom totally revoked.

"I don't understand, Lord. We could have avoided all of this. Now I am cut off and in pain. I can blame no one. I acted on your promptings, and they imprisoned me. Did I hear wrong? Please help me!"

A COMMOTION SILENCED HER, and she listened with growing unease, too tired to get up. Fiza screamed: "Mantri!" but harshly silenced. The little man had become Sonia's companion ever since she opened the school. An orphan who attached himself to Sonia. A shadow of a child with a strong will.

What will become of him? Sonia thought as dread forced her to move towards the door.

"Open the door!" Baaka's voice filtered through, preceded by scuffling, a loud clap, and more screams followed. The plastic wall bulged once more and Sonia screamed for them to stop. Isaac, too, spoke close by, but the door stayed shut. A tall shadow appeared, in its grip a frightening weapon appeared before it came down with a harsh thud. The breakage of bone vibrated through her.

"Stop it!" she yelled, banging against the wall. More shuffling ensued as objects were placed around her shabby wall, closing her in, cutting her off. The act was so final that she fell to the ground. The earth's dust a humble reminder of her position.

What will happen to me?

Why did Tau not help me?

Where are God and Curt?

They have all deserted me.

These thoughts accosted her as she lay there, to tired to cry.

The people she depended on the most, abandoned her. Time's harshness closed in, marking her end with resounding conclusiveness.

29

SONIA'S THIRST MADENED HER. Hunger worsened her turmoil. She drifted between sleep and sickness as hours passed. Her wounds burned with hellish fire. So severe that she wished to amputate it. First the leg, then her head.

How many days had it been?

She tried to pray, but words failed. Longing for biblical support, her memory obscured with years of neglect. She recited Psalm 91 and Psalm 23 often, but no relief came.

In her dreams Curt's faded images left her listless. Her son's face only a mirage; stripped from all the delusions. Even the burned building became a faded memory. A person in white stood just behind it and called her. She tried to move, but knee-deep mud stopped her. She kept sinking deeper into a bottomless pit. Every time she woke, the thirst and hunger reminded her of her predicament.

In vain she tried to get attention, but the attempts remained useless. No one came. She asked for mercy, but received none.

Night time became worse, the heat replaced with smoke from the cooking fires. It trailed inside the hut which ensued a coughing spree. The plastic roof cover changed the dwelling into a sauna. Nausea was the only sign that she still had breath.

She tried to stay focused and pray, but the useless exercise highlighted her weakness. Her words had desiccated into nothing. Her head exploded with agony. Like a drunkard she fell and laid there for hours. Later she crawled underneath the bed, the coolest place during the day. At times she tried to pace the hut, but disorientation kept her in a limped state. The isolation period trapped in a downward spiral.

No one knew her whereabouts. She could die there, be in an unnamed grave and no one would know. The fear so real, it consumed her thoughts.

The weekend was just a wonderful dream she would never experience again. Her mind playing many games with her.

Like now. The reason Sonia woke from her stupor. The scraping at the door. She flew upright, but bumped her head against the frame. Carefully she crawled from underneath and collapsed on the bed. The door opened and an ominous figure appeared and closed the door.

"Who are you?"

The person remained silent, a brooding presence.

"Please," she tried to talk, but it sounded like a frog had embedded itself there. "Water, please," she reached out, hopeful. The person bumped against her knees, and traced up her leg in a way that left her frightened. She slapped it away, but he caught her hand and held it.

"Who are you?" she tried again. A roughened hand touched her face. Panic now in full bloom, she kicked. The explosion it invoked caused dirt to shower her in a reddish dust. All her senses fired up as she fought against the hold. When she tried to scream, a steel grip covered her mouth. More hits followed. Her face turned into a punching bag. She tried to cover herself, but it was useless. He was relentless, and then he pressed into her body.

"Why are you doing this?" she mumbled and received another blow. A soft hissed sound brushed against her cheek.

"Quiet." Every action rough leaving its marks. Her mind switched off as he penetrated her.

"You will tell no one about this." Another hit followed. "No one," he hissed. Once done, he fiddled with himself and left as quietly as he came. She stared into the ceiling, her mind refusing to accept what had just happened.

"THE LORD IS MY SHEPHERD," she whispered, but it did not bring the peace she hoped for.

Curt … He was a phantom of her past. Back then he treated her as a desirable woman.

Did it even happen?

Now, laying on the bed, her legs still open, the fluids drained away. What had she done to deserve this?

"Please Lord, help me."

Her thirst a reminder there was nothing to clean herself, her body turned into an unbending obstacle who objected to every movement she made. The urge to clean overpowered the pain. In her bag she found a forgotten wet wipe package and ripped it open. The action caused her to flinch.

The smell of the man had infested her skin. She hated him.

What would Tau say if he learned that the man he respected, violated her? What would he do?

Why did she think about him right now? The sense of safety she had with Tau had gone. He had deserted her, just as Brady had … just as Curt had.

No, Curt did not abandon me, she reprimanded herself.

She fell back on the bed in a heap, wrapping her body around the self-made pillow. A coldness swept through every bone as she submitted to the tears, and cried herself to sleep.

HOW LONG DID SHE SLEEP? Her head pounded as nausea swept through her. She rolled to her stomach and moved to the side, but only dry heaves left her throat.

Too tired to turn around she went back into oblivion. Her memories dozed every sound. It was only when she pushed deeper into the mattress that she realised she was not alone. A knee pinned her at the spot. Her dress shredded in his wake to have her, and hissed her silence. Once again he did his business in silence.

She became quiet, taking the abuse as tears streamed into the bedding, the only sign of the treachery. The crude language he used while he did his thing would remain with her long after. When he left, she stared at the wall, numbness her only escape.

With the added lack of food and water, she was in a sorry state. Just then her body convulsed, and she retched on the floor—the sour reek of vomit filling the already stale air.

Day and night had become a mixture of murky air, whilst hunger and water drove her into the abyss of insanity. There she could only remember the vileness of one man.

Tired she dozed off, and when she resurfaced Tau sat next to her. His bewildered look did not register. All she saw was her abuser. She scrambled away and fell on the hard floor.

"Leave!" The voice was not hers, but she kept on yelling until he left. Her entire body was a cesspool of pain.

30

IT HAD BEEN SEVEN DAYS since he had seen her, her state nothing like her. Roger released him on day two. He woke in a cage of agony. His fury knew no bounds. He could kill him.

"Where is Sonia?" he insisted upon his release.

"She can rot longer in there," Roger proclaimed once he met him.

"That is inhuman. She does not deserve this treatment."

"She should learn who is in control of this camp."

"What happened to the 'we should treat her like a guest' scenario?"

"She runs my camp as if she is in charge. I will not stand for it," Roger huffed and continued with his work.

He had stomped to her hut when he woke. The guards refused him any entry and he went straight to Roger.

Roger kept him busy with things not befitting his station. Once he could, he paced her hut day and night not knowing how she fared. The hut quiet as a tomb. He tried to remove some obstacles around her hut, but was stopped each time. Even Baaka could not visit her. Now, this.

"Who was here?" he asked Frank who stood in the doorway; his blank face without remorse.

"No one was near her."

"You lie," and Tau punched him. His anger was uncontrollable.

"No one was with her," the other guard said as he held Tau back.

"Why then was she beaten? Who touched her?"

Silence met him as the guards averted their eyes. His distrust grew even more.

The first time he went inside, the sour air confronted his sensibilities. Forced to cover his nose with a handkerchief. When he stepped deeper into the dark, he found her on the bed, her clothes torn, a puddle of dry vomit on the floor. The stench from the corner across the room reeked of urine.

They all had instructions to leave her alone. But look at her! She feared him. Why? She scattered to the corner and clutched her torn clothes like a wild animal.

"Sonia?" Getting up he moved around the bed.

"Don't touch me!" Her swollen face was unrecognisable, one eye shut and black, the other wide in fear. Blood crusted her neck and arms, her lips cracked open as if beaten. Her dress barely covered her pale skin. He watched in horror at the abusive marks across her body. The bruising between her legs flashed before him. Stunned he closed his eyes.

Who did this horrible thing? Quietly he tried to approach her with all the care he could muster.

"Sonia, it's me, Tau."

"Go away!"

Baffled he left, and returned with Baaka. They found her still shivering in the same spot he had left her, slamming her head against the wall. Dust filtered over her. He could hardly recognise the nurse. She had changed into a caged animal too scared for interaction.

Baaka rushed towards her with a cry. Sonia fell in her arms hysterically. Feeling helpless at the unfolding scene, he remained at the back. His heart's distress left him mortified.

Baaka's soft voice drew him back. Repeating herself twice before he reacted. "*Kéngingkeun cai Tau, ayeuna.* (Get water Tau, now.)" When he turned, he bumped into Roger's smirking face.

"Why is the white woman screaming?" he summoned. "I can hear her to the back of the camp."

"Someone paid her a visit while locked up." Puzzled Tau looked at his leader, who looked bored. His non-caring manner baffling.

"That's impossible. I allowed no visitors." He dismissed Tau with a cold shoulder. Something was wrong.

A half an hour later he was back with a prepared meal. Two women followed him. They carried a plastic tub between them, and filled it with water. Sonia's shrieks of fear deafened everything else.

Baaka shielded her the entire time he was there. He remained in the door looming over the women as they cleaned the inside.

He noticed everything. Blood stains soiled the bedding, evidence of her violation. Could it be? His thoughts ran a mile a minute with the different scenarios just to stop at the same conclusion.

To take his mind off it, he reached for the two bottles with bath oils lying on the floor. He sniffed the first bottle, then the second. From the last one he poured into the water. The scent permeating the air, removing the last remaining sourness.

Now and then he glanced across the room with questions, but she remained behind Baaka. Realizing there was nothing else to do, he left, his heart aching for the woman he cared for.

ONCE HE LEFT, SONIA RELAXED. While they were busy she watched in fright. Baaka's body was her only shield against her enemy.

"Come, let me help you," she coached. It took some effort until the buzz cleared. Baaka led her to the bath with great care, where she sank into it with no regard to her wounds.

"Who did this to you, *Mantri*?"

Sonia shrugged, uncertain of an answer. To tell would devastate her friend.

"Can I have water?" Sonia examined her wounds with alarm, especially her leg. It was vital to receive a tetanus shot. In her mind she scanned the list of supplies on hand. It was fruitless. Her memories dazed with the events of her ordeal.

She scrubbed every part of her until the water turned to a muddy red brown, but it was not enough. No soap or water could wash away the embedded filth.

"I will be right back," came the soft reply from Baaka. "I am so sorry this happened to you. Tau was frantic of worry."

She leaned closer and hugged her, but Sonia stiffened.

"I don't need him. Leave me alone," Sonia ordered. Her entire body was on fire. The blinding headache allowed for no sound or memory, her thoughts blank as she continued to clean herself in the quiet hut.

31

MCGEE CONTEMPLATED THE SITUATION with Jillian and her unborn child for days.

Life is precious, this baby is precious. Will Jillian see it?

He and his estranged wife could not hold a civilised conversation about this. She believed Jillian should do what she wanted and offered to pay for the abortion. Curt's anger exploded. The repercussions would cause turmoil and death.

Phillip still waited for an answer when he brushed his head. "I was fifteen years old when I learned about Vicky's pregnancy. At the time she was eighteen. So young, with the world at her feet."

"What happened?"

"We were best friends during that time, but the more I reached out to her, the less she responded. She withdrew and became pensive. Then she disappeared for three days. My uncle and aunt were desperate with worry."

"It must have been hard for them. It's times like these that I am glad I don't have kids."

"I should find you a wife." They chuckled.

"Not happening so far away from civilization." He smirked. "What happened?"

"She visited us on the farm days later. It seems the Vicky I knew was back. We laughed and played, and later we strolled along the gravel road full of jokes. We had a wonderful time." He sighed. "I wished I knew, then I could have stopped her. When the news of her suicide reached me, it devastated me."

"Self-death is never easy," he remarked and took a long pull of his drink.

"She changed. Back then, the fifteen-year-old me could not understand the changes. I do not wish that for my child. I can still remember the last conversation with Vicky." He greeted a soldier before he continued. "I asked her why she was so happy? Her response shocked me, though I did not understand the meaning. 'Oh, I dealt with the problem, she said, now I'm free to go on with my life.'

"What did you do?" I asked.

'You know.' She winked at me with smugness. She was a beautiful woman. Everyone believed Vicky would bring it far in life. She was clever, beautiful and energetic—just like Jill—with an unsurpassed passion for kids and animals." He pinched his eyes. The image of her long legs which swung over the pond remained. The water glistening in the midday sun encircled them in a cocoon of warmth, peaceful and beautiful at the same time.

"I admitted to her I didn't know what she meant. She spelled it out in a distant, no care attitude that left me cold. 'I aborted the foetus' and dozed me with a handful of water' before she ran to the house. By the time I reached the house, she had left." Curt took another swig, tiredness seeped through him with every action.

"And then?"

"She had left a message with my mom. 'Tell him I love him very much.' I never spoke to her again. Later the evening I heard my mother talking to my twelve-year-old brother about it."

"What is abortion, Ma?"

"When a person kills a baby still in the mother's womb," she explained. "The baby needs to stay inside the tummy for nine months. If we end life before its appointed time, we call it abortion."

"But that's not right, Ma," Billy said after a few moments of silence. He too, kept quiet … waiting.

"No, it's not," Mum agreed, her voice quivered.

A week later we heard Vicky had committed suicide. Her parents were never the same after the incident. When I asked my mum why she had done it, she was quiet for a while. Then softly replied: 'Her conscience got the better of her.'

"Your mom explained it well."

"She is a wise woman," he said, his thoughts still with Vicky. He had not thought about her in years. It was a dreadful time in their family's history. No one ever spoke about it or even mentioned Vicky's name ever again, but her experience remained.

"It affected me; I don't want it for Jillian," he said. Each man's thoughts drifted; the military brought order to both.

After a while, Phillip asked: "What are you going to do?"

"I need to talk to Jillian. I cannot leave it there."

"I will pray with you and for Jillian."

"Thanks, Phillip." As he reached for the satellite phone, Phillip stepped out.

THE STRAIN IN HER VOICE gave her away when she answered. His resolve wanted to break, but ignored it. Tenderness would not save this baby, nor her. His words had to be soothing, but potent.

"Pumpkin, just listen to me, okay."

"Yes, Dad."

"To do this will kill every chance of happiness. I understand the situation is not perfect. Life is never perfect." He drifted to Sonia. Thinking of her and what she represented; it gave him the courage to continue.

"I understand, Dad. I am thinking about this." Silence met the heaviness.

"I met a man, Dad."

"Who is he?"

"He is the Executive Officer to the Commanding Officer at the base."

"Who is he?"

"Lieutenant Timothy Blackwell."

He scribbled it in his notebook. "Be honest from the start. He deserves to know." His voice broke.

"Yes, Dad."

"Take care of yourself, Jill. Take his life into consideration when you decide about your future. If this Timothy Blackwell is a man of integrity, he will stand by you."

"I'm not sure, Dad. I will tell him afterwards." It sounded definite as if she had decided; and Curt became cold. He experienced the same sensation when he saw Vicky for the last time.

"No, tell him so that he can be with you," he insisted. "I don't want you to be alone, Pumpkin, not while dealing with this."

After a lengthy exchange, she reluctantly promised to speak to Timothy before she would act.

"I saw Harriet Davies, yesterday. She wants to adopt the baby."

"What did you say?"

"There is no way, Dad. Neil is evil, and I don't want the baby to be close to that kind of evil," she said, almost imposing.

"What was her reaction?" It was Jillian's choice, and he would not influence her in the matter.

"Mrs Davies understood when I declined her offer. She wants to be part of the child's life." there was a moment of silence before she continued, "I like her, Dad. I think she will be a wonderful mother, but I cannot. It doesn't feel right."

Curt listened with mixed feelings, not sure what to make of this new twist in her life. He has never met Harriet Davies, although her name was always on every social paper he had read at home. The Southern Bell had a certain charm about her. She came from a long line of money, everything about her spoke about class and elegance. That was the extent of his knowledge. To be married to Neil had to be difficult.

When he ended the call, Curt sat back in his chair and thought more about his daughter's choices.

HE HAD TO SETTLE THE DIVORCE. Then his thoughts steered towards Sonia. Ever since he met her, his dreams had meaning. She left him with a sense of belonging, filling a hole he did not realise he had before he met her. The promise he made was one he wanted to keep, and he prayed every night for her protection. It was a constant awareness that stayed with him.

During the night's quietness, he relived the moments of passion they shared—a passion that stirred his body and every night he wanted her. He dreamed about her as she laughed. The day at the Barrakka Gardens she was vibrant and happy. She enjoyed the scenery, the way she wrapped her arms around him. He missed her, even though his feelings were wrong. He felt like a hypocrite when he talked to Vivian. He condemned her, but did the same thing in his mind.

He reached for the lamplight before he took the small Bible he had found in the chapel, and turned the pages. He stopped now and then, reading scriptures which caught his attention. Then he moved on to the next chapter, his heart racing with what he read.

He then took a sip straight from the water bottle, thinking about the content. He scrolled through the pages and stopped at specific scriptures in the New Testament—the one confirming the other. Guilt, remorse and shame filled him as he continued. He let the Bible fall on his lap, the thought to stay with Vivian and denounce his love for Sonia too much. That is if he understood the book. It was a tough choice.

Did he misunderstand it? He needed guidance.

"How God?" he whispered with his eyes closed. One scripture stood out, speaking directly to him. "Humble yourself before the Lord and He will give you rest." The message was unmistaken and to the point. This time he could not avoid it and wilted.

"Lord," he cried, *"How can I? This is too much. You ask too much of me."* He glanced through the scriptures. Everywhere he stopped it was relentless in its order, and as a soldier he understood about obedience.

"Lord, you are aware of this woman's actions?"

'My grace is enough for you.' He heard the still voice—so quiet and so specific that he could not ignore it.

"I can't Lord, please don't ask me that." He continued to argue, but it was quiet. Not even an insect disturbed the stillness.

This … and he threw the Bible on his table and left the office. On cue, Phillip met him at the door.

"Colonel, a word, please." The official tone brooked no excuses. In the office each took a chair.

"How can I help, Phillip?"

"This is a personal matter."

"Sure. What's bothering you, Phillip?"

"Nothing Curt, but I sense you are in turmoil. After this afternoon's discussion, I prayed. There is a heaviness on my heart. You want to talk about it?"

Curt stared at the chaplain and smirked. "You and God sure have one hell of a timing." Both men laughed.

"I have been told God works in mysterious ways, Curt. You are on my prayer radar. You have decisions to consider; some please Him, some don't."

Uncomfortable, Curt shifted. He was still angry, disappointed, almost sick. How God expected him to give up his only happiness was not understandable.

"And, what else did He show you?"

"Life and death choices are never easy, Curt. Not when you have lives in your hands. But I believe this is closer to home, correct?"

He went cold. Their friendship goes back twenty years and he knew him as a sincere person. Realising he was still waiting for him, he replied, "Yes, it has."

"How is Vivian?" Phillip asked, taking the wind from his sails. Since the separation he had not talked to anyone about it. Doug might suspect something, one he never concurred or denied.

"Good, as expected."

"You sure?" With this question he stood up and walked towards the window. A dim light highlighted the camp outside. Everything was in order and neat. Further back the desert was hiding in darkness.

"We are busy with a divorce."

"God doesn't approve of that." Both men were peering outside. Curt swallowed.

"Did He tell you what she did?"

"Infidelity is never easy, but you need to forgive her and cancel the divorce."

Curt wanted to throw a punch at him, anything for the pain to go away.

"Do you know why?"

"She is your wife. You made promises to her. God is also testing your faith and your convictions. He wants to promote you, but then He wants obedience."

"It's a high price to pay."

"Sure, but one God expects from a high-ranking official," Curt smirked, his entire body shaking.

"Whatever you decide, Curt. I am here for you and will pray for you to make the right choice. Just as Jillian, it requires you to make a life and death decision." He pressed his shoulder, and with a quick greeting he left. Curt went straight to his room, not returning any salute as soldiers passed him.

32

HE DISMISSED DOUG WITH STRICT INSTRUCTIONS and looked at the pile of paperwork. Just then his phone buzzed. It was Jillian. He hoped for some pleasant news to lift his sombreness.

Curious, he came to the issue at hand.

"What did you decide, Pumpkin?"

"I am keeping the baby, Dad."

He sighed in relief. "This is the greatest news ever."

She giggled. "You sound like the students', Dad."

He grinned. "Well, I am glad about your decision. It is very mature. What happened to the Lieutenant?"

"Oh, Timothy." There was a pause. "He left me."

"Oh, Pumpkin. How do you feel about that?"

"It was painful."

"I am sorry."

He investigated Lt. Blackwell, a product of West Point. At thirty-three he was a decorated straight-A student. He was four years in Iraq and returned to NSA PC. His close-up photo showed a dark blond man, dark blue eyes with a square jaw. The folder said he was six one - fit and healthy. He was on his way to the top with an outstanding rating.

He could not blame the man. It seldom worked with another man's child.

"The right man is out there, Pumpkin."

"Yes, Dad," she answered, not convinced.

"Your studies are almost complete, just hang in there." A dragged-out silence met him.

The road ahead would not be easy for her. The demands of parenthood to a single mother could be devastating, but she had the support if she kept the baby.

He thought about his future in the military. Maybe it was time to go home, to put his life in order - get a nice office job close to home. He was not getting any younger. These thoughts raised through him throughout the call. He was never there for his own kids and the damage was done.

A knock on his door ended the call.

HE NEEDED TO BE ALONE. He could not accept the instructions he had received. In his room he retrieved a bottle of water from the fridge, taking a few long gulps. The rush of coldness did wonders, but nothing for his mind—no refreshing coolness to take away the sharp reality of his life.

He scanned his room, saw every book and folder in stark contrast to his life. They were all neatly stacked on a shelf. His bed was orderly made, everything as it should be while his life was falling apart. His heart ripped to pieces.

He acknowledged the laptop on the desk. It waited with a blank expression. With a light touch against the mouse she waited, leaning against the limestone pillar with a gorgeous smile. The sun tinted her in golden hues; she glowed. Beautiful, sparkling with a zest of life, and his heart belonged to her.

"God no, anything but her!" he called out in desperation. The inkling remained wordless.

"God ... why? Please tell me why?"

'You are committed to Vivian.' The thought dropped in his spirit. He knew this. His shoulders slumped as he gazed at the woman who came into his life like a fresh breeze. She represented more than just zeal. She offered him reformation. He found in her a person of pure gentleness. He would give up the military for her.

God wanted him to let go of all she personified.

'She is not your revival, I am. You can only find newness in me.'

Between Phillip and God's words he was unfamiliar with spiritual confrontation. He always believed in the invaluable Word, though he never believed. So far God or Phillip had steered him wrong. But this? This command was harsh. As a commanding officer, he also understood the value of obedience. He had no choice. He knew it. He was not willing to let her go.

He could still hear her light laughter, the approving look when he caught her watching him. Every move from her graceful body, every feature engraved in his mind. She was his perfect harmony. To let her go was to lose his stability.

Time passed as he weighed the words—the scale tipping less towards her, but more to his family. God was right, but it shredded his heart in minute pieces. It was early morning when he was at peace knowing what to do.

"Lord, forgive me," he whispered. *"I have sinned against you and my wife; with Sonia and with every other woman I had. I am guilty, I see it now,"* he declared. *"I had so much hatred, that I have forgotten my family. Lord, you are my deliverer. In you, I trust."*

He scrolled through the folder and stopped at each picture. He pressed the control shift and it highlighted all the pictures as his finger hovered over the delete button.

"PLEASE FORGIVE ME, SONIA. I MUST SAVE MY FAMILY." With a last look, he caressed the woman's features and removed it. The finality thereof shook his shoulders, but the guilt was gone.

"Therefore, there is now no condemnation for those who walk in the spirit," the words affirmed his decision. He grabbed the Bible, turned to Romans 8, and read the scripture Doug shared with him a while back.

33

Fangak county, South Sudan.

TAU DRILLED THE GUARDS FOR ANSWERS, but their loyalty to Roger stayed intact. He had beaten Frank to near death, but he refused to talk. He needed just one lead to confirm his suspicion, then he would kill the rapist. He stationed himself outside the medical tent, watching each person with distrust.

His relationship with Roger transformed into a silent contest of power. Each time Roger countered his orders. Women and children were fearsome and stayed hidden, the quietness within the camp deafening. Even Baaka remained hidden.

Roger acted suspiciously and refused to talk to him. He found himself outside his trust, and it unsettled him.

Through narrowed eyes he watched Roger as he talked with Antoni, a new guy Tau did not know, his angst building with each passing hour.

Then he saw Sonia walking with a limp, her steps slower. Her entire body covered with a black shawl. She, too, stayed hidden. She had turned into a frightened kitten. Even Isaac kept his distance. She acted like a violated woman.

Who had excess to her in the days of her isolation?

Questions plagued Tau. His own position in jeopardy.

Roger hopped from the boat. He walked with a self-assurance typical of a man who gets his way. Did he have his way with her? The thought angered him. He would kill him, leader or not.

Just behind Roger, the building came into view. He remembered her need to go to that building, the reason she was in this mess. The building stuck out like a sore thumb, his location making it a no-man's-land. Off-limits to every person.

He shuddered at the thought of what could have happened to her if she went ahead. The swamps held no dangers, but they had seen a snake previously. Already a goat had disappeared from its den, then the day before Sonia's isolation a kid went missing. The reason he wasn't there to protect her. After another child disappeared, they found the nest with some remains that morning. They struggled to catch it. Kwame caught it the previous day and fires were lit to celebrate the festive occasion. The swamp was no one's friend. With limited knowledge of the swamps, she could not survive.

He glanced her way where she was busy inside the tent. Already back doing her duties, no matter what happened to her. Her bravery and determination sparked his heart with empathy. Few women would continue. But then, she was not many women.

With a final look he decided to investigate the place. Maybe he could get an idea why she wanted to go. Close by a canoe bopped in the ripples. It took him a few powerful strokes to the island's bank. Nature had taken over the burned-out structure, and Tau ventured closer. The terrain made walking difficult, however his boots were more than ready to take him. The skewed door hung listlessly on a single rusted screw. With great caution he moved deeper into the building. The muddy floor was treacherous, the evidence of whitewashed walls visible behind the soot and dirt. A faded SPLA insignia covered the one wall. The ominous red colour faded to give it a rustic appeal.

Birds scattered, one almost colliding with him in his haste to get away. Feathers rained down and fell listlessly on the floor. Dust motes gave the place a sparkling shine. There was not much inside except for a skewed wooden cross which leaned to the far back of a blackened wall and piles of pews. A small pile of wood lay on one side. It called to him. On closer look shattered glass and bird droppings covered the floor amidst grassy debris. He removed the wood one by one, then gasped. Underneath all the rubble a book waited, untouched. He crouched, picked it up and blew away the dust. Gold letters on the black leather-bound became visible: Holy Bible. He smiled. Roger was correct. She wanted books to read. This would be perfect. Briefly, he brushed through the thin papers. Some words brought back vague memories from a time when he stayed in a similar place.

Once he closed the book, he got up. The white man's religion was irrelevant in the bush.

The book was in excellent condition considering where it was. He grinned. It would delight his woman.

SONIA STAYED FOR AS LONG as possible in the medic. When she closed the flaps after her day's work, she took care of her own needs before she ventured back. When the opportunity presented itself; she threw pain killers in a small container that she hid in her dress's pocket. The constant thumping made life unbearable.

After her ordeal and ultimate release, she had swapped herself, the saline solution the only item available. The fierce cleaning became a ritual as she tried to wash away the assailant's smell, even after three days. She had patched all the bruises, then stitched her leg. Now she took care of it and changed the bandage.

On that first time back she had found a compact mirror on a top shelf, and after a few encouraging words looked at herself. The unknown woman left her disorientated. She had shrunk, her eyes hollowed and black and her skin dried out. It took great courage to touch herself. Her reflection uncommonly and ugly. Her emotions came at her like waves, fierce and violent that she struggled to calm. How long she had remained inside she couldn't tell. But one thing was for certain: she had to move on, no matter how difficult it would be.

She watched as Tau got from a canoe. His ever-present diligence softened her towards him. Each day he slipped in the back, always keeping guard, even with the other security. His observant eyes burned into her. That he could find her beautiful was beyond her. To herself she looked ugly and misformed.

The shock on his face when she woke, said it all. He was just as dumbfounded. Until now she kept him at a distance. Her fear so intense that she automatically shrunk away. She never told him who her attacker was. He never asked, but his eyes portrayed his own turmoil.

Sonia sauntered back to her jail, her limp less obvious. Before its safety helped, but now the plastic hut held agony which imprisoned her.

"Princess." The endearing word broke her resolve and she stopped. Curt ... her heart thumped.

"Hello, Tau," she acknowledged and pulled the black shawl tighter. Hiding behind the flimsy material.

"Can I walk with you?"

"Sure."

"I have a gift, Princess." His tall frame shielded her from curious eyes as he held something towards her.

"What is it?" She blinked.

"It cannot be." She looked at Tau.

"Where did you find it?"

"In the building."

"Tau ..." Then she cried. The awe-inspiring reaction sparked right through her and she fell in his arms. All her fears stepped aside so that she could enjoy the moment. He laughed.

"I guess you like it."

"Tau, this is the best gift anyone has given me in a long time. Thank you." She gave him a small peck on a cheek and took the Bible from him. With reverent care she brushed the gold letters. For the first time in days she smiled.

"T*hank you, Lord*," she gushed in awe. The late afternoon's heat had a harshness to it. Just then an exceptional blue filtered through the haziness and peace covered her in its rays.

She enjoyed the touch for a few seconds before she whispered: "Thank you, Tau."

"IT'S MY PLEASURE."

The wonder as her face glowed with this unexpected treasure left him stunned. Her happiness overflowed, and she kissed him. It felt surreal. The sensation of her lips tingled his cheek. He touched it briefly. As she disappeared into her hut, he followed and surveyed the interior. The changes were immediate. It was the first time he was back inside since he discovered her. Flashes of that day sting his eyes and he brushed the thoughts away. He could not afford to think of that day. All they had was today.

On a turned over bucket a candle flickered and caused long shadows. With her back turned to him she took a seat on a cut-off log. He wanted to talk to her. Now was a good time.

"Sonia?" But her attention was on the book.

"Princess," he repeated. She looked up. The shawl slipped from her face and he lost train of thought. The brief pause gave him time to catch his reactions. Now more than ever he should look passed the physical: "I wanted you from the moment we met." Words failed and he grew silent.

"Sonia," he began once more. Her attention on the thin papers.

"Yes, Tau."

"Will you become my wife, today?"

"Tau." Her reaction left him speechless. His heart thumped. Slowly she put the book down and got up.

"Tau, you are a dear friend—one that I appreciate, but I cannot be your wife."

"Why?"

"It will never work between us."

"I love you," he admitted.

"You don't make it easy for me, do you?"

"Let me show you how much," and he pulled her closer. His lips met hers. When a sound vibrated through the stillness, he broke away. The sting burned his cheek. Dumbfounded he looked at her. She had slapped him. Her eyes burning. He grabbed her wrist in defence, then she screamed. In fright he released her as she crumbled in a heap close to her bed.

At once he followed her, and without thought he picked her up, whispering, "I am so sorry." He took a seat on the bed, rocking her in his lap. "I am so sorry. Forgive me, Princess." His lips showed his love in each tender touch, her skin soft to every touch. When he found her lips, he kissed them. His heart poured into it. He would love no one else.

His pleasure was short-lived when realization dawned on him. She showed no reaction. She did not share his feelings. Big, scared eyes looked at him from a tear-stained face. Her soft wet lips showed no emotion.

"I am sorry, Tau."

Quietly he let her go. She fell to the floor, tried to speak, but words failed as he left her on the ground.

The overpowering need to escape made him blind for Sonia. Overwhelmed with defeat, he changed into an old man. His joy turned into ash. His world had fallen with one sweep to the dust and filtered away. He had nothing else to give.

A simple truth stuck. He was not good enough.

34

THE NEXT MORNING SONIA entered the medic tent, worried. The previous evening's event was still fresh. Last night she caused pain in someone else's life.

He was not at her door.

Would he ever forgive her? She began her work with a heavy heart, first making sure all was good as she set out the registration book and tray of instruments. During the entire day he never showed up. The sun was already setting when Frank took her back. The look from him filled with disdain. By now she was used to it.

Lamya greeted her with a plate that Sonia took. "*Shukran*." (Thank you) Sonia sat on one stump that functioned as a bench and enjoyed the modest food. Baaka joined her. "How are you doing?"

"I am better. So glad to see you."

"How is your leg?"

"I treat it as best as I can."

"I will see you tomorrow." She said when she noticed
Roger, and fell silent. He joined them and stared down at
them with loathing, which changed when he turned to his
wife. Without a word, they walked to his dwelling.

Sonia's anxiety grew each time their paths crossed. She
wished to warn every woman, especially Baaka, but the
hopeless situation stopped her. Prayer was her only
protection.

In the hut she glanced towards the bed. At the bench she
picked up the Bible, her heart in her throat.

"*Do I still hope for deliverance, or should I take Tau up
on his offer?*" the question plagued her. As his wife she
stood a better chance for survival. It would not be
perfect, but safe.

"*I am vulnerable the longer I stay, LORD. Do I have
choices? Please talk to me.*"

She opened at the marker she had left. It is a dried-out
flower she had received from Tau one day. Since she had
not read the book in years, she began at the beginning.
She continued reading until tired and fell asleep, her
dreams a brackish mixture.

The next day a crying woman woke her. Her day started
well before daybreak with the birth. The birth lifted the
mood of the encampment. Women gathered around the
fires singing, they washed clothes and made food with a
joy Sonia didn't feel.

Still Tau's absence was notable. Where was he?

Watching the activities from the tent she noticed the soldiers' movements, except for Roger. The way he acted around her alerted her. With more people in the tent, she stayed busy. At 19h00 she closed the flaps. The headache's hammering forced her to the cabinet. She needed food, a bath and sleep. Her back ached and stretched to ease the stiffness. With listless steps she passed the celebrations. It did wonders for everyone, but she concealed herself. When she arrived at her hut, Roger stood nonchalantly in front of her door, smoking.

"Can I help?" her tone icy.

He beamed in the firelight: "You might. I need relief," his thick accent became alarming as he grabbed himself.

"You have a wife, go to her!" she responded flippant.

"I have, but tonight you will do."

She ducked away the moment he reached for her.

Please Lord, help me. I cannot go through it again.

"Please," she began. At that precise moment Tau Gbadamosi appeared. His tall figure was a welcomed sight. He stationed himself between them to release the hand from her arm, and she attached to him in desperation.

"What's going on?"

283

"Nothing which concerns you. I am talking to the woman. *Ghadar*!" (Leave!) he demanded.

"No," Tau said. He peeked to both and thundered: "It was you!" His jaw clenched. "You are the one that violated her."

People came closer and the music stopped. Sonia shrunk behind him and tightened the wrap, her humiliation seen by everyone.

Roger grinned: "I will not explain myself to you, Tau. I will do with her what I want, when I want."

Tau entered his space with a menacing look Sonia did not see before. The rapid Sudanese flow clipped with a dangerous tone. Noticing a movement, Baaka approached them. Briefly their eyes met. Her sympathetic look erased all doubt from Sonia's mind. This woman knew what he had done.

The two men's voices raised above the rush of people. Yelling ensued and soon each had their own crowd cheering them on. But the men were focused on their opponent, attacking each other with brutality. They had reached a boiling point when Baaka intervened. Bravely, she stood between them. Holding each man's arm. Roger shook her off but she held on and yelled for him to calm. The people turned on her, angry because she had stopped their adrenaline rush.

"Go to Sonia," she heard Baaka shouting to Tau while she pushed against Roger to stay put. Her remarkable strength born from years of defence.

TAU GUIDED HER INSIDE THE hut and shut the door. Out of breath he pulled her into his arms, his body trembling with exertion. He would kill Roger no matter when, but he would have his revenge. His loyalty had shifted, and Roger did not like that.

With the door closed he had sent a message to the entire camp. This is my woman. He would protect her though she did not want him. He could not stand aside and watch.

"Please Tau, I can't do this," she explained, frightened of the consequences, and tried to push him away, but he held her.

"I will protect you from him, I swear." He squeezed her. "I will not let him harm you again."

"What can you do to protect me?"

"As my wife you have my protection. I can kill him or take you away. Without me, you are open to any attack."

His words left her speechless. For a long time she tried to hold on, to be strong through this ordeal. Already she had faced brutal assault. Next time it could be worse. But how could she? She wrung her hands, her situation getting worse every day she stayed in the camp. She had run out of options. Looking at Tau her protector; her eyes messaged her desperation in an unguarded moment. The shawl fell from her shoulders in defeat. His voice, so strong and sure, seeped through the darkness.

"I vow to you; I will always be here for you. We will not repeat the previous mistake. Never again." He moved closer and touched her back. When she slacked against him, he folded her inside him.

Tomorrow would bring its own problems. He was ready, but having her, being with her, was the right place to be, and he would defend it with blood.

35

July 2019, Iraqi desert.

CURT WAS IN HIS OFFICE when Sonia came to mind. It had been weeks since he banished her and kept at it. The impulse to pray stopped him cold. What was she facing?

Why this constant need to pray?

Doug stood aside as Phillip walked in and leaned against the table.

"You look pale," Phillip said.

"Close the door, Doug," Curt said.

"What I tell you two today will not leave this office."

"Agreed." Both nodded.

"I met a woman in Malta." He began and told them about the trip.

"Although the Lord said I should call it off, he keeps on advising me to pray for her. I don't understand it." He sat down and took a sip directly from the bottle. "She taught me Psalm 91, and from that day I pray it every day over her." Both men listened with no interruptions. "God does not release me from this: a persisting feeling that becomes stronger. Can you explain it to me?"

"Do you know where she lives?"

"All I know is that she is a South African. Where she works or lives, I don't know."

"I thought you said you loved her."

"I do … I mean, I did." He pinched his eyes. "The weekend was short and we spoke of everything but work."

"I understand. The nitty-gritty stuff doesn't surface when confronted with love." Phillip said.

"It sounds as if you have experience?" Doug said.

Phillip smiled. "If you believe God is urging you to pray, then we should. God knows her situation."

AS THEY BOWED, GUNSHOTS CLEAVED the air in the encampment and Sonia woke with a racing heart.

"What's going on?"

"Get dressed, I will be back," Tau ordered. As the door opened, gunfire found their mark inside screaming people. Through the opening she witnessed their fall. A fireball lit the heavens and shuttered the earth. Fearful she got up and dressed while dust rained on her. She did a quick prayer as Tau got back.

"Bsre!" (Quick!) he shouted; his boots covered with bloodstains.

"We need to move. We are under attack." Outside the hut the camp was plunged in agony. A woman was raped while a knife found its mark in her breast with each stab. Her assailant's sadistic look filled with satisfaction. Her screams died down when the knife entered her once more, and he got up. Spit found her form, and he gave her one last kick. Sonia charged without thinking, but stopped by Tau.

"Do not let go, keep up."

"We need to help her!"

"She is dead. Let's go."

She stumbled over a body. Another woman's lifeless stare fuelled her into action. People scattered around in all directions. Women screamed and the men that chased them laughed, a diabolical laugh that left you cold. One woman was on fire. The stink of burned flesh, plastic and debris overpowered them. They both closed their noses in haste.

Next to them gunfire ran across the earth and silenced a kid. Another woman fell to her knees, her mouth wide open as blood spewed from her head. Sonia took this all in as Tau pulled her away.

An ear-splitting commotion broke out at the medical tent, and they stopped. Shocked, they watched the fireball escape. A solitary sign of its passing jetted into the air. The movement was so sudden that she bumped into Tau. She tripped, but he held her upright.

A diesel tank's blast ignited everything into an inferno. People yelled in torture; his hold tightened.

"Where are we going?"

"Trust me!" he shouted and ducked a bullet that slammed into a plastic can behind them. The limp caused her difficulty, but she continued.

At the water he yelled. "Jump in!"

"Tau, where are you going?" Kwame called.

"I need to hide her," he informed him.

"She will come with me," Kwame interjected.

"Why?"

"Roger said I must bring her."

"Tau?" Confused Sonia looked at the two men.

"I don't understand, what is this?" Tau asked his friend in a murmur.

"I am just following orders. Your infatuation with this woman is costing us too much, Tau. Let us get this over with."

"You know I cannot do that," Tau said as he pushed Sonia bchind him.

"Do as I say," he whispered, his eyes never leaving Kwame's, both not willing to yield to the other. Kwame hissed. "This woman is not worth it."

"She is worth everything to me. Why are you doing this to me?"

"We have to stop this. This is the only way to do so. Idil will not stop. He wants her."

"You of all people know what he will do with her."

"It breaks my heart, Tau, but there is no other way to avoid this. Look at the camp. Look what is happening to our people."

The commotion had escalated into a horror frenzy as the mercenaries cut through body parts, blood filtered into the ground. Screams echoed through the night and chilled you to the bone.

"Jump in the canoe and get away, Sonia!"

"No, Tau, what's going on?" Her fear was tangible.

A body landed in the water right behind them on top of the canoe. Both sunk into the murky water in a ring of bubbles. Smoke covered the water in an added sinister plot.

"Tau?" Kwame grabbed her and pulled her to him. "Tau!"

"Let her go," Tau growled, his weapon trained on them.

"You will not harm her," sneered Kwame as he shielded himself with her.

"I will kill you before you lay a finger on her."

"No, you won't." Flashed against Kwame he pulled her backwards, away from Tau. She screamed, but silenced when a hand covered her mouth.

"I will come for you, Princess," he shouted as he followed them.

"Don't be foolish, Tau. Once we give her to Idil this will all be over."

"Never. Let her go, Kwame." Determined he followed them back into the commotion with a heavy heart. At the far end of the camp Roger waited for them. Fear masked her face, and he felt helpless.

Once they were with them, he drew his weapon on Roger.

"Let her go, Roger," he demanded. He refused to give up. She would never be their possession to use.

A sardonic laughter pierced through the chaos.

"You will let her go. Get her in the boat," he commanded Kwame.

"No, Sonia, duck!"

"Tau!" she screamed.

The next moment Kwame clutched his leg as he crumpled in screams. She ran, tripped, got up and reached him as a bullet grazed her arm.

"Run Princess, go!" He urged as he pulled the trigger at one of his own men - and she ran.

Strength surged through her as she scuttled into the darkness. At the bank she looked backed. Tau fired a shot and then she dove into the black water when another fireball propelled towards her.

The pitch blackness covered her well as she followed the bank. Roots gave her more cover and at one point she waited between the reeds. When all was clear, she got out again. The rush to get away left her trembling and cold. She did not know what was happening, but had to trust Tau.

Up ahead a young woman fell to the ground. Her screams moved Sonia to action. She could not watch as they slaughtered defenceless people. Getting out of the water, Sonia made sure no one saw her and crawled to her. Once she was closer, she discovered it was Lamya. With only the fiery glows to give light, Sonia observed her wounds.

The sounds of gun fire continued as she examined her.

Lamya had a broken rib and a serious head wound. With trained hands she bandaged her with strips of her own clothing and then concealed her behind some wooden poles, still untouched by the chaos.

"Be still, I will be back," she whispered and Lamya nodded. With a throbbing leg she stayed hidden and saw another woman clutching her infant. Men circled her, one slapped her, and she screamed when another caught a leg.

Not sure where Tau was, she looked around and discovered a piece of steel pipe in reach. While something distracted them she moved unseen to it and picked it up. It fitted her hand perfectly, then she waited. She had no chance against the two men. One grabbed the infant and threw into a nearby bucket, the shrill screams mixed with the horror.

Be calm, Sonia, wait, she cautioned herself.

One man's attention switched to a shout behind him and let go of her leg. The other fumbled with her clothing, but she kicked him. Her next kick landed between his legs and when he went down, Sonia charged forward— her violent blow taking him all the way to the ground. When he looked up, she hit him once more.

"Run," she shouted. Again she hit him. Blood seeped from his head wound. She never felt so empowered as at that moment.

Never would a man do this to another woman if she could prevent it—never! For good measure she gave him another strike as she spewed in rage: "Never again."

"THIS WOMAN IS CAUSING ME MANY PROBLEMS," Roger said when an eerie silence descended.

Tau watched as Sonia disappeared before he returned his attention back to his former leader and friend. Kwame's leg needed medical care, but he felt nothing for him. His betrayal outweighed what he just did and dismissed him.

"Why?"

"Idil offered money for her." Tau took him aside. His anger simmered.

"What did you do?"

"We need the money!" Roger shouted. Tau had never felt so many emotions of anger as that moment. The realization of what Roger did left him nauseated.

"She is not for sale, Roger!" he forced between clenched teeth.

"She is my property. I will do with her what I wish." Nose to nose they glared at each other. Friends had turned into enemies.

"She is mine," he hissed out. "I took her as my wife last night," spittle hitting Roger's face.

"It's arranged." Roger hissed back.

"No!" Tau threw a punch. Then a shot rang out, which stopped them abruptly.

"I will take the nurse, yes." Their worst enemy held a gun to Baaka's head. Blood covered her limped body and torn clothes, a tight grip around her throat held her upright. Tears streaked her pale skin. The very man Tau had saved Sonia from before, had Baaka in his clutch. Tau lifted his pistol, but was hit hard, and the weapon dropped. Pain shot through his wrist, grabbed it and held it against him.

The Mayom leader, Cawo Idil, grinned: evilness poured from every pore.

"You will not touch my wife," Roger hissed.

Idil chuckled: "I already did. And what a fine specimen she is. I think I will take her with me."

Baaka fought against the strain, but he tightened his grip and she stopped as a knife plunged into her side. Her eyes begged them for help.

"I can understand why you love her. Yes." And to emphasise his hold on her, he pulled her closer and kissed the bruised lips. Her body slumped against him; her strength waned to nothing.

"No, I will give you anything." Roger stepped forward. Idil shook his head and lifted her from the ground. Blood soaked the earth as he raised her—wild kicks, the only sign she was still fighting. Roger stopped in his tracks.

"Now that we have established your willingness to do whatever, I will let her go on two conditions."

"What?" Tau dreaded the answer.

"The white woman and the medical supplies. My people need them more than you."

"No!" Tau screamed.

"Yes!" Roger screeched.

"She is my wife." With a deadly look, he silenced Tau, but he refused to stand back and glowered at him. Sonia was his wife. She belonged to him. Why could they not leave her alone?

"Well, now that we have determined my price, I will take it, yes." Idil's nonchalant attitude halted their movements. The two friends glared at each other.

"Get her!" Idil commanded backward.

"No!" Tau yelled as he rushed toward the man, but was stopped with one punch against his temple.

When he woke from a pain-filled dream he sat up. Muddled he spotted Roger in a heap next to him. He, too, groaned. Baaka's face turned away from them. Tau crawled to her, her unconscious body too still. He broke the rest of her. Her swollen face told its own story.

Roger cowered next to him. "I couldn't stop him. He had her again, then gave her to some of his men. They forced me to watch as they used her." Tau felt sorry for Baaka. She did not deserve it.

Was Sonia safe? Where would she be? How much time did he waste just lying there? All around him the camp was in total chaos. Did they find her? Where were Idil and his men?

On the other side of a burning hut three men stood around a fire pit. Another tried to doze a fire without success. Bodies strewn the earth and blood influenced the air in a queasy mess, a sick stench that caught him. Just in time he swallowed when bile rose. He struggled to his feet and saw the store as flames licked it in revenge. It was the last building. If that was gone, they had nothing.

"Help me!" he yelled while he took a bag and struck the first flames. Men ran to him with buckets. Water sloshed on the dirt. His anxiety grew with each smouldering breath. After clearing some debris, he found the supplies were all gone.

Looking back he stood there for the longest time. Everything had changed. Roger ran around, Baaka's lonely figure a summation of their situation. Their survival had shrunk to zero. All because of greed.

"Tau."

He ignored the call, but Kwame limped to him. "He threatened to kill my boy. I had no choice." Tau looked at him, disgust silenced him. "Please Tau, I am sorry." Without answering him, he sauntered in the direction he had seen Sonia last.

"Tau!" To him, Kwame was a dead man. He had nothing to say to a traitor. He could not dismiss the actions.

The sun tinted the sky in a deep red as if the blood had evaporated into it. He looked around, but saw nothing. His heart clenched.

"Where are you, Princess?" he screamed into nothingness. No answer came forth. He followed the bank but found no sign of her.

"I will help you," Kwame interrupted his thoughts.

Through slits Tau looked at his friend.

"Please Tau, let me help." His pant leg was soaked with blood, his arm hung precariously. In the other a weapon hung listless in his grip. The picture evoked no sympathy.

"I have nothing to say to you."

"I understand you are mad at me, but let's find Sonia. She will not survive out there for too long," Kwame stated the obvious, but Tau did not hear him. His attention back on the immediate surroundings. His thoughts consumed with guilt. He did this to her—he and his people. For the first time he really considered her situation. He caused her to lose hope, stripped her from everything and now she was out there. Not for the first time he thought about returning her back to her people.

All he could offer her was danger. She was not made for this life.

"SONIA!" SHE TURNED AROUND and charged him. Kwame had found her first and called Tau as he defended himself.

"You!" She hit him again and again till he captured her arms.

"Sonia, it is me." Tau implored and seized her upheld arm. Looking at Tau first, her arm fell. The pipe fell to the ground.

Her rage had saved her and many others. It was her only weapon that held her upright and moved her into action. Her green eyes had turned into a fire storm, so intense Tau averted them.

"You are wounded," he remarked. Blood covered her drenched clothes and face.

"I am fine," she pushed passed them and trotted away. Both stared at her figure when Tau noticed a man whose head was bashed in and grinned. *That is my girl.*

He followed her, crouched next to a woman. The woman calmed an infant while Sonia examined him. His wails stopped when a breast was pushed into his mouth, the mother to occupied with him to notice the men.

"What type of monsters are this that throws babies like rags and rape women." It was not a question, and he had no answer.

"Is he all right?" he asked instead.

"All are fine for now, but I need more light to be certain." She got up and scrutinised the camp, pipe in hand. Without another word she ran towards one of their own soldiers. Once again he followed. It was as if something possessed her to fulfil her duties and he let her go.

He still could not get over the betrayal. Roger, he could understand, but not Kwame. First the attack on Sonia and now the attack on the camp. They were in a sinister grip he had seen many times, power and greed, the fuel for the unreasonable choices.

How many will suffer because of Roger's stupidity?

These thoughts troubled him as he fired another shot at a man slapping a forgotten child in fury. The child flopped forward and he fired a shot. This time the man slumped down on top of the small body. Blood mixed in their last moments. At the bodies, he watched in detachment.

He gathered some men and together they swept the area. With the explosion, their ammunition was dwindling. He barked a few orders and watched as men scurried away to make sure the camp was rid of the enemy.

Through it all he stayed close to Sonia, making sure she was unharmed. She refused to leave the people and continued long after breakfast. When she found Baaka, they could not get her away. They had found a canvas large enough and carried her to a place where Sonia could work on her. But they knew Baaka's chances for survival were slim.

Inside the store they found another old tent and erected it for Sonia. Some women returned quietly and started with the clean-up. The younger men, who were able, built a new hut with what they could find.

While she cared for his people, he searched for her hut. At the smouldering debris he found only one item of use. This he pocketed and gathered some building material as he looked for a suitable spot. Once he was satisfied, he cleaned the area.

All around him people were now busy erecting huts from the leftovers. Fires spiralled in the air, and some children were already in the water to catch fish.

He, too, began to build a place for them.

His thoughts troubled.

36

Fangak county, South Sudan.

DID HE REMEMBER HER? The ravine was growing wider with each passing day.

Tau was her husband—not by choice, but for survival. She had to accept that. The night before the attack she fell asleep in Tau's arms. Her body protested the closeness. He held her the entire night. No advances. No intimacy. Her first response was to flee, but voices from the other side of their hut reminded her where she was. To keep on fighting did not help her situation. At least he was a gentleman; bush-like but understanding. This small favour she appreciated.

If this was her future, Tau's offer the only safety net. Life could become difficult no matter how much it went against her upbringing. Will people back home understand when they learned about this. She may die, but to be a harlot was not an option. Did she have any choice?

The algorithmic time holder had changed its direction and left her with limited alternatives. Tau Gbadamosi was her protector in a world she did not understand. When he does prompt for sexual intimacy, can she do it willingly?

She took a deep shuddering sigh as she remembered Curt's appreciative stare; the way she felt in his arms, the instant connection they had. A slight smile played on her lips as she drifted back to those moments of ecstasy. When a child yelled, it dragged her back to the swamp.

"Lord, you have forgotten me in this place. Weeks have passed and despite everything, no help has come. I am frightened, hungry and tired; and a bath would be great."

From early morning till late they kept her in the makeshift tent with minor breaks. Even the classes stopped. Tau's business kept them apart. They erected a wire fence after the attack which did not help her mood. Now, more than ever she was caged in. Everyone was on high alert. Silence and time were her only companions.

The disorderly camp righted bit by bit. Tau moved her to another place; sturdier than the one they had. Their belongings scares, but they were alive. Her demolished hut held nothing good anyhow, and she had lost everything of personal value.

She returned to the spot just to find a heap of ash and debris. Nothing was recognizable. The leather bag's buckle she found among the debris, cleaned it. This she wore like a broach on her chest. It became a symbol of her old life, a validation of the old Sonia before the abduction. Gone was the self-assured, independent woman.

She was thankful for the change of scenery, though. Provisions were uncommon with no extra supplies on the way and they were in a desperate state. The women replaced her dress with material they collected. Not much but it covered her. Touched by their generosity. Kwame gave her a brush. It was his way to make amends. Tau found an old pair of shoes, fitting perfectly.

At night she read the Bible, somehow it survived the fire. When Tau presented her with it, her troubled mind relaxed. Some pages were scorched, and the gold letters blackened. The promises it held, her only light. Now, more than ever, she clung to the hope of her rescue. She thought herself stupid for believing for any release. But what else did she have? Curt's memories were slipping away, her love a gnawing reminder of truth at one time.

In moments of quietness when Tau sat with her, he raised questions from the Bible, and she explained. His thoughts riddle with whys, undecided of the faith. He could not understand the purpose of it all, or grasp the love of an unseen God.

"You know how you saved me during the raid?"

"Yes."

"Jesus did the same. He included every person in his plan. Me, you and the seven billion people in the world, past, present and future." He did not move, holding her the entire time.

"God loves us so much that he gave his only son to save us."

"I can never do that." His warm breath tickled her face and she smiled clumsily. She was content in his presence, no matter the circumstances.

"It's difficult to lose a child, but to do it with intent to save another, I cannot understand but accept," she said as his finger trailed her face.

"I will sacrifice myself for you, Princess."

"Tau," she tried to stop the flow.

"Sonia, I have dreamed about these moments many times. From the day I saw you, I wanted you. I will lay down my life for you." He closed the distance and sealed it. The action seared with warm lips.

She wanted to protest the action, wanted to fight, but she also needed the closeness of another. Putting everything aside, all thoughts of home, choices and Curt, she accepted him. She could not hold him off any longer. Her resolve stripped. He had done what many tried but failed, until Curt.

That night he loved her in every small detail and delicate touch. He loved her with so much tenderness that it brought her to tears. And as he kissed it away, she opened her heart—even if with a fraction. His love and care helped to curb the anxiety and loneliness.

They became partners, working together to better the camp.

During the day they worked nonstop, but at night his roughened hands held her—his love making tender, his body strong. Most nights she cried herself to sleep for a lost love she longed for, but could never have. A love she was not worthy of.

They had come a long way. Given time, she could love him. He was a dutiful man, but it did not alter the danger she was in.

She had nursed Baaka's broken body the best she could. Even Roger needed help after the raid. Reluctantly she did her part under Tau's watch. Twice a day he demanded a full report on Baaka, who still lied in a semi-comatose state. With limited supplies she kept her comfortable, but the internal damage was beyond her reach.

His violent reactions to her answers, his aggravation in each blow, kept her on high alert. The looks she received left her fearful. This only happened when Tau was not around.

Her own health was deteriorating. At first she thought it was just tiredness, but the constant headaches were making life difficult and she sweat profusely. Her strength drained with each passing hour.

37

1 August 2019, Iraqi desert.

"SIR, I HAVE GOOD NEWS ABOUT PRIVATE CUMMINGS." Curt leaned back in his chair and took a sip of the bottled water.

"What did you find?"

"Well Sir, Private Cummings wasn't there at the night he murdered Celia White."

"How so?"

"Evidence showed he was at the hotel with another woman. I found a receipt and a witness as proof." He grinned. "I met a friend of Celia White—a school buddy, Vern Braden, she confided to. There was another soldier; one she feared and didn't trust."

"Who?"

"She never gave his name, but his lawyer and I went back to the apartment and searched the place with a fine comb." Now he chuckled with glee, and Curt smiled. "We found a button the police and cleaning staff had missed under the dresser in her room."

"Yes, and?"

"The button is from a man's shirt. We went to the evidence office to inspect TJ's belongings and found no buttonless shirts in his duffel bag. We checked; he handed no shirts in for dry cleaning at the hotel he stayed."

"Do you know who it belongs to?"

"No Sir, but it couldn't be hard to find."

"Why?"

"Since the button belonged to a soldier."

"But not Private Cummings?"

"No, Sir."

"I see."

"Reeves gave the evidence to the police and they are investigating it on their side. Vern also gave his statement. The real perp is out there."

"Did you see Private Cummings?"

"Yes, Sir. He has a tough time in jail, but Reeves promised they will do everything they can to sort this out."

"But why don't they release him?"

"The fingerprints are still a dead giveaway and the judge refused on the lack of supporting evidence. But we're confident we will find him."

"Keep me up-to-date, Doug. I am turning in. Good night."

"Good night, Sir."

THE NEXT MORNING, RALPH handed Curt a Top-Secret Folder.

"What is this, Sergeant?"

"The kidnapping of a Red Cross nurse in South Sudan, end of April. No one has heard from her since."

"Why is the United Nations not overseeing this?"

"They sent the report to all bases, Sir," he explained. "South Sudan is in a delicate situation. No one has men to spare for a search party. The UN doesn't want to jeopardise the on-going peace talks."

"Damn their peace talks." With a grunt he opened the file just to stop and stare. Shock vibrated through him. He gasped and plumped in the chair, his face pale. "No!"

"Sorry Sir, did you say something?" Ralph asked.

"Get me Sam and Alexi," his voice hoarse, and Ralph left the office.

Without looking up, Curt issued more orders. Seconds later Charlie connected him with General Cartwright at the other end.

"You realise you just called me out of a very important meeting." The man sounded irritated, but Colonel McGee did not care. This woman was a priority. All the prayers made sense now. There was no time to discuss anything except her release.

"The IRCI nurse."

"Yes, what about it?"

"And ... we receive word about this, now!"

"You must realise ..." Curt stopped him." Are there any attempts to rescue her?"

"No Curt, "anyone can go, you know the drill," the general affirmed.

"Yes, I do, thanks General." His hands shook as he returned the receiver. Just then Sam, Alexi, and Ralph hurried inside the office and Curt dismissed everyone else.

After an hour Sam and Alexi left, followed by Colonel Curt McGee moments later. He needed alone time.

THAT SAME NIGHT SONIA laid before the Lord in agony. It was a strenuous day. She was not well. Tau was gone for days. Alone, forgotten, and sick she knelt before the Lord with no answers. Without optimism she flipped open at Joseph and his brothers' story.

She read through his entire history until she stopped at **Genesis 40:23**: "The chief cupbearer, however, didn't remember Joseph; he forgot him."

They forgot him. Tears ran down her cheeks. *This is hard, Lord. He was forgotten for two years. How did he bear it?* Every emotion of her turmoil spilled over as she continued to read through the tears.

Two years had passed and then Pharaoh had a dream and the chief cupbearer remembered him. Pharaoh was so impressed with Joseph, he appointed him as second in charge of Egypt. When his brothers returned, they did not recognise him. Then one scripture stood out from the rest.

Genesis 45:4-8

4. And Joseph said unto his brethren, come near to me, I pray you. And they came near. And he said, I am Joseph your brother, whom ye sold into Egypt.

5. Now, therefore, be not grieved, nor angry with yourselves, that ye sold me hither: for God sent me before you to preserve life.

6. For these two years hath the famine been in the land: and yet there are five years, in the which there shall neither be earing nor harvest.

7. And God sent me before you to preserve you a posterity in the earth, and to save your lives by a great deliverance.

8. So now it was not you that sent me hither, but God: and he hath made me a father to Pharaoh, and lord of all his house, and a ruler throughout all the land of Egypt.

"Lord, you have done this to protect him and save his family. Likewise, you have brought me closer to you. I could minister healing to these people. Father, you work in strange ways."

Her depression shifted as wisdom cleared the veil. First, she should forgive Brady and let go of the agony and judgement when he left her. It brought back the pain. She must forgive to have any future.

Baring her soul before the Lord, it felt she had undergone open-heart surgery as He reached in and healed her. Her eyes were blurry and scratchy of all the tears but her spirit renewed.

For the first time she understood what it meant. Her son was in a perfect place. It gave her the peace she needed.

"Brady Scott, I forgive you for leaving me and forgetting me when I needed you the most. I release you of all wrongdoing. I am in the Father's hands. I am remembered."

38

2 August 2019, Bentiu, South Sudan.

AS IF THE UNIVERSE WAS WAITING for her, a C130 lifted from the ground with two black-dressed men and much needed medical supplies for the nearby Hospital in Bentiu, South Sudan.

Pitch dark the scattered stars exposed the movements on the base briefly. With only four people on the ground aware, Operation Gazelle was in full swing. The Iraqi desert silent.

At 04h30 hours the large hatch opened and two bodies dropped from 20 000 feet into the cloud-covered sky. Darkness covered them. In the distance, bombings thundered in the night sky, but it was clear over Bentiu.

The Hercules landed four kilometres away at the National Airline and the two men touched ground minutes later. They gathered their parachutes and gear and disappeared into the thick darkness of Africa.

The flat planes did not give adequate cover, so they stayed low and silent. They changed in civilian clothing, faded denim and shirts—each armed with a knife and their trusted 9mm at their sides. Jackets concealed the bulges, and with bags of proviant over the shoulders they ran.

With hats pulled low they reached the hospital at 05h20 and studied the grounds with keen interest. A small wooden donkey-cart passed them with a green container filled with water, a commodity highly valued. They waited for it to pass before they crossed the dirt road and yard, and stepped into the hospital building.

With the intel provided, the director of nursing was friends with the nurse. She was their only connection. They had to wait for the next hour.

Once they stepped into her office, they wasted no time.

"What appears to be the problem, gentlemen?"

"Sonia Main. When was the last time you saw her?" The blond man's serious tone alerted her.

"Thursday night, the 25th of April. But I told this to the investigators. I am sorry, but who are you?" she asked in a polite but stern voice.

"People who cared about her just as you, Ma'am," came the quick reply.

"When was she expected back?" he continued.

"On Sunday night, but she never showed."

"Who else had insight into her schedule?" the scarred face asked, his long curls moving under the high-speed fan.

"No one. I arranged it with my uncle who took her to the airport. She flew straight to Malta. Her return flight was from Malta to Khartoum and back with my uncle. He met her and saw her entering the plane." This confirms their information. She boarded the plane and arrived back in Bentiu to disappear in thin air.

"And she spoke to no one else?"

"She kept to herself. She has no family back in South Africa."

"No one else knew of the plans?"

"I hope you don't think I had something to do with this?"

"Someone had to have knowledge about the plans to arrange her disappearance. Or did she go off often?"

"I forced her to take time after a personal matter left her restless."

"What was it about?"

"I cannot say. She kept it to herself."

"You can trust us. Any information is confidential."

Haleema watched the two men with years of experience.

"In that case. An observer of the UN spent the week with us. She became even more distracted after that, the reason I arranged the getaway."

"His name?"

"Major Brady Scott."

"Where can we find him?"

"He left his number."

"Can we have it?" She paused, and they kept eye contact. Seconds later she opened her top desk drawer and picked up a small business card. "There you go."

"Thank you for your time," the blond man said. He rose, shook her hand and left.

"I hope you find her!" she called.

"We will find her, Ma'am. Goodbye." The door closed with finality. Haleema sat down and prayed. She prayed for her friend and she prayed for the two men.

"DO YOU THINK WHAT I am thinking?" Sam asked.

"Inside job?"

"Maybe, but inside her house definitely."

"So, we wait."

"Yes, and phone this Major Scott."

"Yes."

"Breakfast?"

"Yes, why not." Sam was always hungry. Except for women, food was his number one passing time. He did it with pure pleasure.

The director of nursing's shift ended at 18h00, so they had time to kill. Next to the restaurant they bought a disposable mobile phone. While waiting for the food, phoned the number on the white card.

A strong voice answered, and Alexi spoke in his heavy eastern-bloc accent.

"You know Sister Sonia Main?"

"Yes, did you find her? Who are you?"

"It doesn't matter who we are, but we are looking for her. What is your relationship with her?"

Sam watched his partner's face for any signs that showed they were on the right path, but since Alexi's blank expression remained, he accepted their food and ate.

"We go a long way back."

"How far?"

"Twenty-five years."

"Were you involved?"

"Yes, why all these questions?"

"We have to follow all leads, Major."

"And now?"

"Nothing. Please tell me, did you find her?"

"No, Sir."

"Do you know of anyone who wants to hurt her?"

"No. Sonia would not hurt a fly."

"Thanks, Sir," and he ended the call.

"Nothing?" Sam asked between bites.

"It seems the Matron is our only lead."

The two ate their meal in relative silence until the phone rang. The blond looked at the caller id, saw it was the number of Major Scott and threw it in the garbage bin. He had nothing more to discuss with him.

SWEAT STREAMED FROM HER face and she shivered with fever. She struggled out of the medical tent to stretch her limbs and fell against Kwame. Her eyes rolled back and she collapsed in his arms. A plate scattered over the hard ground.

Tau arrived that same morning and was eating before he met her. He dropped his plate and rushed towards them. Kwame laid her on one stretcher. Isaac started with the procedure while the two men hovered over them. He scooted them away and closed the sheet.

Malaria had struck once more. Isaac knew the signs. Just the previous night they talked about prevention measures. Now the one person who could help them had fallen ill.

Tau punched his fists in the nearest post and the whole tent shook. He had not seen her for days, and now this.

"Come, Tau," Kwame said. "He will know how to treat her." Tau allowed the bigger man to lead him away. He sat at the fire and prayed as he saw her often did.

His wife needed her God, and he might as well pray to Him for healing. There was a time during their talks she shared what she had read in the Bible. Her excitement touched him. Now he could kick himself. He should have given more attention to her talks.

He found the Bible on their bed and sat down. It opened at **Psalm 103:13**. "As a Father has compassion on his children, so the Lord has compassion on those who fear him; for He knows how we are formed; He remembers that we are dust. Verse 17: But from everlasting to everlasting the Lord's love is with those who fear him."

He paused before he continued. Then he prayed: *"God, I am unfamiliar with you, but Sonia, my wife, knows you. Heal her. Amen."*

He felt uncomfortable talking with someone who wasn't there, but felt a peace he had never experienced before. *Maybe there was something to this prayer thing.*

When he heard his name, he covered the book.

39

3 August 2019, South Sudan.

THE TWO MEN ASSUMED POSITION BEHIND an abandoned building and waited. The matron went into her house at 19h00. Quietly they made themselves comfortable and waited. After midnight a window opened and a tiny figure scrambled out. At the corner he checked the street to both sides before he continued.

They trailed the figure for two kilometres until he joined a group of teenagers, their shadows dancing in the firelight. He crouched and joined the game. Low barks of laughter and ire seeped into the air. Two kids were on watch duty, but their attention was more on the game than the street. From behind the crates of rotten vegetables they had an unobstructed view, especially of the boy.

After an hour he retraced his steps. A bigger boy stopped him. They spoke a bit, then an argument broke out. The older boy shook him and he cried in pain. Pushed to the ground he received another beating.

It was then that they immersed from the shadows at a run. Moments later the older boy was flat on his back.

Fearful eyes watched as the man grabbed his shoulders and whispered something to him. The boy pissed himself and ran in the other direction.

"Let's find out what this fellow knows," he said in an unfamiliar accent. Both men's attention turned to him.

"Take him to his mother."

"Please, Sir," Abasi begged.

"Do you have something to say, Son?" his voice stern.

"Don't tell my mother."

"Okay," and he crouched. The moonlight showed directly on the scars right in front of him. "We will not take you to your mother, but you must answer a few questions."

"Anything, Sir."

"Don't be scared. We are looking for a woman, you may know her?"

"I know many people, Sir."

"This woman works with your mother," Abasi gasped.

"No one will harm you," the man assured him, "but we need to find her."

"Who, Sir?" He stalled.

"You know who we are talking about," came the abrupt reply.

"Yes, Sir."

"We are waiting," the other man said.

"Am I in trouble?"

"No, Son."

"Nurse Sonia?" he clarified.

"Yes, Son. She is missing."

"He said he will kill me if I tell."

"Who, Son?"

"I cannot say his name, but he will kill me."

"No one will come near you. Who took her and why?"

There was a certainty that gave Abasi some confidence. In a small voice he replied: "He wanted to sell her, Sir."

"Who, Son?"

"Please sir, I cannot say."

"And where did he take her?" the questions persisted.

"He mentioned the northern border," he tried to run, but held tightly.

"I know nothing else, I promise," but the men ignored his pleas and asked: "You had to inform him of her plans?"

Abasi nodded. They discussed it amongst themselves and looked at Abasi. "We will walk you home and make sure no one follows."

"Thank you, Sir," and then he ran. They followed at a brisk pace. Just as before, the boy climbed through the window. Once satisfied that they were not followed, they left the boy and searched for transport.

"I saw an abandoned jeep close," Sam said.

"Lead the way," Alexi replied. They jogged to the end of the street and turned left. Across the street the jeep waited for them. A rundown piece of junk, but it served her purpose. Sam scratched underneath the steering wheel and hot-wired it in seconds. Alexi slapped the frame as Sam pulled away. First they had to get their gear, and an hour later they followed the road in a northern direction. The beams of the jeep penetrated the pitch-black night, opening a pathway of potholes and debris. A scene they were used to.

The importance of the mission felt heavy on them. They had never seen the commander like this. If possible, he would have done the rescue himself. It had cost them all their convincing power to keep him at bay. The man was adamant.

Basecamp, Iraq.

"STAFF SERGEANT!" Doug greeted Castledale as he passed him to sit at the next table.

"Sit," he invited and shoved his plate and drink aside.

The table trembled under the sudden weight.

He cut his food. "It has been a while," he said, and took the first bite of the steak.

"Yes, it has," and Doug too savoured another bite.

"You were away on holiday," he said, and Doug nodded.

"Met any women?" he quaffed.

Doug nodded. "Yes, I met a few people. Were you also gone?" he asked without elaborating.

"Yeah."

"It was good to be there, but hard," Doug continued, cleaning his plate with a bread roll as he studied the man under his eyebrows.

"Yeah, I know what you mean," he added and took another bite.

"Amazing how we fight here to keep the enemy at bay, but there the newspapers are full of crime," Doug said matter-of-factly, and Brock nodded in agreement.

"I don't read the newspapers when I am home. I go for the action. So much to do," and he grinned.

Doug pushed his plate aside and took a sip of his cool drink.

"What sort of action are you in?" Doug asked.

"You know," and he made a wave with his fork. "I went to a baseball game, saw a few friends."

"Nothing interesting happening while you were there?" Doug asked.

"No, but the women were hot—especially one," and he chuckled. "A small blond, she was wild, man."

Doug raised a brow and leaned forward. "What about Anna?"

"She doesn't have to know." He winked and cleaned his plate with the last piece of bread. The sodden piece disappeared into his mouth.

"Doesn't it bother you?"

"I'm not married to her," and he looked at him quizzically.

"Yeah, I know, but you know women. They are demanding."

"That's right," and he smirked, "but you need to show them who is in control." He pushed the plate aside arrogantly. "Women want a man to show his strength."

"Now I understand why I have no action," and the man chuckled.

"You are too soft with them. They can handle the roughness, they are not that soft."

"But how? I mean, I don't want to force her," Doug said with interest.

"No man, they love the aggressive side of it. Anna loves that." He leaned forward and grinned. "Especially you know where." He whispered and wiggles his thick brow.

"I thought …"

"Women love that. They moan with delight when you stick it up to them. They cannot get enough," and he sat back smugly. "You should try it, Doug." He gathered his plate and empty bottle.

That is what you think, buddy, he thought angrily. "Tell it to yourself, long enough and you will believe it," he muttered as he too made his way out of the door.

40

"WHAT IS THIS, CAPTAIN BOGART?" Curt asked the head nurse.

"My resignation papers, Sir."

"Why was I not prepped about it earlier? This is short notice?" Vivian demanded he should return home. This was not a suitable time for sudden changes. To find a head nurse was almost as impossible as finding a needle in a haystack.

"It does not matter," she replied. "What matters is that I leave at the end of the week." Her careless attitude was new to him.

"It doesn't give me time," he pointed out and rose to his full height, towering over the thin woman.

"Yes." She tilted her head. Her defiance was obvious in her posture. He wondered why she ever chose her career.

"This will not do." He could barely hold his anger.

"Well Sir, it's done and I am leaving."

Curt plopped on his chair in unbelief. He should charge her with insubordination, he thought. It would teach her respect, but rebuke tapped his consciousness and let it go. "*Sorry, Lord,*" he whispered. *"You will provide a head nurse."*

He stared at the open folder, scanning the contents. His solution stared him in the face and a slow smile grew. With renewed interest he leafed through the information in the file. Satisfied he picked up his phone and gave the number of a man in the head office, and waited. For the first time since he heard of Sonia's abduction, it emanated breakthrough in what seemed a never-ending story of problems.

South Sudan.

SEVEN HOURS INTO THE DRIVE, the sun high and hot in the cloudless sky, they stopped to relieve themselves. A lonely tree's shadow barely touched the road, but they stopped anyway, stretching the legs and aching backs.

They were not young anymore. With Sam's leg a constant problem, he had to walk it off a bit. His knee gave in on a recent parachute jump and he refused to see the doctor. Now and then he would pop a pain pill with no one noticing.

Alexi himself had back problems, and the moment he placed any weight on it, he felt it. But it stopped neither of them. They were the best, proven repeatedly.

At the tree both took a tentative stand. Sam was the first to zip up with Alexi shortly after.

A piece of material trapped in a nearby bush caught Sam's attention right away. Scanning the landscape, he removed the brightly coloured piece and sniffed it. Alexi followed him curiously.

"What did you find?"

"A woman's scarf."

Alexi took it, and just like Sam, sniffed the delicate fragrance, rubbing the soft material between calloused fingers.

"Odd." The perfume a misplaced fragrance so far from civilization, both searched for other clues.

Leaves from a nearby bush rustled. Alexi bumped his partner while the scarf vanished in his jean pocket. With hand signs they moved in the opposite direction and stopped when a small boy appeared, his white toothy grin a paradox against the black skin. He giggled and started to run, but Sam was quick and picked him up.

"Hi buddy," he said with a smile and knelt. His face contorted in pain and switched to his other leg.

"Hi," the little guy said. His English pronounced with hesitation. "Do you want drops?" Sam took gumdrops from his shirt pocket. Opening his hand he revealed the caramel balls. He swept it up and popped one in each cheek.

A small hand reached out, touched Sam's hair and giggled. "Do you like my hair?"

The boy nodded, the cheeks fat with the drops.

"Have you seen hair like this before?"

The boy nodded. The balls clucked against each other.

"When?"

The boy scanned them both. Small fingers shot up of both hands and he wiggled them all.

"Days or weeks?" Sam asked.

"Weeks," the boy said.

"That long, hey? Was it a woman?"

337

"Yes." Again, he touched Sam's hair and let the one loose curl stretch before he released it. It shot back and he giggled. Alexi showed the scarf to him.

"Was it hers?" and the boy nodded.

"Where did she go?" The boy showed in the direction they just came from.

"It cannot be her?" he whispered to Sam. "The boy said northern border."

"Yeah, unless someone else took her," he said thoughtfully.

"How many men were there?" Alexi asked, and three fingers appeared.

"Three men?" and the boy nodded. Sam handed him four more drops which he eagerly took.

"How many jeeps?" Sam asked. The fingers shot up; two.

"Interesting," they both said simultaneously. "And they went that way?" Alexi pointed to the north and the boy shook his head. He pointed to the eastern side. They both straightened and let the boy go. He crossed the road without checking and disappeared in the bushes on the other side.

"We better check the maps," Alexi said, and they hurried to the confiscated jeep. Sam popped a drop in his mouth and Alexi placed the scarf in his pocket.

With the map spread over the bonnet, they traced the road. Someone must have seen three black men and a white woman travelling. They would remember that. She would draw attention to these parts.

Time was of the essence. The C130 would leave in 52 hours. With no communication they had to use what was available and hoped to find her in time.

Back in the jeep Sam took the wheel, and Alexi leaned back and slept. There would be no downtime once they found her. Sam retrieved Sonia's photo from his shirt pocket and familiarised himself with her face.

He grinned as he thought about the Colonel staring at the photo. The distinctive look of longing was unmistakable. He could swear the man was in love.

A slight dimple was noticeable on the woman's face. She should be downright gorgeous when she smiled.

41

Iraqi Desert.

CURT PACED HIS OFFICE IN FRUSTRATION. Radio silence meant he would only receive news once they were back in the Hercules. A three day wait.

How was she? Is she hungry, cold, or afraid? In what state of mind was she? Was she broken in spirit and body?

His patience's threadbare. He needed to get out, or he might lose it.

He stepped out into the late afternoon sun. The fiery ball was not ready to sleep as it poured more heat on them. Mingling with the soldiers he inspected the camp with disinterest. He would do anything to stop thinking about the woman he could not dream about. At the bush pub two soldiers entered, and he followed them inside the cool interior. Loud music greeted him from the speaker attached to wooden poles. A private manned the makeshift counter with stacked glasses. The rest of the men grew quiet, saluted and he waved to them to continue.

"At ease soldiers," he acknowledged and requested a soft drink. Comfortable on an old couch, he took the first long sip. Glorious! He tuned everything out, the buzz, the wait, even the heat disappeared with each sip. This is where Doug found him fifteen minutes later.

IT WAS DEEP IN THE night when Sam finally stopped before the house belonging to the matron, knocking loud on the front door.

The light went on and a man in his late forties opened the door.

"Yes?"

"Sir, we need to speak to your son." They towered over the man as they blocked the door. The man looked at them with curious indifference. Footsteps from the hallway and the soft faint voice of Matron Haleema reached their ears.

341

"Who is it, love?" she asked as she pulled her gown tight.

"Ma'am," Sam greeted, "can we come in?"

"These men are looking for Sonia," she explained to her husband, and he opened the door wider. Sam entered first.

"We need to speak to your son."

"But why?" she asked.

"It will become clear, please Ma'am," Alexi explained.

"Which one?" she asked.

Both men said: "The twelve-year-old."

She gasped softly and looked at her husband, who nodded.

"Okay, let me wake him."

While they waited, her husband ogled them as they studied the interior of the house. Minutes later she appeared with the boy in front of her. Immediately Alexi was on his knees. Sam's knee cramped again and although he said nothing, Alexi recognised the twitch in his jaw.

"Son."

"Please, Mommy," the boy whined and clutched at his mother's gown, but then his father's stern look ordered him to let go.

"You need to tell us who this man is who took Sonia." Alexi tried to stay patient. With a day wasted, it was difficult.

"I cannot," he braved. Haleema caught on quickly and shielded her own shock.

"Why did you do this to Sonia? She is a lovely person? We invited her to our house as a friend and you helped with her abduction. How could you, Abasi? Tell them who this man is, or so help me."

"No," he persisted.

"Let me," said Sam, impatient with the youngster. This was why he never wanted kids. The little characters wanted to rule the world with arrogant, stubborn and undisciplined ways which was not his view of children. And since when did a child tell his parents 'no' when he received a direct command? Brat!

He stepped forward and led Abasi to the corner of the living room, sat down on the chair and pulled the kid in his lap.

Alexi watched as his partner spoke gruffly to the kid. After a while the arrogance changed and he listened. It took Sam ten minutes to extract the information, but when he rose and placed the kid back on the floor, the kid was pale.

"Do you know a man that is called Haji?" Both parents gasped and Haleema pulled her kid under her arm, pale in the face.

The father swallowed and said: "Is he the man you messed with?"

"Do you know his whereabouts?" Sam asked.

"He is an Arabic nomad, leader of his own small faction, the Democratic Freedom Alliance," the husband answered.

"Do you think he sold Sonia Main?"

"Oh my God, William!" Nyanath gasped. The terror on her face told them all they needed to know.

"I hope not," he said thoughtfully. A thought triggered his memory.

"Three years ago his first wife had problems with the birth of their second child. He brought her to me. I warned him if she ever became pregnant again, she would not make it. Her frailty was of big concern."

"Do you think it's the reason they took Sonia?"

"Possibly."

"Do you know where he lives?" Sam asked.

"He has no definite address, but I have heard he has a camp in the Old Fangak County."

"Please find her," Nyanath pleaded with Sam and Alexi as she clutched Alexi's arm. He tapped it lightly.

"We plan to."

As they walked away Alexi asked with a grin: "What did you tell the kid?"

Sam smirked: "I told him I would tell his mother of his gambling problem. He talked quickly," and the men chuckled.

Back in the jeep they studied the map once again. The county started near their location. It was an immense watery zone with endless possibilities. There was only one airstrip, but too short for the Hercules. Determined to find a way, Sam studied the map. She could be anywhere in the vastness.

When the sun tinted the earth, they parked the jeep between thick bushes. Clouds gathered as if in a hurry and brought on a gust of wind. A welcomed relief from the constant heat.

They took the time to eat from their rations and changed to military issued clothing. Ideal for the swamp. Their gear was ready to carry, and the weapons concealed, but within reach.

The landscape changed from barren ground to grass fields. As they followed an overgrown path they observed the area. Armed patrols covered the canals with brief intervals of reeds. It expanded over the water like a grass carpet. They kept in an eastern direction, each step determined to find their mark, staying in the shadows of trees and bushes the landscape provided. They could not afford to be captured by anyone. A woman's life was at stake.

4 August 2019, Fangak County.

"HOW IS SHE?" SINCE SHE COLLAPSED Tau hovered inside the tent with no rest.

"Not good, she has a high fever. I am doing everything she taught me, but nothing seems to work." Malaria reports kept Isaac busy, and they were at a loss. Two women already died.

"She needs medication," the assistant said. A young woman that recently started to help in the tent.

Tau walked straight to the back of the store to Roger's office. He knocked and opened without waiting. Roger had a girl on his lap, his face buried between her breasts.

"When will the next shipment of medical supplies be here?" he demanded. Roger studied him for a while. Softly he instructed the girl to leave. With relief she jumped from his lap and dressed shyly. All the while Roger checked her with a grin.

"She is a sweet thing," he said more to himself.

The door closed. "You must get one for yourself, Tau. Your attention with the white woman is embarrassing and people are talking."

"I have no intention to help myself with a little sweetness while I know Sonia is fighting for her life. She saved your woman's life who is still fighting for her own life. And this is how you repay Sonia and take care of Baaka?" His anger pitched; his foul mood did not help. His life was his business. Let them talk. He was not ashamed of his feelings for Sonia.

"Yes, she did, and I have needs. Baaka will understand." He rose and buttoned the shirt, his face without emotion as he ridiculed him: "You are not exempt from discipline, Tau. Next time you step out of line I will punish you," his black eyes hard and Tau nodded.

Roger opened the door and stepped into the pouring rain. Then he turned and replied: "She will have her medicine by nightfall."

"She will not make it by nightfall." Tau raised his voice in frustration. Roger lifted a brow, clicked his tongue and met the girl. Drenched to the bone she stood unmoveable with eyes down cast.

Tau' s hands clenched in fists. He felt sorry for her, but to stop Roger now was similar to signing his death certificate.

Roger took her hand and disappeared into a newly erected hut nearby. He clenched his jaw in a tight line. Dammit, when will he learn?

42

Iraqi desert.

CAPTAIN BOGART WAS CLEARING her table when Anna asked to leave on her tea break. She agreed and forgot about her. At the end of the day she did one final round before she left.

She inspected each bed meticulously, then stopped at the last one, closed off and frowned. She could not remember a patient in this bed and opened the curtain, just to stop.

Anna was in the troughs of passion, her clothes discarded on the floor and bed. Brock noticed her, lifted his head and passed her a kiss. Shocked she closed the curtain and heard him chuckle. She blushed slightly. With trembling fingers she arranged her hair, a trick she had learned as a young child when she was nervous. Composed once more, she returned to her desk. It was not her problem anymore. The work in London at a local hospital would do simply fine. Her dedication left her with no time for frolicking as she continued her last tasks. When they appeared twenty minutes later, she was still busy with the reports.

Without knocking Staff Sergeant Castledale walked into her office and stopped inches from her. His company raised her pulse as he whispered: "How about it, Captain … wanna try?"

She looked past him to Anna, who helped a soldier with water and then back at him.

"I will report you," she hissed, and he grinned.

"I don't think so, otherwise you would have done it by now." He raised a brow, the confident smirk never leaving his lips.

"I can show you what you are missing out on Captain," and he grinned.

"No thanks."

"Yeah right, Captain, whatever you say," and left the medics. Shaking she sat back and touched her blushed neck. The audacity of the man riled her insides, anger and desire playing havoc in her mind. She pushed it aside and continued with her work.

"I will be gone tomorrow. This is not my fight any longer," she said out loud, gave the office a once over and locked the office for the last time. At the main office she handed her keys in and scurried to her room.

In her mid-forties she still had an excellent figure because of a rigid exercise program, a body she was proud of. In her room she was about to push it closed when it got stuck. When she turned her heart thudded.

"What are you doing here?" she asked, confused.

"I think you know perfectly well," came the voice as he held her throat and pushed the door closed. Like a doll he handled her with skill while her face disappeared into the pillow. She had no defence except to play along.

The next morning Captain Bogart got in the jeep with discomfort. No one cared to ask either. In her normal tolerant manner she simply bore the pain and stepped into the airplane. Hidden underneath the neat uniform of her profession bruises covered her entire body.

Blood had streamed down her as she showered that morning. She had taken a handful of pain pills just to walk. The sergeant never allowed her to sleep and did things she thought were not possible. The violation was so barbaric she would not talk about it, an experience never to be repeated. Captain Bogart already forgotten to staff, soldiers and mostly to her assailant.

HE SIGHED WITH CONTENTMENT. The nurse was better than he hoped. The stern exterior shielded her wild side. Her continuous screams ignited a passion as he buried himself in her. Even her mouth was a perfect climax. She took everything he did to her and more. All the while she kept quiet and followed his instructions to the letter. The skinny woman was a genuine treat. It was a pity he just learned about it. If only his father could watch. He would have loved it.

But, he would find a replacement. For now, Anna would do.

43

AT A VILLAGE THEY SEIZED a dock and waded through the waterways soundlessly. The dense reeds added to the difficulty, and by now the rain was a steady sheet that obscured the world. Forced to stop, Alexi climbed a tree to consider their options. At each village they scanned for any anomalies, but found none. The canals were confusing, the reduced daylight an added obstacle. Their younger self would have found her by now. This frustrated both specialists. To admit that they were getting old, was close to blasphemy.

Sam wiped his face before he examined the map. The gentle bob did not help a tired man either—fatigue added to their discomfort. Soaking wet coldness crept into their bones, Sam's knee tight as he popped a tablet, and Alexi's back pain increased in intensity. To complain would not help their cause as they sailed deeper into the swamp.

Tomorrow morning at 07h00 the Hercules would land; wait five minutes and leave. That was the arrangement. They had no time to waste.

Silently they continued. Not knowing where she was, added stress to find the nurse, Sonia Main. During a long stretch on the water, a brief respite in the downpour cleared the clouds. Just enough to see smoke curling into the darkened sky close by and they grinned. A fair number of trees dead ahead.

"It might protect a camp," Sam said as he lowered the binoculars.

"Let's bank there." Alexi pinpointed a spot. With brute force they moved the dock till it bumped against soft leaves. Sam got out and scoped the place once again through the binoculars. A burned building showed no life and shifted the binoculars to the left. Luck smiled on them when they saw an armed man dashing towards a shabby hut. Sam nodded to Alexi, directing his attention to it.

Following the canal around the small island a two-meter fence rose. It was a sign that they were onto something. The other villages were approachable, unlike this one, which was fenced. Immediately it alerted them and with greater caution approached the bigger island. There was no need for these drastic measurements so far away from civilization both thought.

By now more rain poured down and drenched the earth as they watched the camp—the rain an excellent cover and moved closer. Puddles soaked their stiff bodies further as it added more benefits to their camouflage, but thought nothing of it. Locked on their target time did not give them the lenience to grumble.

This late in the evening the men walked about without purpose. Sounds of children filtered through the downpour well hidden from view. Then they noticed a burned-out truck and a pile of debris closer to the swamp—evidence of a recent raid. On their right was a ragged tent. At the opening a man took a pull from his cigarette. He did not look like a soldier, no weapon in sight. His clothing sagged on him but was neat. The tent was the perfect place to enter and eliminate if need be.

They crawled closer and once certain all was clear, cut the fence with a multi-tool big enough to squeeze through. With hand signs they communicated the next step, then split. Years of working together allowed no explanation between the pair. Each knew what to do and trusted each other extremely.

Sam crawled towards a mud construction where two men played cards. Outside the door a bald man's voice pitched above the downpour. Another had a woman close to him. He was shorter, but his poise evident of his leadership. Could it be the man Matron Haleema and her husband feared? Sam had no way of knowing, but that did not stop to scope the landscape with eagle sight. Every part ingrained in his mind to use when needed.

IN THE MEANTIME ALEXI moved closer to the tent. A stretcher stood at the side. From his vantage point he saw a woman at the fire with two men standing close, their attention fixed on a person further back. He moved silently between a lonely tree, and crate and disappeared behind the tent. The narrow path allowed no room for errors, the blackness of the water ominous so close to the edge.

Through the flaps he had an unobstructed view inside. The man had not moved from his spot, but rubbed his eyes never less. Could he be a medical aid? Alexi wondered. This far from town no doctor would be available.

He counted six beds; all of which occupied. A moan on his right directed his gaze to the sound. A white hand flopped from the bed just behind the closest bed. He grinned. Bingo! He tapped on the throat radio. Seconds later the tap returned. Operation Gazelle was in full swing.

Alexi shuffled around the canvas until he was in line with the bed and crouched. His back stung with the movement and gritted his teeth as he peeked underneath the flaps and waited. Just then the aid stopped at her bed and left moments later. Instruments obscured his view to the rest of the tent. He moved closer, listened. Once certain he was alone, he lifted himself. The sleeping face of Sonia Main rose from the mattress. Pale looking and covered with sweat, he sighed. She was sick, which meant he had to carry her.

"Help me through this, Lord." he whispered. Not one to complain often, this was a tough request.

He scanned the interior once more. With eyes on the aid, he wrapped her in the blanket. She moaned, her breath warm against his cheek. He waited for her to calm, then whispered: "I am a friend. Just relax."

She smiled, an excellent sign that she understood what was happening. Her feverish eyes met his stare.

"We are taking you home," he said. She then moved deeper into his arms. His back acted up, but he forced himself to focus and moved slowly towards the same point he entered and left.

Meanwhile Sam continued with their escape plan. Through an opening he saw a boat with an engine they could use. Satisfied with his find, he placed his gear inside and undo the ropes. He then pushed the boat closer to where he estimated Alexi's appearance would be. His knee screamed with agony, but he ignored it.

Satisfied he went back, stopped, and saw another boat with an engine closer to a plastic hut. This time, armed with his knife, he stayed between the barriers as he watched. Two armed men were deep in discussion, their backs turned to him. Sam moved between the two. With precision slit their throats without a sound and covered the feet with a discarded tarp. With the same knife, he slashed the engine.

Back at the hut baldy stood with clenched fists. The other was not in sight. Next to him a diesel drum gave him an idea. He waited till the man disappeared around the hut and created a wick with an oily rag which he pushed in the drum's opening, giving himself enough time to get away. He lit it and ran back to the boat, hopped in and turned the key. The start-up broke the silence as he roared forward, just in time to meet Alexi with his load. Alexi got in and groaned in agony, but at least they had the nurse.

They sped away as the drum exploded.

44

TAU STOPPED IN HIS TRACKS when he heard the explosion. Scanning the area, he heard the engine and saw the boat as it disappeared into the veil of rain. The hut was on fire, its tongue licking the handmade hut hungrily. He called the two card-playing men and ordered them to extinguish it.

Roger came from his hut, disorientated and half-clothed. Chaos broke out as another gas bottle burst into flames. Women and children came out screaming, but Tau ran to the medic tent. Isaac ran outside, dumbfounded. He passed him without a word. His pounding heart thudded against his chest when he looked at Sonia's bed. She was no longer there. Relief and hurt stabbed his heart. At her empty bed he touched the impression her body made, the outside world forgotten. When a tent flap caught fire close to him, he rushed outside. His will to save the tent gone.

Roger shouted to get the other boat, but Tau shook his head. His reason for living gone.

"Where is the nurse?"

"Gone." He had lost his will to fight.

"Get her!" Like a berserker, Roger ran towards him, his naked torso gleaming in the fire's light. The flames devouring what was still left. Soon they would have nothing. Not even the rain could douse it. The finality of the end of their reign left him tired.

"No, Roger," he yelled back. "Let her go!" His voice sounded hoarse and final, as if he expected this very thing to happen.

She could never stay. It was a knowing that was born after her assault. She would never belong. Not here.

"But we need her!" Roger spouted in anger.

"No Roger, we will be okay!"

"No, dammit! She could show them where we are. Get the damn boat!" he hollered and grabbed Tau, then shook him. Tau held his hands.

The two estranged friends viewed each other with indifference. "The boat's engine is slashed, Roger."

"Fix it!" Haji barked, cursing irately. Whoever took her, was professional. They stood no change.

Crazed, Roger demanded to fix the engine. Thirty minutes later they followed the canal at top speed.

SAM OPENED THE THROTTLE as far as possible, veering through the water. The speed was not enough, but at least they got distance between them and the militia. Alexi clutched the frail body to him with one hand while holding on to the frame of the boat with the other. They kept it up for another hour before Sam eventually slowed enough for Alexi to lose his grip. Sonia stared at him and asked through a parched throat: "Who are you?"

"The Calvary, Ma'am," and he gave her a lopsided grin. She smiled and coughed.

"Water," she rasped. He grabbed a bottle and offered her the drink. When done, she greeted Sam. He nodded a greeting briefly before he turned his focus back to the swamp.

"Thank you! Both of you!" she mumbled. Every muscle ached, but she sat. Alexi covered her and then picked up their weapons.

"Are you thinking what I am thinking?"

"She is a mighty fine lass," Sam acknowledged. "Yep, that she is."

"Our CO is in love with her," Alexi said matter-of-factly.

"He has excellent taste."

"Yep." Both men scanned the area constantly.

"We need to stop!" Sam yelled and looked at the gauge.

"Yes!" Alexi shouted back and moments later the boat came to a slow stop, mooring next to a steep slope where Alexi jumped out. Catching the rope he pulled them closer and helped Sam with Sonia, who had passed out.

Landing on his feet, Sam's face contorted with pain. "Bummer," he muttered and hopped on his foot. Lying her down he stretched the leg.

"You okay?"

"Yeah," he answered and popped two pain pills. He then grabbed a bottle of water and reached for Sonia.

"Sonia, you need to drink water."

She moaned softly. Opening her eyes, he helped her to get water in before she fell back in a trance.

"What do you think?" Sam asked.

"Malaria," came the soft reply, and Alexi walked to the side of the swamp and relieved himself.

"Ready to go?"

"Yeah," and Sam helped Sonia to stand.

Up ahead, the small plane was ready to leave. It was with pure luck that they found the airstrip and arranged for help. The pilot understood what they needed, but was only willing to help until they offered some payment—a good pair of shoes and a flask of brandy the currency. On their approach the pilot started the engine. Time became an enormous factor as they jumped in, with Sonia dangling between them.

They greeted the Sudanese pilot with a quick, "*Salam alaikum*," and minutes later lifted into the air. They watched the swamp getting smaller, honing out the pain they experienced. With no radio contact they could only hope everything would be in favour once they land. Sam had to have dozed off, because the bluest sky was waking him. The height was nauseating, and he closed his eyes.

"Breathe Sam, we are on mother earth soon," Alexi said.

"Yeah, yeah." He hated to fly. Always did.

"How is she?"

"Restless. She needs medical help. She is burning."

Sam swallowed his own thick bile and took a huge gulp of water. Hunger, thirst and tiredness took their toll on him. The pilot silence freaked him out. By 05h00 the sky had cleared and a landing strip was in sight. The pilot spoke to air control and received the okay to land. The sun showed its colours when they touched the bumpy airstrip.

"Ma'a Salama," they greeted the pilot. With just a glimmer of a grin he greeted them. The flask held high. Close by a jeep waited—inside a key was hanging from the ignition.

"Just hang on a sec," Alexi said as he laid Sonia on the back seat. "I need to go."

"You and your small bladder," Sam teased, checking their human cargo. The woman was pale and burning and tried to get water in her. With a cough drops of water dribbled in her mouth, and she moaned slightly.

"We will be home soon, Miss," he explained, and she nodded sleepily. Alexi returned with two steaming cups of coffee.

"Where the hell did you get this?" Sam smiled and took a cup.

"The good fairy," Alexi replied with a wink. "Let us go, time is ticking."

"All aboard." Sam raced out of the small airport and reached the gravel road in no time.

"This is life," Alexi said and cheered the daybreak with his cup. Sam looked at his watch. They had an hour to make it to the airfield in Rubkona.

Stepping on the accelerator Alexi grabbed the framework. The rest of the road was done in tensed silence.

At one point Alexi turned to look at Sonia, but saw something else. "Movement!" he yelled.

Sam looked in the side mirror and sped up once more. The engine kicked into overdrive and they raced along the gravel road. Even though the muddy terrain made it difficult, Sam kept his foot on the pedal. Every fifteen minutes Alexi checked the followers. They did not gain on the gap between them, but they remained behind them. Alexi kept a close watch on the jeep and their charge.

Checking his watch they still had minutes left. Not much, they would make it with seconds to spare, Sam thought. All looked quietly at the forefront. He could only hope it would stay like that.

Ever alert, Alexi positioned himself with his trusted AK47. The followers got closer, but he waited patiently for a clear shot—his mark in the crosshairs, ready to defend when needed.

Sam darted through a series of potholes, screaming: "Hold on!" and Alexi fell backward. Sam swerved, the wheel struck a rock and they flew into the air. Landing on all fours, Sam gunned the accelerator once back on the road.

Again Alexi positioned himself when a bullet slammed in the back of the jeep. Another bullet hit the jeep's body.

"Get us out of here!" Alexi shouted as he aimed for the car's front tire and shoot. The jeep swerved and struck the same rock. The jeep landed on two wheels, balancing for seconds before it landed on all fours. That gave them enough time to gain distance.

With the increased activity on the road they had to slow. Donkey carts were taking up half of the road. Once they passed the people, they continued. When Alexi saw the other jeep once again, he warned Sam. This time it was closer.

Alexi readied himself.

45

SONIA STARED AT THE BLOND MAN. Her muddled mind was grateful for the two that did their best to get her to safety. She winced when they became airborne and fell on the hard bench. The backseat not built for comfort. While awake she prayed fervently for their escape. She thought about Tau and what they shared.

"Thanks for your protection, dear Tau," she whispered. A tear found its way into the blanket.

"Thank you, Lord. Thank you for getting us out." Then she smiled slowly. Just when she thought all hope was gone, hope arrived in two men and she trusted them with her life.

The man with the rifle once again checked his watch.

"Speed up. We are running out of time!" She closed her eyes and just rolled with the jeep's movement, holding on to the seat.

Then, through the chase, she heard another sound, a faint roar, and the jeep responded with speed. They passed a building, the road became smoother. The blond man aimed and fired. This time she heard nothing. The roaring sound deafened everything else.

SAM SAW THE HERCULES at the far end of the runway, its motors roaring. He rushed past the sink hangers and a smaller airplane. A man's show of hand signals compelled him to slow, but he ignored them.

They had to be aboard the moment the bird lifted. He aligned the jeep with the plane's hatch as Alexi once again fired shots towards their pursuers. One man held an SAM7 on his shoulders, the Hercules only meters away. It was touch and go, and he smirked as he fired a shot. The man stumbled backwards and the SAM7 missile sailed harmlessly over them into the air. It landed on the left side of the plane's wheels. When the plane bumped up and roared forward, both men breathed in relief.

The powerful engines were ear-splitting as they came closer, and with determined will power between man, jeep and plane, the front wheels touched the ramp just as the front wheels of the plane lifted.

With added acceleration Sam sped into the plane and stopped just as the hatch closed behind them. Hooks grabbed the wheels during the climb. When the jeep's wheels locked into place, they relaxed. The flight coordinator grinned as the front bars of the jeep touched his trousers.

"That was a good run!" Sam exclaimed, and Alexi grinned and turned. Sonia Main stared back at them. Her smile included every part of her face. With an effort she looked back at the closed hatch.

"Welcome aboard, Ma'am!" the flight operator yelled, and she smiled.

"Thank you, all of you," she said and touched each man's arm briefly.

"You are welcome," he said.

She looked at his chest. LT Price revealed on the ensign and she met his gaze. "Please call me Sonia," she said whilst brushing sweat from her brow.

"What is wrong?" he asked with concern.

"Malaria," she answered.

"When was the last time you had Quinine, Sonia?" Lt Price asked.

She counted the days and hours before she answered, "Yesterday morning."

"Any other drug?"

"No, that was all they had available," she replied.

"I have an emergency case upfront. I will be back in a jiff."

"Thank you, Lieutenant." She leaned back against the hard pad. Relief and gratefulness overshadowed all else.

"Let me help you on a stretcher, Sonia," Sam got out of the jeep, covering his own pain from her.

"Thank you." Her body was trembling with fever and tiredness.

"Here is water," Alexi joined.

"What are your names?" she asked.

"I am Alexi, and our chauffeur is Sam," Alexi replied and both grinned.

She stretched and greeted them with a soft smile. "I thought everyone had forgotten me?"

"No," they both stated, "but are you okay, I mean?" Sam asked uncomfortably.

Sonia replied softly. "There were times that I feared for my life, but it's over." Her drawn look said more than her words.

Both men looked at each other. Worried lines appeared, but they kept quiet. They had seen the bruises on her face. It looked recent. No doubt they had beaten her.

46

Fangak County.

IT WAS LATE AFTERNOON WHEN they finally walked into the camp. Tau left a seething Roger behind. He had no strength left. The plane stripped him of a dream. A brief spell before it disappeared into the blue sky. Numb he stared before him. Words turned to bile which burnt his mouth, and when they stopped he spewed it out.

In his heart he knew she was better off amongst her own people. Her assumption about them correct, they did not fit—their worlds too far apart. No matter what he would have done, it would not be enough.

The way things played out, her survival was dim. Her vulnerability was her biggest flaw. Although gone she left hope behind, imparted knowledge which they could use. They were better off. It was a short-lived relationship that gave him a glimpse of what love was.

Roger's rage did not help matters. His cursing marathon riled him.

"You owe me!" he yelled when they got in the boat. Tau ignored him. His loss was greater than Roger's pettiness.

At the camp reality demanded answers from everyone. The camp's state dismal and their future bleak. Roger's arm needed attention and Isaac dealt with it. For now he was their best medical aid. One shot had hit the leader with the last round, and his arm was in a sling. Blood covered his right side.

At their hut her few belongings were neatly stacked. The bed unmade, her fragrance lingered in the air. Her brush and spray laid on the small table with a handheld mirror, next to it a hair clip.

With the Bible open he read the scripture.

PSALM 23.

The LORD is my shepherd; I shall not want.

2. He maketh me to lie down in green pastures: he leadeth me beside the still waters.

3. He restoreth my soul: he leadeth me in the paths of righteousness for his name's sake.

4. Yea, though I walk through the valley of the shadow of death, I will fear no evil: for thou art with me; thy rod and thy staff they comfort me.

5. Thou preparest a table before me in the presence of mine enemies: thou anointest my head with oil; my cup runneth over.

6. Surely goodness and mercy shall follow me all the days of my life: and I will dwell in the house of the LORD forever.

He bowed, allowing the words to become part of him. Her God promised her safety from them, and He did.

"I will miss you, Sonia Main Gbadamosi." One lonely teardrop appeared, it softened the scarred face. At her meagre clothes he picked up another scarf she wore in her hair, wrapped it around the Bible and concealed it.

Tau watched the surrounding commotion as people tried to clean the campsite; others made fires.

A small hand touched his arm: Fiza. They were the only people who would miss her.

The bond a precious commodity.

PART THREE

LOVE'S

BETRAYAL.

47

5 August 2019, Iraqi desert.

DOUG RUSHED INTO MCGEE'S QUARTERS, an A4 envelope clutched under his arm.

Curt had poured himself an ice-cold drink from his own stash, ready for a break.

"Good news, Sir," he said. "Operation Gazelle has just lifted from the runway. The Gazelle will land in six hours."

The crease between Curt's eyes melted and relaxed the mouth.

"A letter has come for you."

"Thanks, Doug, it's splendid news."

"Yes, Sir."

"How is Gazelle?"

"She has a severe fever, Sir, and..." unsure about the next piece of information he swallowed first. "She is covered with bruises and dehydrated."

Curt frowned; a flash of concern washed over him before he clamped it in the bud. "Alert the medics," he ordered.

"Yes, Sir," relieved. "Will that be all, Sir?"

"You may go, Doug." Curt's shoulders relaxed as a slight smile appeared. He laid back in the chair and thanked the Lord for Sonia's rescue. For a few moments he basked in this before realisation slapped him in the gut. You are a fool; he chastised himself. You should not have brought her here. Look what you have created.

All his worries came alive at once. Though grateful for her safety, it created a new set of problems. Phillip warned him. To get distance would be difficult. He was a married man. No matter how he argued about this, he could not love her. He would have to avoid her at all costs. She must not know about him. He would hurt her.

God, he is an idiot.

"Lord, you are asking too much. Why did you allow me to meet her if I cannot love her? How can it be wrong?" He rubbed his face and felt the wetness. A wetness that left him more vulnerable than he would like. *"Lord, help me stay strong."*

To side-track his thoughts, he opened the envelope. A flashback struck him from a similar envelope which brought on his turmoil. Taking a lengthy breath he let the contents fell on the table. More photos. He cringed in pain and betrayal.

"The woman had no shame, Lord" Ten photos displayed Vivian's affair in all its twisted evilness—this time with another man.

He slumped to his knees. His fifty-six-year frame had changed into seventy-six years. The weight was so enormous that even breathing became difficult. Taking a few deep breaths he reached for the phone.

After five rings she answered, breathless as if she had run or ... He stopped his thoughts mid-stream and pinched his burning eyes.

"Hi, Sweetie." Her voice dripped with honey.

"Why Vivian?" He got out through a dried throat.

"Why what, Love?" Bile rising from the deep he tried to swallow, but it was useless and darted outside. When he returned he heard her breathing.

"Why are you doing this?" Silence met him.

"Did you receive another set?"

"Yes, Vivian." Hurt, betrayal, tiredness and anger balled together, and he quietly asked: "Do you have no shame?" Curt rubbed his head. "How much longer are you going to keep me in this ruse of marriage you are not respecting!" His voice raised with two decibels before he stopped.

She giggled. "But, darling!" She started, but he stopped her mid-sentence.

"Don't darling me, Vivian! SIGN. THE. DAMN. PAPERS!"

"You cannot boss me around like this. I still have use of your name," she said bluntly, this time with venom.

"What use could you possibly have with my name, you dragged through the mud?"

"Business, darling. Everyone loves a war hero, and it opens doors for me. Especially with the bad markets, house prices booming, and fewer people who can afford it."

"You sign the papers, Vivian. I don't want to be associated with you anymore," he shouted red in the face.

"And I said—when I am good and ready." She was silent for a while. "Neil says hi." She giggled as he disconnected.

His confusion wavered. A scripture came to mind: **Proverbs 3:5** "Trust in the LORD with all your heart and do not lean on your own understanding."

"How much must I endure before it will cause a helpful outcome?"

'Until peace becomes one with you,' came the quick reply.

"I have told you these things, so that in me you may have peace. In this world, you will have trouble. But take heart! I have overcome the world." **John 16:33**.

"I trust your word; I will walk in your peace. Please forgive my confusion. Thanks for teaching me. I forgive Vivian and set her free. Your will be done." his heaviness lifted and with clarity he prayed: *"give me wisdom with Sonia and heal her, Lord."*

AT 13H00 HOURS THE HERCULES approached the runway and Colonel McGee waited in his jeep. The medic van stood at the tarmac. Nurse Stalin assured him she informed the staff of the nurse's situation.

From the open hatch Sam and Alexi appeared first. Their tired faces revealed the weight of their involvement; a full report would be on his desk.

The medics vanished in the plane's hull. As one they appeared with an occupied stretcher, the figure covered with a blanket. Curly hair fluttered in the breeze; his heart skipped.

Sam and Alexi approached him and saluted him. When he nodded, Alexi pulled a piece of material from a pocket.

"This is hers, Sir, if you will not mind giving it to her?" he said, his voice strained.

"Thank you, Alexi." He remained robotic. That scarf represented facades of beauty in Techni colours—of a time he had indulged in love and happiness—a time best forgotten.

"How is she?"

"Shaken up, sick, but good considering the circumstances, Sir. She is one strong woman." Sam answered. "Not one complaint all the time. She sure is pretty." For that he got an elbow in the ribs.

Curt's sharp look caused Sam to chuckle, undisturbed at the commander's obvious warning.

"I understand she is single. I will get better acquainted," he teased, and Curt's jaw clenched. "if she stays. She can treat me every day."

385

Alexi bumped him and rolled his eyes. Curt saw this interaction from the shadows of his hat. The bait a tempting morsel, but snubbed the urge to punch him with restraint.

Alexi gave Sam another pump in the ribs. His gaze was a simple message that Curt caught. "Stop that, it's enough!"

But Sam grinned. With mischief written across the face, he shrugged: "Don't you want to do this old soldier a favour, Sir, and let her stay?"

"If she stays it will not be because of you, Sam. I want a full report this afternoon," he said in a hoarse tone.

"Yes, Sir."

"Come, Sam," Alexi motioned and they greeted him.

"WHAT IS WRONG WITH YOU?" Alexi chided Sam, but he chuckled: "Oh, come on man, the man is smitten. Anyone with eyes can see that."

"It's not for you to joke about. He is a married man."

"What does it have to do with anything?" Sam shrugged his shoulders. "Married or not, his wife will not know."

"But God will now leave it."

"You and your God," he humph as he marched to his tent. He could not understand the changes with Alexi. In the past the man had no problems with sleeping around. It became a sport between them. They scratched when the itch became uncontrollable. However, since he came back eighteen months ago, the changes in his friend irked him. They were still partners and Alexi laughed at his shenanigans, but the moment he wanted to have fun, Alexi became bottled up. He had found God. His friend, who never believed in anything except his sniper rifle and the military, was now religious. What was the world coming to?

CURT CONTEMPLATED THE WISDOM TO VISIT SONIA. Standing in the shadows of a truck, he arrived at the medics just before lunch. It shielded him enough from any scrutiny. Ready to move to the door, Doctor Armand Jourdain opened and closed the door behind him, right into the arms of a soldier. The soldier had arrived minutes ago; his back turned to him. He did not give him much thought until now. Their tight embrace told more than he cared to know. What angered him was the doctor's disrespect towards his marital vows. With two kids and the third on its way, Curt shook his head. This part of camp life he never condoned. They walked away hand in hand. He will have to ask Doug about the affair; the man was a walking information desk.

He returned his gaze to the building where Sonia had to be comfortable by now. They delivered her documents that morning. At forty-four she met the requirements involved for the position of head nurse. She was the perfect replacement for Bogart.

Would she accept the position?

In the last two hours he relived their time in Valletta. He prayed to the Lord for strength, to forget, but every time he wanted to leave the shadows, his resolve broke. He would be no better than the doctor.

Earlier the day he strolled through the quiet camp. Teams on reconnaissance left the place peaceful. The dust had settled and the camp was extra quiet. Those on guard duty stared out their appointed sectors, alert as they acknowledged him.

With a last thought Curt entered the medical building.

"Good afternoon, Colonel." Peter Blake greeted him, a nurse from England he didn't know very well, and Nurse Stalin approached him with a soft smile. Until the replacement she oversaw the division.

"Everything all right, Nurse?" he asked more out of politeness as his eyes glanced over the beds.

"Yes, Sir," she replied. "How can I help you, Sir?"

"How is the woman doing?"

"She is sleeping, Sir. Do you want to see her?"

"Just for a moment. I want to leave these papers with her."

"Her bed is over there, Sir." She pointed to an enclosed bed five beds down the aisle. His heart hammered in its chest and he prayed for peace. He had a job to do, nothing more, he told himself. His blank face not showing his inner turmoil, he rushed to the bed.

"If you need me, Sir, I will be at my desk," Anna mumbled.

"Thank you, Nurse." For a few minutes Curt allowed him time to gather himself, then pushed the curtain aside. His gaze locked on the deep brown locks that spread the cushion, locks he enjoyed in the throes of passion. Then he stopped at the bruised face; his heart sank, sorrow filled him and he gulped the guilt away. What did they do to her? He clenched his fists.

On her return from their weekend they abducted her—three months of pure hell while he … How did she survive? She had lost weight, her skin dry and pale. He could see no other bruises, but what about the inner scars? How did they treat her? What did they do with her? Those scars would not be visible—scars she had to deal with alone.

She moved in her sleep. One hand brushed a strand of curls away and he followed the motion hungrily. Her eyes fluttered open and he turned to leave, but stopped when he heard her.

"Curt love, I have missed you," she whispered with a womanly smile on her pale lips. He froze at her confession. A slow smile softened the hard exterior. He lowered and a soapy fragrance floated to him. He closed his eyes and let his lips linger against hers, then straightened. With one last glance at the sleeping figure, he left.

"Please give this to Nurse Main," he said the moment he reached Anna and marched out into the late desert heat— his back rigid, his face blank, but his heart in chaos.

At his quarters he knelt. He had no words to offer except to humble himself before his Creator. He drifted back to the confession she made. He would cherish it.

By the time he got back on his feet, the sun was already showing its face. Too late to sleep, he showered and left for work, peace radiated from him.

48

7 August 2019.

OPERATION GRAY MOSQUITO played a big part in Staff Sergeant Brock Castledale's life. Not because of the operation, or the dead men, but for the woman he met. Her sparkling green eyes and red hair enchanted him.

The relationship with Anna was over. Earlier he demanded his normal fix which resulted in him having his way. Ultimately it also caused the breakup. He had enough of her come-ons just to stop midway. Now she was pulling at his arms as tears messed up her mascara.

"Will you shut up about this!" He stretched his height and pulled on his clothing.

"Please do not go, Brock!"

"I had enough." He shook her like a rag doll. Opening the door he did not give her a second look. He was sick of her games. She simply could not make up her mind about sex. She knew what he liked and the way he liked it. He would not change—for no one. Why this constant refusal he did not understand, but he had enough.

ANNA'S HEART SHATTERED; her love choked the life out of the relationship. Once the door closed, she fell in a heap.

You are pitiful. You deserve this. You act like a cheap bimbo, she loathed herself.

Her love for this man made her blind, but she could not commit to the sickness any longer.

All she wanted was to be in a normal, romantic love relationship where the hero would whisk her away and treat her like a princess. He would make love to her and adore her. Not like this.

Brock was not that man.

ON THE WAY BACK TO BASE CAMP, CASTLEDALE looked closely to his travel buddies. It was then that he noticed the pair of light green eyes again. The soldier's helmet moved back and revealed a redhead. She smiled at him and he returned the gesture. Her name tag revealed her identity. He grinned. Corporal Ellis.

That afternoon he laid eyes on her at the bush pub; and that night he introduced himself in the only way he was comfortable with.

At the tearoom she brushed against him. Mischievous eyes chuckled at his delight. His body reacted, his heart jumped and watched her interaction with every man. For the first time in his life jealousy tucked at his heart and clenched his jaw tight. The emotions so foreign to him he did not understand it.

Later she sauntered to the lady's room and he followed. When she stepped out he grabbed her hand and made way for the exit, his need and want fuelled by his emotions.

He was not even aware that she did not put up a fight. She had her sights on him for a long time. The glee of victory coursed through her when she followed him. Outside he pushed her into the wall.

"How did I miss you?" She was the most delicious thing he had ever seen.

"What is the matter, Staff Sergeant?" Her light green eyes twinkled.

"You have neglected your duties," he said in a seductive tone.

"And what duties will that be, Staff Sergeant?"

"To please your staff sergeant." He pushed his body into hers, the message clear.

She smiled. "How can I please you?" She batted her whimpers and he grinned. Lowering himself he whispered his requirements to her.

She did not flinch or shrieked in fear. She encouraged it. Taking his hand she brought it to her mouth. Her eyes teased him as the first digit vanished in her mouth.

"Your wish is my command, Sir," and he chuckled. She was beautiful.

"I know a place close by," he whispered, his body strained against the confines of his khaki.

"I know the place, Staff Sergeant."

He grinned and captured her mouth as a starved man. She melted against him. It was in those moments he lost his heart.

ANNA GREETED ELLIS ABSENTLY THE NEXT
MORNING. Her attention was not on her work. She still
punished herself for being so clinging, but she missed
him. Though the relationship was not at all what she
envisioned, she struggled to move on. Was she foolish to
walk away? Her thoughts in a jumble about the breakup
and abuse. Her brain told her it was the right thing to do,
but her heart protested. She had to focus on her work,
turning her attention to the taller woman.

"Is everything well?" Anna asked the redhead. It was
time for Ellis's physical, and it was part of Anna's duties.
She took her weight and referred to the chart. "You had
lost weight."

"Yes, Nurse." The corporal flinched as she touched her
arm.

"What is the matter with your arm?"

"Nothing a workout would not fix, Ma'am."

"Please remove your clothing," Anna commanded and
gasped at the bruises on her. She turned her and noticed
the bruises extended to her chest and neck as if squeezed
tightly.

"Were you in combat?

"Sure, was Ma'am. I sure am going to repeat the combat
soon."

"Do you need pain killers?"

"No, Ma'am. I have some with me if it gets unbearable."

"Please look after yourself. You are still a woman," Anna reminded her with concern.

"Yes Ma'am, but I like to play with the boys." She grinned. "To get hurt is expected. It's all part of the game."

"Just remember to look after yourself. Don't take unnecessary risks."

Anna studied her thoughtfully. The bruises looked familiar, as if she had seen them before. At Anna's desk Ellis replied: "Yes, Ma'am."

Anna noted everything in her file.

"We good?" Ellis asked.

"Be careful out there," Anna advised.

Staff Sergeant Castledale appeared in the entrance and she smiled brightly. But his attention was not on her, but with Ellis. It left her dumbfounded. Why was he here and did he know Ellis?

He walked towards Anna and gave her a lopsided grin. "Hi there, gorgeous," he said softly, brushing her cheek with a thump. She believed him … almost. Something was off. Even Ellis looked confused before she left.

"Do you know Corporal Ellis?"

"Of course I know her, Anna," and plopped on a seat. "We work together."

"Yes, I know."

"But …"

"Please do not start with your jealousy. I am here and I came for a visit with my girl." He stopped her protest and she smirked. She did not expect to see him, not after the last fight. He almost looked normal as he used to be. When he returned her smile, her knees buckled and she took a seat.

"I see I still have the desired effect on you."

She blushed. Every time he came closer, she forgot all reason and gave him her undivided attention. He still made her knees weak, her heart fluttering with his touch. She could not help herself.

Nonetheless, the nagging thoughts lingered during the visit. He was jovial and full of playful jokes. His big hands speaking with her, but they could be brutal and then it struck her. The bruises of Corporal Ellis too familiar to forget. She had seen them before. Her own body the replica of his rough play.

Deep in thought she did her work for the rest of the day. She could not ignore the look which passed between Ellis and Brock. It was not a look of colleagues, but of lovers.

49

8 August 2019.

WHEN SONIA WOKE SHE LOOKED AROUND. Only the white walls and hospital bed gave her a clue. She had vague memories of the last couple of days - the rush to catch a plane. Medical personnel drifted in and out from view … and Curt, but it couldn't have been him.

Still weak she reached for the water and guzzled it down. Thankful for the closed curtains, she threw the white sheet from her. They bandaged her right leg, the burning sensation gone. She feared the worst when infection had set in. The rest of her body was healing, the scars lighter. She knew she had malaria, the constant fever and headaches were a giveaway.

The relief of her rescue dawned on her; tears of gratitude fell on her arm. *"I bless your name, Lord. Wherever this is, I am glad you rescued me."*

The curtains moved and a strong deep voice asked: "Can we come for a visit?"

Apprehensive she covered herself before she replied: "Yes."

Two men entered the confines, the blond with lively blue-silver eyes and the other man, darker. His face scarred, but with a beaming smile which diminished the marks. She smiled, with no idea who they were.

"My ego is hurt. The pretty lady does not remember us, Alexi," and he chuckled. The daze curtain lifted, her smile beamed. "Sam and Alexi." She breathed out. "I will never forget you two." Each man gave her a hug before they took a seat.

"You are my heroes," she said and both grinned. "But where am I?"

"You are in the desert, Ma'am," Alexi answered.

"You are not serious," she gasped. "On what continent?"

"Middle East," Sam replied, still with the grin.

"Now you have lost me." She fell back against the soft pillows. Through narrowed eyes she watched them, but both men nodded in affirmation.

"No Ma'am, you are not lost. You are in a military camp stationed in the Iraqi desert," Alexi confirmed.

Sonia was flabbergasted. "But how? I was in Africa."

"That you were, Ma'am."

She interrupted Sam. "Please call me Sonia." She waited for further explanation.

"You remember they kidnapped you?" Sam asked and she paled.

"Yes, I remember."

"Well, our CO had sent us on the rescue mission."

"Your CO is a wonderful man," she gushed with a satisfied sigh.

"He certainly is, Sonia," Sam winked. Scanning them both she could not figure out why he teased her.

"What are you not telling me?" She watched the meaningful glances between the two men.

"Oh, nothing Sonia," Alexi assured, patting her arm, and she frowned.

"How are you feeling?" Sam asked.

"Like a kidnapped, plane-lifted and sick person," and they chuckled. "Confused," she added.

"You will come along," Alexi said. "The key point is your safety."

"Yes, and I am eternally grateful to both of you, your CO and my God."

"Amen," Alexi said.

"I committed my life in Africa." Tears materialized. "The day I received a Bible, I knew God would rescue me, but it was long and challenging days. I honestly believed I was forgotten. There were times I did not know what would happen to me. My life was in constant danger. Only by God's grace did I stay hopeful, even after ..." Her voice broke and the two men looked at each other.

"I have learned valuable lessons there." She smiled. "It gave me a greater understanding of the bigger scheme of things."

"I would love to hear them," Alexi said.

"One day I will share them." She glanced away, uncomfortable and ... The next moment a blond nurse walked in with a bright smile.

"How is my patient doing, today?" Under her arm a brown envelope stuck out.

"I am well," Sonia replied, "still shaky, but feeling much better."

"I am glad to hear it. I am so jealous," she said, looking at the two men. "You had these two men's attention for a long time," and she chuckled as both men blushed.

Sam was the first to recover and winked at her. "You have that right," sending a simple message. This time Sonia turned crimson, and Alexi pumped him in the side with a scolding look.

"As I see it, once the colonel sees her, we will not have her attention anymore," Sam scoffed. Bright red Sonia looked at him, confused. What did he mean?

"Well, our CO was here last night and gave me this." Anna handed Sonia the envelope with the Red Cross logo on it.

"What is this?" Sonia asked and turned it around.

"Maybe you must look," Sam said with a mischievous smile.

A letter fell from the sheave with official documentation.

DEAR MS SONIA MAIN

Re: Request for transfer.

We congratulate you on the new position as Chief Nurse at Camp Apache, Baghdad, Iraq.

As head of this medical facility you will report to Colonel McGee as soon as your recovery allowed. But no later than 12 August 2019.

We notified Matron Haleema at Bentiu Hospital of your transfer. She will be in contact with you.

It is with heartfelt delight that we offer you the position as Head Nurse with the full assurance you will be diligent as you have done previously.

We welcome you back and hope to receive a favourable response.

Kind Regards

G Archer.

Director, Human Resource Department

Geneva, Switzerland,

The letter fluttered to the bed. Sheepishly she looked at them and Anna asked: "What did it say?"

"I am the Head Nurse. I believe right here."

"Serious?" Anna giggled. "Wait till the others find out."

"And will you accept the position?" Another voice broke the giggle fit. No one had noticed the tall man at the opening.

Anna blushed. Sam and Alexi instantly moved away, dragging Anna with them.

Sam winked at Sonia, but she hardly noticed it. She was sure her jaw just dropped. As before his presence spiked her heart before it pumped again. Curt, the man of her dreams, stepped forward and introduced himself.

"I am Colonel McGee, in charge of Camp Apache."

Is he a vision?

Is she still sleeping?

He made eye contact. Time stood still as worlds connected, the hourglass turned, and her world transformed to a multitude of colours.

"Well, what do you say?" he asked softly, and she closed her mouth.

"You!" she began and stopped. Her professional training kicked in and saluted him. "Yes Sir, I accept," her green eyes alive as she took in the military garb. He was just as handsome and rigid as she remembered him.

"Good," he regained his voice. "Your bags will arrive in two days; Matron Haleema managed it all. She sends her love. You will have time to recover and resume your duties by Monday 08h00 hours sharp."

"Yes, Sir," she answered, still stricken.

Her first impulse was to wrap her arms around him, but his formal bearing stopped her. So much had changed. She had changed, her ability to speak with confidence lost.

"I am glad you are much better, but you look tired." His concern was genuine. "I will see you again on Monday morning."

"Yes, Sir, thank you, Sir," she replied automatically and watched the receding back.

Once alone she allowed her mind to take its own flight.

"He is here," she murmured. He was quiet, which was understandable given the circumstances, but he was here. She smothered her joy in the pillow.

Her Curt, thank you Lord for bringing us together. From the small window she noticed the patches of desert, obscured mostly by military buildings. Then the distinct sound of a rotor cleaved the air before it moved away.

She sighed, rolled back and closed her eyes.

50

CURT WALKED OUT AS if the building was on fire. He saluted soldiers, but his mind was with the newly appointed head nurse. He had to forget the butterflies. The promises. All that was said and done. It could never be, he chastised himself.

"Thank you for her safe return, Lord. Thanks for your guidance. Without you this mission was impossible. I praise your name."

Doug met him on the return to the office. "How's the captain, Sir?" he asked just as they stepped into the office.

"She looks better. Jourdain said she is weak but responsive to the prescribed medicine."

"Did she accept the position, Sir?"

"Yes, she starts on Monday," he answered whilst opening a file on his desk.

THE DISMISSAL SIGNALLED DOUG TO LEAVE. The Colonel needed alone time. Ever since he had learned about the affair, he prayed for the colonel. A tough time lay ahead. The situation would be unbearable for both. Would the new nurse accept this and would they adapt? Looking at the colonel's face, he knew the man was serious about following God's promptings, but would love not change his decision? This would be a test of great endurance and faith. One that could cost him dearly.

As he stepped into the midday sun, Charlie met him. It seemed that the alone time was not to be. Her long strides and flushed face said as much.

"Yes, Private?"

"There is a call for the Colonel. It is his daughter," he sighed.

"I will tell him."

"Sir, you have a call from the States," Doug informed him. His sudden return had shocked the man. Clearly he was praying, his spiritual fight a weight only he could fight, but it would not stop him to hold his arms up in faith.

Curt left without another word.

CHARLIE SHOWED HIM WHERE to sit and his daughter's lovely face appeared on Skype.

"Hello Dad," she began with a smile which did not reach her eyes.

"Hi, Pumpkin." He steeled himself. "What's wrong?"

"Mum demands I go for an abortion." Quickly he plugged the earphones in to minimize the devastating news. Right away Doug shielded him from the staff. The corporal's action appreciated.

His daughter's gloomy face and shaking hand revealed her distress as she removed blond strands from her face. She had grown older in the few months since he had seen her. His heart pained.

"When did this happen?"

"Yesterday. She mentioned it before, but now she was adamant. She booked me for tomorrow morning," she sniffed. "Dad, I made my choice. I do not want to abort the baby. Please, what must I do?"

Immediately his mind was directed to a definite knowing. "Listen Pumpkin, I will call you back. I need to make a call; can you wait close by?"

"Yes, Dad, but what are you going to do?"

"Are you still willing to allow Ms Davies to be part of the baby's life?"

"Yes, but I don't see how this can help?"

"Just wait for my call."

"Yes, Dad." Her image disappeared. He patted his pockets, but could not find his mobile. With long strides he went to his office to make the call. On the second ring she answered.

"Ms Davies," he came to the point.

"Yes, who is this?" came the soft reply, and he introduced himself.

"Yes, Sir. How can I help?"

Curt explained the situation to her. Once they agreed to the plan of action, he greeted her, then called his lawyer.

Satisfied he returned and they connected Skype. Seconds later Jillian answered, and he explained the plan.

"Ms Davies and Norton will meet you tonight. Ms Davies wants a part parent ship for this baby and will adopt it. If needed, they will draft a contract."

"But Daddy …," she interrupted him, but he stopped her.

"No Pumpkin listen to me. You still have parental rights, but she will be the co-parent, meaning she can protect you. If Vivian pressures you, Harriet can stop it legally and Vivian can't force you."

"Really, Dad?" she replied, her voice more in control.

"Yes, Pumpkin. If I were there, I could have done it, but I am not and Harriet is willing." He paused. "Is it still okay with you?"

"Yes, Dad. I want to keep the baby." She smiled and rose. "You see, Gramps." She flattened her dress and exposed the hump. He smiled. "You look beautiful, Jillian."

"Thank you, Dad," and she laughed. "The doctor says the baby is growing strong and healthy."

"It's good news."

They chatted for a few minutes longer before he said goodbye and returned to his office. It was already late, but there were matters which needed his attention. When finally done, it was past 21h00. He had to make one more stop before he could call it a night.

Knocking on the door Chaplain Burger opened it with a genuine smile, a towel wrapped around his neck.

"Colonel, and to what do I owe this visit?"

"Can I come in?"

"Sure," and he opened the door wider.

"How can I help?" He hooked the towel on the cupboard door and switched on the kettle.

"I need guidance on a personal matter."

"Sounds like you are a busy man with too much baggage."

"At times it's difficult to hold it all together," he admitted.

"Where to begin …"

"I am ready when you are, Curt," Phillip said and propped up in his comfortable chair.

Once Curt began, he could not stop. At 23h00 he finally stopped and leaned back, the weight of life a heavy burden.

During the conversation Phillip had filled up their mugs twice, keeping their throats wet with the Arab blend they grew fond of.

Phillip prayed often for his friend. Life comes with a manual, but if you did not tap into the Author's mind, it would be difficult to understand. Curt was at a place where he needed guidance and wisdom. He was ready for this day.

"It's a delicate situation you find yourself in." Curt nodded. His throat was dry. Not even the coffee or water helped.

"First off, I would definitely recommend a visit with Sonia. I believe she is our new Head Nurse?"

"Correct."

"You know how to make a tricky situation even more complicated," and both men grinned.

"Once you have met her, you will understand. She is my soulmate, Phillip; I do not know how to exist without her. I made a promise to God, and I will honour that. I swear to you I will not touch her while married. That is why I came to you. Does God expect me to stay with Vivian even after all the deceit and lies?"

"No, God does not expect that, but He requires obedience. You of all people should understand how leadership works. You admitted you made a vow. What is it worth to you?"

Curt lowered his head; the man was right. He promised to stay true. When he stole a glance to his friend and confidant, Phillip continued: "To God this is where your decision will determine your future. Not only yours, but your family and Sonia's. I feel for you my friend, I really do, but God is assessing you. Will you pass the test?"

Curt realised he was in a tight spot. No reasoning would distinguish his words. When he spoke his voice slipped before he continued: "My vow is sacred. I will stay true to it. I will honour God. It is the greatest honour of obedience I can give. But please pray for me, Phillip. Now, more than ever, I need it."

"Of course I will. It will be an honour to do so," Phillip said, holding Curt's shoulder in a solemn moment. Both men went on their knees, and Phillip prayed.

Roughened hands concealed the tears, but Curt laid it all before the Father, leaving nothing out as he committed himself to God.

The echoed declaration changed the energy in the threadbare room.

Finally done, a tired Curt had an unaccustomed sense of renewal. He believed Sonia's life was in God's hands. Therefore he would step away and give God the reigns.

"When you walk out of the door, Curt, you walk into your future with the full assurance God is in control. You do not take it back. Give Him the opportunity to prove what He can do." Curt nodded in understanding and the two men embraced each other. He left shortly after 12h00—refreshed.

Once in his room, he wrote two letters—one to Vivian and one to Sonia. He owed her an explanation. He thought he would struggle with the words, but it came easy. His sincerity was visible in each line.

Just after five he got into a shower and was back in his office. He recognized the Lord's doing in his changed mood, and started his day with praise in his heart.

51

SONIA WOKE AN HOUR LATER in desperate need of a shower. With no toiletries, she had to rely on military supplies. On shaky feet she searched for a bathroom. After three months in Fangak the tiles were strange under her feet, the hard and clean surface something she would never take for granted again. It felt strange to be inside a building—just strange.

"Can I help, Captain?" a nurse asked.

"Yes, the bathroom, please. Where will I find it?"

"Let me show you." He led her along the way and she took a long hot shower. The warm water, soap and overall cleanliness helped to refresh her. Her tears washed the insides where her hands could not.

With a small hand towel she tapped the excess water from her. The abduction left its marks on her as blue, green and purple covered most of her skin. At least her leg felt better, but the scar would linger. Hair dripping she returned to her bed. There she found the blond nurse waiting for her.

"I left you some things," Anna said and pointed to the compact bundle. "It's not much, but we will get supplies soon."

"Thanks, Anna." On the bed two sets of army issued T-shirts and shorts waited for her. A toothbrush, soap, lotion and towel on top with a hairbrush and clip next to it. Quickly she fixed herself when she heard a cough on the other side of the curtain.

"Can I come in?"

"It is Dr Jourdain," Anna explained and widened the curtain opening. An attractive man, about her age, stepped in. His crumpled clothing showed signs of a long shift. Grey hair streaked the black lightly. Otherwise he was still fit and trim.

"I am glad you are up. How do you feel?" Dr Jourdain asked.

"Much better after the shower, thanks Doctor."

"I received your medical results. Do you have a moment?" His glasses pushed to his forehead. With one last look Anna left them alone and Sonia took a seat on the matrass.

417

"Sure."

"Please take a seat." He sighed as if the news were difficult to give, and she frowned.

"Your overall condition is excellent. The malaria is dispersing, but ..." He paused again. "Is there something you want to talk about?" His eyes conveyed a seriousness she could not dismiss and felt a twinge. Whatever the news was, she had to steal herself.

"Not now. What is the matter?"

"Sonia, you are two weeks pregnant. If you do not want this child, you need to speak now."

Sonia gasped. The news stunned her, and she slacked against the pillow. Then she counted the time backwards. Two weeks meant it was Tau's baby. Two weeks ago he made love to her. It helped her to forget the horrible time just days before. Days when her world shifted, and time became a time-bomb with quick choices. Could it only be two weeks?

She had not thought about him since her rescue. He would be excited about the news. He had mentioned it one evening shortly after the union that he did not have children.

"Sonia?"

"I ...," then she stopped.

"Do you want to talk about it?"

She stared at him.

"Were you raped?"

"It's complicated. I need time."

"Sure. I will recommend a speedy decision. I can do it tonight, tomorrow at the latest. No one has to know"

"Give me till tomorrow, please," she pleaded.

"Sure." When he left, her emotions were in disarray. She just sat there, unsure of her next step, puzzled even. What should she do?

How could she abort this baby? They created it in love. Didn't she owe it to the child to live even though it would never know his father? She never wanted to admit this truth, but in her own way she cared for Tau. He must have gone crazy with her disappearance, especially since they had no time to speak.

All the memories charged back. The three months left its mark on her. There were good times, too. The baby was one of it. She could not ignore it. But the baby will always remind her of the time best forgotten.

"*LORD* ..." She fell silent. Tears streaked her face once more, and she covered it with a towel. It was a good thing that the curtain was still halfway closed. To be this vulnerable before strangers was not a good beginning.

"Can I come in?" a very male voice asked softly and removed the towel.

"Sure." And she brushed the wetness away.

"I am Phillip Burger, chaplain on this base." A Green Cross, next to his tag, confirmed it. The ragged face open as he introduced himself. Nature and age were not kind to him, but his gentle spirit shined through. "I believe we have a common bond?" Not following he replied: "We are both from South Africa."

"Please to meet you, Chaplain."

"I thought to introduce myself to the new member of this fine establishment."

She chuckled. "Fine establishment indeed. Please have a seat."

"Are you settling in?"

"As well as can be expected."

"You seemed distracted?" he said when he got comfortable on a chair. She became quiet once more. The news devastated her, but she was not ready to talk.

"Sonia, I realise we don't know each other and you have no reason to trust me, but whatever you tell me stays between us."

She looked away.

"You went through a horrific experience and I wish I could wipe it away, but I don't have that ability," he continued. "I know the One who does." Tears welled up and fell to the bed. She met his sincerity with concern. Knowing he was a South African, what would he think about this? Would he condemn her? At first she wanted to dismiss him but something stopped her and cleared her throat, he listened.

"I just learned I am pregnant."

He took her hand and held it for the longest time. "Do you want to talk about it?"

"I …" more tears dropped, and he handed her his handkerchief.

"I cannot bear to have it, but I cannot bear to kill it either. You see, this baby, as hard as it may sound, was born in love. I believe God ordained this man to be my protector. To abort this baby would be to kill God's acts of faith."

"I like what you said. It seems God revealed much to you during this time."

"He did." She stroked her stomach.

"But it also represents the humiliation and hurt."

"I understand, Sonia," and tapped her hand.

"At times God takes us through incomprehensible pain, but His ways are always far better than our ways."

"I don't understand. These three months were unbearable. The one good that came from this was my relationship with God. I ignored him for a while. Now He has my attention, but the way He does." She stopped.

"We don't always understand, but it doesn't change the truth. God works by adding layers to our growth, each step designed to take us deeper into Him. What you have experienced is not unique, but the fact that you are here shows your victory over the adversity and the maturity to delve deeper."

"God does not throw punches, does He?"

"He certainly doesn't, and your life has meaning. This baby's life has meaning. I cannot tell you what to do. It is your body, but I can tell you to trust Him for He will work it out for you."

"Thanks, Phillip."

"Can I pray with you?"

"Yes, please."

"BEFORE YOU GO, THERE IS ANOTHER matter I want to talk about, if you don't mind," Sonia said once he was done. He nodded and waited. This was a difficult subject, but one she had to address.

"The fact that I slept with a black man in exchange for protection, what does that make me?"

"A woman who made the best of her situation. I understand what you are thinking, but answer me this. Were the people back at home there when you tried to stay alive?"

"No, they were not."

"And, will you return back to South Africa?"

"I don't know my future, I cannot say."

"Let God surprise you then. You do not have to worry about what our fellow countrymen will think. You cannot be blamed for their judgments."

"It just feels like betrayal," she admitted.

"My time away from home had given me a different take on a lot of things. One day we can talk about it, but your choices were just that … yours. This was not about race or political correctness or womanly woes. This was survival. I get that." Again he took her hand and whispered, "You are not a slut either. You did the best you could and for that I admire you."

"Thanks, it worried me. Not sure what to make of it. I never thought my life would turn out like this." Her heart tightened and squeezed his hand before he let it go.

"You are a brave woman, Sonia Main. Few would have survived and stayed positive in a similar situation."

"I don't feel strong."

"Because it is God's strength that runs through your veins. He had given you the courage and the insight and the will to move on. This baby is His way of blessing you."

"When did you become so wise?"

He chuckled: "I walked my road and learned the hard way. God turned my situation around and used me as He saw fit. Every day I am humbled at the way He does. I am still a man with many mistakes, but I stay humble and close to God. He is my Source."

52

Friday, 9 August 2019.

"WHAT HAVE YOU DECIDED, SONIA?"

"I will keep the baby, Doctor."

"Are you sure about this?"

"Yes, I am."

"In that case I will let you sleep."

"Thanks, Doctor." She paused, then cleared her throat. "Do you have to report this?"

"Yes. The colonel wants updates."

"Is there a way that you don't have to tell him right away? I prefer to inform him myself."

"All right then. I give you a week, then I must report it. The colonel's persistency can only be avoided that long."

"Thanks."

Once he left her alone she laid back. She hardly slept last night and stayed in prayer. Keeping the baby was not the ideal thing to do, but it was the right thing to do. He was a blessing from God. From the Word one the chaplain had given, she noticed the many scriptures about life.

At 44 she could provide for the child. He would never know lack. Her age was also factored in, another opportunity might never happen again. Her resoluteness came when she remembered her time with Tau. In his peculiar way he stayed a gentleman. Though he would never know about the child, it was a gift to the short-lived relationship.

Love's reality did not lie in the emotional attachment, but in trust, loyalty and care. She had that in abundance. To be selfish and kill a baby because the situation was not perfect, would annul the relationship and protection he had offered.

If it was about perfection, only a handful of children would survive. To lose another child, one by her own hand, would break her. God regarded her fit to be a mother and formed a seed she could call her own. What others would think about it she did not know, nor did she care. Tired she closed her eyes.

When she woke, a piece of material caught her attention. On closer inspection it was the one she had lost; the colourful scarf bought in Valletta. The surprise was a welcomed antidote, and it confirmed that God was in control. The memento was all she had left of a time so far away. Underneath it was a letter addressed to her.

"Did you sleep well?" Anna interrupted her.

"Yes, thank you."

"I am so glad that you accepted the position as Captain."

Piqued with curiosity, Sonia answered all her questions quickly; and when she finally left she reached for the letter, the sturdy handwriting hard to decipher.

Dear Sonia.

This is the hardest letter I had to write.

I wish we could have met under different circumstances, but we didn't, and I made a mess of things.

The day we met was the happiest day of my life and I thought I could be with you, always, but since I came back my life had changed. I made peace with God, as a result He required obedience from me.

I am still a married man.

This must come as a shock to you. I am sorry about it. I really am.

428

I tried to keep my word and honour my commitment, but it is not meant to be.

Do know that you have my friendship and protection. My door is always open.

Please forgive me.

Curt.

Curt was a married man, and the commanding officer of a base camp in Iraq. The same camp she would serve as a nurse. His presence caused her hopes and dreams to flourish again. They were never meant to be together. Now she felt let down, even used. With a heavy sigh she dropped the letter.

"*You know best, Lord.*" Tears formed and stayed. The futility of it all left her stunned. She touched her tummy. "It will only be me and you, kiddo. I promise you, this time I will take better care of you. With God's help we will make it."

Her dreams were empty, and by the time she woke it was past lunch time. A younger version of Curt entered her cubicle.

"Good afternoon, Ma'am. I am Sergeant Doug Clark."

"Good day, Sergeant."

"I've got excellent news, Captain. Your luggage arrived with a few letters. I've arranged a room for you, and when you feel up to it I will take you."

"That's wonderful news. Can we go now?" Being cooped up was working on her nerves. It was time to go back into the world.

"Sure, Ma'am. You sure you are up to it?"

"I still feel weak, but I need to get out."

"Let me arrange clothes for you."

"Thanks, Sergeant." She did not have long to wait when Anna handed her a set of clean scrubs and followed Doug into the heat into a different world.

53

12 August 2019.

MONDAY MORNING CAME TOO QUICK.

The image in the small mirror reflected a professional person whose life was in order, back to Sonia. She pinned her hair in a French roll; her curly strands enclosed an oval face. Anna's kindness blessed her with a haircut and facial over the weekend. The makeup brush covered the scars impeccably. No trace of her three-month turmoil could be seen.

The first time she saw herself, she felt ashamed. Time left its marks, and she had looked much older than her years. Dehydration, sun, malnutrition and stress could only heal with a healthy lifestyle.

She followed the contours of the small golden emblem which showed her occupation on the breast pocket, another pin with the lamp which she received on graduation day next to it. Right in the middle of the uniform the red cross insignia stood out, her name tagged on the right. She was ready to tackle the day.

The surreal perception of belonging soothed her soul. Since Friday nightmares plagued her dreams, the reason it had started unknown to her. She had to pray before it calmed her emotions enough to sleep. The desk and chair had been pulled in front of the door for security. Why it was there, she did not understand.

She had arranged her room until satisfied with the outcome. Surrounded with all her things it did not have the desired effect, but to have her own clothes helped. She had lost her favourite shoulder bag and overnighter with all the personal items, the beautiful yellow dress and accessories gone. It felt as if it never happened. Only the scarf reminded her of the weekend.

She had read the letters of each member of her former team, a grouped photo with a 'Welcome Home' banner added. She would miss them dearly. They congratulated and wished her well with the new position and glad they found her unharmed, which brought on tears. It was a weekend of cleansing, and she kept to herself. Doug brought plates with food and sat with her until she emptied it. Anna refused to accept her refusal and pampered her. No words were spoken between them.

The defilement stuck to her, but she did not want anyone to know. She would rather tell a lie than admit the truth.

Brady's letter surprised her; and reluctant she read the one-pager. Brady assured her of his love and apologized for his intrusion.

She replied to each letter with the greatest of care, especially with Brady's letter. He was her past. There were no feelings left.

Her thoughts wandered often to Curt McGee. She argued with God about him, but by Sunday night came to the same conclusion as he did. He could offer her nothing. From now on it would be a working relationship only— one she would respect.

Hippocrates once said: "Healing is a matter of time, but it is sometimes also a matter of opportunity." She would use the opportunity to heal and set her life on a firm foundation. The desert was just as good a place as any to do so.

In her natural life, time punched her lifespan with brief moments of genuine happiness just to return to a normal setting. Curt was not the man from Valletta, but her superior. She had to keep her emotions in control. She would be professional. The only way to forget, was to continue with what she was good at … work.

"Lord, help me honour the work you have started in me. help me forget and keep my heart at bay." she murmured before she straightened her bed. As she proceeded to the door her heart thumped loudly. She had to remind herself that she was not in Fangak, but in Iraq. She was safe. Once she opened the door, she breathed the warm clean desert air deep into her lungs before she walked briskly to the mess hall. Greeting men passed her with curious smiles, which she returned with a focussed greeting.

MCGEE WAS ALREADY SEATED when excitement hummed from the door. Doug and Ralph looked towards the counter. Ralph gave a whistle. Unsure Curt looked at the older man sceptically. Did he just imagine it? He could not recall a time where Ralph was excited about anyone before. Then he glanced to the spot of interest and froze, taken back in time when he first saw her.

He steeled himself for today and kept his distance. To tempt fate would be unwise and he avoided her sleeping zone.

He prayed for strength and a sound mind that morning. Now his treacherous heart was doing flip flops. Like David, when he saw Bathsheba for the first time and had her husband killed, he wanted to kill every man who looked at her. He wanted to stake his claim like a cave man.

435

Seated at the right angle he could watch her. Her dark hair framed the caramel skin. Huge green eyes glanced at Wendy, the kitchen cook, then at her plate. The soft smile lit her face.

He scanned the rest of her, a body he wanted to familiarise himself with again. His imagination amok as his hands glided over those curves, taking her into him.

She turned, searched for an empty seat, and found one at the table right in front of him. Their eyes connected and she saluted him. Soulful eyes he got lost in. The moment he blinked the connection severed. The void it left was undeniable. His heart pulsed and pushed blood to all areas, areas better ignored if he wanted to continue. A loud noise disconnected him from the trance, saw the reason for the interruption before he found her once more. A delicate hand brushed an unruly curl away.

Gorgeous.

A sound broke the hypnotic trance, and he turned back to Ralph and Doug.

"Who is she?" Ralph asked.

"The new head nurse," Doug answered and grinned.

"Bummer," Ralph said, and both men looked at him.

Yeah! Bummer, Curt repeated.

"Do you think anyone stands a chance with her?" Ralph asked Doug in a low tone.

"She is open game; single," Doug replied.

Heat flustered Curt's mind and took a sip from his mug. Anything to distract his reactions.

Obedience was better than sacrifice. Curt read during his devotional time—difficult, but doable.

Curt was about to stand when Sam and Alexi appeared with their trays at the same table Sonia occupied. He watched as she greeted them, their conversation lively while they ate.

She did not belong to him and he had no right to feel this way, but he could not help himself. Sam's reputation was legendary, and with him so close he did not stand a chance. He had to move away before he did something stupid.

Her laugh vibrated through him. The pulsing effect left him numb.

You are so screwed, Curt McGee.

54

SONIA SENSED CURT'S ATTENTION. The moment Sam and Alexi took their seats, she could breathe easy. She was aware of the exact moment the Colonel left the mess hall, drinking in his presence in stillness.

Sam pulled a face, drawing her attention back to his plate. She smiled as she darted back to her love. Curt paused at the door. She got the impression he wanted to look back before he disappeared.

IRON SHARPENS IRON: they both had to steel themselves, had to work at it and stand firm. They would get through this separately. They had no choice.

"You certainly care about him, don't you?"

Startled, Sonia looked at Alex. "Is it that obvious?" She diverted her attention to the bottle and took a sip.

"Yes." His open concern arrested her and gazed at the food that became tasteless.

"You know nothing can happen?"

"Yes, I know," Sonia answered, painfully aware of the facts.

"Oh, come on Alexi, why not?" Sam piped in.

"He is married, Sam," Alexi said gruffly.

"Yes, and the two are hot for each other."

"Alexi is correct, Sam," Sonia said. "He is my superior and I will respect him."

"We all know his wife cheated on him, and not only that …"

"Sam," it's none of our business," Alexi stopped him.

"Sonia needs to know."

"Know what?"

"It's nothing Sonia, and Sam, leave it alone," Alexi said firmly.

"She needs to know," Sam continued, but Alexi pulled him. "We need to go, and you, Sam, need to understand why she cannot see him."

"No," his disapproving tone pitched. "It's you and your God again, with all His laws. Freaking hell, man," and his fist hit the table. The mess turned silent.

"You see what you did," Alexi said pointedly at the hall.

"This is not the way. Come, let us go." He rose and took his comrade at the shoulder. "And, Captain Main, welcome to your new home," Alexi addressed her formally and left with a grumpy Sam at his side.

Sonia smirked, not sure what was going on, but watched the two men leave the hall.

Interesting day so far.

She gathered her tray and placed it on the trolley provided before she left the mess. At the door she scanned the area once more. It still felt surreal. Being in the desert in a military camp the last place she ever thought she would go again, but she was grateful.

As she walked through the rows of prefab buildings to her part of the compound, soldiers ran past her. He clearly ran a tidy camp site. Her first impressions of Curt were correct, and she admired him even more. Now, for the military man he was.

Military vehicles roared past her in a flurry of dust. Automatically she covered her mouth and eyes as sweat rolled along her back. The heat making itself known, the climate change something she had to get used to. The dry heat differed from South Sudan's heat. This heat took your breath and scrambled it around, the countless water bottles she had emptied, evidence of it.

There was much to learn about this life. It would test her spirituality, her comfort zone and skill, but she was ready.

At 7h00 Sonia stepped into the cooler interior of the medical facility where Anna and the rest of the staff waited for her.

"Captain Main," Anna said with a bright smile, and Sonia greeted her politely.

"Nurse."

"Everything is ready for your inspection."

"Thank you, nurse."

Over the weekend Sonia had time to study each person's file. The group consisted of four Europeans, Sonia included, Alrich Estie from the Netherlands, Peter Blake from the United States and Anna Stalin from Poland. The four Africans were from different areas in Africa and one from the US. Wayne Morris, Michelle West, Tumi Abara and Leonard Ndlovu, a young man from Swaziland. Two Indians, Amoli Khatri and Vasudha Balakrishnan from Delhi, one from Taiwan: Akemi Huang, one from Jamaica, Brantley Shaw and a Chinese woman, He Liu. Each experienced in their field, two were her age, the rest younger. Their accents were heavy, but they could understand and speak English reasonably well.

She also met the psychologist, an older man, Brett Rogers. A born Scotchman, a stern man that showed no emotion, but his brown eyes studied her intensely. Feeling uncomfortable, she kept the conversation with him to the point. During the fifteen-minute introduction it became clear to Sonia though strict, he had the welfare of each man and woman on staff on his heart.

The tour started at the supply room, then hall, X-Ray-, operating rooms and ER. Everything was as it should be and with an experts' eye. She was satisfied with the set up.

Her office's glass panels had an unobstructed view of the area. A desk and chair furnished the room with shelves stacked with files against the opposite wall and one window.

After lunch an ambulance arrived with two injured men and Sonia rushed to the ER. As a trained theatre sister, she wanted to be present if needed. She could already feel adrenaline surging through her as she scrubbed. A feeling she welcomed.

55

CURT JUST ENDED THE CALL with his daughter when Doug entered his office. It was already deep in the night, with the fan on high speed with no relief. It had an annoyed sound they had learned to ignore.

"Sir." Curt leaned back in the chair.

"Yes, Sergeant." Three missions were of concern, two went bad, and they deployed troops on a rescue mission. One soldier was unaccounted for.

"Two men are in the medical tent. We almost lost Hubert, but they pulled him through. Swanson will report back for duty tomorrow."

"That is good." However, what Curt wanted to ask was: "How is Main?" He worried about her. Even the Lord worried about her. He tried to shrug it off, but could not. This was another kind of danger, a personal matter.

"The Head Nurse did well today," Doug said. "She just left for her room."

Curt frowned … 22h23.

"She refused to go until Hubert was out of the woods," Doug clarified and smiled. "She is good with the men and staff; they respect her, Sir."

Curt rose to his full length. "Then it's time for me to go to bed too. You will let me know if there is any word about Private Simms, Sergeant?"

"Yes Sir, good night, Sir." Curt strode toward his quarters, made a turn at the next alley and stopped in the shadows. Sonia entered the bathroom with a towel and bag. He did not have long to wait, ten minutes later she sauntered out. A whiff of soap and vanilla reached him. He trailed her until she closed her room's door behind her. Moments later scraping sounds broke the night's quietness and he frowned. What was that all about?

Puzzled, he laid it before the Lord and prayed for her healing. When he finally fell asleep, Sonia called his name at his disappearing back—the grassy fields under his booted feet, a yellowish colour. The void in the dream woke him in tears and he cried before the Lord. He was honest enough to admit he could not be impartial to her. He argued with the Lord until peace steadied him. 'My grace is enough for you,' echoed through him at the end, and he accepted the truth.

He prayed for her safety and read Psalm 91 aloud, confessing it over her. The most serene feeling coursed through him as if a shift had taken place in the heavens. Content amid the chaos his life had turned into.

"THEY FOUND PRIVATE SIMMS, SIR," Doug informed him when he entered his office. "He was separated from the rest of his team. They found him in an abandoned building close to deployment point in a frightened state. There were two children with him."

"Glad that worked out, Sergeant."

"Sure do, Sir."

After lunch Sonia walked into his office with a report in hand. "Captain Main, are you settling in?"

"Yes, thank you, Colonel." She coughed, her eyes wide and open. "I never said thank you for the opportunity to serve here at the camp. It was unexpected, but thoughtful."

"You came highly recommended, and I needed a head nurse," he replied with a grin.

"Glad it worked out then," she said.

"Here is my report. If I may, I need to speak to you about a personal matter." Her direct approach impressed him.

"Sure, please have a seat." Doug closed the door behind him.

Curt watched every movement. Sadness lingered in the green pools. He wished he could do more than just stand at the side when she was not herself, even though she tried to hide it. She was far from okay, as she would like everybody to believe.

"How can I help?"

Her hands clutched each other in a tight grip; her knuckles white. When she looked up, they exposed her vulnerability.

"Colonel …" She cleared her throat, and then talked.

Her revelation stunned him, but he listened. The news floored him at first. The way she spoke of her ordeal as if it happened to another person alarmed him. His admiration for her trust and acceptance touched him deeply. Sonia Main had suffered and healing was still an ongoing process.

56

17 Augustus 2019.

SONIA BENT OVER ANOTHER REPORT. With a completed report it would give her opportunity to attend the service. A week had passed. A week where she felt out of sorts, confused.

She was forgetting stuff. Fearful of dark places, she jumped at every little sound. The stacked furniture was an everyday occurrence she could not explain. Each morning she cleared the door before she left for work. She was worried.

Noting last night's casualties, three men dead—one blown to bits, a gruesome task which called for absoluut care. A bile rising mission she completed with empathy. A family back home—wherever home was—waited for the remains of their loved one. The other two were in a better condition if you overlook the torn torso and missing lower parts.

Four seriously wounded soldiers were brought in after a mission went horribly wrong. She did not know the specifics. Her task was the simple part … patch up banged bodies and ready them for the next mission, or ship them back in a tin casket.

This feeling of absolute void and darkness always followed these moments. The remains of what was once a vibrant person affected her, now more than ever. It reminded her of her own mortality—of an unexpected life that grew inside her and of a love unanswered. It had happened twice in her lifetime—first Brady and now Curt. There were others that tried, but she felt nothing for them. The ache in her heart wanted her to hide away in a place where no one could find or hurt her. Her dreams stayed unanswered. Each time another skeleton was added, it disconnected her even more. A future she desperately desired, but never gets.

Last night she wept before the Lord until she fell into a restless sleep. When she woke, she noticed the furniture.

She read about Joseph and his walk through the various stages of his life. In search of answers, she desperately craved. Only one refrain filled her mind—'My grace is sufficient for you'.

Stretching behind her desk it helped to work out the tension and forget her own gloominess. Normal sounds from outside the medical tent floated inside, standard noises for a base camp. She still did not know her exact position, and for the time being she was fine with it. The few women Sonia had met in a camp dominated with men, set her at ease.

Charlie Alvarez was the radio operator in the base. Her Latino heritage shimmered through her olive skin and small build. The pitch-black hair was in a tight bun hidden mostly under her cap. She heard rumours about Charlie. The affair with the doctor was a highlight at base as staff and soldiers talked about it.

The doctor only came once a week. He was a married man who liked to display pictures of his wife and kids, but it was all a ruse.

Wendy was going after every skirt in the camp. From the crew cut style and bulky appearance, she steamrolled her way through the camp with her brusque voice, but she was a fine cook.

She still had to meet the rest; female soldiers that did their duty in quietness.

When the medic van stopped outside, she rushed to the team. Sonia helped a dying soldier to write his last loving words to his wife and child. The child was born during his mission; he would never know his father. Afterwards she closed the blue eyes, removed one dog tag and shoved it in an envelope with the rest of his personals: watch, letter and photo of him and his wife. He would never laugh, eat, drink or love again—to hug his loved ones or whisper words of love in his wife's ear.

Nothing.

For Captain Jean Smith it was over.

Death was a reality in the war zone, one you see up close. They were all acting casual about it, but at night when they were in bed, the minds wandered. For the outside world it did not matter, but for them it was natural, sanely natural.

"Ma'am," and she smiled.

"Yes, Doug?"

"The CO wants to see you right away."

"Thanks, Doug."

"Ma'am?"

"Yes, Doug?"

"Are you feeling well?"

"Just tired, Sergeant," she replied and followed him out the door, report in her hand.

Straightening her scrubs she finger-brushed her hair.

"You look great, Captain," he smiled reassuringly.

"You are a gentleman," she replied, and he chuckled. She knew the word 'great' is far from it. She was not a regular beauty as Anna with her delicate creamy skin and huge blue eyes, framed by long black lashes and a mass of golden blond locks.

At 44 she could not care how she looked for the male species. You lie to yourself; you care what the commander thinks. She shrugged it away and followed the younger man.

In his office the man in question's impressive bulk was neat in every detail. From the grey's golden hues, the straight shoulders and toned legs he was perfect.

"Main, we were waiting for you," he said politely, and she nodded.

"Colonel."

"At ease, Captain."

The moment she sat she handed him the report. A brief exchange of eyes and hands paused as a lightning bolt surged through her and she broke the contact. All the other officers were waiting for them and greeted them.

He cleared his throat and peppered her with questions about the casualties and deaths, which she answered as indifferent as he did.

Two professionals doing their duty, where discipline and order defined each day. Measured by strictness and loyalty to the cause. Defending the innocent and healing the broken bodies with military correctness.

Their love tucked away as it warred silently in the dark.

57

18 August 2019, Fangak County, South Sudan.

"BAAKA PASSED AWAY," ROGER informed Tau. It sounded cold, and with no one to help they watched her decline. The news did not come as a shock.

"*Takziah*." (Condolences) Tau said. Roger sat down, distracted. Quietly they drank the brew Lamya brought.

"You need to find the nurse," Roger said after a while.

"Why?"

"He threatens to take my sons."

"What does Sonia have to do with your sons?"

"You remember the deal."

"*Leres!* (Never) I will never forget." At once Roger became livid. "You will find her. For now I have appeased him with valuable supplies, but it's not enough."

"I don't care. Besides, where must I look for her?"

"She's your woman. You will know."

"I don't." Tau stood ready to leave, but Roger held him back.

"You will get her, or I will kill Sarai." His first wife lived with her family. He visited her once a year out of obligation. Since their marriage she could not produce one child and they believed she was cursed, but to kill her was unacceptable.

"You are a bastard."

Roger smirked. "You get her."

Tau pushed him away and got on the dock. Children scattered around him.

"*Mamang!*" (Uncle) Fiza called.

"Leave me alone, Fiza," he yelled.

"*Mamang,*" but Tau ignored him and pushed the dock from the bank. Why did Roger have to mention her again?

Since she left he tried to forget. He gave all her belongings to the women. Lamya grabbed the yellow dress and paraded in it till Roger ordered her to remove it.

After one night in his old bed, he could not stand to be so close to her and gave it to Lamya. He slept in a room behind the store—far away from all the memories of her. He even took another woman to still the desire. The search meant she would be on his mind constantly.

He could not do it, no matter how much he missed her. Putting distance between him and the camp, he let the pole rest and observed the area.

Allah would show him what to do. He prayed as they taught him, but it seemed futile. Patting his pockets he searched for his cigars. Instead, he found the covered Bible and opened it.

What should I do? He did not love Sarai, but he could not see her in Roger's hands. She would never survive.

But Sonia. He bet she was doing better. The time back between her people would heal her.

He prayed just as he saw her doing it. He needed answers, quickly.

58

18 August 2019, close to Adamiyah, Baghdad.

AT THE SERVICE that Sunday morning, Major Burger welcomed each person in attendance, with a special welcome towards her. Taking a seat in the row in front of Curt he greeted her, which she returned with a smile.

Two men picked up their guitars and began with a well-known praise song. Sonia's soprano voice complemented the tenors and low-pitched voices in a beautiful chorus as they joined. They sang two more songs before they sat, and the chaplain took the mic. He thanked Private Chris Thompson and Sergeant Thomas Banks for the music.

When it became quiet, Phillip gave **Isaiah 58:5, 6** as reference and those with Bibles turned to it.

"5) Is it such a fast that I have chosen? A day for a man to afflict his soul. Is it to bow down his head as a bulrush, and to spread sackcloth and ashes under him? Wilt thou call this a fast, and an acceptable day to the LORD?

6) Is not this the fast that I have chosen? To lose the bands of wickedness, to undo the heavy burdens, and to let the oppressed go free, and that ye break every yoke?"

and **Galatians 5:1**: "Stand fast therefore in the liberty wherewith Christ hath made us free and be not entangled again with the yoke of bondage."

In an authoritative voice he began,
"Each one of us struggles with adversities. Things holding us back to experience God's freedom in full measure. When Jesus was crucified on the cross, His last words were: **'It is Finished.'**

"He has paid the ultimate price so that you and I can be free, but life happens. It wants to rob us of our freedom. Our mind becomes toxic and without realising it, it rules us. It holds us captive in thoughts, actions and words, but today I want to tell you the good news. Liberty has been given to you through the redemption work of Christ. The yoke has been removed. **Philippians 2:12** states, 'Wherefore, my beloved, as ye have always obeyed, not as in my presence only, but now much more in my absence, work out your own salvation with fear and trembling.' Now you need to work with faith to honour your salvation and bring it to completeness. When you trust and obey His word, God will open the Heavens in your life. He will give you the freedom to conquer. Your obedience is a gift to God; therefore make it your own. I want to conclude with this scripture in **2 Timothy 2:7**: 'For God hath not given us the spirit of fear; but of power, and of love, and of a sound mind.' Do not allow fear to steal your freedom, or to put you in bondage and make the work God had started in you null and void. Walk in obedience and the freedom of God's Love.

May his peace guide you, shelter you and set you free. Amen."

SONIA TOOK NOTES OF the message meant for her. Fear ruled her all her life, but after the abduction it became a prominent guest. She needed God's love and freedom in her life before she could have a future of any kind. As he prayed, she felt a gentle touch on her shoulder.

Curt whispered in her ear: "Please forgive me, Sonia," his own voice hoarse.

She turned to him, his eyes pools of regret. "I was unfaithful to my wife, unworthy of what we shared. I never wanted to hurt you."

"Curt," she began by interrupting him. He exchanged seats before he continued: "No, please let me finish. By no means did I want a cheap affair on Valetta. You gave me more than I bargained for, and it meant a great deal to me. But the fact remains, I was not honourable with Vivian or you. Please forgive me."

There was so much she wanted to say. But what she wanted to do was to wrap herself in his arms and love him. She wanted to tell him how much she missed him … what he meant for her during those long, terrifying weeks with no hope.

However, his words dropped in her heart like a heavy burden—the sting of betrayal undeniable.

Lord, let it be according to your word.

"I forgive you, Curt," she finally said. Her emotions were too raw to respond, but she heard him.

"Sonia," and he lifted her head. "I am here if you need help. I feel responsible for you as with every man on this campsite. If you have any needs, tell me."

She nodded and he let her go. His departure left more than a physical emptiness. He had become her world in a heartbeat just to be ripped away. She had to find her strength back and lean more on God.

"Are you alright, Captain?" Burger asked as he took a seat next to her. Only now did she notice they were the only people in the chapel.

"Yes, I am … I am fine," and she brushed the tears away. "Thank you for the sermon. It touched me deeply. I will read it again." She rose.

"Not so quick, Captain." Phillip moved a chair so that he could see her. His sincere face reflected his words. "You can speak about anything and it will remain between us."

"Thanks, but I want to be alone, if you don't mind," she answered and moved away.

"I just wanted to let you know I am here when you are ready."

"Thanks, Chaplain."

"Please call me Phillip." Sonia nodded, her readiness to flee overwhelming. But the man was persistent.

"Can I accompany you to the mess?"

"Not today."

"You need to eat, Sonia," he said and smiled. "You need to get your strength back."

"I am not hungry." She wanted to lick her wounds, but it seemed the chaplain was adamant.

"Will you do me the honour and accompany me to lunch?" Sonia sighed, to give in would be easier.

"Please?"

Come to think of it, lunch would be good. Her shift would start at 16h00, giving her enough time to rest and spend time with the Lord. She nodded, and he allowed her to step out first. The slight gesture appreciated.

TO WITNESS HER DEVASTATION BROKE HIM. He wanted to love her, affirm to her she belonged with him. No matter how hard he tried to honour his wedding vows, he had feelings for Sonia Main, but he made a promise to God.

Now, more than ever, her vulnerability required a man's understanding. He knew she would move forward and make the best of her choices. Her strength was her biggest asset.

"Lord, this is tough. How much more could she take before she breaks?"

He tried to think of his family back home. He was proud to have Vivian as his wife. She was clever, full of life, head strong and loved him. Once. He groaned in anguish as thoughts of their last time together coursed through him. There was never anyone else. In all the years of being away, he remained faithful. He clutched to her as his only source, and it became difficult to part with her. Then the betrayal followed.

God! he groaned as a flashback rushed through him. *"Lord, I promised long ago to love Vivian and cherish her. Help me honour the vow."*

'Deep calls unto deep. Iron sharpens iron. Every tree is pruned and those branches that do not bear fruit cut off and cast in the fire.' The words of Major Burger echoed in his mind of the sermon he had heard three weeks ago.

"Lord, I know you are teaching me a valuable lesson here, but must it be so painful?"

My strength is enough, hide in me and I will give you rest. The soothing words fell on his spirit.

"Lord, I can only trust your work, because I am at a loss, but if you permit me, help Sonia. She is in pain. I am part of the pain she is facing, and she is all alone. Wrap her in your arms, keep her safe."

As he dug into his meal, Sonia walked in with Major Burger right behind her. She looked distant and sad. He watched as she got her tray and sat down two tables in front of him. She greeted Castledale who sat at the same table.

The look he saw on the staff sergeant's face was what he had seen before—predatory, stalking. He would have to keep a close watch on Castledale. Sonia was defenceless and did not need a man like him in her life. Especially after her ordeal.

59

DOUG OPENED THE CUPBOARD doors cautiously. Castledale and his roommates left early Tuesday morning for a search and rescue mission, which gave him a twenty-four-hour window.

He suspected Castledale for a while now. Too many things didn't add up with him. His arrogance grated on every nerve. The men did not like him, and the women feared him. He treated women like scum.

Private Cummings relied on him. The man suffered in jail. The young lawyer was just as adamant not to fail his client. The judicial system obstinate in their decision: Cummings must pay for a crime he did not commit, while the culprit was defending the innocent. How poetic, Doug thought.

He leafed through the grey T-Shirts and black shorts neatly folded on the first shelf. Then the socks and underwear. Shirts and pants hung in a neat row and systematically he worked through them. Nothing.

Nothing was out of place in the room. Each item was stored meticulously as required. His duffel bag hung from a hook in the corner. With a quick glance at the door, slightly ajar and then the window, he opened the bag, but it was empty. Bummer.

Side pockets! He scrambled to open them, but stopped. A noise outside sent him into hiding. The door opened and in a deep voice the soldier said: "He is not here."

"I told you he is on a mission. All hush-hush," another said.

"Oh well, then it's just us," a deep voice said annoyed.

"Let's find out if the blond is available and invite her with us," the sharp guy suggested.

"I would love to get a piece of her." The deep voice smirked and closed the door. Doug could only guess who the blond was, and grimaced.

Without delay he went through the side pockets and felt a soft cloth in the corner of the last pocket. It was a rumpled shirt. As he spread it on the bed he noticed it at once. The second button from the top was missing. Two dark spots were visible on the collar of the shirt. To be certain, he lifted the shirt into the sunlight streaming from the window. It looked like blood. Satisfied with the discovery, he put it in a plastic bag and returned to his room.

Relieved to find his room empty, he spread the shirt open on his bed and captured the images of the spots. Once he was satisfied that the images were clear he sent it to Reeves via the chat platform on his mobile. He inserted the shirt in an envelope, sealed it and addressed it to the lawyer—Colonel McGee's address on top. During a break he informed the commander of his discoveries, and Curt gave his go ahead.

Send as Top Secret and Confidential.

STARTLED SONIA LOOKED AT MAJOR FRANCO TURMEL. He steadied her with a hand on her arm: "Are you well, Captain?" The French accent sounded brusque, but the grin on his face said otherwise.

It was their second encounter in the last two weeks—of average height, their eyes met without effort. They were the same age, but there their similarities stopped. His open face, compared with a sour prune, did nothing for her, although a smile quickly followed. He was persistent and dependable; she had heard. Though it was a characteristic she wanted in a man, he was not the man her heart wanted.

"Yes, thank you, Major. My thoughts are elsewhere today," and placed a strand of hair behind an ear.

He smiled. "I hope it was good thoughts. Maybe of the loved ones at home?" he asked, his gaze lingered on her lips.

"No, I am afraid no loved ones at home," she replied and side stepped him.

But he followed: "How could it be? A lovely lady like yourself has no loved ones; impossible," and rolled his eyes.

She smiled. "Well, it is, no loved ones."

"Incredible. So, what were you thinking of?"

She grimaced and said politely: "If you do not mind, Major, I have work to do."

"No problem, but tell me … if there are no loved ones at home, what is hindering us to get better acquainted?"

Her brow lifted in question. "Is it the best you could come up with, Major?" she asked quite irritated with him.

"Honesty is always the best option, and you should not be allowed to be so sad all the time," he replied.

"Thanks Major, but I prefer to be alone at this point in my life."

"I can't accept it. Join me for a drink at the bush pub."

"Is it true what they say?" she smirked, and he raised a brow. "That you are a bulldog?"

"It's my handle name. It will not do my reputation any good if I leave at the first attempt to get the most beautiful lady in the camp to go out with me."

"I am really not in the mood."

"I am hurt." He clamped his heart with a hand and looked pitiful at her. "Give me a chance, you might like me."

She doubted it very much.

"What will it be?"

She hesitated. "Okay, but only one drink."

"Yes, but of course, we all know women need their beauty sleep."

Amused with the man he gave her a wink and left. She closed the door thoughtfully.

After hours her calendar was quickly filled with invitations after two weeks. She gave it much thought. To sit and mope would not do. For the time being, she only accepted invitations from those she knew and trusted.

Major Burger showed her around the local village on their day off. They had lunch and a wonderful discussion—mostly about South Africa. The deterioration of the systems was a big conversation starter. It escalated to the corruption, the state capture, and the farm murders. South Africa was indeed in a sorry state. People were in uproar and the government in denial. They spoke at length about it until he delivered her back to her room. They had become good friends and Phillip kept it on a friendly basis.

Sam and Alexi also kept her busy and she enjoyed the light banter from both. Even Doug escorted her to supper, and they had extensive talks about anything, but especially about their faith. Although much younger than her, she found him to be mature and fun.

This Major though was more of the romantic kind. His approach was different from others. She had no place for a man.

Her relationship with Curt ended and she had a child to think about. Besides, what man would take her if they knew how soiled she was?

Today she caught a glimpse of sadness in Curt's eyes, a pain she understood well. No matter how hard she tried to suppress the emotions of love, it persisted to grow. To love anyone else would be cheating. She was miserable and lonely, but to replace it with any man would not be good either.

Then there was the other issue which left her fearful of every little bump in the night. She had hoped by now those fears would disappear. Two nights in a row she tried, but she could not sleep. As she stared at the door, her imagination ran wild with unknown assailants who bashed through it. The helplessness reared on its hind legs. The fear of violation, the rejection when no one came to her rescue. The utter loneliness in those weeks caged in between swamp water and the shadows of the nights. It was a wonder she could still function during the day. Those few days in lock up burnt her from within. The odour of her rapist followed her with determination she could not shake.

So far she kept it bottled inside. A couple of times Phillip steered the conversation in the general direction of her ordeal. Prompting her to talk about it, she deliberately ignored it, but it kept her awake. Ignorance's bliss better than the alternative.

She would be all right. She had to. She could not allow her fears to rob her or control her. She was stronger than that. She brushed against her stomach. Inside her the baby's development kept her going. She owed it to him to stay in control.

A knock on her office door brought her out of her reverie. The steel grey eyes of Dr Brett Rogers pertinent gaze swept over her and she forced a smile on her lips.

"Yes, Doctor?" Sonia was convinced she could not fool the psychologist. He was one of the best in his field—had written two best sellers about a soldier's psyche. He knew people, but he said nothing other than, "they need you in the ER. They brought in a young private. He lost his foot and they can't console him."

"Yes, of course, Doctor."

Screams filtered through the swing door. Once she opened it, blood pools covered the floor in an ominous manner. An abandoned shoe laid next to the trolley as two men held him. Blood squirted from the leg, what was left of it. His blood-soaked clothes clung to him.

Once they cleared a path for her, she bowed over him and smoothed his hair. He was incredibly young, maybe eighteen years old—still a child that belonged with his family and in college. Confronted with a difficult challenge at this age made things worse, with a long road to recovery his only option.

She hated the blasted war.

In a calm voice she addressed him. At first he ignored her in his pain induced frenzy. The thrashing became quiet and he listened. Blood red eyes looked at her pleadingly.

"Please don't let them take my foot," he implored her.

"I want my foot back." The helplessness of the soldier; pitiable. In the one soldier's hand a bloodied boot showed the remains of the foot. She swallowed and met his eyes with heartfelt pain.

"What is your name, Private?"

"Shaun, Ma'am, please give back my foot. I want my foot!" He pulled her closer. "I need my foot!" Then he screamed again.

"Shaun, can we talk for a few moments?" she asked gently. His gaze shifted towards her.

"Shaun, Anna is going to administer a pain killer. While she does it, we will take great care of you. But your foot, son, there is nothing left. It will be more trouble if we leave what is left of it. Believe me when I tell you, it will make life simpler. You will adapt, and one day you will be a wonderful husband and father, no matter if you do not have a foot. Your foot does not define you, but how you take it from here, will. You are a brave young man. I know your parents will be proud." Tears streamed into the bedding and he closed his eyes without comment.

Anna administered the drug and soon he fell asleep. With whimpers of confusion and pain on his thin lips, they took him to the theatre.

His career in the military was officially over. With rehabilitation and care he could continue a normal life.

"Thanks, men," she said as they relaxed their hold on him. Not much older than their friend, they stood bewildered in the way. She gently tucked at each blood smeared arm and led them away and left her staff with the wounded soldier.

"Let's get coffee," she suggested and escorted them to the small office where she pointed to the open chairs. They sagged into the seats. The shock had paralysed them as they held their heads; eerily pale. One, Private Jenkins' face, had a dry blood smear across his cheek.

"It was so quick," Jenkins muttered. "I mean, the one moment we were in the Humvee chatting," and he blushed, "and next, kaboom." Jenkins swallowed.

"Are you okay, Soldier, or do you need to go to the bathroom?" He shook viciously, his broad chest moving under the strain.

His hands shaky, his age apparent.

"Can I offer you something?"

"No, Ma'am," he whispered. Meeting her for the first time, the fear so real she could smell it.

"I will book you off for the day," she started.

"No, Ma'am," he interrupted. "I will be fine."

She looked at him, then at Nolan who stared outside the small window, his jaw clenched in a bitter line.

"Private Nolan, are you fine?"

"Yes, Ma'am."

Just then Corporal He Liu walked in with bottled water and three cups of steaming coffee. They sprang up and stretched clumsily. "Thanks, Corporal," they mumbled and drank the water like starving men before they took the coffee.

The CO appeared and signalled to her through the glass panel. She excused herself and followed him to the outer door. The heat was a welcomed relief after the despair.

"Are they fine to answer questions?"

"Yes, Sir, they will be fine. Just take it slow with them, they had a tough time."

"We need answers, and they are the only two survivors."

She gasped in shock. "Do they know?"

"I doubt it," he admitted. "It happened too quickly. The rescue crew found them with their mate in their arms clutching one another. They had no idea what happened."

The roar of a truck passed them and they stepped aside, closer to each other. When he returned his gaze, she saw the man she loved. His indifference changed and he removed his shades.

"How are you?" His voice just above a whisper. Her world stopped and leaned closer.

"I am well," she replied. Thankful for the closeness he offered. She needed it.

"Promise me you will ask for help when you need it," he pleaded, and she looked away.

He reached out and touched her. "Sonia, promise me."

She nodded. "I will." His attentiveness did flip flops in her stomach. All she wanted to do was to step into his embrace—stay there forever. All would be fine, then.

But no one moved closer, their body warmth the only connection they could allow. Their arms folded as barriers between them, not one willing to step away. It was difficult not to reach out, not to touch. Sonia closed her eyes and whispered:

"I miss you," she admitted. It seemed so out of place, but it was true. It was a foolish thing, but she did miss him. Not trusting herself any further, she stepped back and broke the intimate connection, his hand hanging in the air.

With a quick step she was back in her office, leaving him at the door.

He too left, his mind a blank. His heart in pieces.

60

IT WAS AFTER 19H00 WHEN SHE finally left the medical tent and bumped into Major Turmel for the second time that day.

"Again I am startling you, Captain," he murmured, and she glanced at him wearily.

"I am so sorry, please excuse me."

"Not so fast, Sonia. We have a date."

"Not tonight I am afraid," she replied and started to walk, but he kept her pace.

"Sorry, I don't want to argue with you, but we do. I am going to hold you to it. We will enjoy a supper compliments of the government, then we will go to the pub for a few drinks to relax and have fun."

"I am not in the mood," her voice rose a pitch. A headache was threatening since lunchtime. She needed a shower and bed.

"Now come on, Captain."

"No, not tonight." She picked up her pace, but he blocked her way.

"I am afraid no is not the answer I want. I have waited a long time for this, and we will have it." His fingers clasped her arm in a stronghold. All her fears rushed back. Only years of training kept her intact and she looked at his hold, beaming a message in rage.

"Maybe another night?" He released her and stepped back. The moment he let go she walked away. Fear gripped her as she practically ran to her room and caged herself inside.

The next night she came out earlier and Major Turmel waited for her once again. The man was persistent she had to give it to him.

"Major Turmel," she sighed, and he grinned.

"Captain Main, how about dinner and a drink?" he asked, but before she could respond he continued: "Please, I know you had a rough day, but you will make this old soldier happy to dine with. It becomes lonely and a fine young lady like yourself will lighten his mood. You do not have to talk, I will do all the talking."

She smiled wanly. "Okay Major, you convinced me. Can I at least freshen up?"

"Excellent, sure you can." He held out his arm gallantly and she took it warily.

"I can see why the entire camp is talking," he started as he accompanied her to her room.

"And why is that?"

"I will be the envy of every man."

"I doubt it, but thank you for the compliment."

"It is true."

"Flattery will get you nowhere," she said with a half-smile.

He grinned. "On the contrary. I think I am getting somewhere with you."

They stopped at her door and she said thoughtfully: "Don't bargain on it. I will be right back," and left him standing at the door.

A shower would be her preferred choice to freshen up, but her stomach cut her short and combed her hair. She added some colour to her lips and met him outside.

As they walked into the mess hall twenty minutes later, he helped her with a tray of food to a table in a quiet corner. They made small talk about their respective days. Sonia had to admit it was good to sit and talk, even though his expectations was clear she enjoyed the light banter. In his own way he set her at ease.

In the pub they joined a small group at a table where the light conversation continued, and she relaxed. A private brought them drinks and they continued with their conversation about family, their countries and the choices which led them to a solitary life.

Because of the noise they moved closer to hear each other, not noticing the light blue eyes watching them from the dark corner of the pub.

JEALOUSY SURGED THROUGH HIM.

He should not feel the emotion; to feel so possessive, but he was appalled. How many were after her?

Sam made it clear how much he liked her. They were often in each other's company. Major Burger took her out two nights ago and now Major Turmel joined the gang. Didn't they know she belonged with him?

He was a mess. He was unreasonable.

He must let go but he had her first.

Did she allow any of them to touch her?

Did she respond in the same manner?

God help me. Angry with her, with him, the Major. Yes, the entire world.

"I can't bear this," he grunted, pushed his table aside, paid his bill and left. The mere thought she could be with another man disturbed him.

The next morning Curt snapped at every man that entered his office. Phillip, his first victim, was startled at the unjustifiable act. Turmel was next in line, his expression alarmed, and he could not blame them. Each walked away with a stack of reports to complete. It would occupy their entire day since he wanted it back first thing the next day.

As the day continued his mood grew worse. To avoid the medic tent became harder to do. There were things he needed from her to complete the report for headquarters.

After more deliberations with himself, he gave Sonia a good run around. He barked orders and in her usual calm manner she addressed each issue. It aggravated him even more and by the time he wanted to leave, Sam Gerber appeared. His bright smile and charming greeting left him furious.

What was wrong with all the men in the camp?

With sure strides, he disappeared in his office slamming the door in Doug's face. With shaking hands, he opened a bottle of water and drank deep and long pulls—his head pounding. Just then his satellite phone buzzed. It was Jillian. Her sweet voice stilled him and while they talked, he could feel the anger dissipated.

He groaned as he recapped the day. He was a complete fool—a fool in love with a woman he could not have.

"Lord, how am I supposed to cope with this? She is tempting me around every corner. Her bright smiles, her fragrance, her body—it all tempts me. Lord, I will be honest with you. I never wanted a woman so much as I want her. I am trying so awfully hard to be the man you want me to be, but I'm making a mess of things."

A knock on the door got him out of his muse, and he shouted: "Enter!"

"Do you have a moment, Sir?" Burger asked in his normal polite and calm way.

Curt motioned. "Come in."

They stared at each other. Curt's clenched jaw and balled fist did not shield his gaze as it threw daggers at his best friend. Phillip took a seat, not flinching with his higher than thou attitude.

"Can I be open and frank today?" the chaplain asked with no hesitance. His hand rested on his knee, calm and open—the stance of no hidden agenda.

"Yes," Curt agreed reluctantly. Philip's cunning ability to read people and get right to the point caused a raised brow.

"How are you, Curt?" A loaded question. He decided to play it casual, but it did not mean he had to be friendly. At this point he was making advances to his woman. God, listen to yourself. To differentiate was killing him. He knew he was at fault. Not Phillip, not Sam, nor this Turmel fellow.

"Good, thanks," came the abrupt reply. He hoped the man was not there on a social visit. He could not do it, not now.

"How are things at home?"

"Crazy, but they will survive," and he smirked. Get a hold of yourself. You are not ten, Curt McGee.

"They offer up a lot to have a loved one so far from them."

"True." Where was Phillip going with this?

"And your marriage?"

Curt shifted in his chair, his eyes sweeping over his desk before he returned to the steady gaze of his friend. "It has its moments."

"Care to elaborate?" The man was persistent. "I see you are on edge Curt and I am a brilliant listener. Whatever this is, can be sorted and you can move on. You are irritable and the men talks."

"Nothing, I can sort it myself," he said annoyed, not used to being in the corner like this.

"Frankly, Curt, I don't think so. You have reached the end of your rope and as a chaplain I will not do my work if I let this slip. Next time Doctor Rogers will walk in."

Curt rolled his eyes and grinned. Rogers brooked no nonsense, not even from him. Once he had you in his sight, he did not let go. The reason he had put him on Sonia's tail.

Moments of silence filled the office. Curt rose and sauntered through the confined space, agitated with the situation and the man in front of him.

He hated it when Burger was doing his mojo on him. He threw a curveball at him. "Do you have a relationship with our head nurse?"

The man's gaze was unwavering as he answered. "She needs a friend right now. She struggles with the after effect of an abduction, trying to sort out her own fears and exertions of the past and the unrealistic hold of a man she fell in love with."

Curt stared at him in disbelief.

"Who is the man?" He swallowed, tried to look away, but stopped himself. Guilt stirred his gut.

"She does not say, but I can guess." His brow lifted as he stared pointedly at him. "Now, you evaded my questions long enough. Get to the point and spit out your troubles so that we can have the Curt McGee back we respect."

"Bummer," he muttered.

"You don't want her to find a friend or to receive healing she desperately needs. You want to be selfish and keep her for yourself while you are committed to your wife. Your jealousy is an evil which drives you to this unreasonable point. You have no right to be jealous. You made your choice."

Curt swallowed hard. "I try, but it's difficult. My heart refuse to let go."

"Yes, it is hard," Phillip admitted, "but it doesn't make it right. Did you forgive Vivian, Curt?"

Curt turned his head before he said, "I have. The pictures are a constant reminder, though." He removed both envelopes from his locked drawer and handed it to him. Burger took it, removed the pictures and looked at the first one. Slowly he placed it back and handed it to him.

"Yes, it is hard for any man. And you are far away. I believe there is a war brewing inside of you. Your desires are not met, and you fight and quarrel with everyone. Even me," and he grinned.

Curt was once again startled with Phillip's perceptiveness. Through all the years together, they experienced difficult situations and he was used to his insight. But to be on the receiving end of his bluntness, was hard, even shameful. He knew the man was right.

"Especially if you have feelings for another woman," and he looked at him perplexed.

"You are smitten with our head nurse. Jealousy makes you forget the right conduct in camp and the vows you have taken with your wife. The word states in Proverbs 6:34, 'For jealousy makes a man furious, and he will not spare when he takes revenge.' And in James 4:1-2 'What causes quarrels and what causes fights among you? Is it not this, that your passions are at war within you? You desire and do not have, so you murder. You covet and cannot obtain, so you fight and quarrel. You do not have, because you do not ask."

"I hate it when you do this," Curt interrupted him.

"Yes, I know, but you need to hear the truth," he said. "This cannot go on. 'Do not be conformed to this world, but be transformed by the renewal of your mind, that by testing you may discern what is the will of God, what is good and acceptable and perfect.' **Rom 12:2**."

Curt dropped back in his chair. Burger's precision left him speechless. He had read these same scriptures, reprimanded himself, but he did not want to listen. He groaned in agony.

"Please pray for me," he admitted finally—his eyes burning.

"This is why I am here, Curt. I see the turmoil you are in and it will be my pleasure to help you. I understand where you come from," and Curt nodded.

Ten years ago, Burger was at home when he found his wife of three years in bed with a good friend. He had a tough time of accepting and moving on. He was still waiting for the perfect woman.

"Let's pray," and both men bowed.

61

31 August 2019.

SONIA WOKE WITH A THROBBING HEADACHE, the sun setting in the west. Grabbing her bag, she scratched around until she found the pills and popped the lid. Two capsules fell on her hand and she swallowed them with a mouthful of water. The bitterness spirals down her throat to her stomach to do its work.

Last night's shift was tiresome, and she only left after 12h00 that afternoon. They admitted several cases of the flu, stomach aches and cramps. Three soldiers were part of a collusion and bled all over the ER. Then, to make matters worse, Colonel McGee demanded additional reports. It kept her busy the rest of the morning, her timetable stretched to the limit.

The nightmares had intensified. Concerned about them, she made an appointment with Major Burger for the next day. Her fibs did not fool Dr Rogers either. Uncomfortable under his stare she avoided him. He prescribed sleeping pills to her, but she had not taken them. She pulled the desk and chair away from the door before she opened it and enjoyed a refreshing shower.

An hour later she received the reports from Anna.

The night shift was uneventful, giving her enough time to read a letter from Major Scott. He asked to see her one more time to talk. According to him they did not part well and would love to resume their friendship.

The man had lost his marbles. She could never allow him back, not even for friendship. Some of her nightmares were because of him. Gisemba occupied the others. The fear it could happen again left her sweaty. When she was awake the thoughts were manageable. Skilled military men surrounded her. No way could he get to her, but her mind refused to accept the fact.

Taking a quick break during the lull, she slipped out to the loo's on the other side of the mess.

Outside she connected with a wall of hard flesh. Steel arms surrounded her and she struggled with a yelp.

"Sonia, it's me," came the deep voice of Curt.

"You scared the living daylights out of me." She pushed him away.

"I am sorry. I didn't see you until it was too late," he explained.

"How are you?"

"Well, thanks. Please excuse me."

"Wait, please," he said in a low tone and held her against him. She looked at him, then at her arm and back to him. He lowered his arm and it disappeared into his pants' pockets.

It was essential to get away from him. The thought hammered away and ignited another pain. One, no pill could help and best forgotten.

"Please Sonia, how are you really?" His concern swept through her and she drank it in like a dry sponge. Hearing her name on his lips caused her heart to jump. A fleeting euphoria of a lover's kiss. So exquisite, but so wrong. She closed her eyes and will him away.

CURT HAD RECEIVED THE REPORTS from Major Burger and Rogers, and her lack of response troubled him. After Burger set him right two weeks ago, he avoided her totally. Tomorrow he leaves for the States to sort his life. He had long talks with Phillip and God. When he saw her in the mess hall earlier that day, he could not believe his eyes. The dark circles, lifeless eyes, hunched shoulders and pale skin signalled her pain.

And now she was here in his arms. His own heart did a backflip. Drinking her in.

"I am well. Please, I need to return to the medics." The blank look she gave him stirred him. Her tensed body and guarded expression revealed more than she said.

She was shutting him out and he could not blame her. She needed a person with the ability to listen. If only she would open. Why must she be so stubborn?

SHE WANTED SO MUCH TO RUN back and love him, but words or actions at this point would be futile. No, it was for the best.

Walk away. Do not look back. You are not meant to be together.

But why was her heart and body so stubborn?

Why don't they want to accept he was not for her?

Because Sonia Main, he has your heart right in the palm of his hand. That is why.

The moment she stepped back into the tent, more soldiers were admitted, and by the time Sonia came up for air the dayshift had started. But where was Anna?

By midday Anna was still a no show and she asked the staff, but no one had seen her since the previous night.

Dead on her feet she left to go straight to her room. Her feet moving automatically, reaching her room, she fell on the bed and slept.

The sun was already high, hot and extremely bright when she forced her eyes open. Looking at her watch it was close to 17h00. She reached for the capsules, drinking three pills and dozed off.

SOMEBODY WAS SHAKING HER. It seemed only minutes later. She slapped it away, but it persisted. Wild and fearful she smacked at the hands which held her. From afar someone called her. She pushed with all her might, but nothing helped. The grip held her tight.

"Sonia, wake up!" the person yelled. Then everything came into focus. Doug's anxious face stared at her and she groaned.

"Sonia?" Her name woke her completely.

Worried eyes looked at her.

"Yes Doug, I am fine." She felt stupid for acting out. How did he enter her room? Furniture was askew, the door opened at a slight angle.

"I had to push them away when you didn't respond," he replied.

"Why was the furniture in front of the door?"

"I don't know," he replied, puzzled at the state of her room.

"You worry us, Sonia."

"I am fine," she replied again and placed her feet on the cold cement.

"You are not fine, Sonia. You are shaking. It does not look fine, to me. Besides, you are late for your shift." She cleared her throat, and he passed her a bottle of water.

"I will be okay, Doug, promise. Why are you here?"

"Anna is in a terrible shape." His concern edged his voice. Feeling lightheaded she pinched her nose.

"Are you well?"

"What about Anna?"

With a heavy heart he replied. "Anna was attacked."

She stood, but dropped, taking in deep breaths. She rose again, this time slower.

"Are you up to it?" He reached for her.

"Thanks, Doug," she finally said and leaned on him.

"Are you sure?"

"Yes," and with a quick glance at her image she brushed her hair. The scrubs creased, but it had to do.

BRUISED AND BATTERED ANNA was lying in the hospital bed, her normally silky skin now pale, stricken with pain and fear. Both eyes swollen and an ugly cut marred her face from her forehead to her jaw. Her right arm was broken. Her left wrist, three ribs and an ankle broken and her insides in such a mess that they doubt she would ever have kids. At one stage Anna opened her eyes and mumbled her attacker's name before she slipped into a comatose state.

Silence cloaked the entire base. The thought of rape by one of their own to unfathomable that the soldiers' silence was the only way of support they could give.

Sam paced the medics outside, swearing loudly as he vented. He would kill the bastard when he found him. Treating women like scum had never sit well with him. Alexi found it difficult to control him and prayed softly for peace and that they would find the culprit.

Once the name of the attacker became known, there was no stopping Sam Gerber. Turmel gathered a team of men to search for Brock with Sam as the team leader. Brock was a trained soldier who knew the area well. It would be difficult but with Sam and Alexi taking the lead he would be found.

Corporal Wayne Morris had found Anna in her room. It was unlike her not to show up for her shifts and searched for her. Her hysteric state forced him to call Charlie for help. She did not allow any man near her. At the medics they sedated her.

With the doctor in the village they had to wait. She needed an urgent operation.

NOTHING LIKE THIS HAD ever happened before in any camp they stationed her, Sonia thought. Not that it never happened in other military camps, but this case highlighted the importance of abuse again. She took a seat next to Anna's bed and stayed there until the doctor arrived. The memories of her own ordeal written in bold as she kept vigilance over her colleague.

Anna thrashed on the bed in such fear that she wet the bed at one stage. Sonia administered a sedative and when she calmed, she cleaned Anna quickly.

A plan formed, one she had to address with Phillip. He would know how to begin. Then she prayed.

62

1 September 2019, Chula Vista, San Diego.

"JILLIAN."

"Dad!" Long, slender arms encircled him. He hugged her fiercely, feeling the bump of his growing grandchild pressed into him. Her blond tresses ticklish, she chuckled and kissed him soundly on a cheek before she stepped away.

"Mark."

"Dad!" He greeted him with the same appreciative tone. His son's hard body had grown and by the looks of things, he matured into a handsome young man.

"How are you two?" Mark took his duffle bag from him and proceed to the exit. He followed them to the parked SUV.

"We are good, Dad," Jillian replied and brushed over her stomach. The T-shirt she chose shifted and revealed a pierced belly button. Her low-cut denim showed even more skin.

Mark's faded denim and black T-shirt stretched over bulky arms. At the same height as him women stared after him. One winked at him and Mark smiled. Even he got a wink or two from younger women and Curt pressed his sunglasses deeper onto his nose.

"How is everything?"

"Well as can expected," Mark replied.

Mark took the wheel and followed the I-15 South towards their house. The familiarity added its own ease and they chatted away the twenty-five-minute drive. The amazing views were a welcome sight after all the sand, and Curt realized how much he had missed the place.

Mark slowed and turned into the driveway, a house he bought fifteen years ago on recommendation of Vivian. Neatly trimmed shrubs lined the garden, and a tall tree covered the front lawn creating a peaceful setting. Roses fringed the edges beautifully. The cobbled path led up to an ornate wood door. The whitewashed two-story house evidence of luxury.

Vivian was at the front door, beautiful as always. Dressed in black pants and a red silk shirt, it complimented her darker locks and skin. The make-up showed off her best attributes with bright blue eyes, high cheekbones and full lips. Her slender figure the result of years of hard work in the gym, the stiletto's doing wonders for her figure: every man's dream.

But for Curt the picture resembled pain and betrayal. He had hoped for a good night's sleep before the confrontation, but it was out of the question. His struggles with her infidelity left him helpless. Seeing her brought it all back.

"Sorry, Dad," Mark said. "She overheard the conversation," and parked the car. With a last look to his children, he got out and followed the path with some heaviness.

"Oh love, just look at you. You look marvellous," she drawled it out in her honey voice.

Curt greeted her with a peck on the cheek. She wrapped long arms around his neck and turned her face to offer ruby red lips.

Help me, Lord, he cried inwardly. She was the woman he loved and cherished all the days of his life. The woman he vowed to give a second chance. He tried, he really tried. He simply could not continue with the mockery.

Burger was certain there was a reason for the delay, but he could not see it. Phillip suggested using this time to solve their differences, even if it was hard to look past the betrayal.

Now she was here, on her tiptoes, smiling up at him as if butter could not melt in her mouth. Out of pure necessity he kissed her and stepped back. Vivian continued to babble on as if all were right between them. They entered the cool house where a feast awaited his arrival.

They talked … well, she talked, and they listened. When her mobile phone chirped, she walked away with a swing. He caught the children's rolling eyes and knew who it was. His heart squeezed with so much pain that he excused himself, walked to the spare room and closed the door. All he wanted was sleep, shut down and forget about his wife speaking to her lover on the other side of the brick wall.

They had nothing to add to what they already said. Two strangers in marital misery.

Back at base camp…

STILL IN A DAZE, ANNA HEARD HER NAME.

"Anna, you are safe." When she finally opened her eyes, emeralds gazed down with all the love she needed. The dream she had was so vivid that she could not distinguish between dream and reality. All the while the smoothing voice of Sonia Main filtered through, and finally, she slept.

"She is in a terrible state," Sonia said as she turned to the psychiatrist.

"Yes, it would be best to get her comfortable and back to the states for evaluation and healing."

"Yes," she agreed. "A month ago I requested another nurse from the CO. She will be here in a week," she replied.

"That's good news. I doubt Nurse Stalin will come back," he said thoughtfully.

"After the attack I doubt it myself," Sonia sighed and straightened the sheets. "It will be a pity; she is an excellent nurse."

"Yes, the men loved her," and he grinned.

She could not believe the man was capable of any form of emotion, but she made no remark and stated, "I will get the paperwork ready for her transfer."

"Thanks, Captain."

With one last glance towards Anna, Sonia pinched her eyes. The headache had emerged into a full-blown migraine. Her jaws tightened and she ran for the bathrooms.

Ten minutes later she stepped into the hallway. Dr Rogers waited for her. "Is everything, all right?" he asked.

"Nothing a pain pill and sleep will not cure."

"How long are you struggling with migraines?"

"It's only fatigue, nothing more," she brushed it off, but he saw right through her in the same way her father did all those years ago.

"They do not need your help right away. Therefore," and he led her to the ER, "I am prescribing you a cocktail and you will sleep this off, do I make myself clear!" His steel-grey eyes restrained her. He motioned for Morris to assist.

"We need a cocktail," he ordered. Wayne looked at her peculiarly and she handed him the key. She was familiar with the migraine cocktails.

"Doctor, I cannot stay away so long."

"We need you healthy, Nurse. You need to rest." Another bout of nausea stopped her reply as she doubled over a dustbin.

504

"There - there," the Doctor smoothed her and pressed a cool cloth against her neck. When she felt a bit better she straightened. Before she could object, Wayne administered the medicine with a grin on his face.

"Wayne will accompany you to your room. Sergeant West will cover for you. Dr Jourdain will make sure you are fit for duty before you are allowed in. Then, young lady, the two of us will have the long-awaited discussion ... the one you try so hard to avoid."

"Yes, Doc," she muttered, feeling small in the presence of the foreboding man. She needed help.

Michelle was a qualified Nurse, excellent in her duties and the men respected her.

Before she could argue, Morris had her at her arm. Her last sane thoughts were: The new nurse could not come quickly enough.

63

San Diego, California, United States.

CURT SPENT THE SECOND night with his children alone. Vivian left shortly after supper to show potential clients a new house, but she only arrived back after 04h00.

"Who sees a house at ten at night?" He was restless since she did not show.

"Don't worry about it, Dad."

"Thanks for supper," Jillian said as she kissed him goodbye.

"We are used to it. She will be back," Mark said as he greeted him.

In the living room he took a seat and prayed. His heart was breaking—she did not even try. By the time he stopped, he heard the key in the door. She passed him and seconds later the main bedroom door closed. His heart was heavy with the treachery in his own home. Exhausted he finally fell asleep. Two pain filled emerald eyes reeled in front of him. A smoky daze covered the rest of her face. I upset Sonia, Curt thought as he lay awake.

He brushed over his stubbled face. Turning to the digital clock, he shrugged the sheets from his sweaty body. With his running shoes on he left the house in the early hours of the day. The simple exercise helped him to relax, the openness on the road, the quietness of nature. Vibrant and relaxed. A light sea breeze tickled his nostrils.

It normally helped, but as he paced himself on the uphill, his heart and steps were in sync. "Sonia, how I miss you," he whispered.

Back at home he showered, and by the time he entered the kitchen Vivian was making breakfast—one of the few things she could do well. He forced a smile on his face and approached her. She looked up and smiled. Normally it would have curled his toes and made his heart jump, but the feeling was long gone. He was there to make amends. He forced himself to place a chaste kiss on her proffered cheek.

"Hi Darling, did you just wake?"

"No, I have been up a while," he answered and popped an apple piece in his mouth.

"Running?"

"Yes."

The one syllable conversation did not distract him. His mood was weary. She was still beautiful, still graceful in her actions and way of dress, but could not ignore the hard lines around her eyes and mouth.

"I hope you had a wonderful time with the kids?" she said conversationally.

"Yes, it was good to visit with them," he replied, taking a sip of water he poured. She was busy cutting bacon pieces and placed them in the pan to fry. The muffin mixture was ready and waiting to add the meat once done. The aroma hung in the air as he waited for her next question.

"I hope you didn't wait for me?" she asked with no shame in the dark blue eyes.

"No, I was praying," and she lifted one manicured brow.

"Praying?"

"Yes."

"Why, did you find religion?" and she scrambled the bacon pieces around in the pan.

"No, God found me," he said matter-of-factly. Again she looked at him.

"Why did you pray?"

"For us," came the immediate answer.

"For us? You mean me and you?"

"Yes."

"Why?"

"Because whatever is going on between us, can't continue. I need closure," he said.

This got her attention as she glanced up at him and blushed. Vivian McGee never blushed. Her no-nonsense attitude did not allow an insignificant blush of shame, but his answer clearly took a back. Her eyes flicked back, turned the plate knob and removed the warm pan. She placed the pieces on a paper towel before she added it to the mixture.

Silence hung between them as she added the muffin mixture in the prepared pan and placed it in the preheated oven. Silently she stood with her back turned to him. Curt decided it was time to end the silence.

"Where were you last night, Vivian?"

"I told you. To show a house to potential clients."

"Till four in the morning?"

"Curt, I am a grown woman," she started, but he interrupted her. "Yes, and married. Where were you, Vivian?" he insisted, his patience wearing thin.

"I went to see a friend."

"Neil Davies?"

"Now listen, Curt," she started impatiently.

"No Vivian, let us get this straight. You are my wife. I do not share my wife with any other man. If you do not accept this, you know what to do," and he straightened to his full length. "Do I make myself clear!?"

"I am not one of your soldiers you can order around. I am your wife," she snarled, her face contorted into ugly lines.

"Exactly! My wife, not a whore."

When she slapped him he grabbed her wrist and pulled her to him as he seethed out, "What will it be! Wife or whore?" His voice cold and detached.

"Mum, Dad?" Mark called out from the front door and he let go of Vivian's wrist. She rubbed the tender skin and took a deep breath.

"Hi, Son."

"Are you okay?" His eyes flicked between the two of them. Wisely his son said nothing, even when he focused on him briefly.

They planned the previous night to go to the beach. Jillian had classes, but Mark took the day off to spend time with him.

"Where are you going?" Vivian asked, her face not showing any signs of the fight they had.

"To the beach," Mark answered. "Mmm, what smells so nicc?"

"Savoury muffins," she replied and turned to the oven just when the alarm went off.

"Nice," Mark replied, and took out plates and knives to set the table.

"Can you drop me at the office?" Vivian asked. "My car is in the repair shop."

"Why, what happened?" Curt asked, raking over her.

"It's normal service, they collected it this morning," she quipped.

"Yes Mum, of course," Mark replied and cut into the warm muffin, the bacon and feta mix created a juicy and tantalising aroma. Vivian poured coffee for each, all the fragrances working together to create a serene atmosphere. But it was far from the truth.

Silently Curt asked for wisdom since the conversation was not over … not by a long shot. What threw him the most was how casually she continued as if nothing was amiss. Her actions and voice were pleasant and calm, but the brief twitch in the left corner gave it all away. She was nervous.

His wife still had not answered him, and he was angry. If Mark did not show up, it would have been hard to maintain his patience.

The interruption was God's way to keep him calm, he knew it. He came home to sort out his marriage. He did not want this thing to linger between them once he returned to base. As he watched mother and son arguing about the latest girl in his life, he wondered if she listened to herself. Preaching to him yet seemed to see no fault in her conduct in the marriage.

Once the breakfast was over and the dishes cleaned, they left with Mark at the steering wheel. Vivian sat directly behind him as she continued with the conversation. There was no opportunity to raise the topic again, and reluctantly Curt followed them into the Mustang.

Tension rose in the confined space of the car. Vivian clearly wanted to say what's on her mind. Mark clutched the wheel to keep his composure, but she was not one to give up a fight or lose. With grand finesse she told him exactly what she thought of the Maxi, Curt had yet to meet.

During the twenty-minute drive, Curt had to commend his son for holding his tongue. Then finally, with blood-shot eyes, Mark had enough. His anger flared.

"Will you stop this? Maxi is a decent girl!"

"Mark!" Curt yelled as he made a U-turn right in front of Vivian's office.

A truck slammed into them with a sickening screech of metal hitting metal. The car with its occupants swooped away into traffic. Another car hit them, they rolled. The car twisted. It became a metal tangle and when silence fell, the smell of oil and petrol perforated the warm air. People rushed to help, others called the paramedics. Histeria mixed into the fray.

But they knew nothing about it.

64

Iraqi desert.

"PLEASE HAVE A SEAT," Dr Rogers motioned. Reluctantly Sonia took the seat opposite him.

It was the first time she entered his office. It looked like hers, just bigger, with the same governmental issued desk and chairs. No soft music to calm the nerves and no plush sofa.

There were no family photos, just like her. A few certificates from prominent universities and his master's degree in Psychiatry hung in black frames against the one wall. Shelves on the opposite side displayed medical books neatly stacked and used. His desk was clinically clean with no papers strewn around, only one open folder in plain sight. Her photo laughing at her.

"Thank you," she replied.

"How do you feel today?"

The concoction they gave her knocked her out for twelve hours. When she woke, she felt disorientated. She visited Anna first, but she slept, and Michelle confirmed she was doing all right. Her flight was booked for 14h00 hours.

"I am feeling better. Thank you, Doctor," and she grinned sheepishly.

"Tell me about the nightmares?" he came straight to the point. Her pulse quickened. Phillip urged her to talk about her experiences. He summarised that it influenced her healing. With her past as the deciding factor, it would trap her if not dealt with. Except for the doctor and Curt, no one knew about the pregnancy. Being in this position felt vulnerable, and she wondered if open-heart patients felt the same.

She squinted out the open window. Soldiers with fully rigged gears on their backs got into a Humvee outside the office. Officers hollered commands and more men scattered around to accommodate the never-ending flood of orders. The sun left them in a daze of white heat. Dust coloured the sky and someone sneezed.

Sam got into a jeep, his rucksack looked heavy. He and Alexi would be gone for a week, leaving her alone. They had become good friends and visited at regular intervals.

It all looked so normal. Only she was not part of the business.

"Captain?" His voice startled her and met his gaze. Her fingers fidgeted.

"When did it start?"

"I always had nightmares; since the age of eighteen. It just became more frequent after the abduction. Worse." she finally admitted.

"Why did you have them before the abduction?"

With difficulty Sonia swallowed. This would be the first time she would speak about it to a stranger. She had guarded all her grown-up life as a shameful experience she didn't want to be reminded of. "I mostly dreamt about my son."

"You have a son?" He looked through her folder. The deep frown increased.

She stopped him. "He died during birth," she clarified.

"When?" he asked in a low voice.

"Twenty-five years ago. I was only eighteen at the time, living on the streets of Pretoria when he was still born," she answered, the small image still in her mind, fresh as yesterday.

"I am so sorry to hear this," he added softly. She nodded, brushing the tear away.

"Do you want to tell me more?" He broke the silence after a few moments to gather herself.

"Not much to say. I believed a man loved me enough to take care of me and the baby, but he left. I had no one to turn to and ended up on the streets. I was saved, but for my son it came too late." Quietly she stared at her hands. "The images still haunt me. It is bearable, but just before the abduction it started up again."

"Why?"

"My path crossed with Brady, and I had to tell him about his son. It was difficult. He and his wife are struggling to get pregnant."

"How does it make you feel?"

"Oh, I don't know. On the one hand I feel terrible, but I take pleasure in his pain." She met his gaze. "Does it make me a bad person?"

"No." Dr Rogers replied, his tone softer.

"Then the abduction." She said practically, as if it had happened to someone else.

"Yes, then the abduction. What frightened you the most about the entire ordeal?"

"Rejection," she simply stated, "to be forgotten." The last part came from a deep place of hurt.

"Like on the streets," he pointed out.

"Yes." She hiccupped. This time tears spilled over and she lowered her head. For a long time her cries were the only sound as Dr Rogers gave her the time she needed.

"So you lock yourself in?"

Surprised she looked at him, but his face stayed blank. The thought was so outrageous, but it stared her in the face. She was locking herself in. The thought so profound that she fell silent. Searching herself.

"Yes, the fear of getting lost—not being able to defend myself."

"This gives you security?"

"Yes," she admitted.

"You are amid trained armed forces with thousands of men who will protect you, and you feel fearful." Not a question, just an observation, and he leaned forward, his elbows resting on the desk.

"I know," and she blushed as the ineffective and wasted thoughts hit her, "but it comes automatically," she defended her actions.

"There was no one to protect you. Ever."

"No."

"But yet you hoped they would save you?"

"Yes. When I received the Bible from Tau, it gave me hope."

"And when they rescued you, that hope was fulfilled?"

"Yes."

"But you placed the furniture in front of the door?" Uncomfortably she shifted and chuckled nervously. "Silly, I know."

"No, not silly, just sincere," he admitted. "You are still struggling with the tragic loss of the baby, abandoned by your lover and the daily harassment by your abductors. These factors all came together as one messy cake. You feel fragile and unprotected, even between all these men." He looked to the outside world and she followed his gaze. Heavily armed men marched passed the window, ready to go into action.

"I am not big on religion, but I believe your God brought you to a place of safety to teach you how to trust again." His eyes flicked back to hers and he asked, "Are you willing to trust Him?"

"Yes," she whispered, his words hitting home. Just after she arrived the Lord said so much in the first service she joined. And, although she confessed it with her lips. Her actions spoke otherwise.

"God has not given me a Spirit of fear, but a Spirit of love, joy and a sound mind." She quoted the well-known scripture.

"Yes," he agreed. "Did you not tell me how the commander prayed for your protection and how you were kept safe during all those weeks in the heart of Africa?"

"Yes."

"So, was it all a lie?"

"No," she admitted, her eyes wide with awkwardness, and she swallowed.

"When I am afraid, I put my trust in you. In God, whose word I praise, in God I trust; I shall not be afraid. What can flesh do to me? Ps 56: 3-4, I believe," Dr Rogers stated, and she smiled, her green eyes striking to life.

"Unless something else happened, which makes you doubtful?"

Uneasy, she avoided his stare. Touching her stomach, she thought of those few days. Where was God during that time?

"Sonia?"

"Isn't our time up?"

"We still have a few minutes."

The clock's hands loudly ticked each second away. Each second robbed her of the peace she needed, but her doubts and fears had the upper hand.

"Our time is up." He said after a while and moved away from the table.

Grateful to get away, she thanked him.

"I want to see you again—same time, same place. Unless you do not address everything, it will steal your peace."

"Yes, Doctor."

In her office she prayed,

"Father, I still have much to understand, but thank you for bringing me to a place of safety. Please forgive me. I lay all my fears before you. You are my refuge and my strength."

She was about to stand when the overwhelming sense to pray for Curt and his family overpowered her.

Reciting PS:91 over them.

Her voice was firm and convincing.

65

3 September 2019, Base camp, Iraq.

"THEY ANALYSED THE SHIRT YOU SENT. The traces of blood belonged to Celia White," and Doug chuckled with relief.

"The court forwarded an arrest warrant to your camp for the release of Staff Sergeant B. Castledale into our custody." Reeves' voice was hoarse with excitement.

"What does Cummings say?"

"Relieved. The judge is signing his release forms as we speak."

"Great!" Then he toned down, Reeves was unaware of the missing Brock. So far the search delivered no results. Four fruitless days met with frustration.

"There is one snag in this," Doug finally said.

"What?"

"Staff Sergeant Castledale has disappeared after molesting a nurse to near death. We are searching every place." This wasn't good PR for the military. Curses met his ears as Reeves muttered obscenities, Doug waited patiently. "So far he has not left the country," he assured him.

"I want this man," Reeves spat.

"Yes, believe me, we are too. He faces a Court Martial."

The man groaned and then clicked the phone. So much for his honesty, he thought.

Captain Main passed him on her way to the mess hall, and he ran to catch up with her.

"How are you doing?" he asked.

She smiled when she saw him and replied. "Much better, thank you. Looking forward to the new nurse arriving tomorrow."

"Was she not supposed to come on Monday?" he asked surprised.

"Yes, but I asked the Major nicely," and she batted her eyelids.

"Do you know who it is?"

"Not a clue, but they assured me she is well qualified and ready to join us."

They gathered plates, dished up their food and took a seat. As always their conversations turned to the Word and what they have discovered.

AFTER HER APPOINTMENT WITH DR ROGERS on Tuesday, she had a discussion with Phillip after supper.

"I am glad you are better, Cap."

"I feel much better."

"Why did you want to see me?"

"Fear has a hold over me. I need to deal with it." She had a long, hard talk with herself. Being fearful made little sense any longer. It caused so much emotional pain that her body was acting on it. The migraines were not from God, but robbed her of her peace. She could not be useful if she could not control her own fears.

"Do you want to tell me more?"

This time she told everything—from the first day of her abduction to her pregnancy. Once she was done, he prayed with her.

"Sonia, I want you to take this bottle of oil," and he handed her a small bottle of golden liquid.

"This is olive oil. I want you to apply it to your door post and window. Take authority over this fear and trust God completely. This represents God's anointing, protection and favour."

She opened the bottle and breathed it deeply. The fragrance reminded her of the day she went to the building.

"I remember this smell just before the lockup. Why did God not protect me then?"

"I wish I can wipe it away, but, Sonia, you did nothing to deserve this. Evil walks around and sees who he can devour. You were at the mercy of this man who felt nothing for you. He deliberately cut you off from your protector and harmed you. That is downright evil, but God will defend you. You might never learn the how, but God will defend you. That is his promise to you according to **Deuteronomy 22:25-27**.

25: But if a man finds a betrothed damsel in the field, and the man force her, and lie with her: then the man only that lay with her shall die.

26: But unto the damsel thou shalt do nothing; there is in the damsel no sin worthy of death: for as when a man riseth against his neighbour, and slayeth him, even so is this matter:

27: For he found her in the field, and the betrothed damsel cried, and there was none to save her.

"God heard your cries and sent Tau to you. You do not have to feel guilty for that. You were in a very unhealthy and troubled place. You did what you had to do to protect yourself. This child is the fruit of that protection and it will never happen again. God has sealed it. You can accept it as God's gift to you."

Sonia allowed the words to wash over her.

"Forgive yourself," he finally broke the silence. "You don't have to feel guilty. Never. God is on your side."

"Evil has tried to stop my promises."

"Yes, he tried and failed. Here you are. Healthy, protected and loved."

She smiled.

"Can I serve God's meal to you?"

"I believe I'm ready to receive it," she replied.

The entire encounter while they broke bread and drank water instead of wine, lifted her spirit.

She did as he told her to do, and that night she slept peacefully.

The table and chair stayed against the wall each night after that. Her dreams dominated by a certain tall man. Rigid and proud he called her, and each time she woke, confused, not sure what to make of it. But she prayed for him and his family. It was the right thing to do; she was convinced of it.

66

RELAXING WITH A BOOK, Sonia had found in the pub, the first book in a while, a loud explosion broke the silence. Sonia scrambled out of bed and stood outside as soldiers rushed past her. Walking to the corner of her building she noticed Doug and called him.

"There was an explosion at one of the gas lines and we have to check it out. You stay here, Ma'am, and sleep."

"You will let me know if you need help?"

"Yes, Ma'am, go to bed," and he jogged away.

She stretched and got into her bed, crunched the pillow under her and fell asleep.

Suddenly a weight pressed on her. Startled she opened her eyes to feel a warm breath against her face. She could see nothing in the darkness, the sliver of moonlight not enough to identify her attacker. Pushing with all her might the man laughed wickedly. Recognition shot through her and fear captured her breath. The sound from him, ice cold. She shivered uncontrollably.

"You!" she mumbled, her mouth covered with an enormous hand. The sudden intrusion of light left her blind, and she blinked. When she finally focused the fugitive stared at her with a smug grin. Fighting against the hold, he pinned her securely underneath him. The sour smell of liquor confronted her nose.

"You can try as much as you like, but no one will save you. No one is close, not even Doug, and I will have my way just as I imagined it."

She tried to scream, but it did not help. His hand smothered her.

"You will not scream." The sound roared in the room and she kept her mouth shut. He lowered himself until their noses touched. "Understood!" he hissed, and she nodded.

"You learn quickly. Now let me see what we have here." She moaned helplessly, kicking with her legs. When he rolled his eyes in pain, she knew she had kicked a sensitive spot, and he slapped her again. Blood trickled along her lip and smeared her face.

"You bitch," he growled and with one swift move he turned her around and pressed her face into the pillows.

"*Please Lord*," she whispered with a cry, "*not this.*"

"What the hell!"

"Sam!" She tried to scream, but her head was still in the cushion, curses drowned everything else out. Then the weight lifted.

She pushed herself to turn as a table broke. Sam and Brock were in a tight hold. Sam punched Brock in the gut, which gave him momentarily the upper hand. Followed by a kick Brock fell on the floor; his face hit the cement with a thud. Sam was on top of him, slamming his face into the floor.

"Sam, stop! Stop!" But he did not listen as he pounded into her attacker mercilessly.

The next moment another big body sheltered her vision and slipped her sweater around her shoulders. She shivered, screamed for the person to make it stop as the fight grew in intensity. The room became a pool of confusion as the two men fought. When Sam got the upper hand, he pushed hard against Brock, slamming his head into the cement floor with a sickening thud. Groans of determination mixed with her screams. The entire time she was kept away.

Then silence—like someone had covered her ears with earplugs.

"There now." She recognised Alexi's smoothing accent as he patted her. "It is over." More voices entered her room, and soon she felt a prick in her arm and slept.

How long she was out she could not recall before she woke, startled—unsure of her surroundings, her dream gone.

"Sonia, it's me. You are safe." The same words of her dream were repeated. However, it was not Curt, but Dr Rogers.

"You are safe, Sonia," he whispered, brushing away the tears. She was still in her room covered with a sheet and blanket.

"Staff Sergeant Castledale is gone. It is only us."

She must have fallen asleep, because when she woke it was midday. The sun was streaming into her room and she shoved the covers from her sweaty body. This time she was alone. She sat up straight, reached for the bottled water and took huge gulps of it. The soothing water refreshing to a dry throat.

Her room was wiped from any traces Brock could have left. Numbly she placed her feet on the floor. It all happened so quickly that Sonia was unsure about most of it.

Two raps startled her, and she rose. "Yes?"

"It is us." Alexi and Sam stood with a nurse her own age next to them. She blinked. It could not be, but when she opened them again her friend stood before her.

"Lee Ann!"

"Yes, my darling," the blond replied with a laugh, concern covered the corners of her lush lips.

"When they told me who was attacked, I had to make sure. And here you are, Sonia Main," and the two women hugged each other.

"I guess you two know each other," Sam said dryly, and both women chuckled. Sonia introduced Lee Ann Buys to them.

"We were in nursing school and applied at the Red Cross after we attended a conference. Then we split. This is the first time we see each other in what … fifteen years?"

Lee Ann nodded, "Yes, fifteen years. You have not changed a bit. Just as lovely as ever," and Sonia blushed.

"I can say the same for you."

"You lie and you know it. Look at me, I gained at least five kg since the last time we spoke."

"Well, if you ask me, the five kg sits in perfect places," Sam quipped. Sonia slapped him against the shoulder and Lee Ann blushed.

"Hey, it is true. Skinny women were never attractive," he explained seriously, and Alexi agreed wholeheartedly with a grin.

"Please come in and excuse my friend," Sonia said.

Alexi took the only available chair and Sam and Lee Ann sat on the unmade bed.

"Can someone tell me what happened last night?"

Alexi started. "Sam was here first before he could harm you," and she looked at Sam, who met her gaze.

How will she ever repay this man who came to her aid, twice?

"What happened to him?"

Alexi reached for her hand and held it tight.

"Brock is dead." Alexi's cold answer left her speechless, "What!?"

"The bastard is dead," Sam repeated, his voice equally cold. She

looked at Lee Ann who shrugged her shoulders and then at Alexi.

He nodded and squeezed her hand.

"Tell me what you have done," she whispered, looking at all three.

534

"Sam was the first one who noticed something was wrong, a sixth sense if you like," and Sam smirked. Killer instinct is the correct term, he thought.

"He asked what if the explosions were a diversion because we were all there, the camp practically unguarded. Doug said he spoke to you and sent you back to bed, and then we ran. Sam kept on saying it did not seem right. He was the first to get back. By the time I reached your room, he was already pounding into the man while you were screaming."

Sonia listened in utter shock. It happened so quickly that she thought she had dreamt it.

"When I finally got him of him, he was unconscious. He died this morning from head wounds."

She looked away, wiping away the tears and then turned back. "Thank you," looking at both men, "I couldn't believe what he tried."

Sam was facing prosecution, but she did not have to know it, not yet anyway, they all decided.

Sonia turned her attention to Lee Ann. "I can't tell you how good it is to have you here. You are a God sent," Sonia said once settled.

"I don't know about that, Darling, but it is great to finally work with you, for sure," and she chuckled delightfully. Both men grinned.

"Are you up for lunch, because I am starving?"

A low groan emanated from Sam as he stated, "A woman after my heart."

Sonia grinned. "Yes, I believe I am. Just give me a moment to freshen up?"

"Yes, Darling, we will wait outside, right boys," and they nodded.

Sonia shook her head. Alexi and Sam were far from boys. They both towered over them, but sheepishly the two agreed and followed Lee Ann, especially Sam.

When the trio stepped outside, Alexi walked aside to answer a call. It gave Sam the opportunity to speak with Lee Ann.

"So, any man waiting I must be aware of?"

"Boy, but you are blunt," she remarked with a chuckle, her blue eyes meeting him with a mischievous glint.

"Well?" and he chuckled. "No time in wasting," he agreed and raised a brow in question.

"No, there is no man waiting anywhere," she finally admitted.

"It's hard to believe."

"That it is, but still the truth."

"Why, is there something wrong with you?"

She laughed. "I stand under correction. You are plainly rude, Sam Gerber."

"Well?" Sam could not remember the last time a woman fascinated him from the start, and although rude, it was better to get to the heart of it.

"No, nothing is wrong with me. There was just no time for any lasting relationship if you must know."

"I understand," and silence fell between them. Not the awkward kind, but the mutual understanding kind before he said. "Drinks later on?"

"Yes, why not? Then you can show me all the attractions," the meaning clear as she looked at him with appraisal. He chuckled and stepped closer so his hand could brush against the delicate skin of her lower arm, the rest covered under the usual uniform of medical staff.

"I like you, Lee Ann Buys. What kind of surname is it anyway?" he asked in a low tone.

"South African, the origin I believe is Dutch," and she swallowed, the man affecting her more than she cared.

"It suits you," he whispered, his breath warm against her lips, nearly touching her.

"Thank you," she whispered, the electricity intense as sparks lingered between them. Everything else forgotten. Almost.

Just then Sonia appeared in the door and they parted, but the result was still shimmering between them.

Both Sonia and Alexi looked at the couple, stunned, and then grinned. Sam was smitten. They never thought they would see the day that Sam Gerber would lose his heart.

67

5 September 2019, Military Hospital, San Diego.

CURT WOKE WITH ANTISEPTICS which stung his nostrils and gasped. The oxygen tube was uncomfortable, he tried to remove it. His attempt thwarted by a gentle hand.

"Daddy," Jillian's voice broke through the cobwebs.

"Jillian, Pumpkin," he whispered. The youthful face filled with concern. She looked tired.

"Don't talk, Dad, just be still. The nurse will come to help you."

"Thirsty." A glass with a straw appeared before him. Gladly he took the soothing icy water. Tiresome he laid back on the cushions. The worried expression on his daughter's face reminded him where he was.

"What happened?"

"Don't you remember?" Her voice broke. Now he noticed her red swollen eyes, her pale face.

"Pumpkin?"

"Mum is dead."

He gasped in shock. "Mark?"

"He is still alive, but they are not sure if he will make it."

"No," and he tried to get up, but his right leg was heavy, his body tight. Only then did he notice the cast on his leg. Bandages covered his chest and right arm.

"I am so happy you are awake. For a moment I thought I have lost you, Dad."

"I am not planning to go anywhere soon, Pumpkin," he consoled. He reached for her, their hands meeting in a tight hold. Vivian was dead, Mark fighting for his life.

The accident hurried back, brakes screeched, then an overpowering BOOM, the smell of gasoline and then nothing. He closed his eyes and swallowed.

"How long was I out?"

"Two days," she admitted. "I am so glad you finally woke. I was so scared. I didn't know what to do."

"It's okay, honey," and kissed her small hand.

"Grandpa said we don't have to worry; all arrangements are done. The funeral is tomorrow morning." More tears fell. "I cannot believe she is dead. I wished her dead at one time." Her voice was small.

"Don't do this, Jillian, this is not your fault," he assured her with a slur.

A nurse approached. "Do you have pain, Sir?" He flinched when a hand brushed against his ribs.

"We will make you comfortable. Please excuse us, Miss, but we have to care for our patient."

"Yes of course. I am glad you are awake, Dad."

THE SUN FILTERED THROUGH his room when Curt opened his eyes. A ray touched the sheets warming his bed. The coldness faded and he thanked God for his life, earnestly asking to spare his son.

"Lord, there were so much unfinished business between me and my wife. Now she is gone." His voice hitched, the guilt of not doing enough. Their last angry words towards each other.

A deep voice nudged him back. Immediately he recognised his father-in-law. It smoothed his aching heart.

"Curt, do not blame yourself." He met the concerned eyes of Markus Kent. "I know what my daughter has put you through. I had discussions with her about her choices, but she was not willing to consider it. Nor thought it was a problem, not even a sin. She thought she had the right to have affairs. This last one she didn't even hide." His heart opened for Curt to see.

He always liked his in-laws. Markus and Janette Kent were two caring, loving soles—God-fearing people who did not only talk, but walk the road they preached. Even her brother, Gustav, was a good man, loved his wife since day one, but Vivian was different. She refused to be captured in a box and did her own thing. At first it drew him to her, but it also drove them apart.

"I think it was God's way of taking care of a stubborn heart," he finally added.

"I never prayed for this," Curt admitted, choking on a sob. He genuinely cared about her. She was his wife, friend and lover. She was the mother of his children. He shared with her twenty-five years of memories.

"I wanted to fix things, the reason I came. I had a challenging time coping while she was gallivanting around. It feels I have failed her."

"I know, Curt. Your salvation is truly a blessing to us. You did the best you could. You are not to blame. Your prayer of restoration is heart-warming. We prayed as well, but she was not willing to sway."

"Something happened overseas which led me to a commitment to the Father. There were just too many unanswered questions." Silently he looked at the white ceiling. "I had a tough time accepting the facts of my marriage. I came to restore what was left."

Markus tapped his hand without commenting. What was there to say, after all?

Curt's heart was heavy and he whispered softly. "I met a woman a few months ago and fell in love with her." What a crazy thing to admit to anyone especially your father-in-law, but it was out before he could stop it and grinned sheepishly.

"I am so happy to hear, Curt. We prayed for you often enough to find the happiness you deserve. Vivian cared only for one—herself. We will never stand in your way to pursue this love." He smiled reassuringly. "Tell me about her."

Curt smiled. For the first time he could speak openly about Sonia. The guilt gave way for a new life. Breath-taking slow he spoke about her.

"She is beautiful." His eyes sparkled.

"But of course," and both men grinned.

"She is the head nurse at base camp. She has the most beautiful emerald eyes you can drown in, long curly hair and a perfect body."

"Mmm." Markus smiled with a hint of approval without comment.

"Loving, stubborn and strong. A stunning smile." Both men chuckled. "I miss her."

"Does she love you?"

"I hope so." He stared out the window. "I pushed her away. I wanted to give my marriage another chance. I vowed to stay with Vivian and pushed Sonia away. I must believe she still loves me. I need to phone her, tell her."

Markus stopped him. "Careful, Curt. You need to heal completely first. You were knocked out cold for two days. Be patient. If she is the love of your life, she will be there. That you wanted to stay and do what you had to save your marriage, proves your integrity and tested your obedience." Silence fell between them as Jillian and Janette joined them.

"How is Mark?"

"His condition didn't worsen," Markus replied.

"I need to be with him," he insisted.

"I will get a wheelchair," Markus offered. Once the wheelchair appeared, Curt's disdain was visible.

"Come on, Dad, it's not that bad." Reluctantly he took a seat in the obnoxious thing, being this helpless foreign.

They took him up a long corridor, then took a lift to the second floor before they reached ICU. The staff allowed him entrance. The first thing he noticed was the relentless beep of the monitor above his bed. Pale and fragile, lips blue, eyes closed. Bandages covered his head, crisscrossing the right eye. Cuts and bruises covered the open skin. His normally fit and bulky body covered in casts.

"Good morning, Colonel. I am Dr Samurai." The lanky man towered over Curt, his head covered with grey. The glasses sat low on his nose which gave him a strictness, his tan evidence of an active life.

"I know it looks serious, but he is out of the woods. He has no internal bleeding and his spine isn't broken."

"That is good to hear."

"His lung was punctured by two ribs, which was our primary concern."

"Has he woke since the accident?"

"No, he hasn't. The swelling on the brain is the reason. We keep him sedated to help with the healing. He is stable for now."

"Thanks, Doc."

"We will monitor him closely. He is strong and healthy, which counts in his favour. We will keep you posted."

Curt reached for the hands around him and on signal they chained together as he prayed.

68

Basecamp, Iraq.

LEE ANN WAS ON HER WAY back to her room. Her shift ended four hours ago, but they were swamped and she stayed. To work with a co-student after all the years, was the highlight. Many had married and left the Red Cross to pursue a family. Only two remained of the original group. She remembered Sonia Main quite fondly.

Sonia had changed from a terrified little girl to a mature woman. Her managerial skills laced with precision and care. She was reminded of the Matron back in Pretoria. She had the same dedication to her staff and patients and well loved.

Sonia was a silent and strong woman. Back then she never mingled with the group, but Lee Ann remained close to her, protective. When the other girls spoke nastily about her, she defended her. Although never close friends, they connected.

Her dedication had paid off. She was an inspiration and comfort for most. Now they were colleagues in a military basecamp off all places.

Only when she felt a touch, did her attention return to the surroundings.

"Hi, beautiful." She grinned and looked up in coffee-coloured eyes, sparkling with mischief.

"Hi," she got out. "You scared me."

"I was next to you, but you were so deep in thought that you didn't see or hear me. I am not sure if I offended you."

"No, I was only thinking," she admitted with a smile.

"About me?" His closeness raptured her chest. He stepped even closer and his lips brushed against her forehead. He smelled of desert, and sun. It woke the desires for more.

"No," and his expression soured. This was the first time they saw each other since the day they met. He was handsome in a rugged kind of way. His dark hair was already showing grey, it suited him.

"Now I am really hurt."

"Don't be, I do think of you often." Crow feet appeared under the soulful eyes, the scar on his face softer.

"Good to know." He glanced at the row of locked doors. "Which one is yours?" His voice trembled with desire and her own body reacted.

"Two doors away."

"Are you tired?"

"Yes, but I believe you can help me with it."

He grinned. "Oh yes, Baby, I definitely can," and he placed a kiss on her lips.

Once inside her room with the door closed, he pushed her against the door. "I believe you wanted to see some of the attractions this place has to offer?"

"Yes," she said breathlessly.

"Well, let's start with the tour then," and his lips covered her own.

"MAJOR TURMEL HAS ORDERED SAM'S ARREST." Doug informed them.

"Why?"

"He allegedly killed Brock with his fists."

"No!" Shocked Sonia pushed her plate away.

"He saved my life."

"Turmel feels it appropriate."

"He doesn't like Sam."

"Where is he?"

"Here he comes." Doug showed towards the door. Lee Ann accompanied him.

"It seems the two of you are getting it on?" Alexi said.

"At my age I have no time to waste, and she is available and willing."

"Every time I think this man cannot be blunter, he astonishes me." Lee Ann piped in as they sat across from each other—Lee Ann next to Sonia.

"But you like it. I do not mince my words and I say what needs to be said."

Just then two military police stopped behind Sam. Their serious faces brooked no argument.

"Sam Gerber, you are under arrest." Sam pushed his chair away. The group stared at them.

"Why?"

"For the murder on Staff Sergeant Castledale," said the tallest of the two.

"On what charge?"

"Manslaughter."

"But …!" Lee Ann called out, Sam glanced towards her, turned and went with them without a fight.

The mess hall grew quiet. Everyone knew what happened.

"But he defended me," Sonia said.

No one replied.

69

7 September 2019, Bentiu Hospital, South Sudan.

TAU LEANED AGAINST A TRUCK. The shadows concealed his presences from the onlookers. It was already past 19h00. The director of nursing normally leaves at 18h00 and did not appeared yet.

Time was running out. He needed information and this was the only place he could find it.

A donkey cart rumbled passed him as he crushed his cigar with a boot, then he crossed the street.

In the hospital he searched for any information to the office when he overheard a nurse who had to meet the matron. At a distance he followed, swerving through the busy hallways. Visiting hour made it easier to blend in.

When they entered the adjoining building, it became quieter and he fell back. At the second door she stopped and he waited patiently. Half an hour later the matron and nurse left without noticing him.

He waited for a minute longer, then tried the door. It was not locked. Once inside he went through every drawer but found nothing. A file cabinet caught his attention and he opened the drawer marked STAFF. Within a minute he had Sonia's file. Making sure he was still alone, he took snap shots of all the paperwork and removed the photo.

"Hello, Princess," he whispered and put it in his jacket pocket, making sure all was as he had found it before he left.

In his vehicle he switched on his phone and scanned the shots. Finally he found a letter and stared at it.

"What are you doing in Iraq?" He sighed. The situation in Iraq was not ideal and increased the scale to problematical. If she was in a military facility, he could not talk to her. No way would they allow him entrance.

What will he do? Roger was adamant. Just the thought of what Idil could do with her, had him cold.

Kwame informed him of Sarai's capture just that morning.

"What must I do?" He removed the photo from his pocket. It was a younger picture of Sonia. A rough hand touched the screen's face. She was even prettier than he could remember, his dreams overwhelmed by her presences.

He was ernest when he made that promise to her. No harm would come to her. But the situation he found himself in was difficult. He had to play for time.

He started his jeep and crawled into the traffic. A military truck in front attracted his attention. Then, smiling, a planned formed and he dialled a well-known number.

IT WAS MUCH LATER in the night that the two friends met. His agitation growing with every hour. He could not sleep or eat. He just wanted to get it over and continue with his life.

"This is betrayal. Roger will hang you," Kwame stated.

"He will kill everyone if we don't intervene. You know this. Can I trust you?"

"I have your back, but are you certain there is no other way?"

"*Pasti.*" (Certain) The car filled with cigar smoke as both men slumped back. Keeping their thoughts for themselves.

"How is Hilde treating you?"

"She is good to me." Hilde came into his life shortly after the rebuild of the camp. She offered him companionship and he offered her protection. There was no love, but she was a kind woman. What more could a man want?

"You miss her still?" He knew who Kwame referred to. Tau caught his only friend's gaze. "*Hirup Jalan terus.*" (Life goes on.)

"*Éta yakin henteu.*" (It sure does.)

He would never confess how much he missed her. Every heartbeat longs for her. Each time he closed his eyes, he saw her.

"Here is he now." Kwame pulled him from his thoughts.

The smugness of the man irritated him, now more than ever. He knew full well he had them by the throat. Roger sang according to his beat.

"It surprised me to receive a call from Roger's lieutenant." His men laughed with him.

"Did you bring the woman?"

"She is in the car."

"Where are the diamonds?"

"First the woman."

One man opened the door and dragged Sarai out. She landed with a thud on the ground.

"Bring her closer," Tau demanded.

They pushed her towards him, but Idil stopped her. She trembled, a fearful face covered with blood and tears.

"What did you do to her?" Tau seethed.

His evil laugh echoed through the empty building. No words were needed.

"I said she must be unharmed."

"She is still intact. Keep this up and I will damage her in such a manner you will never want her again." His men grinned and Tau clutched a fist.

"You have good taste in women, I must admit. It's a shame we could never taste the nurse."

"You will not touch her!" He threw a small packet to him. Idil caught it and opened the bag … light caught the uncut diamonds. Enough to still his quest for now.

"Sarai!" he called and Idil pushed her towards him. She fell and he helped her.

"You will leave us now." This was not a question, but Tau wanted to get away from him before he did a stupid thing.

"Sure. It was nice doing business with you. Until later."

"Get in the jeep. Now!" he commanded, trained eyes on the small group. They were totally outnumbered. All he could do was to get away. He didn't trust this man.

"I will have the nurse, Tau—with or without your help. This only buys you time."

Kwame and Sarai got in and with a last look Tau got in, his weapon trained on them.

"You will leave her alone." He seethed and the man's diabolical laugh followed them out of the building.

"This was too easy," Kwame said when they sped away.

"I know, but this was the only plan I could come up with."

He looked at Sarai; up close her bruises looked severe. She did not meet his gaze and pushed herself into the seat.

"Go to the matron's house."

"What must we do there?"

"She will take care of Sarai. I cannot take her to the camp."

"She is your first wife. Of course, you can."

"No, the nurse must patch her up and send her to her uncle. I have arranged for it all."

"I hope you know what you are doing?"

"No man will get their hands on any woman of mine, ever again."

At Haleema's house they stopped. In Sudanese he gave her a quick rundown of what he expected. When she protested he stopped her. He had no time to argue the point.

One knock on the door and she opened it without a word.

"Back to camp?"

"Yes."

"I hope this will not backfire on us."

"Sarai didn't look good."

"No, she didn't."

"We got her just in time."

They sped away into the darkness—an oppressive gloom that tried to choke him. He hated what he had become. With all his crimes he could add betrayer and diamond thief with it. His life was over when Roger would learn of this.

70

9 September 2019, Military Hospital, San Diego.

FOUR GRUELING DAYS PASSED as they waited for Mark to open his eyes.

"Where am I?"

"You are in the hospital, Son," Curt informed him.

"Why, what happened?"

"There was an accident."

"Are you okay, Dad?"

"Yeah, I am good, just a broken foot." He tapped against his cast."

"Mum?"

"She didn't make it." A silent tear vanished into the cushion.

"Mum's funeral was on Friday," Jillian said.

"What day is it?"

"Monday, the 9th," Curt replied.

"I am so sorry, Dad."

"It is not your fault, Son. No one blames you."

"That's right, Son," Markus said as he hovered over his grandson.

"You need to get well, Honey," Jeanette said.

"Gramps," then more tears rolled into the bedding.

"It's okay, Boy. You will go home in no time," Markus assured him.

"Get well soon. We will see you tomorrow."

"Thanks, Grams."

"You need to go too, Pumpkin."

"Yeah." Mark's eyes dimmed.

"We all will go so that you can rest. We will talk again."

"Thanks, Dad."

Outside his room Jillian stopped. A young soldier waited for them; one Curt had seen only in a picture.

"What are you doing here?" Jillian's aggressiveness aimed at him.

"I heard about the accident and thought to come," he said self-consciously.

"Now that all is good, now you come," she sneered.

"Jill," Curt stopped the flow. He was not in the mood.

"Dad, meet Lt Timothy Blackwell."

"Colonel," he stretched.

"At ease, Soldier."

"How is Mark doing?"

"He just woke."

"I am dead on my feet, Pumpkin. Good night. I will see you tomorrow."

"Good night, Dad."

"Colonel."

Curt never thought they would hear from him. Slowly he sauntered the hallway to the exit, the cane tapping with him. He could only hope the man was sincere.

At home a Get Well Soon card waited at the door. When he opened it the name was enough to upset him. None other than Davies signed it, wishing them all the best. At first it aggravated Curt tremendously. He did so much damage to his family.

"Let it be, Son. Don't fret about it."

"This is one pain I do not know how to deal with."

"You don't have to. Let God deal with him."

"Are you all right?" Jeanette asked.

"Yeah, I am going to lie down."

"Then we will see you tomorrow."

"Thanks for everything," Curt said.

In the spare room he laid back, his leg throbbing. The Davies name brought back ugly memories.

At Vivian's funeral he arrived, unashamed. Lucky for him he stayed in the background.

Harriet Davies introduced herself to him. A fine woman attached to a scoundrel. He could not see them together.

The day of the funeral Markus had picked them up. Together with family and friends they stood at her grave. They passed a bunch of red roses to him which he threw on the casket and said goodbye.

"I forgive you for all the heartache you caused, Vivian. I hoped to work things out, but time was against us. Maybe now you will find peace," he murmured. This was not the way he envisioned closure, but it brought peace back into his life.

Neil Davies had reached for him, but he ignored him. There was nothing he wanted to discuss with his wife's former lover. No words could resolve what had taken place. They would go on.

When he got into the car, Curt looked back to where the man knelt next to the grave, a handkerchief in his hands. He loved her, he thought grimly as they sped away. A toxic love that left a bitter taste.

The house was empty, devoid of anything warm and inviting. The next day he phoned the real estate agent for an appraisal. Jillian helped to pack all her things and gave it to a church outreach centre. His guilt, numbness and tiredness replaced with a quiet peace.

Now the house was an empty shell with nothing he wanted or cared for.

Then he smiled. God's promise all those months ago settled in his heart. "I WILL MAKE A WAY IN THE DESERT, ONLY BELIEVE."

Joy filtered through him and for the first time in a long time he laughed. It hurt as hell, but it felt good.

71

13 September 2019, Chula Vista, San Diego.

"PLEASE TAKE A SEAT PRIVATE," Curt addressed T.J Cummings. He phoned early morning and asked if he could speak to him. It pleased him to learn his hunch was correct and the young man was not guilty, but they could not leave the AWOL matter. It was a serious offence, and he wondered what the young man wanted.

Boxes lined the walls on both sides of the living room. For the last three days he packed in between visits with his son and Jillian. The Realtor and he agreed on a price and they put the house on the market. The sales sign outside announced it in bold red letters, URGENT SALE.

He had pressed for time. He wanted to return to camp and if Sonia would accept him, make her his. There was no doubt in his mind.

His appointment with General Andrews would steer his future in the right direction. It was a long time coming, but he was tired of the desert, and being absent from his children's lives. Soon to be a grandfather, he wanted to be close.

General Andrews had asked him frequently to take a position as Commander at the San Diego camp and he rejected it. He felt his duty was better served overseas.

Curt loved the city, the beach. The pulsing life vibrated through his pores. He was confident a certain young woman would be happy here as well. Now he could give her the family she wanted.

The baby would have a home. Taking the responsibility of another man's child was a hurdle to overcome, but if it meant he could have her, then the baby was not an obstacle. He would support Sonia all the way.

He grinned at his image in the mirror while shaving. You are a silly old coot. But he could not help himself, the joy it gave him was plastered on him.

His study was the only place not packed, and he led the private inside. "I am so glad to hear of your acquittal. You must be relieved."

"Definitely, Sir. Freedom never meant so much to me," Cummings said. "I will never take it for granted again." Laugh lines creased his mouth and eyes and McGee smiled.

"What can I do for you, Private?"

First, my condolences on your wife's death, Sir." Curt waved

him to silence and said quietly. "You know I have to report you. The Military Police are still looking for you."

"Yes, Sir. The reason I came. Starting over, I have to set things right beginning with the military."

"I do not get it, Private. Why leave? You had a bright future," a question which bugged him often.

The younger man met him without wavering. The eyes serious, devoid of any lies. His hands folded, but relaxed. He had a back bone, Curt thought as he waited.

"While I was in jail, I had a lot of time on my hands thinking about my life and the choices I have made. Wrong choices had put me into harm's way. If I stayed I would have never learned what I have when I was an inmate."

If nothing else, this man grew up quickly. To admit a wrong choice put him directly in harm's way must be difficult to come to terms with. His calm exterior showed he made peace with it. To be punished further would be a crime.

"It was a stupid reason," he continued. "My girlfriend just found out she lost the baby. We were so excited about that—to be a father," and his eyes misted. Curt could relate. He almost lost his son.

"You were in meetings and Sergeant First Class Ralph refused to give me clearance. I had to go to her. Her parents called and said sorrow overwhelmed her so much that it scared them, and I simply walked out." He dropped his eyes briefly.

"It was stupid, I know, but the weekend in question I was with Tracy and we got married. I love her. The murdered girl was a friend of a friend. I hardly knew her, but I helped her with her car trouble. This man must have seen us together and took the opportunity to hide his crime. If it were not for Tracy, I would have not made it alive out of prison. She saved me on many occasions from myself. If there is any way I could make this right with you and to the military, Sir, I would do it in a flash. I want to make it. I am a good soldier."

Curt nodded. A plan formed as he listened, and asked. "Do you want to return to the desert or stay in the States?"

"If possible, stay, but I will go wherever Uncle Sam sends me. I do not mind. All I ask is an opportunity to prove myself. You will never be disappointed in me again, Sir."

"I believe you, Private," Curt said. He had learned his lessons at such an early age, how fortunate for him.

"Okay, Soldier. I will see what I can do. I am at Headquarters tomorrow." His leg felt stiff and painful from the sit and stood.

"Thank you, Sir. That is all I ask, Sir." He was on his feet and saluted him, which he returned.

"We will speak soon."

"Yes, Sir … thank you, Sir," and he walked him to the front door.

72

"HOW ARE YOU, MCGEE?" General Andrews boomed in the office as he closed the door behind him. The General's office was typical of him. Mahogany furniture dominated the space. Shelves covered two walls from ceiling to floor. It held leather-bound books, honouring plaques and achievements throughout his career. A collection of photo frames of VIP's in the political arena were in a small group. The rest was with family and friends.

He never had children, but loved his wife. It was plain to see in all the photos and this added a warmth to the workplace.

He met Eleanor three or four times. The photos were not display pieces, they were truly in love. All his spare time was spent with her. Two paintings, both from the Rockies on the opposite wall, were painted by her. It was their favourite place which they visitcd often.

"I am well, Sir," Curt replied.

"The flight?"

"Good."

"It's a damn pity about your wife, Curt." This was the closest he would come to condolences as he could not stand Vivian. Then he did not understand the animosity.

"Thank you, Sir."

"Take a seat, man."

"Thanks, Sir," the plush deep leather chair a welcome offering,

The dark wood desk occupied with folders and a laptop on the side. The files neatly stacked in perfect piles from important to top secret. Sticky notes covered an open folder which he closed once seated.

"Can I offer you something?"

"Bourbon will be perfect." The General turned to a small table with a crystal carafe and tumblers pouring them each two fingers straight up. The General handed his glass.

"I tell you; it surprised me to hear from you. Never thought you would consider the offer." A year ago at a fundraiser Curt and Vivian attended, the General cornered him. They offered him the position of Commander since the present Commander was ready for retirement. Then he turned it down without a second thought.

"What changed your mind?"

"My life has taken a dramatic turn and I want to be close to my children," he admitted.

"Domestic. Curt McGee turns domestic." He chuckled and Curt grinned. "I never thought I would see this day. You have fine children." He raised his glass in salute and Curt did the same. "I hope there is a woman involved."

"In fact there is, Sir," and he smiled sheepishly, "the reason I had to see you."

"Good for you, Curt. Who is she?"

"A Red Cross nurse."

"Ah, a ministering angel. I admire Florence Nightingale tremendously," and Curt smiled. The General's interest could be seen in his study at home. He read every available book about the historical figure. His wife was a nurse during the war in Afghanistan, where they had met. He became fascinated with Ms Nightingale's accomplishments.

"She truly was, and Sonia is."

"Sonia, hey?"

"Yes, Sir, but there is a catch."

"Tell me, and it's done," and he leaned forward, his glass on the table.

"She is a South African."

573

"Consider it done. Do you have her file?"

"Yes, Sir." Retrieving the file from his briefcase, he handed it over. In silence General Andrews opened the file.

"But this is the abducted nurse you rescued?"

"Yes, the same person," and he grinned. "I met her before her abduction during a weekend breakaway. Then it wasn't possible to offer anything, but now I can."

"A lot of things make sense now, Curt, you devil." A smile creased his face and Curt grinned.

"I would like to hear the story and meet her," he said as his personal assistant rapped on the door and reminded him of an urgent matter which needed his attention.

"I have to go, leave it to me. I will let you know when the paperwork is ready."

"Thank you, Sir. Just one more thing, General. I will leave another matter on your desk. When you have a free moment, we can talk." The General nodded—both stood, swallowing the last of their drinks. They exchanged firm handshakes and left.

He could not wait for his life to begin.

73

October 2019, San Diego, USA.

"COME ON, MARK, YOU CAN DO THIS." His therapy started since his release from ICU. There were days it did not go well, but Curt vowed to stay until Mark was back on his feet.

Today was a difficult day and he refused to cooperate.

After four weeks of hospital food, probing doctors, nurses and the overexposure to medicine, they discharged him. He moved in with Curt, where friends and family visited each night.

His last week in hospital his mood changed when he met a pretty young thing who visited him. It was all by chance.

Lindy was looking for a friend's room when she stumbled into him, and from the first meeting a spark kindled. Lindy could not have come in a more opportune time. It gave Mark the will to put his back into it.

Maxi, the former girlfriend, left after the accident. One thing Vivian was correct about.

At home, the therapy continued with Curt monitoring his progress akin to a camp commander.

"I am tired, Dad," he whispered as sweat dripped from his face, his t-shirt soaked.

"I know, Son, but you are so much better. Besides, Lindy said she is coming over. It will be great fun. We will have a barbeque. I plan to make my favourite hotdogs."

It perked him up right away and continued with the last set. Exhausted Curt helped him to his room.

"Will you be okay in the shower?"

"Yes, Dad," and he rolled his eyes, agitated. "I am not incapacitated."

"Never said you were, Son," and he tapped him lightly on the shoulder.

"Finish up. I am almost done with the salad, and you can light the fire." Immediately a smile appeared on his son's face and Curt left him in his bedroom.

Curt's own injuries healed satisfactorily, and other for the cast on his leg he was fit. The house was sold to a young couple who would move in by the end of October. They packed most of the things which would go in storage. It consisted of antique furniture he gathered. Heir looms from his own family.

Vivian's artwork was sold, her belongings divided between her parents and the children. He placed her jewellery in a safety box for the day Jillian would want them.

He had a talk with both about her memory, even if she did not deserve it. It was also a conversation which caused him to phone a lawyer.

"One day I will know the full truth of what truly went on in this house," he had begun after the Lord pressed it on his heart, the silence thick with resentment. "Honour her as mother and forgive her."

"Never, Dad." Mark moved away, but he stopped him.

"Mark, listen, I know this is difficult to hear now. Believe me, this is not an easy topic for me either. I had to forgive her, just as you should forgive her." He paused and waited for Mark to sit.

"If you want any life with Lindy, or any other woman, you must forgive her."

"I don't know if I can, Dad," Jillian said, her five-month-old tummy growing—a reminder of her ordeal.

"I know it is, believe me, but if you do not, this chain will choke you and instead of peace, it will haunt you. This will influence every choice you make. I do not want this for you two. I want you to flourish, to grow and live a life without the baggage."

"He molested me," Mark seethed. "The man touched me in ways I struggle to get out of my mind."

"I am so sorry, Son. I wish I were here to protect you."

"It's not your fault, Dad," Jillian said.

"Thanks, Pumpkin, this is one guilt I will live with for the rest of my days. I plan to fix the situation, be here."

"Mum never stopped him. He is sick," Mark spat, not ready to hear the message of forgiveness.

"The good book teaches us to forgive, to accept God's grace and He will give you peace."

"Why did God allow this to happen to us?" Jillian murmured.

"Why didn't he stop him?" Mark's bitterness choked him.

"God does not intervene when he does not have permission to do so. Maybe He intervened, you just did not realise it. I don't know, I wasn't here."

"Exactly, you were not here. You are our father. You were supposed to protect us, but no, you protected the world while evil roamed inside this house," Mark flared and left the kitchen.

Lord help me, give me wisdom. I do not know what to say.

"Gramps visited one day," Jillian said after a while. "Neil was about to take Mark to the room when he showed up unannounced. Neil was angry and left."

Curt listened; the silence did not hide the anxieties.

"I can remember other times people would pitch up during these sessions. They were evil, Dad."

"I am so sorry, Jill, I really am. Why did you never tell me?"

"They threatened us."

"How long did this go on?"

"It started when their relationship began and stopped when we moved out."

"The entire two years?"

"More like one. I came over to visit and study here when he raped me one afternoon, when Mum was late."

"Will you be willing to testify about this?"

"Yes, I will."

"Mark?"

"I believe he will."

He contacted a lawyer on Saturday who specialised in this. He would fight for his children. This man will not get away. Now more than ever he knew he had to come back. He would be there for them.

His thoughts drifted to another woman he missed. It would not be easy, not by a long shot, but she would support him - an awareness that stuck with him.

His eagerness to return, get things sorted and come back only thwarted with the thoughts of Sonia. He had to do it right this time. He missed her. Then he can take care of his son.

October 28 was two weeks away. Would Sonia be in Valletta?

As he prepared the lunch his cell phone rang.

"Phillip, this is a welcome surprise!"

"Listen Curt, you need to contact Sonia."

"What's up?"

"She is having a tough time. So far she does not know about your wife, but the woman's pining gets on my nerves. Turmel and Ralph aren't helping either."

"What do you mean?"

"The two fight about her." He chuckled on the other end. "You should see it. Jealousy ran rampant. This is not what upsets her, though. She says nothing, but she misses you."

This is the best news he had received. Did she still love him? Even after all the things said between them. How could it be?

"I am waiting for news from the head office. It involves her. I am coming back."

"It's the best decision you have made in a long time. I do not know how she feels, she never talks, but whatever you plan will be good for her. She does not belong here. If you understand the meaning."

"Yeah, I do." He remembered her file. During one conversation back then, she had said she did not have a house she could call home. According to her file she left South Africa right after her training. That must be twenty-one years of drifting around.

"Lord, I know you will help me, not only because of my selfish desires, but because she deserves a home—a place to settle. Remind her of the promise. Let her be in Valletta on the 28th."

74

THE DOORBELL CHIMED, and he said goodbye. Lindy greeted him with a cheerful smile, the young brunette the best antidote his son had found. He certainly liked her. Clothed in a low fitted denim, it showed off her toned body. The white tank top displayed a belly ring.

"Hi, Colonel McGee," she greeted. She insisted to call him on his rank. Her dad died two years ago after an ops gone bad, leaving her and her mother alone. Her mother was seeing an older man stationed at the Air Force Base. Captain DW Steele had a long rap sheet. Lindy asked him to check on the man. According to Lindy, the captain was serious.

He met the mother during Mark's hospitalisation. She was a school teacher at the local high school and taught drama in her free time.

"Please come in Lindy, Mark will be with us shortly."

584

She held out a warm dish. "I brought potato bake. Mark says he loves it."

"Yes, he does." He sniffed the rich flavours of cream, cheese and garlic. "It sure smells good," he commented and closed the door. "I will show you where to put it."

She followed him through the house to the kitchen at the back of the house which had a beautiful view of the beach and sea.

"You have a lovely place," she commented. Just then Mark entered the kitchen and they greeted each other enthusiastically.

Soon the fire was lit and they relaxed on the patio. Curt laid back on a deck chair listening to the conversation with only half an ear as the children continued with the barbeque.

Once the kitchen was cleaned, Curt excused himself to visit Jillian in her dorm. She was not feeling well, and it gave him an opportunity to get out.

When he arrived her roommate was still out for the weekend. She was still sleeping which was unusual for Jillian. She looked pale and sweaty; and she was burning.

"Jillian!" he called out. Shaking her, she stayed unconscious—whimpering with pain. Sensing something was wrong he had her in the SUV, calling her gynaecologist.

Doctor Pamela Wright waited for him with a gurney at the hospital door. They rushed her inside and he sat in the waiting area. While he waited he called Mark first and then Timothy. Following his gut on this one he knew it was right when he arrived ten minutes later. While they waited Curt got to know the younger man.

"Tell me about yourself?"

"I have four sisters with the names Belinda, two years my junior." Curt smiled. "Jolene is the oldest, then Carolyn, and the baby in the family, is Lucille."

Curt chuckled. "Clearly your parents loved the sixties music."

"Yeah, we had so much teasing about it growing up, but love it. We heard it so much that it's part of us."

"Where do they live?"

"They are scattered across the country. Jolene is married and has two children," he answered, his love for his siblings noticeable.

"My parents live in Miami. Once a year we gather for a well-deserved family visit. This is the only time we are all together."

Doctor Wright finally appeared and focused on the startling news.

"You came just in time, Colonel McGee. If it was later, she could have gone in severe shock followed by a coma—the chances of a miscarriage a real possibility. Her heart rate is unnatural. When did you notice something was wrong?"

Timothy replied. "She complained of cramps three days ago, mostly over her chest, but said it was heartburn and took tablets to ease it. I thought nothing about it after that," he grinned sheepishly, "as both sisters struggled with it and it seemed not important."

"It can be overlooked, but it was not heartburn. Stress is the primary culprit in Ms McGee's case. The recent events had taken its toll on her."

"Did she discuss it with you?" Curt asked.

"Yes, she filled me in some of the details. I will keep her for observation."

"Yes, of course," Curt agreed.

"I also recommend an in-house therapist."

"Anything to help, I appreciate."

"And the baby?" Curt asked.

"The little tike is doing well," she smiled. Surprised at the news he stared at her. "You can already discern the sex?"

"Yes, Sir, she is carrying a boy."

"Oh, my word," he clipped it out. "It's wonderful news."

Doctor Wright allowed them visiting time, and both men took position next to the bed.

"I am sorry for scaring you, Dad," she apologised in a small voice.

"You had me there for a while, but you kept the best news from me," he chastised with a smile.

She blushed and whispered. "It slipped my mind with Mum and Mark."

"I will not hold it against you."

"Thanks, Dad."

"A son," he whispered and kissed her on the cheek.

They spent ten minutes more with her. When her eyes got droopy they left, and Curt and Timothy went their separate ways.

On Tuesday, 15th October, the Police arrested Neil Davies.

75

---

15 October 2019, Fangak county.

TAU LOOKED AT THE YOUNG GIRL who occupied his bed since Sonia left. From the time when he had taken her in his care, she flourished; became more confident, which he enjoyed. Earlier that day she had informed him of her pregnancy. It was the best news he had received in an exceptionally long time.

He watched her from the small window inside the small hut, the only place with adequate light. While she prepared their food, he took the time to read the Bible.

He found the content difficult to understand, but certain chapters spoke to him. His English challenged with the strange words or their meaning and wished someone could explain it. Those he understood pulled at his heart as if it was written for him and he found it peaceful, serene even.

The orphanage he grew up in was burned down years ago. The nuns had left in a rush after the militia killed the priest. Their country in turmoil since he was a youngster. He knew nothing else, but the content of this book gave him the peace he needed.

"Tau!" he heard Roger and covered the book in its hiding spot.

"Tau!" This time Roger was closer, and he stepped out in the midday sun.

"Yes?"

"What's the matter with you sitting in your hut?"

"Why are you looking for me?" Tau asked.

"Idil demands payment," Tau flinched. He had hoped the time he bought would stretch longer.

"He wants the woman or will wipe us out, completely this time."

"You know she isn't here, Roger."

"I don't know what you have done before, but you better find her."

"And how do you suppose I find her? I do not know where she is. Surely another nurse will suffice."

"Idil wants no one else Tau, you know this."

"I can't see how it will be possible."

"You will make it possible, you hear me!" Roger's voice carried across the camp. Tau shuffled nervously under the angry stare. Why couldn't they just leave her alone? She had suffered enough.

"Get her, Tau. Time is important. Go, now!" His voice boomed over the swamp.

"There is still much to do here, I cannot leave. Besides, who will look after Hilde?"

"I don't give a damn about your problems. You will find her. You will only return once Sonia is in your hands. Do I make myself clear?"

Looking at Hilde, he knew she had heard the entire conversation. Soft eyes beseech him to go.

"I want her delivered to Idil." Roger followed him inside and Tau's jaw clenched tight. He loathed the man. There was a time he respected Roger, but not anymore.

"I do not know where she is. I doubt she is at the Bentiu hospital. The foreigners took her away. She can be anywhere in this world."

Handing him a small bag, Roger barked. "Get her. This will be enough. Fly if you have to, but bring her back."

Taking the black bag he opened it. Inside were rolls of money. He nodded, got his own bag and threw in a few personal items.

"I will look after Hilde, Tau. Just get her," he said on a softer note. "Keep in touch. I will play for time."

Tau listened without a word. When Roger stepped out he removed the book from its hiding place and placed it in the bag.

He was in an awkward position, Hilde a bargaining tool Roger would use without hesitation.

76

15 October 2019, Iraqi desert.

"WHAT IS GOING ON WITH YOU?" Sonia was deep in thought, the report forgotten. Since Lee Ann arrived ten minutes ago, she showed no interest in the two soldiers which had to go for rehabilitation.

"Nothing." Misty eyes briefly met brown ones and Lee Ann frowned.

"Come on! This is not nothing." Her voice raised an octave. "You have been out of it for weeks now. Spill it, girlfriend," her voice was stern.

It had been seven weeks since Curt left, 49 days, which chafed her nerves. Not knowing the devastation. She had hoped, but it was a useless exercise. She was exhausted. She could not forget him. The more she thought about him, the stronger her feelings grew.

Stupid, but her heart pranced when she received news, or heard his name. Lovesick; dreaming about him constantly. Missing him severely.

Her conversation with Phillip settled her fears, a long overdue conversation. Phillip listened without condemnation when she revealed the rape and pregnancy.

She was not to be blamed for what had happened to her. She accepted it as an act of evil, and not because of something she did. The baby's birth a seal to God's protection, a forever reminder of His word. Her own rainbow. She even looked at fitting names. She never expected the excitement she felt with this baby and could not wait for his birth.

Would he love her even though she carried another man's child? Ever since her rescue, she had to deal with the questions.

Why did God allow the abduction to happen to her?

Why did He allow the rape?

Why was she forgotten?

What was the reason for her pregnancy?

Phillip's sincere responses helped her to put all in perspective. He assured her any man who genuinely loved her, would accept her no matter the past. She was still beautiful and treasured - her hope for a better tomorrow alive.

She had to forgive the man several times in fact. She prayed often for Tau and hoped he would read the Bible; that God would reveal himself to him.

"Sonia?" Lee Ann asked once again pulling her back. She closed the door. "Please girlfriend, what is the matter?"

"I love a man," she blurted.

"Wow! It's splendid news, honey," and she smiled. "But what seems to be the problem?"

"He is married," she said bluntly.

"Oh, it can be a problem."

"You think. But he made a promise back in April." Lee Ann raised a brow, "and I do not know if he will honour the vow. If, in fact, he is divorced."

"Do I know him?"

"No," which was the truth. Curt was gone before Lee Ann arrived.

"Who is it?"

"Colonel Curt McGee."

Lee Ann opened her mouth, then closed it. "You mean the commander of this fine establishment?"

"Einste." (Indeed)

"Well, I never … "

Sonia blushed.

"Where did you meet?"

"At Valetta."

"Malta?"

"Yes."

"Beautiful Island. I love the place," Lee Ann agreed.

"Yes, it is."

"What was the promise?"

"To sort out his life and we will meet again. I had to wait for him. He even booked the same rooms."

"And now?"

"I haven't heard from him. I do not know what is going on. Did they sort it out? Do I have a chance? Must I go?"

"For when are the rooms booked?"

"We are supposed to meet on the 28th."

"Of this month?"

"Yes." She met her friend's gaze.

"Go," Lee Ann blurted out. "If the rooms are booked, then go. You have nothing to lose. A paid weekend? It sounds like good odds."

"Yes," she said with her smile growing slowly. Sonia watched a helicopter lift, the noise drowning all else.

"Well?" Lee Ann asked once quietness was restored.

Sonia shrugged her shoulders nonchalantly and sighed just to answer the knock on her door. "Come in."

"Captain, they need you in the ER," Michelle said, "I

am coming."

"We will talk later," she told Lee Ann and followed the younger nurse.

77

"HOW DO YOU FEEL, PUMPKIN?"

"Better, Dad." He had spoken to Dr Wright who assured him she was fine.

"Are you ready?"

"Yes, my bag is packed. If you do not mind, could I crash with you? Dr Wright booked me off for two days."

"But of course, Pumpkin." He helped her with her shoes, her movements already hindered by the growing babe. Then he took her bag. "It will be nice to have you all for myself before I go back," he said as they followed the corridor.

"When must you leave?"

"I booked my flight for the Red Eye on the 24th."

"So soon?"

"I stayed far too long already. There are people counting on me, too," and he smiled.

"I know, Dad, but I am jealous. They can spend much more time with you, and so far this vacation wasn't good."

"No, it wasn't, but at least I could spend it with you. I like Lt Blackwell. He is a fine young man," and he opened the double glass doors at the entrance for her.

"Thanks, Dad."

"I have parked the car nearby, then you don't have to walk too far."

"You are good to me, Dad; I will miss you," and she kissed his cheek.

"I will miss you too."

"Is there a future with this young man?"

She smiled softly. "I don't know, Dad. With the new job and baby, I don't want to add more complications."

"I see."

"He is nice, and I like him, but I sense nothing else with him. I am not sure he is into me or I into him."

"When the time comes, you will know." Stopping at the red light, he glanced at her before he returned his attention back to the road. Both were thinking of the people in their lives, each with decisions to make.

Curt and Jillian had talked about her life. The world of relationships had changed for her. She struggled with trust after what Neil did to her. She did not want any man close to her. By December, this baby will be born. The work at the financial firm was not the best, but it afforded her experience. She would stay at least a year before she would venture to New York, work her way up with the ladder. Men did not surface in those plans. And Timothy was dedicated to his work. There was no future for them.

When the SUV parked in the driveway, her father broke the silence. "I am glad you are here. I need to discuss something with you."

"This sounds serious."

"Yes, it is. It involves all of us."

Jillian decided to make macaroni and cheese the way he loved it, rich with different cheeses melting together in one savoury flavour. With a dab of garlic, not overwhelming, just enough to enjoy, and a green salad.

WHEN THEY WERE FINISHED and the plates pushed aside, Curt cleared his throat.

"I need to discuss this with both of you, and I hope you will give me a moment to just tell it as it is."

"You know you can, Dad," Jillian said reassuringly.

"Thank you, Pumpkin."

"I met a woman a few months ago."

"Dad?" Both gasped, leaning on the table. It wasn't news they expected so early on.

"Her name is Sonia Main. We met at Valletta right after your mother's …" He cleared his throat. Since her death no one talked about her. Each struggled with their own pain. It was a challenging time for all of them.

"I have struggled with my feelings and pushed her away. Honouring my marriage vows was of the utmost importance. Since Vivian's death, I can offer Sonia a future. I have spoken to leadership, and they offered me a Commander position at the training facility, which I have accepted. I want to bring her with me."

Silence fell among the three; both brother and sister looked at each other momentarily and smiled. As one they declared: "This is good, Dad—really great!"

Jillian rushed to him and hugged him. "You deserve a new beginning," she whispered.

"Thank you, Pumpkin," and he gave her a hug.

"Does she love you?"

"Yes, well, I hope so. The last time I saw her I told her there was no future for us."

"Oh no! What did you do, Dad?" Jillian drooped, a frown between her manicured brows.

"It's a long story," and he told them how they met, his struggles, how he found God.

"It was important to obey the voice of God, no matter how tough it was."

"Dad, you are a great guy and of course she will wait for you," Mark said eventually, shifting his weight.

"I hope so, Son."

"Any woman will love to have you. You just need to be confident," Jillian replied.

"Thanks, Love, your acceptance means a great deal to me."

"My new position will begin on 1 December, so I still have a few days left to convince her." He grinned.

"That means you will be back for Christmas and for the birth." Jillian clapped her hands.

"That's wonderful, Dad," Mark replied.

"The realtor is looking for a new house for me as we speak. Sonia had a rough time and I want the transition with the minimal hiccups to ease her into it."

"Tell us about her?"

"Do you have a photo?" Jillian's excitement was bubbling.

"I have one."

The conversation continued and when Jillian yawned, he stopped.

"Sorry, Dad, but I am pooped."

"Thanks for listening to this old man."

"You clearly love her. I hope she knows how lucky she is."

"I am the lucky one," he insisted.

Later, in their individual beds, all three reflected on the changes that had happened.

Both Mark and Jillian realized their father was on a different path than them, their family unit disrupted by hurt and deceit.

Would they ever be a family when he returns?

Would this new woman accept them?

78

"YOU ARE GOING SONIA?" They were busy with supper, talking, when Alexi joined them and the conversation turned to Sam.

"Any news from Sam?"

"Nothing. They are busy with the investigation, is all Turmel says."

"I still cannot get over it. The man saved my life."

"It is unbelievable."

"An officer contacted me, I have to give my statement," Sonia informed them.

"For me as well," Alexi admitted.

"We can only pray."

"The man is going bonkers," Lee Ann said.

"When did you talk to him?"

"I pushed for clearance until they let me call him. He is not doing well all cooped up."

"I can believe that. Sam enjoyed his freedom and open spaces."

Sonia could swear she saw a mistiness in her friend, but averted back to her plate as she took a bite. Then the table turned towards her.

"You didn't answer me. Are you going?" Lee Ann continued with the conversation.

"Where?" Alexi looked at both women, baffled.

"Valletta," Lee Ann answered.

"What happens in Valletta?"

"It is nothing," Sonia replied in a whisper, staring at her plate.

"It is not nothing, Sonia," Lee Ann said brusquely. "She has an appointment this weekend with her soulmate. They have not seen each other in six months. Now she has misgivings about it."

"Is it who I think it is?"

"Our commander."

"You should go," Alexi said, and Sonia flicked to him almost desperately. Her heart thudded in her chest.

"That man has prayed for you. He had a tough time staying away from you. I don't think you realize the ordeal he suffered," he informed her.

"And, Sam will agree with me."

"See, three to one," Lee Ann said with a triumphant smile and sat back.

"I will think about it." Sonia removed her tray and left the mess hall.

"HOW ARE YOU DOING?" Phillip had to repeat the question before Sonia responded.

"I am well thank you, Phillip, yourself?"

"Good."

"Thanks for the sermon. It was touching."

"I hope it was more than that," he replied with a grin.

"Definitely, you gave me much to think about."

"Care to join me for lunch?"

"It will be wonderful."

Finally, seated at a table, he asked. "So, what are you up to these last few days?"

"Busy," she sighed and took a bite of the lasagne.

"The shifts were long and daunting."

"I believe so. Two of our soldiers passed away."

"Yes." Voices increased as more soldiers entered the eatery.

"When is your next free weekend?" he asked.

"Next week," she replied thoughtfully.

"Are you going somewhere?"

Looking at her plate, she said hesitantly. "Yes."

"Where?"

"Valletta."

"Were you there before?"

"Once before. It is a beautiful place and so peaceful." Over the past seven days Sonia's brain worked overtime, evaluating each scenario—the sensibility to go. Was she opening herself for another heartbreak? Should she take the chance?

After a restful sleep, she was convinced to go. The sermon confirmed her thoughts. Get closure - if for no other reason than to be sure.

She dreamed of Curt. This time his arms were outstretched, calling to her, a welcoming smile on his face. His arms were wide open and she ran to him. When she woke she looked around in search of him.

She had to believe it was meant to be. Curt would be there, waiting for her. A sense of confidence allowed her to be light-hearted for the first time since April ... peaceful.

Phillip's sermon touched on inner peace which came from knowing the truth, and she made notes. One scripture captured her attention, Colossians 3:15, "And let the peace of God rule in your hearts, to which also ye are called in one body; and be ye thankful."

God's peace lived in her. He was her restorer. He would come through for her no matter what.

"I was thinking of going there myself, but so far work kept me busy," Phillip said and she smiled. "I will bring photos."

"I would love to see them." Once done with lunch they stepped out. Major Turmel stopped them at the door and Sonia gave him a disturbed glance. Burger said his goodbyes and left her with the man.

"I was hoping to go into town. Care to join me?"

"Not today."

"Why not?"

With renewed poise she said, "I love another man. There is no point in taking this further."

"I thought you said …"

"At the time I was, now I am not."

"Do I know him?"

"I believe you do. Good day, Major."

24 October 2019

"SO, THIS IS IT," MARK SAID.

"Yes, it is." For one last time Curt looked at the house they shared, the empty shell's ghosts best to forget. They took a few pieces to Jillian's apartment, and the rest stored. The oppressiveness made way for calmness.

"We are looking forward to meeting Sonia," Markus said.

"Bring her home," Jeanette added.

How they really felt about the changes he did not know, but they supported him with each decision. Without them the last couple of weeks would be difficult.

They removed the cast the previous day and he walked freely. Though stiff, the exercises helped get him to stay in peak condition. The doctor's report of full recovery was a bonus.

"Well, let's go," Mark said. With a final thud Curt closed the front door for the last time and gave the key to Mark. He would deliver it to the realtor later. Jillian would meet them at the airport.

"Markus and Jeanette, thanks once again. I will see you soon." He greeted his in-laws and got in the car.

The long-awaited paperwork arrived the previous day. He had to report for duty on the 1st of December 2019. His successor would join him on 1 November, which means the month would be jam-packed. Personal time would be non-existent.

How would Sonia feel about the changes he had made?

Did she still love him?

Did one of the men take his place?

Sam was a known womanizer. He would turn on all his charms to catch her. Major Burger, although a good friend and chaplain, was still a man, seeking a woman to share his life with. He had seen the looks when he thought no one was watching.

Then there was the biggest pain of all … Major Turmel. He was adamant to win her over. It looked like she welcomed it. He cringed; he hoped not. "*GOD* ..." he prayed silently.

These questions plagued his thoughts while he went ahead with his plans. Determined to continue he stuffed the required documentation in his shoulder bag. It included her residency and work permit paperwork, which needed her signatures.

All he could do was to trust God for favour with her as well as being in Valletta, the long trip a hurdle to overcome, but vital. He could hardly wait to see her.

Sonia a treasured part of his future. He needed her as much as his next breath.

PART FOUR

LOVE'S VICTORY

79

28 October, Valletta.

SHE ARRIVED EARLY at the hotel and booked in the same room. Though tired, the impressive view oozed through her and she dragged the offered beauty deep into her lungs.

"It was a long road. The last six months had brought on many changes, Lord." Sonia wiped the tiredness away. *"You made this all possible and kept your promises, Lord."* A hand fell on the slight bump and cupped it.

"My future is in your hands."

Insecurities played with her on the 24-hour trip. Their last meeting did not go well. Then she had pushed him away, and he was angry about the time she had spent with Sam and Alexi.

Their unusual meeting and courtship followed by the strain of not knowing. Was their love enough to pull them through? Her heart was in a permanent longing.

She was excited, yet careful, not sure what to expect. Before her trip she wanted to cancel it, but Lee Ann convinced her otherwise. If she did not, she would always wonder if he pitched.

"God, please let him be here," she whispered.

The rising sun kissed the water in soft golden hues, illuminating the sail ships floating on the quiet waters. The place was just as she remembered.

Inside her room the coffee-coloured duvet invited her to relax, and after a shower she fell into the embrace. A small bouquet's fragrance filled the room with delight. Being in a male dominated environment, you lose touch of the womanly side.

After a three-hour nap she visited the spa and indulged in the massage. Kneaded thoroughly, they dealt all the knots and bumps with. It also eased the constant flutter. The facial experienced a welcomed part of her preparations. Six months' harshness fell away and revealed a softer side. Her reflection smiled at her.

At the pool the conversations kept her thoughts busy as hotel staff scurried around. The hotel was fully booked.

All the time her heart asked … Where was he? Her stomach in turmoil—couples highlighted her loneliness.

By supper there was still no sign of him. She ate and returned to her room. The entire day she refused to give into the void of his presences, but could not ignore it anymore. He was not coming.

Her dread turned to sobs during the shower. She was exhausted and fell asleep, woke again, and checked the clock for the umpteenth time. The floodgates leaving a mess in its path.

At 21h59 a knock stopped her cries, and she listened. A soft tap followed. "Who is there?" Her voice was small and detached, hoarse, but no one answered.

Another round of taps followed and abruptly she got from the bed where she basked in her sorrow, and opened the door.

Her world stopped. Overwhelmed with emotions she stared at him—his body rigid, his eyes pleading—his jacket, side cap and glasses at his feet. There were tired lines around the eyes and mouth. She took it all in with one look and whipped her face.

He smiled sheepishly and said softly. "Hi Sonia, love."

"You came?" Her hair cascaded around her shoulders and she brushed through them, absently wiping away the tears.

"Yes." He straightened his back. His chest seemed broader, a muscle in his jaw the only sign of his tensed feelings.

"Why?" Her heart wanted to believe, her body trembling.

"To offer you a future," he simply answered. She was in his arms in a flash, sobbing with relief this time—touching him as if she did not believe it.

CURT HAD TO BRACE HIMSELF at her sudden impact, but just to feel her body pressed against him, he did not mind. This was what he waited for all these months. Every struggle was worth it.

Using the commercial flights he lost his duffle bag. The flight was delayed for several hours, leaving him stranded on the European continent. He wanted to scream with frustration. He caused a scene at one place and it frightened the poor assistant into silence. When he stepped on the Valletta airport tarmac, he could kiss the ground. Instead he rushed to the hotel.

This was what it was all about. This woman in his arms. How he missed her. He would never let her go again.

When she kissed his face, he carried her inside and closed the door with a foot.

There was so much to discuss, but they needed this connection more. The last six months were hard on both. They were finding shelter in each other, as it should have been from the beginning.

"Does this mean it is a yes?" He finally pulled her away, drinking in every contour, appreciating the bright green eyes filled with promise … for him.

"Yes," and she continued with the path of kisses. They fell on the bed, refusing to separate as she held on.

"Never leave me again," she whispered when she finally calmed.

"Never, you are mine, Sonia love," he assured her once again.

"I love it when you call me that," and she pressed another kiss on his lips.

"You are mine," he whispered and kissed her breathless.

All the months of turmoil forgotten as they basked in the love that looked impossible, marvelling at the thought of a future together.

When they finally breathed again, she whispered. "You came."

"Nothing could hold me back."

"You love me?"

"Yes, I do."

"My chief," she chuckled, light-hearted and carefree.

"Yes, your chief." Her possessiveness was a marvel to enjoy.

"I love you," she choked out. A lonely tear followed her contours.

"I love you," and he kissed her softly. She sighed in contentment, the evidence of the tears still on her face.

"I am sorry for what I have done," he whispered thoughtfully.

"I understand."

"Do you?"

"Yes, and I love you even more." She kissed him once again. Her heart opened as she trailed the lines of his face.

Foreheads pressed together. He closed his eyes and revelled in her touch.

"Are you hungry," she asked much later, and he nodded. He was famished. She ordered a plate of sandwiches and disappeared into the bathroom, washed her face and dressed in a T-shirt and pants. They had a lot to discuss in the few hours left—so many questions to ask.

Back in the room Curt was stretched out on top of the covers wolfing down the food. What a glorious sight, and she leaned against the doorpost, smiling. The relaxed figure revealed a confidence which stemmed from an inner peace. Now more than before she marvelled in the good-looking features in the man he was.

When their eyes met, he returned the smile and patted the mattress next to him. She bounced on it, kissing him on the cheek. His stubble gruff, but she did not mind.

"You are truly here," she whispered.

He placed the half-eaten food next to him and turned to her, whispering, "Yes," and kissed her.

"There is so much we need to talk about." He brushed her hair, touching her face.

"Yes," she gasped as his hand trailed her neck to her collar- bone, so soft as if she was porcelain, his thumb brushing her lips. "I can't believe you came."

"It was touch and go for a moment," she admitted. "I didn't know if you would come."

"I am sorry for putting you through this."

"I am too. It was so long." Wetness was her only expression as he held her.

"Don't, please."

"I can't help it. I missed you terribly. I was so afraid," and another tear joined his mate.

"I never imagined it will be so difficult, but this means we will be together."

"Yes." A sob shuddered through her.

"Love one," he whispered, and she moaned as he captured her mouth.

80

WHEN SONIA FINALLY LET go of him, he finished his meal while she updated him on the current situation in camp.

"Did you hear about Brock?"

"No, what happened?" They ordered a fresh pot of coffee and took in the view, the sun touching the new day.

"Brock is dead, and Anna sent back after the assault."

"How did that happen?" He frowned. Why did Turmel not inform him of this?

"Sam got him in time and was killed."

He sucked in his shock. "Was Sam arrested?"

"Yes. Everyone is angry about it. He saved my life, Curt. That man is a saint."

"And Anna?"

"He did his worst on her, she needed an emergency operation."

"Did he attack you?"

"He tried, but Sam was just in time. You know, just a few days before that, God gave me a promise of protection. This time evil didn't stand a chance."

He pulled her closer. "If Sam didn't kill him, I would have." He squashed her into a bear hug. All he was told was that they dropped the charges against Cummings, but not informed what happened in his camp. Turmel owed him answers and pushed it aside. His woman was here. She needed his undivided attention, which he applied liberally.

"What happened at home?" Sonia asked when they laid back exhausted, but not willing to sleep.

"Vivian passed away."

Sitting up she looked at him. "Mark is all right after a tough time and my leg is all better."

"You mean you were also hurt?" She gave him an overall glance, and he drew her back to him.

"I broke my leg; they removed the cast on Thursday."

"Why didn't you call?"

"I was unconscious for two days," he said and she gasped.

"I could have lost you?" She wrapped her arms around him.

"No, never." The genuine fear in the green depths real. "You brought me back. I dreamt of you calling me," he said.

"I really missed you. I had the same dream days ago of you calling me. I prayed so much, not sure what to do. Lee Ann, Alexi and Phillip all convinced me to come."

"Who is Lee Ann?" he asked, confused.

"She was my best friend in college, we studied together in South Africa. She is the new nurse. You will meet her."

"I am happy for you."

"The Lord is good," she admitted.

"He is!"

He held her tighter and continued, "I had a lot to deal with after I woke, my bruises healed quickly. My in-laws arranged Vivian's funeral while my son fought for his life. Jillian was in hospital for observation. She is pregnant with a boy."

Sonia chuckled. "So, you will be a gramps soon. It just shows how old you are."

"I am not that old," he pouted.

"To be a grandpa you need to be old. In theory you are," she laughed.

"I will show you old," and pinched her down on the mattress.

"I am in love with an old geezer." He covered her mouth with a kiss.

"So, you have two children?" she asked out of breath when he let her go.

"Yes. Jillian has just completed her degree and Mark is twenty, still unsure of a lot of things." For the first time he could open his life to her, and she listened. He talked about the rape and molestation.

"I missed you, Sonia, so very much. There were days I wanted to call, but I first had to deal with my family and all the issues her death brought on. I wanted to approach you with a clean slate."

"I like it when you say, 'Sonia love', I feel special."

"Because you are special to me." It was true. She was never far from his thoughts, planning their future, hoping she would agree. In all these weeks he exercised control and did the things needed.

"And your son, how is he?"

"Better. When I left, the doctors assured me, he would make a full recovery. He is strong," and he smiled.

"Like his dad," she said, and he grinned.

"It was touch and go. I thought I was going to lose him," and she wiped away the anguish.

"There is nothing as bad as losing a child." He looked at her, surprised. He thought he knew everything about her. This was not in her file.

"What do you mean?" his voice hoarse.

"I lost a son once," and he shifted up straight, his eyes piercing into hers.

"When?"

"Twenty-five years ago, during birth," she replied, taking a sip of water to cover the rising flow.

"You didn't tell me," he whispered.

"I try to forget the little face on the pavement."

Now he was alarmed, his own grief gone, shocked even.

"What did you just say?" She looked at him in dismay.

He pressed her into him, shielding her as she told him about Brady and how they met. Moving in with him at eighteen and learning about her pregnancy.

628

"He just left one day and never came back. I ended on the streets as I had nowhere to go." In a tearful sob she said, "He died on the pavement in Pretoria. He was born too early because of malnutrition and the abuse I suffered. A good Samaritan took me to hospital where I was nursed back to health."

"You are the bravest woman I know."

"Not really. I just learned to survive."

"How did you become a nurse?"

"Matron van der Walt helped me to join nursing school. When I graduated, I applied with the Red Cross and here I am."

He pulled her closer once more. His heart ached as he whispered words of comfort to her, soothing her.

"I didn't know this, it had to be horrible. I wish I was there, I would have helped you, Sonny." He took her mouth with a whisper. "Now you are more beautiful than before," capturing her mouth tenderly, love overflowing.

Her heart soared with the love for this man she wished she could have known back then.

When he finally released her, he sat up straight, taking her with him—his closeness stable. "I need to discuss our future with you, if you are willing."

"Our future?"

"Yes, I want you in it always. While I was in the States, I had an offer and accepted it, but I want you next to me." He kissed her. "I want you close. You are my future."

"When I leave, I want to take you with me. If you want to have this old man as your husband, of course," and he grinned.

She slapped him softly. "You are hot and sexy, and I will be proud to be in your future," she said, kissing him in answer.

"When will you leave?" Just the thought of him leaving again …

"Don't cry, this time you are coming with me. Would you consider America as your new home?"

"Yes, yes, yes!" she beamed without hesitation, "because you are there," and he grinned.

"We leave at the end of November," he whispered. "Your residency and work permit are approved, if you want it?"

"You did?"

"Yes."

"You are terrific, Curt McGee. So, are you asking me to marry you?" Merriment twinkled in the green depths.

He laughed and said, "I guess I am," and she kissed him in response.

"Does this mean, yes?"

"I guess," she whispered, and he laughed.

"You are mine, Sonia love; I will protect you, love you, provide for you and never ever leave you."

"You are mine, Curt McGee, I will love you, care for you and keep you warm, giving you all the pleasure I can," his body reacted.

She was ready, open to have his way with her, accepting him. He struggled with the reactions coursing through him. He already had her and wanted more, her lithe body eager. She met him with no wavering. But he wanted it differently. It was more than just an act. Especially after what she told him just now. He would never use her in that way. She was far more precious to be used.

"Marry me now, here, today?"

She had no doubt about any of it. God promised a way in the desert and now it was blooming, but before she could give in there was one last topic to discuss.

"What about this pregnancy?" and she touched her budding stomach.

"I will be a father to this child, there is no doubt in my mind. He will carry my name."

"God, you are the best."

He chuckled. "I am a man as any other with many faults, but God worked in me these last couple of months. I have no doubts about his plans for me/us."

"Then the answer is yes. I will marry you here, now, today."

Warm breaths sealed the vows, and when she broke free, she uttered. "You are a terrific, wonderful man." The rest of her words stopped by his ever-seeking mouth, saying what his body could not.

"You have my heart, Sonia Main. From the moment I saw you, I loved you," he whispered.

"I love you Sonia," and she sighed.

81

Lover's sacrament.

TO BEGIN WITH A NEW FAMILY WAS A DONE DEAL. Curt mentioned this to his older children. They loved the idea.

While in hospital they gave him a bill of good health. When the doctor playfully suggested he should consider another child, the wheels in his head turned. He knew the woman he wanted to have one with. Once this baby was born, he desired another. Meanwhile he could practice all he wanted.

Later, tired and relaxed, they rolled on their sides. With Curt's arm draped around her waist, they fell asleep, the closeness a unique experience which made them whole.

Curt stirred first, the sun shining directly on him. The lunch hour had come and gone. Their flight booked for 21h00, so they had no time to waste.

What would it take to get married in Malta?

He looked at the love of his life and without waking her he got his phone and called the front desk. On the balcony the radiant glow greeted him. It warmed his insides.

"Sorry, Sir, it's not possible. You need a Certificate of No Impediment and your Birth Certificate. The court will not allow any marriage without those papers," the desk clerk informed him.

"Are there other ways around it?"

"No." Frustrated, he searched the outstretched water for calmness.

"Can I help with anything else?"

"Can I speak to your manager?"

"Hold on, I put you through." Seconds later, a woman answered.

"Good afternoon, Ma'am. My girl and I want to marry today. Will it be possible?"

"Do you have a Certificate of No Impediment and your birth certificate with you?"

"No, we don't have it."

"Then I am sorry, Sir, it will not be possible." Her thick accent sounded off handed.

"Not even with special permission?" Curt pleaded.

"No! Just hold on please," and a song interrupted him.

"What's going on?" Sonia's arms snaked around his body and he squeezed her.

"I am holding for the manager." She smiled and kissed his chest.

"Hallo, Sir, are you there?"

"Hallo, yes. Can you make me a lucky man today?"

She chuckled. "I am afraid it won't be possible, but we can arrange a ceremony for you with a priest. When you go home you can officiate it. How does that sound?"

"Do you want to be married by a priest?" He whispered and Sonia chuckled.

"Is that our only option?"

"It seems so."

"Then we do it."

"Sir?"

"Yes, a priest is fine till we get home. What time and where?"

"Armanno will meet you at the desk in one hour and take you to him."

"What costs are involved?"

"You can work it out with the priest."

"Thanks."

He relayed the message and Sonia disappeared into the bathroom.

"Where are you going in such a hurry?"

"To get myself ready, of course?"

He sighed, stepped into the bathroom and closed the door.

"How long do you need?" he asked once he joined her under the spray.

"An hour is too short, so …" Her words cut off as he stepped into her, "I guess …"

"You talk too much," his lips busy with a seductive dance, which she did not mind.

An hour later they walked to the front desk—Sonia dressed in a navy dress she had added on a last-minute hunch and Curt in his military uniform.

"You look perfect," he said to his blushing wife-to-be.

"You look dashing yourself, Sir," and saluted him. With hands glued together they met the driver.

"Armanno, how are you?"

The older man beamed. "This is wonderful to meet you. So, you are the two who want to marry?"

"Yes, Armanno," Curt replied.

"It's a pity we can't make it official, but a blessing is just as well, yes?"

They smiled. "For sure," Curt replied.

"Then we need to go." They followed him to a white SUV parked at the entrance.

"My brother-in-law agreed to the ceremony. You understand it won't be legal?"

"We understand. We will do it all proper when we are at home," Curt assured him.

"Good, good." They parked in front of an old cathedral, its limestone walls towering over them, and Sonia drew in her breath. The Baroque architecture well preserved, a marvel of its time. The ancient wooden door opened and they walked inside.

"This is beautiful," Sonia whispered as she looked around. Elaborated artwork covered every inch of the inside walls. The holy ambience stopped the word flow.

"Follow me," Armanno said and took them deeper inside the rich gold, painted and tapestry folds.

"Have you ever seen something so beautiful?"

"Once or twice." Curt teased and she giggled, slapping her mouth shut when Armanno's fierce look found her.

They entered a smaller office where a priest waited. The rich blue panel walls fit for royalty. Armanno introduced them and told Curt the fee, which he paid with a smile with an added extra tip.

They kneeled in the presence of God, touched by the beauty of it all. The priest held both their hands in his as he prayed. They did not understand a word of the prayer, but their spirits agreed with the clergy. He served them the holy sacrament and smiled once done.

"There, he is finished," Armanno said and helped Sonia to her feet.

"Thank you, Armanno. Thank you, Sir. This was so moving," Sonia said.

"Where to now?" Armanno asked?"

"Can we have a few moments just to walk around?"

"Sure, you can. I will wait outside."

"Thanks, Armanno."

Words could not describe the serenity they experienced as they sauntered through the cathedral, memorised by the craftsmanship in every detail. Curt's cell phone camera worked overtime.

"I could not have hoped for a better union than this." Sonia said when they finally got in the car."

"This was an unique experience. I am glad we did." Curt pulled her closer and kissed his woman soundly.

"Lunch? I know this beautiful place at the harbour," Armanno said.

"That will be wonderful."

Once at the restaurant, Armanno introduced them to his wife. She had prepared a feast for them.

"We cannot allow the newly-weds to set off in the sunset without a proper feast, no." Armanno chuckled.

"Thank you for the lovely meal," Sonia said, and Armanno translated to his wife.

The platter, with an array of fish and vegetables, well prepared and the wine a perfect complement to the dish and the older couple's company.

At 16h00 hours Armanno delivered them at the airport, and they walked to the same gate with the same destination.

Ready for their future—times algorithm in tune with their hopes and dreams.

82

HE DROPPED SONIA OFF at her room after twelve. She was exhausted. During the flight they got some shuteye, but with Curt's bulk it was hopeless to relax in the confined space. They decided to remain in their separate rooms until they made it official. Only then would Curt arrange for her things to move.

She still could not believe the wonder of it all, praising God as she gathered her toiletries for a shower.

On her return Doug met her with a boyish grin, handing her a note. "What is this?"

"Don't know, Ma'am," he said winking. "I am glad it finally came together."

"Thank you, Doug. Did he tell you anything?"

"No, but he is glowing," and she giggled.

"I never thought I would see the day the Commander would glow, but it looks good on him."

"Did he tell you his wife passed away?"

"We haven't talked yet. I assumed they completed the divorce and didn't want to pry."

"She passed away; almost lost his son in the same accident."

"Is he all right?"

"Yes, he recovered."

"I am happy for you."

"Thank you, Doug," and he left. She unfolded the piece of paper. The CO's neat handwriting welcomed her.

My Sonia

Thank you for a lovely time. You made this old man ten years younger just being with you. Please dream of me.

Your Curt.

With a satisfied smile she fell back on the mattress and kicked her legs in the air. The emotions he created in her made her feel sixteen again. She touched her lips where he had spent most of his time and sighed, closing her eyes in wonder. She would sleep peacefully, her dreams true.

Curt McGee was everything she wanted.

"JUST THE PERSON I WANT TO SEE!" Major Turmel's voice boomed over the camp. Heads turned and Sonia waited for him to join her.

"How can I help you, Major?"

"I was looking for you the weekend, but they told me you left!"

"Yes, I did." Although she could sense he was waiting for an explanation, she deliberately withheld the information.

"I am hurt." He touched his heart with droopy eyes. The look just did not do it for her.

"I wanted to show you around," he mentioned it a few times, but each time she had an excuse. Now more than ever.

Without another word she continued to the office for her weekly report. She was looking forward to it. Just being with him, even if they could not speak to each other was enough.

With long strides he caught up and followed her, reports in hand.

"What will it take to get you going with me?" He lowered his voice as men marched passed them.

"Major, I am not interested or available."

"I have watched you; there is no man in your life." They stopped at McGee's Office and Doug allowed her to enter. She sighed softly, pleased to get away from him.

Curt was sitting at his desk signing paperwork and looked up just to close the folder.

"Welcome back, Colonel," she offered.

"Thanks, Captain Main," he said with his eyes fixed on the man right behind her. He nodded as the Major greeted him.

Tension grew exponentiality and he ordered them to take a seat. Two seats were open, one next to McGee and the other at the other end. He showed her to sit next to him. When all was seated, he thanked them for the kind words of condolences.

"Let's begin, Major Turmel." Their knees brushed against each other. Sonia struggled to keep her composure natural. She listened to each officer's report. Notes were shared and questions asked, and soon the hour meeting ended. When it was her turn she relayed her report—an overview of the medics, what they needed and the wellbeing of the patients.

When they filed out Curt held her back, unnoticeable. Turmel stood next to her and showed her to go.

"After you, Captain Main." His tone was polite.

The colonel barked from behind. "Captain Main has a private matter to discuss with me. Please excuse us."

"Of course, Sir," and he left, closing the office door. Swiftly she was turned around and kissed thoroughly, her arms wrapped around his neck. How they would stay away from each other, they did not know. Every minute spent apart similar to a year with no contact.

"This feels so good," he whispered. "Finally I can have you all to myself," and kissed her.

"I thought he would not leave," she said out of breath.

"Is there something I need to know about him?"

"No," she replied, "I love you."

"I like the sound of that." He gave her a slap on the bum.

"I have to go. I have meetings all day. Will I see you tonight?"

"Yes," and she straightened herself quickly. He picked up her cap and handed it to her, stealing another kiss.

"Thank you, love," she whispered, and with one final peck she left.

Outside Major Turmel waited for her and she groaned inwardly.

"What did he want?"

"It's personal, Major," staring him down like a wayward child.

"Can we have lunch?"

"No," and he held her back.

"Is there hope for me, at all?" His gaze searched hers.

With renewed confidence she replied. "No, Major, none," leaving him at the door.

83

7th November 2019. A Day to Remember.

"PLEASE COME WITH ME, MA'AM," Doug said politely just after 13h00. His face serious, but a lop-sided grin tweaked the left corner of his mouth.

Last night when she and Curt met, he had a similar smile. When she asked him about it, he blew it off with nothing. They even called it an early night.

"Why?"

"Just trust me," he said whilst accompanying her to a jeep. Gallantly he opened the door. Inside, Alexi sat at the steering wheel with a huge grin.

"All will be revealed in due time come on, just enjoy the surprise," Doug said.

"Okay but ..."

"No buts, you are under orders of the CO," he demanded. She raised her brows but let the tone slip.

The Russian's eyes avoided her and she laughed. He gave her a lopsided grin, without a word and they continued towards the village at an easy pace. The air buzzed with excitement.

The entire day Lee Ann acted all evasive and had to leave earlier. Now the men were acting weird.

The town was busy but they got to a well-known spot in good time. At the tearoom Alexi patted her on the leg and got out. Walking around the jeep he opened the door. As the afternoon warmth hit her, she stepped out. Made sure the head scarf covered her and followed him into the clay building. He nodded towards the owner who said nothing and led them to the stairs.

They followed the stairs down the narrow dim hallway until they stopped at the second last door, knocked, and opened the door.

Lee Ann waited for her.

"Can you tell me what is going on?"

"You need to get dressed," she ordered with a smile.

"You have an hour to get ready. In the bathroom you will find a collection of bubbles."

By now Sonia was fed-up with the orders and silent treatment, and stopped when pushed.

"Excuse me, but I demand to know what is going on. Why are we here and why do I need to take a bath?"

Alexi sniggered. "Lee Ann will help you." Sonia looked at Lee Ann, astonished. Grinning she asked her friend, "What are you guys up to?"

"Nothing, but be ready in an hour," Alexi commanded and winked for Lee Ann before he closed the door. It left her with a smiling Lee Ann who went to the en-suite bathroom and opened the taps.

Whistling? Is Lee Ann whistling?

"Lee Ann?" Sonia looked at the black bag against the cupboard. Since no one was filling her in, she stepped towards the bag.

Maybe it would reveal its secrets and without warning Lee Ann stopped her hand the moment she touched the zipper.

"No peeking, *agie*," (an Afrikaans word for a curious person). She tried to be stern, but failed miserably in it when she snickered.

"You heard the man. Get in the bath," she parroted Alexi.

"I want to know Lee Ann."

"In an hour you will know, trust us. Please, girlfriend. Go on." and she almost dragged her to the bathroom where a bubble bath awaited her. The mixed fragrance of vanilla and lavender accosted her to silence.

Looking at the preparations she turned, "I don't like to be bullied," she began, but Lee Ann interrupted her once again.

"Tick Tock, time is ticking. You don't want to be late, do you?"

"Late for what?" she asked with her hands on her hips.

"Where is Curt? I mean, Colonel McGee?"

"He is waiting for you. You will see." She winked and closed the door behind her.

With no other choice but to indulge in the bubbles, she dropped all her clothes and was in the warm bath, quickly.

It was one big secret; everyone was in on except for her. Come to think of it, she did not see Curt all day as well. Whatever was going on, she would give them a piece of her mind afterwards.

Once done she wrapped a soft towel around her. Back in the room a table with makeup, brushes and a hair dryer waited.

"Come, please take a seat." She directed her to a small chair. "Why all this secrecy?"

"Trust me, you will enjoy the surprise. Hush now, I need to concentrate," she said with a grin.

"You enjoy bossing me around," Sonia said playfully.

"Not every day that I can do so, Ma'am," she answered, pressing her back on the chair. Under her touch, Sonia's thick hair framed her face in soft curls. Some refused to budge, but she dutifully managed them.

Sonia watched every move thoughtfully. Now and then their eyes met. Sonia's questioning stare said it all, but Lee Ann continued with the whistling.

Since when did she whistle?

Next up was her face, and she demanded Sonia to close her eyes. Lee Ann did the facial in quietness. Brushes soon followed and after a while she asked Sonia to look in the mirror. Sonia had to admit she looked beautiful. The mirror showed a glowing face of a woman in love; it brought on a smile, highlighting the green eyes and kissable lips. She felt like a bride being prepared for her wedding.

But no, it couldn't be, could it?

"Lee Ann?" she tried.

"Fine weather we are having," Lee Ann changed the topic. "Reminds me of home, don't you think?"

Deciding to play along Sonia replied softly. "It has been a while. I haven't been in South Africa for over five years." She admitted, "but yes, it reminds me of home."

"You ever want to go back?"

"Nothing is there for me, so no, I have no reason to return."

"Same here. Both parents died. Brother Dirk lives in England now and my sister, Lizzie, lives in Australia."

"Are you and Sam serious?"

She giggled softly, blushing brightly. "He is a fine specimen, for sure. I really like him. The case makes it difficult, but I believe in his innocence."

"I hope you two can work it out," Sonia encouraged. It was difficult to be alone all the time. Life should be shared with a loved one.

"We will have to talk to the colonel about the case."

Scented cream was liberally applied while they talked. In the dry desert weather, moisturiser was an essential part of her dressing ritual.

Meanwhile Lee Ann unzipped the black bag, just a little to put her hand inside. White under garments with garter and white sheer stockings appeared.

"Why girlfriend, where did you get this?"

"Contacts, my dear friend, contacts," was all she said.

The entire time the preparations were done in silence, but the twinkle in Lee Anne's eyes were unmistakable.

Whatever it was, she liked it so far. If it included a commander who held her heart, she would not mind, Sonia thought, her own smile spreading with an endearing fondness.

While she dressed her legs, butterflies fluttered inside her stomach—not the romantic kind. She ran to the toilet and reached it just in time. Morning sickness had started.

"Is all well with you?" Lee Ann knew nothing of her pregnancy, should she divulge the secret? Maybe at another time.

"Stress," she laughed it off.

Back in the room the zipper was opened entirely, and a white dress appeared. The delicate lace garment revealed the secret.

"Lee Ann, is this a wedding dress?"

"Girlfriend, you need to wait for your lover to reveal such essential information to you. You heard nothing from me." She locked her lips, throwing away the imaginary key.

In awe Sonia watched as Lee Ann unzipped the long zipper and held it out. Carefully she took the first step inside, the silky satin caressing her skin while Lee Ann pulled it upwards. The perfect white dress sheathing her like a glove, the bump visible, and she touched it briefly.

This time it is different, kiddo. This time we are cared for.

Her reflection showcased bare caramel shoulders as the dress enhanced every curve beautifully. At the bottom a bow, done in a golden cream material, snuggled her hips. It came together in front with embroidery pearls in a delicate pattern. The rest of the gown flowed to her feet, silky soft and beautiful.

If she had to pick out a wedding dress, this would be her choice. Running her fingers down the material she stared at her image. Twirling around bubbles of giggles erupted from her throat.

Alexi had to knock, because when she finally saw him in the room, he was dressed in a tuxedo, smiling.

"You look beautiful, Sonia," he said appreciatively. It was the first time he called her by her name. His eyes sparkled with wetness.

"If only Sam could see you now."

"He would have loved this," Lee Ann said and wiped her face.

"Thank you for all you have done," her hands running over the sheer softness once more.

Alexi held out a thin black box, his hands shaking.

"And this?" Astonished, she looked at them, her voice only a whisper.

"Come on, Sonia," Lee Ann exclaimed. Sonia opened the box, her hands shaking. Inside was the most beautiful platinum choker she had ever seen. A mother-of-pearl teardrop hung in the middle in a beautiful setting of small diamonds. Alexi took it and she stepped in front of him. Once he placed it around her neck, tears ran.

Lee Ann squeezed her shoulders. "This is my wedding day?" They met her gaze without comment.

"This is my wedding day!" She repeated, but no one denied or confirmed.

"Stop crying, Sonia, you will ruin everything."

She could not help it. "It's so beautiful." Barely touching it her fingers followed the choker, her voice breaking.

Alexi cleared his throat. "We need to go."

"Thank you, Alexi and Lee Ann."

"It's a pleasure, my dear," Alexi acknowledged. "It's a gift from us."

"I will treasure this always." She turned around and kissed him smack on the lips.

"Come Sonia, we need to fix the mess you made," Lee Ann said, also dabbing away the tears. "You still need to put on shoes."

"I will," Alexi offered, and Lee Ann handed him the white stilettos with white ribbon lace. Bending he strapped them on as she held his broad shoulders.

Lee Ann fixed her makeup, leaving no trace of her breakdown a moment ago. Alexi held out a white mantle with gold decorating embroidery which covered her shapely body, a hood over her hair.

The dress code was still strict once you stepped out of the room into the public eye.

An hour later she hooked unto Alexi's arm, Lee Ann right behind her.

"This feels so real," Sonia said, "I feel like a bride meeting her groom. I never imagined it will be like this."

No comments came from her entourage, but the smiles said it all. Butterflies fluttered through her entire body, this time the good ones.

In the back seat of a black SUV they sped away, Alexi behind the steering wheel once more.

"You hold out on me," she reprimanded him softly.

He grinned. "That is how the CO wanted it."

"I never thought this could actually happen."

"You deserve it—you both do." His own was voice husky. "Make each other happy."

"I will," she vowed.

Behind them Lee Ann exchanged her own clothing in her jeep. The jeep swerved precariously until righted it again.

In less time they were back in the camp, stopping in front of Curt's quarters. Doug waited, also dressed neatly in a tux. Opening her door he helped her out.

"You look beautiful, Captain."

"Thank you, Doug."

84

ALEXI REMOVED THE HOOD and mantle from her shoulders. He handed her one red rose with a white ribbon, which she held carefully. Inside, her love was on his knee, dashing in his military's uniform.

His action confirmed her thoughts. He had done this! Their eyes locked and her world changed—gone was the old life. This was it. With him. Soft music accompanied her inside.

"Sonia Deborah Main, will you do me the honour of becoming my wife, today?" All eyes were on them.

Touching his face she bent, gave him a lingering kiss and without thinking twice she said, "Yes, Curt McGee, I will."

His smile glowed as he straightened. People clapped while whoops filled the air. They decorated the living area with white candles, balloons and roses. Creating a pathway to a small patio as their guests surrounded them.

Phillip waited with a grin. The full impact of what they were about to do, hitting her. The tears were unstoppable, the moment too big.

"You are a wonderful man, Curt McGee," she said, and he grinned sheepishly.

She turned to Alexi. "You are giving me away?" He and the Colonel were about the same age. Stepping in as a father figure, she could not have asked for a better person for the role.

Mystified, she whispered, "Thank you Alexi." He too thumbed a tear away.

Handel's march began. Alexi gave her a quick peck and handed her back to Curt. Her heartbeat increased. It was the most beautiful moment. Curt's nod started the proceedings. Their hands clasped together.

Song of Solomon Chapter 2.

"He brought me to the banqueting house, and his banner over me was love.

Stay me with flagons, comfort me with apples: for I am sick of love.

His left hand is under my head, and his right hand doth embrace me.

I charge you, O ye daughters of Jerusalem, by the roes, and by the hinds of the field, that ye stir not up, nor awake my love, till he please.

The voice of my beloved! Behold, he cometh leaping upon the mountains, skipping upon the hills.

My beloved is like a roe or a young hart: behold, he standeth behind our wall, he looketh forth at the windows, shewing himself through the lattice.

My beloved spake, and said unto me, Rise up, my love, my fair one, and come away."

"Father has brought these two people together in love. They had to face many trials to be here. I believe there is a banquet table waiting for them. It consists of enjoyment and love.

As a pastor I watched them grow, laying down this love when God wanted obedience. God was faithful. Through it all, He protected them. Their love is strong and alive. God promised them a stream in the desert, and it came together with perfect reconstruction timing. Together you will be an oasis of God's love, a testimony of his faithfulness."

Sonia and Curt listened to the words as they gazed at each other, united before their friends and God Almighty. It was everything they hoped and dreamed of.

Fifteen minutes later Sonia Deborah Main became Sonia D.M. McGee, wife of Colonel Curt McGee. Her heart swelled with pride as he wrapped her in his embrace, kissing her with a hunger she felt right through—her skin glowing with him so close and she whispered, "I want you so much right now."

"I don't think they will love the show," he replied huskily. She giggled as a blush spread across her neck. The group started to laugh, clearly hearing what she had said.

"Sonia love, you are mine," he whispered and kissed her.

"You are mine," she repeated softly, "and might I say, you look dashing."

"Thank you, my love."

CURT'S SPEECH INCLUDED ALL—thanking Doug, who made everything possible in such a short time. Their small audience whistled in agreement. Then he turned to Lee Ann who had put in the extra effort with the dress, transforming his new wife into a beautiful princess. Lastly he fixed his gaze on his newly wedded wife, and told her how beautiful she looked.

A toast followed with more whistles and cheers which brought them back from their moment.

"This was all so sudden," she said softly when everyone's attention was on the food.

"Do you mind?"

"This was perfect … unexpected, but perfect." Her smile took his breath away. Now there was no more denying she was his wife.

When he noticed Turmel's attention, he had to act. Doug informed him that the man was persistent during his vacation. Now it was a clear sign to any man to stay away. He would never share his wife.

When he spoke to Phillip yesterday in preparation, they had a long chat.

Phillip asked him if he was over the infidelity and he could honestly say he was. He confided in Burger just before he left about the binge he was in after the breaking news, his bitterness and betrayal towards Vivian.

Together they went through the incidents, and not only did he have to forgive her and Neil, but himself. His guilt played a significant role in his life, leaving his children who suffered during his absence.

It was tough to face the realities and get rid of all the commotion it caused. Cleaning his rooms he reached for the photos that stopped his world and burned them. Once the ashes blew away, a weight lifted.

Before the accident he suffered with chest pains. At first it alarmed him since the doc said it was his age and he could be a heart attack candidate. But in his gut, he knew it was not the case.

Everything had changed. He could breathe easily now, the chest pains had dissolved completely. He would not project his insecurities towards Sonia, but he would protect what was his, making it official for all the men and her.

The celebrations continued until nightfall; by then Sonia was tired. Covering another yawn the small group said their goodbyes.

Curt escorted them out the door and closed it. When he turned around she was still in the middle of the living room, watching him with a smile. Slowly he walked to her, stripping his jacket and laid it over the headrest. Their eyes never leaving each other, conveyed a simple message.

"Did you have an enjoyable time?" he asked when he took her in his arms.

"This was wonderful. Not even my wildest dream could muster this."

"Now you are my wife."

"Yes, I am."

"Do you want to go to bed?"

"If you will not mind, I am tired," and another yawn escaped for emphasis. She covered her mouth.

The last two days were busy, the excitement of the day adding to her tiredness. There was so much she wanted to say, but words failed her.

"Tonight I can hold you—in my book it is perfect."

"Perfect indeed."

"Come this way, Mrs McGee," and he led her to their bedroom.

Since her arrival she had not looked at her new living quarters, and she examined it with interest. The small apartment comprised a living area, kitchen, bedroom, bathroom and patio with a small, enclosed garden. There were two deck chairs on the patio.

The furniture was a military issue in the standard brown and greens which could be rectified to make it more of a home. The furniture consisted of a sofa, two armchairs, coffee table and small table. There was a desk and chair in the corner, with a laptop. A small bar fridge in the kitchen sported a microwave as well. The double bed looked inviting. For now, it satisfied her just being there with her love.

When they entered, all her belongings were stacked in three bags. When she looked at him, raising a brow, he whispered, "I can't let my wife not have her things with her, could I?"

She shook her head, and he closed the door.

When the door clicked her ears perked. Her tiredness evaporated and excitement took its place—her heart rate did a tango. It would be the first time since they were back that they would be united again.

Fixated on the broad shoulders encased in a white shirt, the tie long forgotten. The black dress pants hugged his narrow hips, showing off long muscled legs.

Strolling towards her, he took her hands and twirled her around. "You are a vision. Mrs McGee."

Her smile said it all and he stopped her, her back towards him. Unzipping the dress he took her hand and she stepped away from the garment.

She was indeed a vision in her girdle and satin underwear. She was practically shimmering in the soft light.

"Perfect, just like my dreams."

Their love withstood many hardships, a true testimony of their faith.

Tested like silver in a refiner's pod.

85

"FOR AN OLD MAN YOU ARE GOOD," she could not help but to tease much later. He kissed her chastely on the forehead, laughing.

"I think you need to sleep before this old man gets more ideas." She pressed soft lips against his chest and relaxed into him.

They fell asleep exhausted and were only awakened by the sun high in the sky. Startled she came up, and he brought her back to her spot.

"No work for today. You are off duty, Captain McGee." She fell back laughing. "It has a nice sound."

"How about another round," but her stomach's grumble had a word about it as well.

"Later, let us eat first." Moving away from the bed he followed, grabbing two new robes to cover them, one for him and one for her, a wedding gift from Lee Ann.

"I never thanked you for yesterday," she said as he tied the robe around her waist, and he furrowed a brow.

"What was last night then?"

"Foreplay," she said cheekily, laughing as she stepped outside.

"Then you better come and fix it," he grinned, "yeah?" and he grabbed her playfully. "Now say thank you properly."

Wrapping her arms around him she kissed him tenderly. "Thank you. Now we are glued to each other. Where you go, I follow."

"Glued together, always." Another rumble disturbed the duo and she snickered.

"Come glue, let us see what our guests have left. I hope there is more cake. It was delicious."

"Yes, it was."

The food was no longer on the table outside. Investigating the small kitchen, they found two plates of food covered on the countertop. The cake was in a plastic container.

"Here love, the food is here!"

"I am coming!" She dashed passed him to the bathroom.

Just then a knock vibrated through the small apartment. When Curt opened it, Doug was waiting with a huge smile. Walking in, he congratulated him.

"Where are you?" There was no sound from the bathroom and Curt frowned.

"Sonia?" He found her bowed over the toilet.

"Sorry," she said.

"What's wrong?"

"Morning sickness," she replied.

"Oh," and he closed the door.

He switched on the kettle as Doug brought him up to speed.

When Sonia joined them, she looked pale and Curt gave her a cup of tea which she gratefully accepted. Their eyes met. What she saw scared her.

"Tell me how you got everything together?" Sonia asked. The baby-topic a discussion for later.

"Wendy and her staff did the catering,"

"Compliments to the chef."

"Do you want to eat now?" Curt asked as he indulged in the leftovers, but she shook her head.

"Thanks for everything, Doug, you definitely have a gift."

"I will do it anytime for the colonel and the captain."

When he left Curt asked, "How do you feel?"

"Better, thanks."

"When did it begin?"

"Yesterday."

Silence fell between them while Curt closed the remaining food.

"Do you want to talk about this?"

"Not really."

"Curt, please talk to me." He glanced up and put the milk back in the fridge.

"Curt?" He walked around the small counter and stood before her.

"I love you with all my heart. You know this?"

"Yes."

"My wife's infidelity has broken me; I will not lie. When I burned those pictures, I completely forgave her." He stopped and moved away.

"Curt?" She rose and wrapped her arms around him. "Please talk to me. I want to know what you think."

"With all that has happened, I forgot about the baby."

He touched her stomach. "It brought back so many ugly things," he finally admitted.

"I know this is difficult, but this little guy is here. I feel responsible for him."

"I know." He pulled her to the couch, right on his lap. "The thought that another man had his hands on you just drives me nuts."

"I am yours, always. No matter the past." She touched his cheek. "This baby is God's closure to us. I had to accept His way of protection. If not for Tau, I would have died."

"God ..." He groaned and hugged her with a fierceness that left her in pain.

"Tell me what happened."

"Are you sure?"

He nodded.

"The leader kept me in a hut for several days without food or water while he defiled me. He broke me. It took me a few days just to become sane. I had no other choice but to accept Tau's protection." She kissed him softly. "Do you understand?" It was the first time that she spoke openly about that time.

"I do ..." he sighed, "but it's difficult."

"No," and she brushed a tear away.

"I want this baby to be loved. I don't know God's plan for him, but God saw it fit to give him to us."

"You are amazing."

"I am just a normal woman. If I had a choice my life would have looked differently, but now it is in God's hands."

"Amazing and wise," he said and kissed her.

"I love you with all my heart, Curt, never forget that."

"Thanks, love," he finally said. Then he moved them both and announced, "Come, you need a warm shower."

"Why, do you think I stink?" She sniffed at herself with a snicker.

"Don't start woman." He growled playfully.

They spent a good half an hour underneath the warm spray. He occupied her time in the most delicious ways, their passion and delight soaring as from the moment they had met.

86

All roads lead to Sonia.

TAU WANDERED THE STREETS of Pretoria
aimlessly. He had been to Iraq over the weekend of the
26th of October but found no trace of her. He had no
intel about her whereabouts, the military camps so well
guarded he could not get close.

His search brought him to South Africa. His first night
he stayed hidden as Xenophobia madness broke out
around him. Being a foreigner was not perfect timing for
a search.

South African blacks were out to kill any outsider. He
found himself amid it the moment he stepped on the
paving just outside the Gautrain station, in midtown
Johannesburg. People were flinging rocks and burning
rubbish. A fuming mob targeted and stripped foreign
businesses from their products. Some barely escaped.

The next day he made way to a taxi rank but realised his mistake as a brick hurled at him. He missed it by inches and ran away, getting behind the police who tried in vain to disarm the mob. Screaming, wailing and gunshots caused a cacophony in the enclosed space.

Rubbish littered the streets while many of the drains overflowed. The smell was so unbearable that he had to get away. He ended up close to Ellis Park Stadium. A taxi took him to Rosebank where he got on another Gautrain train to Sandton.

He had to stay alive, his unborn baby's life dependent on that. They warned him at the airport, but he thought nothing about it. He had to go to South Africa.

Roger was true to his character and left him a message on the burner phone. They used Hilde and the unborn baby as pawns in Roger's sick mind. Every night he received a call. Roger's patience was running at an all-time low as he reported back.

His second visit with the director of nursing back in Bentiu led nowhere. The only information she could give was that Sonia was originally from South Africa. Even after trying to intimidate her, she refused to surrender the information. Leaving her in a bewildered state he went straight to the airport. He had no other choice but to follow every crump of information he could find.

The reason he was in Pretoria. For the last two days he walked the streets without an inkling. His search on the internet delivered no news. She had no social footprint.

Roger breathed down his neck which did not help the matter.

Deciding to return to his hotel, he knew he had to get more help. His search was leading nowhere.

At the cafeteria he ordered food and scrolled through his phone while he waited. He still had to get used to the smartphone. He did not understand most of the functions, but ended up in his Gallery, in any case.

Documentation he had taken came into view and he studied them. One letter caught his attention and he zoomed it bigger. It was a letter dated from 2001 from a Matron van der Walt. In it she mentioned Sonia's name. At the bottom it was signed, Sally van der Walt, Steve Biko Academic Hospital.

Could this woman know where Sonia was?

He opened the search engine and searched the hospital. Corner of Steve Biko Road &, Malan St, Prinshof 349-Jr, Pretoria.

"Here is your food, Sir," the waitress said and he made room for her. Since it was too late he would pay it a visit the next day. Hopefully he would find a clue there.

87

IT WAS A LONG DAY. Soldiers streamed in a constant flow through the medic. She managed it in a breeze, her high spirit flowing to those in her care.

Knowing the man she loved was with her, that he was close and his heart belonged to her, was pure bliss. Even Dr Rogers stared at her approvingly during their ten-minute tea break, smiled, but said nothing.

At 21h15 she got back to their rooms, exhausted. When she switched on the lamp, a small white card greeted her. Next to it was a small box in a red heart shape on her pillow. Opening the letter with the masculine handwriting,

"Meet me for dinner at the mess," she smiled, "Your Curt."

I wonder if it is an order, she thought, her eyes sparkling. She could skip, only years of practise kept her on earth.

She dashed to the shower—having her own accommodation still new. No more sharing with others.

He did not say the time, but knowing him, every step she took, he knew.

She brushed through the uniforms and decided on a pair of brown slacks and a cream tank top with leather sandals. Taking extra care with her face and hair she made sure she looked good enough.

In the corner of the big empty hall candlelight displayed the setting table. Her husband, dashing in his uniform, waited for her. The entire walk met with an appreciative stare. When she reached him, he gathered her in his arms and kissed her breathless.

"I have missed you," he whispered.

"Yes, I did too." He chuckled pressing another kiss on her lips before he let her go. "You look beautiful."

"Thanks, my love."

He took a seat across from her. "How was your day?"

"Busy, but you know that," he chuckled.

"You know all my secrets," she added.

"You bet you beautiful curls I am," and she shook her head playfully.

Doug appeared, greeted her and served them. It was not the normal menu; the BBQ steak done to perfection with apple salad and bread rolls on the side. She thanked him.

"This looks delicious."

"We must thank Wendy."

"How was your day?" she asked, biting into a piece of the juicy steak. Her hunger had increased and her waste expanded. Except for the morning sickness that appeared around lunchtime, she was in good health. Taking her prescribed vitamins with diligence, the headaches dismissed completely.

"Busy; a lot of problems to sort out."

"I never thought of the mess as a romantic setting."

"It's one advantage of being the chief."

"I can see that."

"Do you mind?"

"Not at all. I think it is beautiful and very considerate of you."

"You deserve special treatment," he said matter-of-factly. She beamed.

"I want to start fresh. I don't want any baggage that will hinder my future." She met his watchful gaze. A brilliant smile appeared on the handsome face. "I can pursue your love." He moved until he sat next to her and held her for the longest moment. "Since the day I saw you at the hotel, and again when you arrived at camp, I loved you. I am sorry for all the pain I caused."

"No need to apologise. We are together now. I understood you had things to sort out," she replied softly, his manly cologne tickling her nose.

"We first had to get right with our Heavenly Father before we could have this," pointing between them.

"Did you know almost every man was in love with you on the first day you walked through those doors," flicking his eyes to the double doors. She shook her head in disbelieve.

"They were, even Ralph wanted to court you. Doug told them you were open game. I was furious with him. I wanted you."

"I dreamed of you, of this." He looked at their clasping hands. "I never wanted another woman after I met you. I had a tough time with God. When he said I should forget you and honour my vows, it devastated me."

"And I made it even more difficult."

"You didn't know about the marriage."

"Still, it wasn't my place."

"You are not to blame. It squarely rested on my shoulders," he demanded and kissed her to silence. "My love," he whispered.

"You call me love," still surprised in the manner he related his feelings to her, unashamed.

"I love you. Ever since you stepped into my world, it has changed for the better," his voice husky.

"This is all so new to me." Never did a man cared for her this deeply. Never did a man offer her a future and set it in motion.

He grinned. "You don't give me much choice in the matter."

"Nope, I was afraid you will run, and I wanted you more than anything in my life."

"You definitely know how to impact a girl," and he chuckled.

"Yes, I am known for that." This time she chuckled.

"You are not old, you know," she said, changing the conversation.

"No?"

"Nope, how old are you?" Now he laughed at her.

"Fifty-seven," and she gasped.

"Your birthday?"

"21 December."

"A Christmas baby." He laughed. "You know how old I am?"

"You are 45 years old, your birthday is 20 September. But it does not matter, does it?"

"No, it doesn't."

"This is all so beautiful."

"Yeah, this is beautiful." Lifting her on his lap, her head was on his shoulder.

"I meant what I said. I will not hurt you, nor leave you behind," as if reading her doubtful mind, he continued, "Do you believe me?"

"Yes." How long did she wait for a man like this? As a liberating woman, independent, she should feel trapped. Even offended at his presumptions, but she did not. It felt right. She nestled against him and savoured the moment.

"The mess has lost its appeal to me," she whispered into the silence and he chuckled as he stroked her back.

"I could never come in here and not think of this," she added.

He looked around the immense hall with its cleaned tables and chairs neatly packed in rows. The bright florescent lights switched off, the candles highlighting their little corner giving them both an amber glow.

"I know what you mean," he agreed and brushed his lips across her forehead. "This is much better."

"Yeah," and she laughed.

He squeezed her tight and heard her yawn. "Are you tired?"

"It was a long day," she replied, her body soft and relaxed against him.

"Let's go."

88

11 November 2019.

SAM'S TRIAL STARTED WITH MUCH TENSION. Many thought his arrest unjustly, others were glad they incarcerated him.

Cooped up in the DB, Sam had no contact with Lee Ann. She worked herself to the brink of falling asleep on her feet. The love bug had hit hard.

Sonia had a word with Curt about the two lovers, and the restriction lifted. Her time in isolation gave a better perspective and understanding, the value of support a vital necessity.

Manslaughter was a serious offence.

The defence had to prove the reasons for the arrest.

Alexi Krasnorada, Sonia Main McGee and Dr Rogers testified.

"The court has taken all the evidence in consideration. Each testimony showed Staff Sergeant Castledale brutal obsession towards women." Colonel McGee stated— Major Burger and Sergeant First Class Ralph represented the panel.

"From a psychiatry perspective Dr Rogers had shared his knowledge with this court. Staff Sergeant Castledale had a traumatic childhood."

"We included Nurse Anna Stalin's medical report and statement. It showed the mindset of the staff sergeant at the time." He took a sip from the glass.

"The defendant could not prove maliciousness at the night in question. Sam Gerber protected Captain Main from his brutality. We find the accused, Sam Gerber, innocent of manslaughter." Applause shattered the silence, Turmel's disgust clear as he watched Sam.

"Thanks, Colonel. I knew I could count on you," Sam said. Curt nodded. Lee Ann kissed him, a public announcement that they were together.

"Please have a seat."

Everyone became quiet. Curt cleared his throat and took another sip before he continued.

"I have a few words to say about violence against women." He found Sonia across from him. She smiled. This case gave him the opportunity to address the matter.

"Violence against women are an abomination. In camp their tenacity and strong will cannot be faltered. They are true soldiers. They protect others with their lives therefore need our respect and protection. This is not the opportunity to violate her and think you will get away with it.

Women are the source of life. Nurture them. Raising a fist against her shows your disrespect towards all women. During sexual encounters rough play is acceptable only with the woman's consent. You have no right to force yourself on her.

See a woman as God sees her. She represents the Bride of Christ. As her husband he protects her, care for her and love her." He cleared his throat once more. "When you do, she becomes your most beloved treasure who will care for you. She will stay by your side through your life as your biggest support. Her wisdom and insight valuable.

When you violate a woman, you violate her essence. When you break her, she crumbles and becomes a nonentity. A woman who sees herself as nothing, has lost her sparkle. Even her will to stand.

Take care of her, love her and protect her. Never ever lift your hand in anger against her."

Silence fell across the hall. Sonia pinked away the tears, then stood and applaud him. All the women joined her, followed by the men in attendance. Her pride grew exponentially.

That night she basked in his love. Time stood still for an eternity as she accepted him in each loving act.

12 November 2019.

"WHAT'S THIS?" CURT ASKED Alexi the next day.

"My resignation. I want to go home."

"Are you sure about this, Alexi?"

"I prayed about this. It is time to reconnect with my wife and daughter. I am getting too old for this." He chuckled. Curt could not believe it. The ex-KGB sniper came a long way. At sixty he could understand his reason.

"What are your plans?"

"I bought a farm two years ago. I am exchanging my weapon for a plough. I want quietness and openness."

"You sure will miss the heat," Curt grinned.

"Mother Russia is in my blood. I cannot ignore her voice. Besides, by the looks of it Sam is also moving on. That hottie has his attention. I never thought I would see the man so smitten."

"You two came a long way. I am honoured to have you in my company. We will miss you."

"Thanks, Colonel. We had fun under you, for sure. In Africa I realised these old bones could not handle it anymore."

"I understand." They shook hands and Alexi stepped outside.

"CAN I HAVE A WORD, COLONEL?" Sam stopped Curt on his way to lunch.

"You want to walk with me?"

"I ask permission to leave, Colonel. I have personal business to attend to."

"How many days?"

"Three, Chief." Curt observed the man. Since his release he had changed.

"You want to talk about it?"

Sam looked around, uncomfortable. "I have it bad, almost as bad as you."

"What?"

"You know … women."

A light switched on and Curt grinned.

"So, Sam Gerber, the womanizer, is in love."

"Not so loud, Chief." He scanned the area.

"No reason to be so secretive. Everyone in the camp knows about you and the nurse."

"You must admit we are a perfect fit."

"That you are. You have my permission, Sam. After what you have done for my wife, I owe you this much."

"Thanks, Chief."

"Thanks, Sam."

When he joined his wife they stole a kiss.

"Guess, who I ran into today?" Sonia said.

"I think I know, but tell me?"

"Your replacement came for a visit."

"Colonel Powers?" The arrogant man struggled with a little man syndrome and Sonia was glad they were leaving.

"He is a highly decorated officer. The camp will be in good hands," Curt said.

"Will you miss this?" Curt looked around, greeted the men and took a bite from the pie Wendy had made.

"A little," he said, "but it's time to take care of my woman and my children. I have been away long enough."

"Lucky woman." He grinned and squeezed her hand.

"This will be my first Christmas in civilisation, you know." Sonia said.

"I didn't know that."

"I never had a proper Christmas meal. Be ready for a full-on Christmas feast, complete with fruitcake and lots of cookies."

"You are a woman after my heart." She giggled.

"Where will we live?"

"San Diego." Curt said, when she said nothing he continued, "For now we will live in a house supplied to me. We can look around and decide where we want to live when we are there."

"Tell me about the place."

"It's the most beautiful city, I believe. Breathtaking views, a beautiful shoreline. The vibe is something you can only experience. I think you will like it."

"I cannot wait to make it my home."

"Colonel," Doug called.

"Yes, Doug?"

"Urgent message, Sir."

Taking the message he skimmed it, gave her a peck and hurried out the hall.

"I guess lunch is over," she said to no one in particular.

89

29 November 2019.

"WHERE IS LEE ANN AND SAM?"

"They asked for personal time," Curt replied, distracted with his paperwork.

"I am off to bed."

"I'm almost done with these reports. Keep my spot warm."

Tomorrow was their last day in Iraq. While Curt was busy she had written a few letters - one to Haleema and one to Sally van der Walt. She had so much to share with these two women and poured her heart into the emails, their constant encouragement and support encouraging.

Today her replacement took over. A brilliant woman full of laughter and a positive attitude. She had all the requirements needed. The soldiers were in excellent hands.

This gave her time to pack and do her last rounds. The four months at camp held a special place in her heart. She learned to trust God and found the peace she searched for all her adult life. She made wonderful friends and got married. She sighed.

The long-time dream remained a lost hope until God restored her from the inside out. The bonus was the new life growing in her. A miracle of protection and love.

"What are you thinking about?" Curt moved in next to her.

"About my many blessings."

"Am I one of them?"

"You are the main blessing. Without you, nothing else would matter so much as it does."

"I love you, Sonia love."

"I love you, my chief."

"GUESS WHAT?" LEE ANN said the next day.

"What?" Sonia had just closed the door of their quarters for the last time. The jeep took all their bags to the helicopter.

She lifted her hand and wiggled the fingers. A small gold ring with a few diamonds pranced on the second finger.

"Are you married?"

"Yes, I am officially Mrs Lee Ann Gerber."

"I am so happy for you."

"Now we are both hitched."

Sonia snickered. "What are the plans?"

"Sam and I will remain here for another year. Our vacation will be a family meeting event, then back to Ireland. He has a family farm waiting for him."

"It seems you two had discussed every detail."

"We have. The time he was in the brig gave us lots of time to talk." She blushed.

"I am happy for you. This means goodbye then."

"Yes, it does."

"Do you and Curt plan for a family?"

"Yes, we do. In fact, I am pregnant," she admitted and blushed. The surprised expression on Lee Ann said it all.

"But isn't he too old?"

Sonia burst out laughing. "No, the man is more than capable, believe me." Silence fell between them as they walked past the mess to Curt's office. Then Sonia stopped.

"It isn't his."

"Excuse me?"

"This is not Curt's baby."

"How, when …" then she became quiet.

"You mean this baby happened during your kidnapping?"

"Yes."

"Why didn't you abort it."

"Because this baby saved me." Time to explain the entire story had run out. She owed no one an explanation. In the eyes of the world this was Curt's baby.

"Does the commander know?"

"Yes, he does."

"And he is fine with it?"

"Perfectly fine.

698

"I really admire you, my friend, because if it should have happened to me it would be gone."

"I had the choice, but decided against it. Curt accepted it."

"I stand corrected, you are both amazing people."

Inside the office the staff greeted them and Doug asked them to come closer.

"Today we say goodbye to the best Commander I had the privilege to work with.

Captain Main, we got to know you as a kind woman and could not asked for a better wife for our chief. May your years together be blessed, and our Father's grace go with you. You will be both missed."

Cheers broke out and Doug raised his hand. "As a token of our appreciation we have bought you a gift. We hope you can use it in your new house."

"Thanks Doug, this is thoughtful of you. We appreciate it," Curt said. After more greetings Sonia and Curt got in the helicopter.

"This is it," he said when they were buckled in.

"This is it. Thank you, Lord."

"Amen."

90

A new home.

THE FLIGHT WAS LONG and difficult on Sonia. Morning sickness was an all-day experience for the last two days. Dr Jourdain assured her it would be over soon. At eighteen weeks she really hoped so.

It was already late the afternoon, the winter sun basked the earth in pale pinks against the backdrop of grey hangers.

Feeling sleepy he almost carried her from the plane. "Mrs McGee, your new home awaits," and she smiled up at him.

Suddenly two bodies shuffled her away with excited shouts, and she stepped away.

He showed her photos of the children and she recognised them. Watching the trio the similarities were noticeable. The daughter was a petite version of Curt with a belly ready to deliver any day now. His son was bulkier than him, but with the same piercing eyes she loved.

When he finally broke their hold, she broke the awkwardness.

"Hello Jillian and Mark."

"Ma'am," both said.

"Please call me Sonia." They had spoken over Skype the day after their marriage, but reality was different, the situation difficult. As she told him once, they were part of him and she would love them as such.

"This is my wife, Sonia McGee." He said looking at her as she smiled, "and these two are my joy, Jillian and Mark McGee." Their greeting was polite, but reserved. Curt drew her in and reluctantly they placed an arm around her waist.

It would take time to get used to her. She understood it.

"It feels good to be home."

"I have missed you guys." Releasing his hold on the children, they stepped back. Watching them she realised they were not accustomed to him holding another woman and she stepped back.

"We missed you, Dad," they spoke in union. Jillian had a degree in Financial Management. Mark's muscles showed his occupation as a contractor.

Walking to the SUV waiting for them the sergeant stretched, opened the door and they got in. Curt saluted the young woman and followed. Driving away from the hanger, Sonia observed the new camp which would be her home for the unforeseeable future.

Their eyes met as he spoke to his children. On the question in his stare she mouthed to him she was okay, observing the rest of the outside world.

After about a fifteen-minute drive they reduced in speed. Sonia observed the brick home with curiosity. The neat exterior welcomed her and she stepped out. The chilliness caught her by surprise and Curt snuggled her closer.

"You will get used to it. The weather is like your South African winters."

"I don't mind," Sonia assured him.

"The moment we are settled, we can search for a new home. One of your choice."

"This is perfect."

All their stuff stood together in the corner of what seemed to be the dining area. Hers was the smaller pile, she never had earthly belongings to begin with.

The winter sun streamed through the living area.

Passing the pile they visited each room as the children followed them, conversing with each other softly, no doubt about her. But she did not sense dislike, just curiosity.

The children would not share the house with them although there were enough rooms. They both had their own accommodation in town.

A truck pulled up.

"The movers are here. I arranged for the furniture to be delivered. The rest we will have to buy—curtains for one."

"Perfect." She chuckled.

Sonia continued with the tour. A tear finds its way into the scarf and she wiped it away, overwhelmed with the emotions.

"Thank you, Lord, for bringing me to America. For this house." Then she stopped. Her house. She had a house. Awe inspired her to tears. She never thought it would become a reality. Running her fingers over the walls she could only thank God. Her gratefulness broke out in a song.

When strong arms drew her into a loving embrace, she leaned against her husband. "What is it, Sonia?"

"This is my first home," she sobbed, "my very first home."

He lifted her face. "Our first home," and kissed her.

"Yes," she whispered.

"Since I left my parents' house I never had a home before. A place where I could hang a framed picture or a place to kick off my shoes. Always a stranger. But this, this is beautiful," and she threw her arms around him.

"Here are a lot of walls you can cover with many photos," he replied.

"And serve my favourite man."

"Of course; as you have mastered my heart. Fair is fair."

"My heart will always be yours."

Then he looked at her tummy, stroking it tenderly and asked. "How do you feel?"

"Tired, really tired."

"I will arrange for a bed for tonight. Will you be okay alone?"

"Sure. I can investigate the place more. Get my bearings around this."

"Thanks love," she finally said, "for all of this."

He kissed her and left her alone.

She was finally home. The thought sank deep into her soul; a void filled. No matter where they would finally end up, this house broke the ice.

A new country, new house, an adoring husband and baby. What more could she have asked for?

THAT NIGHT SHE CUDDLED into him in the curtainless bedroom. He watched her sleeping. The beautiful smile weakened his knees, and he remembered the first day he saw her, the same day he had lost his heart in the elevator. It was only eight months ago, and now, she was his wife, his life. Tracing her high cheekbone, she sighed contently as she shifted closer to him.

He was one lucky man.

"Why was she crying, Dad?" Jillian had asked when they went with him to the shops.

"This is her first home, Pumpkin. She's emotional about it."

"It's strange to cry about it. Don't they have homes in South Africa?"

"Of course, they do. Sonia had a tough time since the death of her parents and never had a home till now."

"That must be a long time," Mark said.

"Her parents died when she was sixteen. Since then she is all alone." Silence ensued as they paid at the till, all three lost in thought.

"Please help her to feel welcome. I depend on your guys," he said once they were back in the car.

"How is the baby?" They have not spoken the last month and he had to catch up.

"Good, growing, as you can see," stroking the bump.

"You and Timothy?"

"I am not ready for any relationship, Dad. I called it off."

"And Lindy?"

"She is still around. Will see," Mark said.

He was worried about both, but had to trust that God would guide them. For now he had to concentrate on the new workplace, his wife and baby.

He touched her tummy tenderly. For a fleeting second it irked him. It was another man's child. It was an inner struggle he could not allow to fester. He made a promise and would honour it.

"Help me remain true to my word, Lord. Help me to love this child. This is an innocent child, a child you saw fit for Sonia to carry. Help me to support her without this apprehension."

ON SUNDAY, THE YOUNG SERGEANT, Vicky Gomez, was at the door promptly at 06h45. He reported in and met his new aid, none other than Lt Timothy Blackwell.

"It's good to see you, Lieutenant."

"Welcome, Colonel. Good to see you, Sir." He was surprised to learn about the young man's appointment as his personal assistant. He could not be more pleased with the choice. They talked about certain changes as Timothy showed him around, and by lunch they left the office in search of his wife.

When he left that morning she was still asleep. He could not wait to see her.

91

Steve Biko Hospital, Pretoria, South Africa.

TAU RETURNED TO THE hospital two weeks later. The director of nursing was on an extended holiday.

He used the time to explore and learn more about South Africa's culture and the history.

On the day of her arrival a nurse informed him she was on her rounds and he had to wait.

In the hour many staff passed him without a word. Finally, after he knew every crack in the floor of the long hallway, an older woman marched up to him. Glancing his way she stepped inside her office, closing the door. Taking a deep breath, Tau knocked.

"Come in."

"Matron van der Walt?"

Seated behind a small desk covered with piles of files she looked up from her work, a comprehensive book open before her.

"How can I help?" Huge green eyes looked curiously at him.

"I am sorry for troubling you. My name is Tau Gbadamosi. I understand you know Sonia Main."

"What do you want with her?" A slight reluctance caused her posture to change on guard.

Will she know about Sonia's abduction?

"I am trying to locate her, it's a matter of life and death." He had no other explanation to give, and a half truth was better than a lie.

"Sorry, but I don't see what Sonia's whereabouts has to do with you. Please go or I call the security."

"Please don't call them. I mean no harm, but it's important to find her."

"I cannot help you, Mr Gbadamosi. It is private. I have no right to disclose it to any stranger crossing my path."

"You don't understand, Matron; it is life or death." Tau pleaded. Other than get the information with force he had no other reason to give.

709

She clearly did not trust him.

"Unless you do not give me a proper reason, I will not divulge Sonia Main's address to you. Please leave."

"Ma'am, please. Can I sit down and talk to you for a second?"

"Mr Gbadamosi, please leave this instant." She got up and reached for her phone. He had to go. He could not afford any attention from the authorities.

"I do apologies." He left the office in a hurry.

Roger's demands increased with every passing day. Last night he could hear her screams over the phone. His back was against the wall. Her abuse haunted him. It was a miracle that she had not lost the baby yet. But how long could she hold on?

He took a seat in a coffee shop across from the hospital and monitored the personal gate. Time for niceties was over. He had to get an address.

He could not blame the woman's reluctance. After what they had put Sonia through, she was correct in not trusting him.

Two hours later a light blue Hyundai left the hospital grounds. Her number plate coincided with the one Kwame gave him. According to her schedule she would be back the next morning.

He paid his bill and entered the hospital grounds with a group of visitors slipping past the security guards without notice.

Visiting hour left the administration building relatively empty. The few staff left too busy to take interest and he got to her office with no problems.

Her office door was locked. Looking around he removed a small tool from his pocket and opened it. He waited until his eyes were accustomed to the darker interior. All the files were stacked in smaller piles and the book lay on the side table, closed, the computer's dark screen next to it. From his pocket he retrieved a small flashlight. Hospital related paperwork covered the surface. Frustrated he glanced through the interior. No personal objects were anywhere, even her table was clean. He investigated the cabinets without luck. The very last drawer at the bottom had a tissue box and an exam pad in front. Old, disregarded envelopes were neatly stacked in one corner.

Glancing through them there was nothing of interest. He could see in the far back a handcrafted box, and opened it. Inside were a few pictures. One was of her and Sonia. An incredibly young Sonia, and he smiled. How he missed her.

"Where are you, Sonia? What happened to you?" Back at the desk he touched the mouse. The white light flicked on. The matron's email box was open. The very first email was from Sonia. He read the letter thoroughly, read it again just to understand the content before he looked at her signature. In the email Sonia gave a lot of personal information. That information brought him joy as he read it again. How he longed to hear those words from his wife, but it could never be.

He read the signature again. Captain Sonia Main, a military address underneath.

Confused he realised he never really knew Sonia. He scribbled down the address and left the office.

He had to speak to Kwame.

According to this they were on the wrong continent.

92

"ARE YOU GOOD TO GO?" Curt asked. Sonia struggled out of bed early. Morning sickness was doing its worse on her. She took a long soaking bath and had a cup of tea, the only thing she could hold.

"I am all right. I will make an appointment today with a paediatrician."

"Good. Let me know when, I want to be there with you." The SUV pulled up. "Vicky is here."

"Thanks, love." With their bags in hand they locked the door behind them, greeted the young corporal and got in.

"How are you feeling, Ma'am?"

"I am well. This morning sickness is taking too long." She sighed and sat back in the seat. She never thought she would ever resent going to work. Being on her feet all day left her swollen at night.

A week has come and gone, and Sonia was surprised how well she adapted in the domestic routine. The staff helped a lot during the transition phase. The doctors and nurses were professional and direct.

She had met officers' wives earlier in the week during a luncheon. Their curiosity was palpable. Some were friendly and tried to make her feel at home. Not being used to so many people around her, she observed mostly.

Curt's work kept him busy till late. She went to his office on Tuesday to meet his staff, impressed with the organisational operation behind the wooden doors. She really liked his aid, Timothy Blackwell. Curt spoke very highly of him.

Night-time was their time while they prepared food, talking about their day, doing bible study and prayer. The children came over on Wednesday for a pizza and movie night. Viewing the interactions between Curt and his children, Curt was not his usual self.

A busy weekend lay ahead. Jillian was moving in. Curt invited his in-laws for Sunday lunch. Mark would also join them. He assured her that they would accept her and was looking forward to meeting her.

Overnight her life had changed from being single to a wife and stepmom with responsibilities. The domestic life was daunting, but she liked the interaction.

What did bother her was the slight distancing from her. Maybe it was just her own emotions that changed constantly, but something was different.

In many ways they were still strangers. Could that be the reason?

Could it be that he had doubts about them?

Does he resent the baby?

With a quick prayer she said goodbye to Curt, and Vicky delivered her at the Military hospital.

At work the fast pace day helped to curb her fears and she prayed often for peace of mind. During a break she finished her correspondence and was called for an emergency.

This kept her on her feet later than normal. By the time she got a car to go to the local store, she was dead tired.

"Hello, Sonia," a woman sauntered towards her with a baby stroller—the two-year-old sleeping.

"Hello Bea, how are you?" she greeted the younger woman.

"Are you going to the market?"

"I need a few things for tonight," Sonia replied. Bea was one of the wives she had met—a young couple with a toddler and another on the way.

"Then we can go together." They entered the market and did their shopping.

"You and Curt should come for lunch on Sunday. A few of us will be there."

"We have a full house this weekend, but thank you for the invitation." They exchanged cell numbers, paid for their groceries and left.

Sonia just stepped back outside when she had the sense of being watched. She scanned the parking lot and the park on the one end, but saw nothing out of the ordinary and got back in her car. The uneasy feeling creeping up her back while she drove away.

"I don't know what this is, Lord, but thank you for being with me."

"CURT!" SONIA CALLED.

"In here, love." Leaving his study he stopped in the living room.

"Good God man, but it is good to see your ugly face again."

"Yours too," Phillip greeted.

"How did this happen?" Curt asked Sonia. She was watching them with a big smile and then, when the two men broke their manly hug, hugged her husband.

"It is a surprise. You needed a familiar bonding."

"A very pleasant surprise, indeed."

"When Sonia e-mailed me, I was about to take a vacation, but did not know where to go. So I have accepted her invite," Phillip explained, "and here am I."

"It's good to see you both. You look happy."

"This woman is good to me."

"You can see how good, actually." He patted his belly to show the pound he had gained.

"It suits you."

"Let me show you your room before we get comfortable," Sonia interrupted. "Forgive all the boxes, it still needs to be unpacked."

"Is it okay if I stay here for a few days, Curt? Otherwise I can make other arrangements."

"You are more than welcome to stay as long as you can," Curt confirmed.

"In that case I will stay, but only for a week. Then I want to explore this country of yours before I return."

"Perfect."

Later, with steaming mugs of coffee in hand, Curt spoke about the latest family news.

"Neil Davies's case is coming up."

"I am glad to hear that. This man should pay for his crimes."

"Two other women stepped up as witnesses. This man is a real piece of work," Curt said.

"Violence against women is getting out of hand. Your little speech after the hearing showed immediate results," Phillip relayed.

"How come?"

"You remember Corporal Charlie Alvarez?"

Curt nodded.

"She broke up with the doctor. He had another fling on the side and Charlie was diagnosed with Aids. His wife also left him."

"You are not serious," Curt said surprised.

"Charlie was in quite a state, but after they had helped her, she changed her ways dramatically. You will not believe it is the same woman."

"Good for her," Sonia said.

"Lee Ann sends her love as well."

"I received an e-mail from her yesterday. It seems marriage life in base camp works out for the two."

"Indeed, it does. Sam handed in his resignation. Turmel and Powers had joined forces against him."

"Sam mentioned he wanted to quit after a year, but it's good. It's time to move on," Curt said.

"Lee Ann is happy about it. They will leave at the end of January."

"How do you feel, Sonia?"

"Good, the morning sickness finally stopped. Now I eat everything I can find," she giggled.

"You look beautiful," Phillip complimented her. Sonia caught Curt's gaze. She had seen it once before, just a quick glimmer before he shields it. Does he not trust me?

"I will quickly set the table."

"I am glad you are here," Curt said. "It's good to see you."

"Camp is not the same since you left. In fact, the primary reason I am here is to see what is next for an old burned-out soldier like me."

"I'm sure the Lord knows exactly where he wants you."

"Indeed. For now I will enjoy your country. I haven't been on a road trip in a while."

"How is Jillian?" They gathered around the table as the conversation continued.

"She is due any day now. This Davies man is making life difficult for her."

"In what way?"

"He keeps on contacting her, even from prison. No is not in his vocabulary."

"What does he want?"

"He wants to continue the relationship. Now that Vivian is out of the picture, he is set on her daughter. That she carries his child, gives him entitlement, so he thinks."

"But why don't you get his wife in?"

"Harriet Davies?"

Phillip nodded and Curt continued, "You know, I have forgotten about her. You are correct, I should call her."

"Do you think he will face jail time?"

"The lawyers are optimistic. They have enough evidence against him."

"We will trust God for complete deliverance for her."

"God really came through for you two this last couple of months. He required much, but the fruit is visible. I am proud of you."

"Thanks, Phillip."

"I really feel I want to do something here, though not sure what. I stay tuned in to the God's small voice," Sonia said.

"That is the best way. Be still and know. Both of you have powerful testimonies. At the right time you will be released," Phillip said.

"It's late, I am going to bed." Sonia said.

"Have a good night."

"Keep my side warm, love."

"Sonia looks good, but how do you feel?" Curt laughed softly. He missed this man more than he realised. He switched on the kettle and took mugs from the cupboard.

"She is doing well. The new environment is helping her, and she adjusts well."

"She has a lot of adjusting to do."

"True." He added milk and sugar and after he had stirred it, gave Phillip his coffee.

"What are you thinking?"

"I struggle with the baby. I get jealous when a man just looks at her. I call her often just to check up on her."

"Do you think she cheats on you?" Curt took a sip and burned his tongue.

"I try not to, but then I think of Vivian and what she had done."

"You need to forgive and forget, Curt."

"I struggle with it. I try. I really do. It's difficult."

"Sonia is not Vivian. Believe me when I tell you that woman only has eyes for one man, and that is you."

Curt smirked, his heart warm, but the uncertainty clawed at him.

"I realise the baby is difficult to explain," Phillip said.

"Yes, it is. In retrospect, it makes little sense that she was willing to be with a man for protection." Curt finally spit out what was troubling him.

"We cannot judge her. We were not in her shoes." With just the clock's ticking, they drank their coffee.

"It is difficult. I will honour my promise, but how do I explain it to family and friends? This baby is not mine."

"You can't think like that. It is not right towards Sonia or this child, you know it."

"I know."

"All I can say is—let God do His work. He will work it out for you. Stay connected with Him."

"I am really glad I can talk to you about it. I was afraid to talk to Sonia—fearful of how she would react."

In the hallway Sonia tiptoed to their bedroom and closed the door softly. She could not fault Curt. He had valid reasons, but God would make a way.

93

TAU SAT OUTSIDE THE HOUSE for more than an hour. Wait became second nature to him.

It gave Tau time to study the Bible without fear. During a church service in South Africa he accepted Jesus as his Saviour. He received a scripture that gave him the peace.

Zechariah 10:6.

"I will strengthen the house of Judah, and save the house of Joseph, I will restore them because I have compassion on them. They will be as though I had not rejected them, for I am the Lord their God and I will answer them."

The Bible opened with simplicity. His values changed and now he knew what to do, convinced about the next step.

A friend had sent him a text message with the news of Hilde's miscarriage and disappearance. He knew she was dead. Roger's temper was Hilde's demise.

He shed no tears, his course determined.

He once promised Sonia he would lie down his life for her, and he was ready.

The house and area differed from Fangak County. He could never offer her this. She deserved it.

Just then a black SUV pulled in and two men got out. They walked around the vehicle. One man opened the front door and there she was. Sonia! Beaming.

Staring at her, his heart somersaulted. Surveying her body, his heart ached. She was pregnant. After all this time she had found happiness. His child's future was in excellent hands.

This must be the man she mentioned. A wrenching pain so fierce pulled his heart, mixed with joy he let it go. She was happy.

When they entered the house, he locked the rental and crossed the street.

His mind set with a definite plan. He would not put her through any turmoil ever again, but for his plan to work he needed her husband's help. They could arrest him, but he would offer his life for her. He had nothing to lose.

Knocking on the wooden door he waited patiently. Once the door opened it reached the point of no return.

AFTER A STRENUOUS TIME in the shops Sonia burrowed deep into the pillows, Sonia heard the knock. Knowing Curt would open it, she closed her eyes.

Thirty minutes later, feeling refreshed, she freshened up. Voices filtered through the living area and trotted towards it to halt. Time stood still. An infinity passed in a second before it continued its path.

The man she thought she would never see again was in her living room. She swayed. Curt was with her in seconds, holding her upright. He helped her towards a seat and a glass of water was given to her. She guzzled it down in one swallow, her green eyes never leaving him.

CURT CAUGHT HIS WIFE JUST IN TIME.

For Sonia this meeting was worse. He had no time to prepare her and he was worried.

If not for Phillip, a man's life would have ended by his hands. He had a tough time calming him when he learned his identity, the shock a continuous vibration while he listened to what he had to say.

Seated across from them one of her abductors came clean. How he found them was not clear, but he would get to the bottom of it.

Tau Gbadamosi was anything but what he had expected. The man looked human, even earnest. He matched him in height, a warrior from the broad shoulders to the rigid body. The dark eyes brimmed with sincerity.

The bond that Sonia and he shared, reasonable. He was her protector and father of the child—a child he promised to take care of as his own.

"Sonny, speak to me." His wife had not moved since she stepped into the living room; transfixed on Tau. Powerful emotions played over her face, her posture closed off.

What will this do to her?

"Why are you here, Tau?" she asked, her muffled voice distant and wary.

"I realise it must be a shock, but I had no choice. Your life is in danger," Tau explained. His own rigidness shifted as he looked at her. In that one look, Curt understood the reason he risked everything.

Curt's concern for his wife was greater though than the feelings of this man and stopped him. Gbadamosi already gave him the information they needed. There was no reason to upset Sonia further.

"Sonni, let me get you out of here."

"No, I want to hear what he has to say." Her voice rose with each word. "Tau, why are you here?"

Curt looked at Phillip for help, but he shook his head. He held her hand and prayed quietly.

"Roger Gisemba is here. He wants to take you back to Cawo Idil. Idil is threatening Roger with the destruction of the camp. He already caused the death of my unborn child and its mother. I am really sorry to barge in like this, but it is crucial to warn you and your husband." His accent was thick with emotions. Sonia's body stiffened.

Although Curt never met the two men, he hated them, especially Gisemba. He would kill him himself.

"Why can't this man not accept I am not part of his bargaining chips?" Sonia's voice broke.

Tau rose. "If possible I will come back tomorrow. Sonia is upset. The last thing I wanted to do is bring her this news, but you must know. I owe her." His tone was genuine as he met Curt's sharp gaze, and Curt nodded.

Phillip accompanied him to the door. Minutes passed and then Phillip hunched in front of them. Sonia's crying quieter, her body shivering as she rocked herself.

"Sonia, this must be a tremendous shock to you, but I'm thrilled that he gave us this news. I believe the Father wants to heal you completely. Roger will fail. You are safe here."

"How can you say that?" Sonia sprang up, her anger torpedoed towards Phillip as a floodgate open and angry words hit him. All her fears bunched up. He listened quietly and prayed softly. When she turned away she shivered and was off balance. When he reached for her, she shrugged him off. A door slammed—so fierce and violent, it left them in silence.

"She didn't mean it …" Curt tried to explain, but Phillip stopped him and smiled reassuringly.

"Don't fret, Curt. I know Sonia by now. This was an enormous shock; she was caught off guard. Don't worry about it."

SONIA TREMBLED ALL THE WAY TO the bathroom, vomited and sunk on the floor. Just then the baby kicked in the side, and she rubbed against it.

Seeing Tau in her house broke her defensive walls. She had no more words. Her worst nightmare had become real. All the despair, the rape, her nightmares and pain crushed her with one blow. Soon the bed was soaked.

Much later, when darkness coloured the sky, she noticed Curt. He stroked her back. Every fibre reached for him and she pulled him closer.

"Make love to me," she begged him.

"I will do anything for you, love, anything you want."

Curt captured her mouth and poured all his love into every touch—their love making a healing drug which consumed them.

She absorbed it, quenching her fears till it sated her. Exhausted she fell asleep. When she woke she was all alone.

"Why, Father?"

"Why, now?"

"Please help me."

Wiping away the tears, she waited for God's peace. Taking up her Bible, she began where she had left that morning.

Job 5:19: "From six troubles He will deliver you, even in seven evil will not touch you."

"Lord, thank you for not leaving me in the dark, for giving me this lifeline. Sorry for doubting your word, lord. Thank you for your promises. Thank you that no evil will touch me or my unborn son. Not one of my household will be harmed. Thank you for wisdom and clarity. The evils of hell will not prevail. In Jesus' name."

"You are safe, Baby, no matter what. Daddy and Mommy will keep you safe. No harm will come to you," she whispered.

94

SUNDAY MORNING A GLIMMER OF SUN broke through the clouds and touched her bed.

Curt was not in his usual spot and she rose.

She found the men in the kitchen, praying. She hugged Curt with so much love she thought she would burst.

"Good morning, love," his embrace tight and she kissed him.

"I will make coffee," Phillip interrupted them and she smiled.

"How do you feel?"

"The baby kicked last night for the first time." She took his hand and pressed on the spot. Another kick caused them both to laugh.

"This baby is happy," Curt said.

"Indeed, he is."

"Here you go. Tea for Sonia and coffee for us."

Taking a seat Sonia wanted to talk to Phillip. Her explosion was unnecessary.

"Don't worry about it," Phillip stopped her.

"I had no right."

"You had every right."

"Will he come back today?"

"Yes, he will." She nodded. A knock emphasised it.

"I will open." Phillip said.

Numb she watched as Tau entered her house. The shock had made way for curiosity.

"Sonia!" he greeted. He had changed. The same fierce man, but his arrogant persona had shifted.

"Tau." Her emotions heightened with his closeness. The baby kicked and she calmed it. Each stroke an act of love. Did he recognise his father's voice?

"Hello, Tau," Curt said.

"Any news?"

"He is in town. My informant told me he is on his way." Another knock broke the tension. This time Curt answered it. The children could not have come at the worst time.

He greeted them and then got his cell phone.

"Hello, Mark and Jillian," Sonia greeted them.

"Let me introduce you to Phillip and Tau."

"We brought Jillian's things," Mark said.

"You know where to put it," Sonia said, and the two disappeared down the hallway, each with a few bags.

"I called the gate. They will be on the lookout for him. Please give them a description." He handed the phone to Tau. When he stepped aside, Sonia looked at both men.

"What will happen now?"

"We have to deal with this quickly. With all of this, I have forgotten about the children. My in-laws are also on their way." Sonia giggled, a nervous ring that just bubbled over. Her life was in danger and she had lunch to prepare.

Can life be any more complicated than right now?

"The security is on high alert. They would check each vehicle. If they get past them, they will not get far."

"Do not underestimate Gisemba. He is a leader with a name for a reason," Sonia warned.

"He is messing with the wrong group," Curt replied.

"No harm will come to you or the baby, you understand!"

"Yes, I do, but I cannot sit still. I cannot be here. If he gets through the children's lives will be in danger."

"What's happening, Dad?" Mark asked.

"I need to make another call," Curt said and followed Tau outside. A chill crept up her spine. A helpless emotion she did not care for.

"Sonia?" Mark interrupted her. She owed them an explanation.

"A few months ago …" Yelling from outside interrupted her, and she got up. At the window Tau and Curt's bodies obscured her view. A jeep pulled up.

Moving towards the door Phillip stopped her. "Stay here, Sonia. Curt will handle this."

"I want to know," and she pushed him away.

"Sonia, listen! You cannot go outside."

A gunshot broke the silence and more yelling resulted. Sonia rushed past him.

"Curt!"

The front lawn had become a war zone. Soldiers were trained on a target. A man shouted.

"Curt!" she called, his bulk not visible. She pushed through. More hands tried to stop her and then she screamed. "No! Please God … No!"

"Princess!" Tau appeared, followed by a shot. It happened so quickly, but to the trained ear two shots rang out and two men fell to the ground. Tau grabbed and pulled her with him as he slumped to the ground, his white shirt stained. The growth so quick she could not stop it.

"Tau. Talk to me!"

"You are safe, Princess," he mumbled before his eyes closed one last time.

95

"I HAD LEARNED A LOT FROM LIFE. It is true what the Bible says. For everything there is a time. A time to live and a time to die. A time to mourn and a time to be joyful. Everything we do is measured in time. We cannot escape it."

Sonia skimmed the group until she found him. The man she loved more than life itself. Curt had asked her to speak at the opening. All the brass was sitting in the front. General Andrews and his wife in attendance.

"We start our lives with big eyes and a romantic notion of rainbows and red roses, but when life hits you it teaches you to be a human being. It removes all the glamour thereof and instils values in you. My life is not unique." She brushed a wayward curl to the side. Her tummy pressed against the podium and her feet swollen. "My life has started the day I met Colonel Curt McGee. Before that it was a series of survivals. The day at the elevator I had no knowledge how my life will change." Curt blew her a kiss, some snickered.

"I met God, my protector in the swamps of Fangak County as a warrior. This man protected me from the moment I met him until the day he sacrificed his life for me. Between God and Curt I had no choice but to overcome all the obstacles presented to me." She caught Curt's encouraging smile.

"This is not easy for me but the lessons I have learned of great value. My story begins when I was sixteen years old. The death of both my parents shortly after each other had sent me into a bleak existence. Distant family took me in their care. At seventeen I met a young man. This changed my life completely." Sonia cleared her throat, and took a sip of water, all eyes fixated on her.

"When I announced my pregnancy, he left. With no financial means to pay rent, I was evicted. I landed on the streets. There I had to learn to do many tricks just to get food."

Jillian's attention turned towards her. Their eyes locked and smiled, little Curt sleeping in her arms.

"Sometimes those tricks caused me severe pain. The last trick led to the death of my baby. The attack left me close to death." She looked at her husband, still dashing in a wheelchair, silence the only other sound in the hall.

"A good Samaritan helped me to become a nurse. When I graduated I applied with the Red Cross and was sent to different war zones across the globe. My life became a sequence of moves with no real foundation or house to call my own. It was only once I met Curt that a dream became reality—unaware of the difficulties we faced.

God protected me even during my abduction last year. Brutally raped and sold, God saw it fit to give me one protector amongst the abductors. Tau Gbadamosi paid the ultimate price on December the 15th, 2019 when he saved me and Curt. God's faithfulness a beacon for us all." She sidestepped the podium where everyone could see her growing belly. At twenty-four weeks, her health had improved a great deal.

"I accepted God's redeeming grace and carries Tau's baby with pride. Though he will never know his actual father, Tau's actions will live on." She waved for Curt to come closer, and Mark helped him with the chair. She lowered and kissed Curt. A whistle or two broke the quietness and she smiled.

"This man agreed to father this child." Whoops echoed and Sonia blushed.

"That he took me as his wife knowing my story is a miracle. As a woman we have to make choices with the limited resources we receive. We cannot judge a woman when we do not know her story. Only God can change our views. When we tap into him He removes the stones and implants hearts filled with mercy, grace and understanding.

There are thousands of women that need our understanding. They are helpless against the world. A cruel world that will take until she has nothing more to give.

Therefore, as a step in that direction, I declare the Diva house open. Diva house women will be accepted and not judged or be forgotten. We will nurture them until they become the women God has created them to be. Handmaidens who are worthy to love and be loved and have a home of their own.

A brooding war against God's love is always at hand. It is only by accepting His love that we can finally be free."

The end.

CONTACT

Thank you for reading this book, please leave a review on
Amazon or Goodreads.

Connect with the author at www.kreativcollectiv.com and
sign up for her newsletter.

www.ingramcontent.com/pod-product-compliance
Lightning Source LLC
Chambersburg PA
CBHW022346020726
47500CB00002B/145